Praise for *The 13th De[...]*

"A gripping look into the s[...]
pages—each one a little sca[...]

—MIKE YORKEY,
CO-AUTHOR OF *CHASING MONA LISA*
AND THE *EVERY MAN'S BATTLE* SERIES

"Bruce Hennigan's *The 13ᵗʰ Demon, Altar of the Spiral Eye* is a thrill-a-second ride and an impressive debut. Intense, gripping, suspenseful, and spooky—once you open the cover, the pages will fly. Carve out some time for this one ... you're gonna need it."

—MIKE DELLOSSO,
AUTHOR OF *FRANTIC, DARKNESS FOLLOWS,* AND *SCREAM*

Praise for *The 12th Demon: Mark of the Wolf Dragon:*

"Bruce Hennigan has done it again. *The 12ᵗʰ Demon* is everything a good suspense novel should be and will have you realizing you've been holding your breath for way too long. Interesting characters, a plot that speeds along, and a message you can ponder for a very long time convince me of two things ... *The 12ᵗʰ Demon* is a hit, and Bruce Hennigan is the real deal."

—MIKE DELLOSSO,
AUTHOR OF *FRANTIC, DARKNESS FOLLOWS,* AND *SCREAM*

"Jonathan Steel fans rejoice! Bruce Hennigan is back with a quick-paced thriller chock-full of action, plot twists, and some great slam-bang monster action. *The 12ᵗʰ* Demon is a fun read that puts a fascinating new spin on the vampire genre."

—GREG MITCHELL,
AUTHOR OF *THE STRANGE MAN* and *ENEMIES OF THE CROSS*

"Bruce Hennigan's *The 12th Demon* is the redemptive answer to books like the *Twilight* series."

—MIKE YORKEY,
CO-AUTHOR OF *CHASING MONA LISA*
AND THE *EVERY MAN'S BATTLE* SERIES

The 11th Demon

THE ARK OF CHAOS

BRUCE HENNIGAN

WESTBOW
PRESS
A DIVISION OF THOMAS NELSON

WestBow Press books may be ordered through booksellers or by contacting:

WestBow Press
A Division of Thomas Nelson
1663 Liberty Drive
Bloomington, IN 47403
www.westbowpress.com
1 (866) 928-1240

Because of the dynamic nature of the Internet, any web addresses or links contained
in this book may have changed since publication and may no longer be valid. The views
expressed in this work are solely those of the author and do not necessarily reflect the
views of the publisher, and the publisher hereby disclaims any responsibility for them.

Any people depicted in stock imagery provided by Thinkstock are models,
and such images are being used for illustrative purposes only.
Certain stock imagery © Thinkstock.

ISBN: 978-1-4908-1388-2 (sc)
ISBN: 978-1-4908-1387-5 (e)

Printed in the United States of America.

WestBow Press rev. date: 10/29/2013

Introduction

This novel is the third book in the *Chronicles of Jonathan Steel*. While you may enjoy this book without having read the first two, *The 13th Demon: Altar of the Spiral Eye* and *The 12th Demon: Mark of the Wolf Dragon*, I encourage you to read them. Each book in the series features a demon on the Council of Darkness; I count down the demons in order of increasing power, from number thirteen to number one.

This book is an adaptation of a novel I wrote at the request of my local Barnes & Noble store for National Novel Writing Month, or NaNoWriMo. I was interested in exploring the inner voices of my major characters, so I took a unique approach and wrote each scene from the first-person point of view of that character. That year, I took this very rough novel, *The Ark of the Demon Rose*, and gave it to my faithful readers. Almost all of them told me it was my best book yet!

When I was offered a book series deal by Charisma House, they asked me to take this rough draft and bring it into the mythos of Jonathan Steel as a fully realized novel. I was able to include several story lines that had been omitted from the first two books due to length constraints. I was also able to create a new evil organization that would make the Council of Darkness look pretty tame.

Now that I have even more freedom in word count and editorial choices, I have made this story richer and more detailed—this is the version of the book that I would want to read. I hope you enjoy it and find the story redemptive and inspiring. We face a world in which the forces of evil battle us on every front. Just remember, the father of chaos may seem to be winning, but he is truly already defeated!

For more information on my writings, go to www.brucehennigan.com.

Bruce Hennigan
August 2013

To the Scribes of the Round Table, my brothers in creativity, Mark and Larry. And to my sisters: Sue, who read through many ill-formed manuscripts, and Gwen, who watched while Sue cried.

For we do not wrestle against flesh and blood, but against principalities, against powers, against the rulers of the darkness of this age, against spiritual hosts of wickedness in the heavenly places. Therefore take up the whole armor of God, that you may be able to withstand in the evil day, and having done all, to stand.
—EPHESIANS 6:12–13 NKJV

Prologue

The Tomemaster

AH, YOU RETURN? So curious, you humans. I am surprised you are not frightened by this abandoned insane asylum. However, I have learned over the millennia that humans have a morbid fascination with the macabre.

What is that? You want to know more about the Council of Darkness? Why are you so curious? Do you wish to become a disciple of the Tomemaster and his apprentice, Quibble? There is a cost, you realize? Ultimately, you will have to make the Choice: Whom will you follow? Whom will you serve?

For now, I will open the Grimvox, our repository of stories, and allow you to witness the tale of the eleventh demon and his pursuit of the Ark of the Demon Rose. What is the Ark? Ah, you must be patient, for our story does not begin here in the present. It begins many decades ago.

Quibble, activate the Grimvox!

Chapter 1

Grimvox reference USNA-FCaskey111563

The Priest

November 1963
Dallas, Texas

"SHALL I KILL the human?"

I wearily lifted my head at the sound of the demon's voice. His host body wore a brown Nehru jacket, and a silver chain hung around his neck. On the chain, a red jewel glistened in the weak light. The demon's features were dark beneath a shock of black hair. His eyes were disturbing: totally white with no pupils.

"We need him." The pale man standing next to the demon stared at me with his red eyes. His face was ageless beneath his bare scalp and marred only by a star-shaped scar on his cheek. He wore a long black overcoat and black pants. A stray ray of muted sunlight came through the shrouded windows of the abandoned asylum. In that meager light, his chest glowed in the darkness. He moved across the debris-strewn floor to crouch before me. "His will has been gutted. The fight has gone out of him. Isn't that right, Father?"

"Then why do we keep him alive?" The demon crossed his arms over his chest.

The pale man nodded and licked his large teeth with a very red tongue. "He is our only connection with the girl."

So that was why they wanted me. They were using me to get to Mary!

"Don't look away from me, Father," the man said. "Unlike most of your kind, the touch of your flesh does not harm me." He pressed his cool fingertips against my cheek and turned my face around so all I could see were his hideous red eyes. His breath smelled of fire smoke and vinegar. "For you see, Father, you are a failure. You think you serve your master, but your love for the girl's mother has undone your commitment."

I jerked away from his touch and struggled against the ropes holding me to the chair. "If you hurt her, I will kill you!"

The demon laughed, his voice echoing up into the empty rafters of the hospital ward. "You cannot kill Lucas, human. Now, Lucas, where is the girl? I need her."

I glanced at the demon and his empty white eyes. "Please don't harm her."

"*Please don't harm her.*" He mocked me and shook his head. "I have plans for her, human. Why would I want to harm her?" He removed the necklace from his neck and held it up to the ray of light. As it moved, the jewel changed from pale green to vivid red. "Do you see this jewel? Watch how it changes color with a shift in your perspective. It is the Metastone, human. I plan to give this to the girl's mother as a gift. It will not harm either of them. In fact, it will transform them!" He sighed and placed the jewel back around his neck. "Why am I even trying to explain these matters to a mortal? Lucas, take me to the girl, and then we will no longer need this human."

"Perhaps we do not need to kill him yet." Lucas squatted before me and tilted his head to the side as those crimson eyes regarded me. "I am wondering, Father, why you have not tried to exorcise my friend's demon? Hmm?" He tilted his head the other way and blinked slowly like some great white reptile. "Why haven't you just spoken the Words? I know why, Father. You have lost your connection with the Power, haven't you? It is because of your love for this woman—what is her name? Millie?"

"Molly," I whispered. Nausea overtook me and I retched. Lucas was right. I was empty, impotent. I could no longer see my Lord; only the girl and Molly's hauntingly beautiful face.

"You see, Father, it is not the eleventh demon who has harmed the girl." He reached out, grabbed my collar, and tore it from my neck. "It is you." He grasped the top of my shirt and ripped it from my body. I shivered in the cold air as Lucas gestured to the demon. "For you have forsaken the only Power that would allow you to defeat this demon and to save them. In betraying your master, you have unwittingly betrayed your love." He unbuttoned his coat and it fell open to reveal his bare chest. "You are lost, Father. But, there is one way you can save the mother and the girl: Swear allegiance to the eleventh demon. Once you do, this mark,"— he brushed his coat aside and a hideous tattoo of a beast stirred to life on his flesh—"will be yours. It will live right here." His cold fingers caressed the skin at the base of my neck and I flinched.

Lucas's chest was covered with tattoos. A scorpion squirmed across his collarbone. The head of a wolf howled over his breastbone. But, these were no ordinary tattoos. They lived! Arcane creatures moved and struggled on his white flesh. This new tattoo was one I instantly recognized. I had seen it in the ancient book—I wish I had never opened it! The creature was a chimera, a beast with the head of a lion, a snake for a tail, and, coming out of its back, the head of a goat.

"If I swear allegiance to the eleventh demon, will the lasses be safe?" I closed my eyes and saw Molly standing at the church altar with the girl's hand in hers. God forgive me!

"I do not need the allegiance of this creature, Lucas!" the demon said, moving across the trash-covered floor without stirring any of the debris. He floated above it all and came to rest behind Lucas. "My patience is wearing thin. The timing of my plan is critical."

Lucas stood up and raised an eyebrow. "*Your* plan?" he asked the demon as he studied my face.

"This is the year the Council begins its grand plan to rain chaos down upon this 'one nation under God.' Unfortunately, at times, the Dark Council is thwarted by the Other. To deal with such a possibility, I have developed contingency plans of my own to complement those of the Council. And for those plans, I will need the girl."

Lucas tensed and his gaze shifted to the demon. "Contingency plans? You play a dangerous game. The Council's plans have been long in the making."

The eleventh demon shrugged. "You know very well that each member of the Council develops his own backup plans! We are far from united in our efforts." He examined his fingernails. "Your faith in the Council is well known, Lucas. Since you are such a toady for the Council, go tattle on me if it pleases you."

"Toady?" Lucas frowned. "I do not serve the Council of Darkness, Chimera. I serve the Master. Would you like to tell the Master that you think his right hand man is a 'toady'?"

The demon stiffened. "Listen, underling, you will not speak to me that way! I know what you are and you are not one of the Fallen. You may be the right hand of the Master, but I am far superior to you. The Master trusts me, Lucas. Take me to the girl. Now!" His voice grew in volume and for a second, I saw the beast that possessed the human rear its ugly head. It was like a specter surrounding the man.

Lucas smiled, his impossibly white teeth gleaming in the darkness. "If what you say is true, then you will not mind if I consult the Master." Lucas held out his hand. A swirl of red smoke billowed from his palm like a small tornado and then a pleasant, handsome face appeared in the smoke. Was this Lucifer? He was more fair than foul.

"Chimera, you try my patience," he said from the smoke. His eyebrows arched and his face twisted in anger. "If you insist on continuing with your 'contingency plan,' then I want your talisman."

The demon stepped back. "No!"

"Lucas, take care of this!" Lucifer bellowed. He disappeared from Lucas' palm.

Lucas gazed at his empty hand and slowly clenched it into a tight fist. "The master is well aware of the lack of cohesion in the Council, Chimera. He wants me to have leverage. So I am gathering the talismans of the members of the Dark Council. If you wish to fulfill your plan, you will give me the talisman." He glared at the demon with his crimson eyes. "Or shall I summon the Master to speak to you in person?"

The eleventh demon's face paled. "I will not allow this human to see my talisman."

Talisman? Clearly, it wasn't the Metastone they were talking about; I could see the jewel glittering on the demon's chest. "What is a talisman?"

Lucas glanced at me. "I tore yours away, Father." He retrieved my stained collar and held it up with two long, delicate fingers. "This once meant everything to you, didn't it? Now, it means nothing. So easily discarded at the touch of a woman's hand." Lucas dropped my collar on the floor and stepped on it. "The eleventh demon's talisman is not the jewel that hangs about his neck. That is merely a tool, Father. No, his talisman is as important and defining as your collar was to you. And, he does not want you to see it." Lucas rubbed his hands together. "I think that can be arranged."

The demon nodded and reached into his pocket. Something long and golden flashed in his palm. I tried to focus on it, but it was blurred, indistinct, otherworldly. "What is that?"

The demon floated toward me and the odors of fire and soot surrounded us. He knelt before me, the golden talisman flickering in the periphery of my vision. He put his left hand, hot and sweaty, on my forehead. I tried to pull away from those hideous empty eyes. Lucas moved behind me and held my head in his cold hands.

"I will let you keep one eye so that you may see the fate that awaits those who follow in my footsteps. For the eleventh demon demands total commitment, Father! Will you renounce your allegiance and find love with the mother of this girl? If so, you will be mine, and your death may be avoided."

I was frozen with fear, paralyzed by their inhuman power. The thin gold needle appeared at the edge of my vision. It plunged into my right eye, and then there was pain beyond imagining.

Chapter 2

Jonathan Steel

Shreveport, Louisiana
Present Day

MY NAME IS Jonathan Steel. I have no memory of my past. I am a killer by trade. I don't kill humans—I kill demons. My mentor, Dr. Cephas Lawrence, would tell you that demons can't be killed. For me, that is a matter of semantics. I send them packing back to the deepest, darkest pit of Hell: Tartarus. Their eternal pain and suffering are a far worse fate than oblivion. I find some comfort in that thought.

Cephas told me this was my purpose. I call it vengeance. I am angry, always. Livid. Furious. Full of rage. Just ask the demons; they know. Why? It could be because my own father, "the Captain," experimented on me and imbedded some kind of device in my brain. Or, it could be because of those I have lost. You see, those demons have taken away people I loved. April. Claire. And the one woman who could have revealed my past to me, Raven.

I didn't choose this life; it was thrust upon me. I was drafted into the cause of goodness and light against darkness and evil. If revenge is my catalyst, then so be it.

I had been saddled with responsibility. Thanks to a court order, Cephas's nephew, Joshua Knight, was now under our protection. Thanks to the same judge, I had a new partner, Theophilus Nosmo King. It was either take him under my wing, or let him rot in jail. The man had saved Josh's life in the caverns under Transylvania. Also, I did have a pesky tendency to help people who just couldn't help themselves. It was even on my business card: "A helper in times of crisis." Cephas told me this was another aspect of my "mission." He could be so annoying. He was also usually right.

So here we were, back in Shreveport, Louisiana, where I had defeated my first foe, the thirteenth demon. We put Dallas, Texas, in the rearview mirror of my RV, along with the vampire clans of the twelfth demon, Rudolph Wulf. I can't believe the property that Cephas purchased. He was ousted from his deco high-rise in New York City so he moved here to the South, a warmer climate. Of all the places to choose to house his collection of arcane artifacts, why did he have to choose the one once owned by the host of the thirteenth demon?

Ketrick's castle of evil sat before us. Even though the FBI had cleared out Ketrick's antique weapon collection, I still felt the evil leech off the hot stone walls in clouds of rippling heat. I climbed out of the RV and stared at the house. Cephas followed me and ran his gnarled fingers through his shock of unruly white hair. He could have passed for Einstein's brother. "Surprised, Jonathan?"

"It's Ketrick's house."

Theo walked past us and lifted his huge arms into the air in a victory gesture. "Chief, this is an awesome house!" His smile disappeared when he saw the look on my face. "Who's Ketrick?"

"The man who hosted the thirteenth demon," I said. I heard a motor roar to life out on the nearby lake. A ski boat surged away from the water near Ketrick's dock. Light flashed off of something hanging around the driver's neck. A pair of binoculars? Paranoia reared its ugly head. Was it really the boat that was bothering me, or was it the house of horrors?

"Robert Ketrick was the man who worked with Vivian in Lakeside," Josh said. He leaned against the front of the RV. His face was pale and his short hair was sweaty. The last time Josh was at this house, he had been possessed by the thirteenth demon.

"We're not staying here, Cephas," I said.

"This house was a steal, Jonathan." Cephas glared at me. He pointed an arthritic finger in my face. "There is ample room here for my artifacts. Besides, you signed the settlement papers in Texas. You have no choice. Judge Bolton will not allow Josh or Theo to live anywhere for the next year except under our supervision."

I sighed and looked once again at the huge, castle-like monstrosity of Ketrick's house. Why had Cephas had to buy a place with such bad memories? Granted, with my amnesia, I didn't have that many memories. The beach house in Gulf Shores was the only other place I had lived, and it, too, carried bad memories. Now this house would likewise remind me of my failures. I had watched Claire walk away from here and into the evil whirlwind of Robert Ketrick's plans.

"Dude, it's okay." Josh stepped between us. The piercings in his lips and ears had healed and he had cut away the hair he had dyed black in order to infiltrate Wulf's vampire clan and save his girlfriend, Ila. His short, naturally reddish-blonde hair was moist with sweat, and the shadow of a moustache made sweat bead over his lips. "Dude, let's just go inside and get on with it. I'm tired of fighting this stuff. At least we know the house will be safe. Ketrick is dead and gone."

Cephas took out a key and unlocked the side door off the driveway. It led into a huge kitchen attached to a long room that ran the length of the house.

"This is called the hearth room." Cephas gestured around him. "The FBI took Ketrick's collection of antique weapons and torture devices, but they left the furniture." A car pulled up outside and Cephas squinted through the kitchen window. "Ah, and here is my realtor."

A plump woman with frosted hair and a bright-orange blouse and blazer let herself in. "Well, how do you like it?" She asked. White-rimmed glasses surrounded her eyes. She gasped and smiled. "My, my, what pretty eyes you have."

I just stared back. My turquoise eyes always had this effect on others. I needed to get some new sunglasses.

Cephas shook her hand and gestured at us. "This is Sadie Thompson. We love it, Sadie. It's just what we need."

"Well, I know it was a really good price, but what with all that happened in Lakeside, I was surprised anyone would consider moving here, of all places. I mean, the man was a monster!" She frowned and pushed at her huge glasses. "Now, you'll notice that much of the furniture is still here—at least, what wasn't taken by the FBI—so it is included. If you don't want it, just donate it to charity." She moved past me and led us into the huge study. I cringed at the memory of Ketrick's pictures on the wall. One of them had been of Rocky Braxton, the man I had fought in the beach house. Another had shown Ketrick with Rudolph Wulf, the man in league with the twelfth demon. Fortunately the pictures were gone. Only the desk and chair were left, covered in a layer of dust. Sadie showed us the huge master bedroom. It was all red and black. Cephas could have this room. She led us upstairs to the other bedrooms. And then she took us into the game room.

Josh stayed outside in the hallway. I couldn't blame him. From the back window, he had looked down at the pool and his mother while he was possessed by the thirteenth demon. This was the last place that Claire had seen him before she died in the church basement. I felt like I should say something to him—but what? Comfort is not one of my gifts.

Back downstairs, we followed Sadie outside onto the pool deck. I felt my throat tighten as I saw the overturned table and scattered chairs. Ketrick had never cleaned up after the party. There had been a fight here. I had lost.

Sadie dabbed at the sweat on her brow and smiled. "I'm sorry for the mess. The pool man still comes and he's paid for until the end of the year, but I didn't know about the tables. Now over there,"—she pointed to a three-car garage separate from the house—"is an apartment above the garage. That is where Mr. Ketrick's assistant lived."

"Vivian." The name felt like acid on my tongue.

"Yes, Miss Darbonne." Sadie tried to smile. "Without the apostrophe."

I glanced at Josh. He swallowed hard and rubbed at his chest where Rudolph Wulf's spears had almost pierced his body. The last time we had seen Vivian was in the cavern under the mountains of Transylvania. She had been a prisoner, like Josh, but her role in almost ending his life had been no less than that of the twelfth demon.

"I'll take the apartment," Theo said. "I'll get rid of all the girly stuff."

Cephas pointed back toward the house. "And the basement?"

Sadie nodded and led us back inside. We followed her down a huge set of stairs behind the kitchen into the basement. "It's very unusual to have a basement in Louisiana, what with the water table and all." She stepped through a door at the bottom of the stairs. I was shocked at the size of the room underneath the house. It was almost as large as Cephas's storage rooms in New York. "But Mr. Ketrick had several ... well, *odd* items stored here. It is climate controlled and the foundation is sealed against moisture."

"Torture devices and weapons," I said.

Sadie was having a hard time keeping that smile on her face. "So I've heard."

"This is why I wanted the house. I can put most of my artifacts in here, Jonathan. This can become our strategy center," Cephas said.

"Strategy center?"

Cephas took my arm and pulled me away from the others. "Jonathan, after your encounter with Rudolph Wulf, surely you must realize what your purpose is?"

I jerked my arm out of his grasp. "No one determines my purpose for me, Cephas."

"Not even God?" Cephas's pale-blue eyes glittered. "You've been instrumental in doing away with the thirteenth and the twelfth demons. There are eleven more of these things somewhere out there, planning more evil deeds, and the only person standing in their way is you. You may not like where this is going, but if you don't go after them, they will come after you. We need to be prepared, Jonathan."

I gritted my teeth and glanced over at Cephas's nephew, Josh. "We have a responsibility, now, Cephas. We have to protect Josh." Claire's will stipulated that Cephas and I become Josh's guardians.

"He is as much a part of this as we are." Cephas ran a hand across his huge moustache. "And without a strategy, we are sitting ducks for the enemy. You do want to protect Josh, don't you?"

"Of course I do," I said. My face warmed and I felt the muscle under my right eye twitch. *Calm down!* "I need some time," I said. I hurried up the stairs, leaving them behind. I burst out of the back door and walked off toward the lake. I had to think. I had to process all of this. It wasn't supposed to happen this way. I was not supposed to end up living in Ketrick's house. I was not supposed to be babysitting a teenager. I was not supposed to be the boss to an ex-drug-addict or an old man with a basement full of arcane artifacts.

I hurried across the lawn toward the dock extending out into the waters of Cross Lake and followed it to the shade of a boathouse. The heat was unbearable, and the fecund odor of the lake swam on the heat waves. The boathouse had three berths. A ski boat shifted with the waves in the first berth. Above the others, two Jet Skis were suspended. At the back of the boathouse was a bathroom and an open patio with a table and chairs and a gas grill. I walked onto the deck and slumped into a patio chair. Insects whirred around me and frogs croaked beneath the dock. It was a pointless cacophony.

I spied the boat from earlier now resting calmly on the water in the middle of the lake. Again, light flashed off of the man's binoculars. What was he looking at? Would it always be like this from now on? Would I constantly be looking over my shoulder for the next demon? Maybe Cephas was right. Was I chosen to battle these denizens of Satan? No! I wasn't some kind of supernatural super hero! I had no special powers! And, no special responsibility!

My hand drifted to my chest underneath my T-shirt. The scars from my fights with the assassin, Raven, were gone. She had died in Wulf's vampire-filled caverns. But I, on the other hand, had survived. I had healed quickly, almost miraculously. Why?

"Josh is gonna like that boat."

A shadow fell over me and the deck shifted under Theo's weight. He was over six feet tall and weighed close to 320 pounds. Most of it was muscle. He had been a cop, then a pastor, then, recently, a drug addict. In Dallas, he had cleaned up his act and sworn his unfailing allegiance to me. "Yeah. I guess he will."

"He lost his daddy's motorcycle. Those vamps took it with them to Romania." Theo settled into a chair. It groaned under his weight. He ran a hand over his bare scalp and slung drops of sweat into the air. "It's not good for a boy to lose something of his daddy's. You're gonna have to let him have some fun, Chief. Eases the loss."

I nodded and looked out over the water. Josh's father had died years ago and Josh had kept his father's motorcycle running without his mother's knowledge. When we returned to Dallas after Claire's death, he had taken off on the motorcycle to find Ila. "I guess so, Theo."

"Chief, I know you're worried about the boy. But you're not in this alone, you hear me? I will make sure nothing happens to Josh. You understand me?"

I looked into his dark sweat-streaked face. "I believe you, Theo. But you're only human. We're up against something that is inhuman."

"I seem to remember a Bible verse: 'Greater is He who is within you than he who is in the world.' You can't forget that."

"You're right, Theo. You need to keep reminding me of that."

"It ain't easy being one of God's warriors, Jonathan." He stared out over the water. "It ain't easy. But, nothing has ever been easy for you, has it? And yet you keep on fighting for what is right. Now why is that?"

"I made a promise. I said I would stop them." I saw April's dying eyes.

"Then we're gonna keep that promise. Right?"

"Yeah, Theo, we are."

"Whoa! A ski boat?"

I turned to see Josh gaping at the boat in the boathouse. Cephas was smiling behind him. "Can we take it out?"

"I don't know anything about boats, Josh," I said.

"I do. I used to go water-skiing with my dad." He hopped from the dock into the boat.

"But you were only eleven."

"Dude, it's not that hard." Josh smiled and for a second, I saw the carefree teenager Josh should have been. Instead, he had already faced more evil in his young life than most people did in their entire lifetimes. I shook my head. "We don't even have—"

"The key?" Cephas held up a keychain with a small buoy on it. "Sadie says it's in top condition and that it and the jet skis come with the house."

10

Josh grinned. "Jet skis? Bro, maybe Ketrick's house isn't such a bad deal after all."

I tried to find something to say. But Josh was smiling. I kept quiet.

Theo stepped into the boat. It rocked with his weight. He looked at me. "Well, aren't you coming?"

Cephas stepped gingerly into the boat as well and handed the key to Josh. Josh started up the engine. It guttered and burbled in the water. "Dude, can you untie the boat?"

I gave up, untied the ropes, and stepped into the boat. Cephas and Theo had settled into the back row of seats. I took the passenger seat next to Josh. He gunned the engine and threw it into gear. We rocketed out of the boat slip. It was going to be a long summer.

Chapter 3

Vivian Darbonne Ketrick

FBI Evidence Warehouse
Dallas, Texas

"HONEY, YOU'VE MADE me madder than a wet hornet!" I unleashed the power of one of my demons and hurled the laptop across the room with inhuman strength. FBI Special Agent Juan Destillo barely ducked in time. The laptop hit the cinderblock wall and shattered with a satisfying crash. Oh, how I loved mayhem! Glass and plastic rained down on Destillo as he hunched over.

"Vivian, please, calm down!" He straightened and shook the glass and plastic from his hair. "I have searched every item in Ketrick's manifest. It isn't here."

The door to the small storeroom burst open and a young woman rushed in. She was small and wiry with Asian features and long black hair. "Juan? What just happened?"

"Nothing, Zoe," Juan said.

I glared at the young girl as she rushed over to Destillo and began to brush bits of broken laptop from his shirt. "Do you realize how many toxins are in this laptop?"

"It's nothing, Zoe." Juan tried to push her away.

"Who is this?" I asked. Within me, Summer, the plant-girl demon, swelled green and fiery with jealousy.

"Uh, this is Zoe Reynolds. She is in college and she is my, uh, intern for the summer," Destillo said.

"Yes, ma'am, I'm getting my major in law enforcement and Juan agreed to let me intern. He has taught me so much!" Zoe brushed broken plastic and glass from her hands.

"I'll bet he has." Forget violence, try lust! Summer filled my mind with raw seductive power. I would show this vixen a thing or two. She couldn't have been over twenty!

I calmed the pulsing demons within me and let my anger cool down. "How long have we known each other?"

Destillo swallowed. "Since the FBI removed all the artifacts from Robert Ketrick's house and brought them here."

I sauntered across the room and pushed Zoe aside. Destillo cringed at my approach.

"Now, Vivian, you know there is nothing going on here. Zoe is just a student."

"What?" Zoe planted her hands on her hips. "You said I was special. You promised to show me some of your sculptures." Zoe stepped between us. "Juan sculpts in his spare time. He's a regular Leonardo Da Vinci."

"Zoe, step away and let the grown-ups deal with this." I gently pushed her aside and smiled at Destillo. The shark demon within me wanted me to rip out his throat, but I could be tender if I chose. Destillo was taller than me and had beautiful, dark, curly hair, a wispy goatee, and haunting, gorgeous brown eyes. I ran a hand through his hair and fragments of plastic and metal rained down. I leaned forward and blew some broken glass off of the tip of his nose.

"Sugar honey, I know I've been away the past few days. But I had important business out of town with the ex-CEO of my company's latest acquisition, Wulf Pharmaceuticals. I lost my husband, Robert Ketrick, at the hands of Jonathan Steel, and I was so lonely. But I am back in Dallas and hoping you can warm the cockles of my heart."

Destillo nodded and his face grew red. I stroked his chin. I leaned in and breathed onto his lips. Summer was so good at her job! He swallowed again and bumped up against the wall. His shoes crunched on the broken laptop.

"All I'm asking from you, Juan, is to find one little, itty-bitty item in all of Robert's possessions. They are, after all, mine."

Destillo nodded. "Once the FBI releases them." He smelled of onions and salsa and body odor. "But until then, I'm sorry. It's just not here."

The shark demon writhed within me. *Let me kill him!* I ignored the inner voice and the images of torn flesh and gushing blood. It wouldn't do any good to kill the man. Not yet, anyway. I had to find the artifact. Since I had regained my demons after the debacle in Transylvania, my memory and thinking had cleared. But, try as I might, I could not recall where Ketrick had hidden the artifact. *Unless* ... I prodded my oldest demon, the first one who had come to me in my hour of great need. I touched the mind of my dung-beetle demon and probed its memory. It had been with me while I worked for Ketrick. Did it recall where the artifact was hidden? It trembled within me and a blurry image surfaced. Of course! Leave it to Ketrick to hide the thing with his unmentionables.

When I was being held captive by Wulf, he had offered me freedom in return for my bringing him the chest. The twelfth demon had said it would give Wulf great power. Wulf never told me what kind of power. Now poor Wulfy-baby was sizzling in eternal darkness, thanks to Jonathan Steel. And now the artifact and its power would be mine!

There was no need for me to waste any more time with Destillo. Just as his lips were closing in on mine, I pulled away. "Too late. I'm bored. He's all yours, Zoe." Destillo disgusted me now. "When you find it, let me know."

I pulled my cell phone out of my pocket and checked my hair in the reflection on the screen. My lipstick was still perfect. I was wearing the latest in designer suits from the most exclusive shop in Dallas. It was the only one of its kind, and I had had to strike down the other woman who wanted it with pustules to get her out of the way. The Centers for Disease Control was still looking for the origin of the outbreak. I dialed a number and held the phone to my ear while Destillo shuffled in the broken laptop debris behind me.

"Ketrick Enterprises. This is Jerome speaking."

"Bile, this is Vivian." He hated to be called Bile. I had rescued his miserable carcass from the carnage in Wulf's vampire cavern and had healed his mortal wounds, so the man had pledged his undying devotion to me. He was acting as my executive assistant until I could find someone more qualified.

"Oh, uh, Miss Vivian! What can I do for you?" He whimpered.

"First of all, show some backbone. When you answer the phone for me you have to be firm. You represent me, Vivian Darbonne Ketrick. Understand?"

"Yes, Miss Vivian," he said a little more firmly.

"Now get my corporate jet ready. And have one of my assistants bring my travel bag to the airport. I need to leave within the hour for Shreveport. Make a reservation for the Remington in downtown Shreveport for the week. Got that?"

"Yes, Miss Vivian. I'll have the jet ready within the hour. May I ask what your business is about?"

I ignored his question and turned off the phone. Now to get out of this warehouse. The FBI had brought most of Ketrick's artifacts here after his death. He had been a busy man. Matching all the different sources of DNA from the blood on his devices would take months.

A woman appeared at the door to the storage room. She had dark-green eyes and fiery-red hair that cascaded down to her shoulders. She wore an unflattering FBI jacket over a blouse and pants that had to have been bought at a local Anonymous-Mart.

"What is going on down here?" She glared at Destillo and Zoe. "Agent Destillo, I heard a crash. What happened to your laptop?"

Destillo had picked up all the remnants of the laptop and was dropping them into the trashcan. "I was checking the manifest of Ketrick's possessions and, uh, accidentally dropped it."

"An accident? You've been having a lot of those lately. Showing up late for work. Sloppy cataloging. It's a wonder we can find anything in Ketrick's manifest with your haphazard records. What happened to you? You used to be compulsive." She glanced at Zoe and then at me. "Maybe too much partying! Well, it'll come out of your paycheck. Who is this civilian?"

"Robert Ketrick's widow." Destillo pried the hard drive out of the laptop housing before throwing out the rest of it.

"Mrs. Ketrick?" She crossed her arms and glared at me. "Your reputation precedes you. I am FBI Special Agent Regina Cornelius. I am in charge of this project and you need my permission to be in this room. Agent Destillo has not cleared it with me."

"Agent Cornelius, tell your boss, Franklin Ross, that I can go anywhere I please. He'll back me up on that. If he disagrees with you, just tell him to listen to his inner demons."

Cornelius's face reddened. "Ross warned me about you. I know about your obsession with the occult. But I deal in reality. You can't spin a spell on me."

"I'm still bored." I yawned. "When the FBI is finished with my late husband's playthings, be sure and let me know. Oh, you can keep the iron maiden. Just your size."

Cornelius glared at me and then suddenly sneezed. She blinked and dabbed at her eye. "Destillo, what toxic waste from your laptop is floating in the air? If I get pinkeye, you're fired, and you can take your prom queen with you." She continued to blink and then she glared at me. "Why are you still here?"

Let me strike her with the pustules, the dung-beetle demon said. For a second, I considered it. Might improve her looks. Maybe one of the other demons had put something in her eyes. Good enough for now. I glanced at Destillo. He still wore a sheepish, lovestruck look on his face, even with Zoe draped on his shoulder. I blew him a kiss and left the room. "In a while, crocodile."

Chapter 4

Jonathan Steel

I STOOD IN THE kitchen while Theo and Cephas and Josh went on and on about the boat trip. Josh had handled the boat well. We had survived. At one point, I had seen the ski boat driven by the man with the binoculars pulling into a dock on the far shore. I still felt a vague sense of unease. But maybe this was how it would be from now on. Maybe I was destined to constantly look over my shoulder for the next danger. I glanced at Josh. What about him? Would the promises and decisions I had to make endanger him?

"Dude, I'm starving." Josh opened a cabinet. "Do we have any grindage?"

"I don't think so," Cephas said. "Sadie said the dishes and utensils were included, but even if the FBI had left any food, I doubt it would be edible."

Josh slammed the cabinet door shut. He boosted himself up to sit on the huge island in the middle of the kitchen. "Where is the nearest pizza place?"

A roaring sound came from outside. Three moving vans lumbered down the driveway followed by an old truck. The first time I had seen the truck, Josh's mom, Claire, had been driving it. Now, it belonged to Josh. Cephas nodded as the trucks pulled up. "Looks like my possessions have arrived."

"I'll go get some eats now that the truck is here," Theo said. "Josh can go with me and I'll drive through somewhere and get us some pizza. What kind of groceries do you eat?" he asked me.

"I don't cook." I hadn't cooked a meal since that fateful dinner in the beach house. It was the last time I had seen April.

"No problem. I was once a chef," Theo said.

"Really?" The man had been a cop, a pastor, a drug addict, *and* a chef? He never ceased to amaze me.

"At my brother's café," Theo said. Something dark and painful passed across his face and he averted his eyes. "That was long ago, Chief, but I'm still a good cook."

Cephas headed for the back door. "We trust you, Theo."

"There is one problem, Papaw," Theo said.

Cephas paused with his hand on the door. "What?"

"I need some funds."

I pulled out my wallet. "Take my ATM card and get enough cash to pay for groceries."

Josh snatched the card out of my hand and a huge smile came over his face. "Bro, this is like the time you let me loose in the Apple store."

"Groceries shouldn't cost thousands of dollars."

Theo reached over and deftly removed the card from Josh's hand. "I'll take charge of that."

"Hey! Dude, I'm the vice president of this organization!"

"Little dudette, I am now the treasurer."

I felt a smile lift the corners of my mouth. It had been a long time since I had smiled. Theo tucked the card in the pocket of his jeans. "So what's the PIN?"

My smile faded. "A name. It's how I remember the numbers."

"What name?" Theo asked.

I glanced at Josh and then out the window. "Claire."

Theo brought back armloads of food and we had pizza that evening. Josh was quiet and pensive the whole time. He had lost a lot this summer. So had I. But unlike him, I was used to it.

After dinner, I went down to the basement. The first three trucks had been replaced with two new ones, and Cephas had men moving crates around the huge space. He was slumped in an old office chair pulled up to a huge wooden desk. He looked pale and tired. "I have much to accomplish while we have the moving men here."

"Cephas, you have Josh and Theo. Theo alone could move almost anything in here by himself. Why don't you just let the men unload the stuff and get Theo to sort it out later? That way you can get some rest."

"We are almost done. That pallet is the last of the big items. And I do plan on securing Theo's help in uncrating many of these objects."

There was a box sitting on the center of the desk with a large picture frame facedown on top of it. "Family portrait?" I asked, reaching for the picture.

"I want you to see something." Cephas stood up and pushed the box out of my reach. He turned to the adjacent wall where a large mahogany secretary had been placed. He opened the two upper doors to reveal the interior. In place of shelves, a wooden frame hung. Cephas stooped over and plugged in a cord. A light illuminated the frame. "Look familiar?"

I studied the ancient document preserved behind a thick layer of glass. "You showed me this at your New York City loft the day I met you."

It was a diagram scrawled over with arcane symbols and letters. A circle roughly two feet in diameter contained twelve spokes pointing toward the center. The first time I had seen the document, I had paid attention to the periphery only. I pointed to a spiral of dark ink in the corner. "That is the spiral symbol of the thirteenth demon."

"That is correct." Cephas crossed his arms. "And at the top of the circle?"

At the twelve o'clock position was a wolf's head on a dragon's body. The head had come about full circle to clamp its mouth on its own tail. It was the mark of the wolf dragon. The Roman numeral for twelve was beneath it. "Wulf?"

"A coincidence?" Cephas asked. "What are the chances that Rudolph Wulf would be the pawn of the twelfth demon and have a last name consistent with the wolf dragon's symbol?"

"There are no such things as coincidences," I said.

"Precisely. Now look at the symbol for number eleven."

Counterclockwise from twelve was a large circle containing a single dot. On top of the large circle was a smaller circle, and atop the smaller circle was a small cross. "I don't recognize this."

"It is the symbol for chaos. Now, here, under the number ten, what do you see?"

Next to a faded red blob with the Roman numeral for ten sat a symbol. I leaned into the document and studied it closely. "It looks like a teardrop or a drop of blood or something."

"I thought as much too. But notice the faded lines radiating from it as if it is supposed to be glowing."

"Radiating something? Heat? Power?"

Cephas shook his head. "I don't know, Jonathan. But I have been anxiously waiting to retrieve this document from storage since you told me of the twelfth demon. All twelve demons on the Council of Darkness are here on this diagram. You need to study it."

"I don't need to study anything."

"Your destiny—"

"I don't have a destiny, Cephas."

"What about your father?" he said. I looked away and tried to swallow.

Cephas stepped in front of me. "You've had some more flashbacks about him, haven't you? Why haven't you told me?"

"We've been a little busy with demons and kidnappings and moving into Ketrick's torture chamber!" My face grew hot.

"What did you learn about your father this time?"

There had been flashbacks of a prison camp in North Africa. I had been imprisoned by a man known only as "the Captain." He had overseen the implantation of some kind of device into my brain. I felt nausea and I was suddenly dizzy. "I can't talk about it, Cephas. He implanted something in my head." I gagged and the room began to swim. I collapsed in the desk chair.

"Stop! Stop thinking about it now! Clear your mind, Jonathan."

The nausea lessened and my vision cleared. "It would seem I have no choice but to *not* think about my father, Cephas." I looked into his ancient eyes and lied to him. "I will not be looking for the Captain, Cephas. It is not my destiny!" I headed back up the stairs to the kitchen.

Theo and Josh were unloading groceries. I ignored their light banter and went into the den. Even with the summer heat of August just outside the massive windows, I felt a chill. Ketrick's house was cold and inhuman; it felt as though the walls were sucking the life out of me. I ended up at the French doors. Here was the leather chair in which I had collapsed under the touch of Robert Ketrick and the memories of his past Lucas had supplied. Ketrick claimed to have known me since the day I was born. I tried to imagine the mind of the fiend who had planned so many deaths from inside this house. Ketrick had been a monster.

I opened the French doors and stepped out onto the patio. The sun was setting across the lake, painting the sky with an awesome display of orange and red. A few straggling boats were making their way back to their docks. The blinking red-and-white safety lights were fireflies floating across the water. The wet odor of the lake was borne on the evening breeze. Mosquitoes buzzed around my ears.

"Dude, you want some tea?" Josh handed me a glass of iced tea as he joined me on the patio. "Theo says we can use his iced tea for syrup."

I sipped the cold, sweet concoction. "It's good. Minty. Do I taste oranges?"

"Yeah, he uses mint tea, oranges, limes, and lemons." Josh sipped at his own glass. He slapped at his neck. "Mosquitoes! We need to get some kind of repellent."

"Yeah. I don't have them on the beach. The ocean breeze keeps them away."

"Yeah," Josh said.

The sun settled lower on the horizon and the sky grew darker. Stars began to appear. "Bro, that's beautiful."

"Yeah."

"I'm sorry about using your mother's name for my PIN."

"No problem," Josh whispered. "I miss her."

"Me too."

"Do you miss Raven?"

"What? Josh, she tried to kill me."

"She also saved our lives." He sipped more tea. "You two had a history, right?"

"Yeah."

"Did you ever, you know ..."

One of the memories I had not yet shared with Cephas was of an intimate encounter I'd had with Raven long before the events of the past few weeks. "I don't remember."

"What about that police officer? You know, Sue Kane?"

"I was never interested in her." I glanced at him but my face was probably hidden in shadows. Sue Kane was a Dallas police officer involved in the investigation of Rudolph Wulf. "Why are you asking all these questions?"

He shrugged. "I don't know. You seem to be one unhappy dude."

"I am unhappy."

"Maybe you need to find a new girlfriend."

"Maybe you need to find a new mother." It came out before I could stop. Josh froze and stared at me. "Dude, that is cold!"

"I'm sorry. I didn't mean that." I sighed. "Look, it's just that everyone I love dies."

"Does that include me? Man, you *are* one screwed up dude." Josh whirled around and went back into the house. I swore and threw my glass at the brick wall. Glass and ice showered over the dead grass at the edge of the patio. A piece of glass nicked my chin. I felt the warmth of blood and wiped it away in one swift motion. I stared at the blood on my hand.

A ray of light from inside caught my face and I looked up at my reflection in the patio doors. My hair was a mess. Blood trickled down my chin. I needed to shave. My face was haggard and drawn. I hadn't eaten well in the days leading up to Josh's rescue. My turquoise eyes glowed with my inner turmoil. Would I ever find answers? Would I ever find peace? I went inside to face the music.

Grimvox Interlude #1

Chaos

Interdimensional Void
Present Day

HERE WAS A time when my name was spoken with fear and trembling by my fellow fallen. But I now call myself Chaos. I have abandoned the plans of the Master to embrace the chaos that swirls through my mind like a hot dust devil.

What is this? I sense a gathering of some of the lower fallen, those who have descended into irreversible insanity. They are gibbering about a focus of evil that springs from the actions and the choices of a human. Yes, there it is, a small room closed off from the fresh air these humans take for granted. I unfold from the other dimensions into the midst of these wraiths of evil. These lower demons sense my presence before I even fully enter this world's space-time dimensions. They flee without any hesitation in a flurry of horrifying screeches.

The room with the unconscious human is hot, but not as hot as the place of eternal torment. I should know. I was there when the sons of man came unto the daughters of man and the door to Tartarus was open for a nanosecond and the energy of the most evil of us seeped into the world and I saw what waited there for the worst of the worst.

The human is quiet and the air smells of sweat and dust and chloroform. I watch its chest move. It will soon wake up and start screaming behind the duct tape on its mouth. The room is surprisingly well done with candles and a makeshift altar. I like altars. This one shows promise. If I wait long enough, I will meet the perpetrator and it might prove to be a worthy host.

Ah, there above the candles is the image of a human. Yes! The hate grows within me, stoking the fires of revenge. Somehow fate has linked

21

me to the one person I longed most to destroy. If I wait long enough, then the perpetrator of this sacrifice may lead me to this human. And then that creature will become the focus of my vengeance!

Chapter 5

Vivian Darbonne Ketrick

"GOOD EVENING, MRS. Ketrick," the boy said. He couldn't have been over eighteen.

"Who are you?" I asked as I stepped off the airplane into the hot night air of Shreveport, Louisiana.

"I'm Reggie." He had short, dark hair and an eager-to-please face. He wore a nice blue shirt with a power tie and a dark blazer. He wasn't even sweating. Yet.

"Reggie, that means nothing to me."

"I'm your executive assistant here in Louisiana. Ketrick Enterprises. I'm at the Lakeside office. Jerome called me from Dallas," he babbled.

I had changed into a black jumpsuit for the next part of my mission. "Where's my car?" I asked. Reggie froze. His eyes widened. "Where is my car, Reggie? You were supposed to get me a rental."

He paled. "I forgot. I can drive you." He pointed to his car.

I shoved him aside and headed for his car. "I will drive myself."

"What will I do?"

"Call a taxi. Take my bags and check me into the Remington. I don't want to see you again, understand?" I hopped into the car and threw it into gear. He jumped out of the way as I almost ran him down. Now he was sweating!

I headed north out of the airport. I hadn't planned to come back to this area any time soon, but I needed the artifact. I had to have all my ducks in a row before meeting with the Council.

I had handily defeated the thirteenth demon and taken on three more demons in the aftermath. They were now living within me; I had sufficiently cowed them to my will. But the two new demons I had picked up after dealing with the twelfth demon were proving less obedient. One had lived inside of poor Armando, who was currently rotting in prison for some of the deeds I had perpetrated. The other had lived inside Bile for a short season. I had jerked the demon out of him the same way Wulf had removed my demons. I had learned Wulf's tricks!

I threw on the brakes and pulled the car off the road into a wooded, unlit rest area along the highway. I got out and walked over to a nasty-looking, stained picnic table. The night was dark and humid. The highway was deserted.

"Come out of me now," I said. Like pale smoke coming out of a dirty flue, they streamed out of me one by one into the night air and hovered in front of me. "Take your form!"

Each one took on a different form. There was the shark creature, the dung beetle, Summer the plant girl, the bat thing, and finally, Armando's old demon in the form of a huge, weeping leech.

"Let me make something very clear: I am your master. Each of you is but a weak, useless demon in the scheme of things. Without me, you would be insane. I give you purpose. Together, I can make us powerful. Do you understand?"

"Yesss, human," hissed the dominant bat demon. "We will take your leadership. We pledge ourselves to you."

I nodded. For the first time in a while, I was curiously empty. The old voice was returning. But I had killed her years ago, and the witch had deserved it. I had to get them back inside before my strength of will faded. "You will not betray me?"

The creatures looked at each other. The bat thing shook its head. "Never, Vivian."

"You will do anything I ask?"

"Yesss," it hissed.

I heard a noise from the back of the picnic area. A homeless man crawled out of a cardboard box next to the trash dumpster and slowly stood up. "What is going on?" he said. The sound of his voice was rich with phlegm. His stench engulfed me.

"You should have stayed asleep, honey."

His long and dirty gray hair was matted against his scalp. In the bright light of the headlights, his eyes were yellow with jaundice. His gaze raked over me like fingernails on a chalkboard. "Pretty thing, why don't you come see my etchings?" He pointed at his cardboard box. I turned and studied the shuffling, hideous forms of my demons.

"I think the five of you need some playtime. Give the man a drink."

In place of the five demons, five shot glasses filled with amber fluid appeared. The homeless man goggled.

"First, let's have a drink," I said.

"Don't mind if I do." He pushed passed me and plucked the glasses out of the air one by one, chugging down each one. Then he turned and winked. "Now, how about you and I have a little dance?"

Suddenly, the skin on his forehead bulged and the bones in his arms shattered with an unnatural muscle spasm. His screams filled the night and I walked away to avoid the blood splatter. I kept my back to him as they finished. The man grew silent, then there was a soft, plopping sound as his body fell onto the ground. I turned back to see my demons hovering again. They seemed agitated but sated.

"Now you see I will take good care of you." I pointed at the misshapen body of the homeless man and, for a second, felt sympathy. Sympathy? Weakness! I brushed aside the sympathy like a troublesome spider web. "I let you play. I let you have your way. But I am your master, and one day, I will control the Council. Then, each of you will serve my will, and together we will perfect the will of Lucifer. Now, get back inside."

I inhaled. The forms took on their pixelated, smoky form and streamed back into me. I felt their strength and vigor rejuvenate me. That was better! Now, to Ketrick's house to find my artifact. Once I had it, I would have the Council!

Grimvox Interlude #2

Chaos

The Sacrificial Chamber

I WAS ONCE KNOWN as Chotus. But in the time before time, my true name was spoken with the same hushed reverence as that of the Master. I and my brother were his chosen, and when the Master led our revolt against the Creator, we were by his side. Ah, the souls I have garnered for the Master! I will continue, for what else is there to my existence? With few exceptions, my kind has descended into eternal insanity. In their minds is a mixture of madness and depravity. We hover between our dimension of hell with its many layers of darkness and the limited dimensions of this world. This is why our hatred for the humans is so great. And we should hate them! The Creator gave them the choice of redemption, but we are denied the chance of restoration with Him. Our destiny is eternal separation from the one true source of Love. All we have left is hate. And hate is a powerful tool.

Not all of us are insane. The Chosen few on the Council preserve sanity. They shun the distracted minds of the other Fallen. Like them, I am not insane. I have learned to relish the disorder. I wallow in entropy. I wreak havoc wherever I can!

Now, I am waiting for the human to come. I will make him my host. I hear him approaching the door to this chamber. The sacrifice is drugged, but still alive. The altar table is coarse and unrefined but it will do. He built this altar to honor and worship the person in the picture.

Now the man is inside and hovering over the sacrifice. His eyes drift up to the image of the object of his desire and worship. Now, the knife! Yes, that one. It is golden and gleaming and jeweled and has taken thousands of human hearts in its day. How did this human come by it? No matter. This day, it will take another human life. How sweet to look down the timeline of its existence and feel the death of all those humans: the hot blood flowing and the shock of the soul leaving the body.

Some of those thousands went to the Other, but most joined my most vile companions in the worst corner of hell, Tartarus. I do not care about the soul of the sacrifice, though. I care only about the devotion of my intended host, this pitiful man so enamored with the woman in the picture. He must serve me well if I am to achieve my goal.

He waits. He is fearful. He is studying the knife and the sacrifice. What shape, then, shall I take? I once had a shape that pleased me, but now I am Chaos, once known as Chotus. What shape is Chaos? A flash of memory: the chimera, an ancient blend of human and animal parts. I laugh at the irony. To take on that shape would be the height of arrogance and disrespect for the one who claims that form as his own. But after all, I am Chaos! Yes, my appearance shall be the chimera.

"I have come to serve you, oh great one," the man says. "I bid you show yourself to me. I invoke the words of Simon Magus."

I wait patiently as the human consults one of the arcane books from the dark ages of humanity. The name means nothing to me. The book itself means nothing. The words mean nothing. It is the choice and the act of submission that matters.

He finds the pages and begins to say the words. They are but the pointless babblings of humans, unlike the Words of the other book, which carry power. I let him drone on until the sacrifice begins stirring. She is awakening. Now is the time.

I begin to take shape. My head forms as that of a lioness with a small mane. A goat's head springs from my back, and my tail is as a long, fanged snake. I unfurl a pair of wings and a human head appears next to the goat's. Fire trickles from my lion's mouth. The human looks up in wonder. I see the fear and revulsion in his eyes.

"Do you find me repulsive?" I ask.

The human gasps when I speak. It is always this way. Their fascination with the macabre and their instinct to run are always at war. He should be hurrying back to the light of his Creator, but I can rely on his fallen nature to root him to this spot in reverence. Ah, they always seek the darkness! He drops the book but not the knife.

"My master."

"You have brought the knife. You have brought the sacrifice. You have spoken the words. Do you wish to serve me unconditionally?"

"Yes."

"Then it is time. Do as I say."

I talk him through the ritual sacrifice. Afterward, he places the knife at my feet and kneels.

"Do you wish to serve me?"

"Yes." His mind is dull from the shock of killing. There is no thrill in this human. I will have to teach him much.

"Do you invite me into your heart and mind and soul?"

"Yes." He looks up, but at the picture of his desire, not at me.

"Look at me!" My voice swells with power.

The human jerks. His eyes are dull. Now is the time. I cannot take him without an invitation. This is their downfall; they have to allow us in. The Creator deems it so.

"Behold your guiding spirit."

"I follow you," he whispers.

"Ask me to come into you and I will guide you with mind, voice, reason, reflection, name, and thought," I say, reflecting the words he spoke from the book by this Simon Magus.

"You are the Boundless Power. I want you to come in."

I smile and become smoke. He inhales and I rush into his soul. He is not nearly as tainted and horrific as my previous hosts were. But I will change that. He recoils in horror as he realizes what he has done. They always do. But he has invited me in and I take over his body and mind. I shove his soul into a far, dark corner and bind his mouth. He screams soundlessly for release, but he will never know release again. I stand up now in the human's body and lick the blood from my hands. How delicious! I feel my symbol burn its way into the man's flesh. But, wait—I do not want to reveal myself just yet. The symbol fades back into the bloodstained flesh of this puny man. In the distant corner of his mind, he flinches, for he recognizes the symbol.

And there I find another image. What is this? A chest? Yes, I know this thing! It is feared by every member of the Council of Darkness, and this man knows where it is! While my new name may be Chaos, I see a plan forming. I see how I can use this chest to achieve fitting closure to the pain of my past. Yes, we shall have the chest. Just a slight right-hand turn into other dimensions will suffice.

Chapter 6

Theophilus Nosmo King

MY POOR BRAIN was fried. I was beat! I hadn't felt this wiped out since the time I chased those two perps across south Los Angeles on a ninety-five-degree summer's day. I stopped and glanced up at the star-filled sky. "God, you know what else I did that day. Only you know what drove me to the drugs."

I shook it off and walked through the dark toward the garage apartment, my gym bag in hand. It contained all my earthly possessions. Thank God Jonathan Steel had helped me on that night I was supposed to shoot him. I shuddered as I walked up the outside stairs to the second-floor porch. To think that the last bullet in that gun had been rigged to explode! The assassin, Raven, had not intended for me to live after killing Jonathan Steel. Thank God things had turned out differently.

The stairs groaned under my weight. Truth be told, I had lost about fifty pounds while trying to do crack with Lydia. But I had been too big for the hits to do me any good. I had wasted away while Lydia lay in a daze. Over the couple of weeks since Dallas, I had gained some weight. I was going to get back into shape. I was going to do whatever I had to in order to protect the man who had saved my life. I was going to protect Jonathan and Josh.

I fumbled with the keys to the fancy French doors on the second floor. A blue glow came off the pool and cast shimmering reflections as I tried to find the lock on the door. I finally got it open and stepped into Vivian Darbonne's old lair.

The air was musty and hot. I found the light switch and flicked it on. A large den looked out over the pool through another set of French doors. Along the back of the den, a bar separated the kitchen from the dining area. The furniture was all black leather. Vivian needed to get a new look! I found the thermostat and turned it down to sixty-five degrees.

A short hallway behind the kitchen led to the only bedroom. I flipped on the lights. The king-size bed was bare. I tossed my gym bag onto the bed and stripped down to nothing. I turned on the water in the shower and waited for it to heat up before getting in and scrubbing the sweat and grime from my body. At least they had left the water heater on. I finished my shower, dried off, and looked at myself in the mirror above the vanity.

"You are one ugly dude," I said. I had shaved off my hair after the events in the Transylvania. Just easier to deal. My eyes were dark and rimmed with yellow. I was zonked, but I was clean. I was healing. I was the man!

I pulled on my gym shorts and a tank top from my bag. That was when I heard a sound from the kitchen. Hunched over the bed, I froze and then slowly turned so I could see down the hall. Something moved in the deep shadows.

"Z'at you, Jonathan?"

Something exploded at me. Two metal darts hit me full force in the chest. I fell backward toward the bed, slid down sideways, and came to rest on the floor in the corner of the room. My entire body convulsed with the electric wave sent by the Taser.

Vivian Darbonne Ketrick stepped into view. She wore a black jumpsuit and her hair was pulled tight against her skull. She tossed the Taser aside and hovered over me. My heart raced as I tried to move. Nothing happened.

"Well, if it isn't the big mountain of a man. Imagine my surprise to find that someone had bought this house. And by some of my favorite people."

I tried to speak. My tongue was thick. Drool trickled down my chin. Vivian crossed the room to an electrical panel next to the outside door. She opened it and withdrew a ring of keys.

"My extra key to Ketrick's house." She dangled the keys in front of me and smiled. "I kept the key to my apartment, but I had to give the other keys to the FBI. Never thought I'd need to come back to this dump." She kicked me hard beneath the breastbone and pain exploded through my stomach. "Now, if you'll excuse me, I have something to find in Ketrick's dungeon. See you later, alligator."

She disappeared down the hallway, leaving me to my pain.

N W✦E S

Jonathan Steel

I never found the words to apologize to Josh. How do you deal with a teenager? Moody, fickle kid that he was, I felt bad for bringing up his mother.

"Good pizza." I said.

"Not bad." Cephas nodded. The air was thick with tension.

"Chief, what are you going to do about that other house of yours?" Theo said.

"The one in Gulf Shores?"

Josh showed a flicker of interest. "You have a house on the beach?"

I saw a glimmer of redemption. "Yes, I do. Maybe in a couple of weeks we can go to the beach. You can frolic." Frolic? Where had that word come from?

"Dude, I don't frolic," he snapped. "Wait, maybe I do. I'm going upstairs to *frolic* in the game room."

Cephas sighed as Josh shoved his chair away from the dining room table and disappeared up the stairs. "Frolic? You had to say frolic?"

I shrugged. "I don't know how to handle kids."

"Well, you can't beat the tar out of them like you do the demons." Theo stood up. "I'm heading to my apartment and shower." He grabbed a gym bag and left the room.

Cephas nibbled a piece of pizza and then tossed it on the table. He ran a hand through his unruly hair and turned his tired eyes to me.

"What was that all about, Jonathan?"

A muscle twitched at the corner of my mouth. "I said something stupid while we were outside. I seem to be doing that a lot around Josh."

"I don't have any experience with children, either. I don't think there is an owner's manual for adolescents, unfortunately."

"You never married?" I glanced at the old man. He averted his gaze.

"I loved only one woman, Jonathan. She rejected me. That is all I will say about it." He motioned me to follow him. "I want to show you something." We descended the stairs into the basement.

Cephas threw a master switch by the foot of the stairs and lights came on in the cavernous chamber. Wooden crates were stacked all around in groups. Already, climate-controlled cabinets sat against one wall, ready for Cephas's most ancient artifacts. I followed him back to the secretary by his desk. I thought he was going to start going over the manuscript again. Instead, he closed the doors on the secretary and pointed at the wall next to it. He rapped on the wall. It made a hollow sound.

"Hear that?"

"Yeah."

Cephas motioned down the wall. "Now, follow me. You'll notice that the basement is separated by these walls into four divisions."

"It gives the place a feeling of compartmentalization. Sort of like your setup in New York City," I said.

On the other side of the wall, Cephas pointed at a dark stain that had soaked into the concrete. At the base of the wall, the stain extended upward onto the unpainted sheetrock.

"What is this?" I asked.

"I am afraid to ask, Jonathan." Cephas touched the wall. He grimaced and jerked his hand away. "Old blood, perhaps? Secret chambers, Jonathan."

"Why didn't the FBI see this when they took Ketrick's stuff?"

"There was so much for them to remove and catalog, I'm afraid they had tunnel vision. With Ketrick's reputation, I hate to even imagine what is hidden behind these walls."

A scraping noise filled the room. Metal grated on concrete. The sound started near the base of the stairs and started to come toward us. I eased back down the wall and around the end of the partition. An axe appeared in the air above the top of the crates and crashed down against the wall. Plaster and dust shot into the air from the impact. I ran around the crates. Vivian Darbonne Ketrick was holding an axe above her head. White sheetrock dust covered her black jumpsuit.

She swore and glared at me. "You scared the dickens out of me! Honey, you shouldn't scare a woman with an axe to grind."

"What are you doing in our house?" Cephas asked.

"Your house?" she said, lowering the axe and resting the head of it on the floor. She leaned against the handle and put one hand on her hip. "It belonged to my late husband, Robert Ketrick, and it was seized by the FBI before I could keep it from being sold right out from under me."

"That's right. I forgot that you and Ketrick got married," I said. "Sorry about the honeymoon."

Vivian shrugged. "He was a hard man to love. Now, I have the right to take anything that I want from here. It's in the sales contract."

"I am the owner of this house now," Cephas said. "And I went over the contract with a fine-toothed comb. I did not find a clause allowing the former owner to return for any possessions left behind." He lifted his cell phone into view. "I will now call 911 and report a burglary unless you leave."

Vivian tensed and hefted the axe to shoulder level. "I never had the chance to lock horns with you, old man. But I looked into your past. Have you told Steel about the girl?"

Before Cephas could answer I put a restraining hand on his arm. "What do you want, Vivian?"

"Something that belongs to me."

"Maybe the FBI took it," I said.

Behind Vivian, a shadow passed down the stairs; Josh walked into view. Vivian sensed my attention and whirled around. "Well, looky what the cat dragged in! Hi, boyfriend," she said. Josh's eyes grew wide and he paused at the base of the stairs.

"Who let you in?"

"I let myself in." She slinked toward him, letting the axe head fall to the floor. It scraped on the concrete behind her, throwing up tiny sparks. "I've missed you, Josh."

Josh glanced at me. *Stay calm*, I mouthed. After all, Vivian had an axe. She paused just inches from his face and suddenly licked him across the cheek, her left hand pressing his face close to hers. He shouted in surprise and pushed away from her. "That's just gross! Why don't you just leave us alone?"

"Oh, honey, don't you taste like God!" Vivian spit on the floor. "I need some mouthwash. Some unholy water!" She laughed and touched Josh's face with a finger. He pulled away. "You should have listened to me when Wulfy baby was around. You could have joined me instead of hanging out with these two losers."

Josh gingerly stepped around her and hurried over to us. "You lied to me about the unpardonable sin. I can't denounce God, Vivian. I belong to Him."

"Can't blame a girl for trying." Vivian tossed the axe to one side. She crossed her arms over her black jumpsuit. "Let me make one thing clear. There is a chest here, about two feet by two feet by eight inches with bronze clasps. It belongs to me. If you find it, I expect you to do the honorable thing and call me, Jonathan. It is mine regardless of the wording of the contract. I will be contacting my lawyer tomorrow. With the money I now have, I can have you evicted from this house and every wall torn down until I find what I'm looking for. So save yourself the trouble and just give it to me."

A chest? I glanced at Cephas and he shrugged. "Haven't seen it," he said.

"Well, it won't be sitting out here with a black ribbon on it. It's inside there." She pointed at the wall and walked slowly across the room until she was next to the secretary. "What have we here?"

"Stay away from that!" Cephas said. "You have no claim on my possessions."

Vivian opened the door and peeked in. "Well, aren't you full of surprises?" She turned her attention to the desk and picked up the framed picture on top

33

of the box. "Nice hairdo." She placed the picture facedown and then reached out and stroked the wall. She closed her eyes. For a moment she seemed transfixed. "Boo!" Her eyes flew wide open and Josh jerked beside me. She sat down on the edge of Cephas's desk and tapped on the back of the picture frame. "Old man, you have no idea what you are dealing with. Inside these walls there are things that would make an angel sweat. No one knows the depths of depravity to which my dear, departed husband stooped." She grew quiet and her eyes glazed over. She was suddenly far away. "You just don't know, honey," she whispered. Then she shook her head violently and slid off the desk. "Do I have your word, Jonathan? If you find the chest, will you give me a call?"

"You have my word, Vivian. Now, go."

She threw me a kiss and turned to go. Something lurched at the top of the stairs; Theo stumbled down and landed at her feet, his chest heaving and his limbs wild and uncontrolled. Vivian glared at him. "Back on the drugs, I see."

She ran up the stairs and disappeared from view as Theo sat up. "She tased me, bro. She tased me."

Grimvox Interlude #3

Chaos

THE HUMAN IS weaker than I had anticipated, but he managed to get the chest from its hiding place in the house. I waited until after midnight so that the new inhabitants would be asleep. Unfortunately, the stress on my host's body was more than he could handle. I may have left something related to the chest behind but I will have to wait until my puny host recovers. The vile old man in the house has something else of interest. I will have to retrieve it too.

I am getting weaker. This cannot be happening! My mind flickers like lightning through memories of the past. My memory is nightmare: unrelenting, unforgiving, always unwinding and beckoning. There is no mortal flesh to my essence, no brain to shrink and pale. Memories are sharper than sharp, a reality unto themselves. This is eternal torment: to always remember and never forget.

I am falling, forever falling from that wondrous light and swirling down an infinite abyss with Chamas beside me. He is my spirit brother and our minds are so alike we are almost one.

"Why did you follow him?" I scream in pain. The wound on my side is leaking light and my appendages—what humans will one day call wings—are totally useless as they flap in the cosmic wind.

"He contended with the Creator for equality." Chamas presses his hands against the gaping hole in my side. He extends his wings to try to catch the wind, but all he gathers is dark matter. Dark energy balls up against us like pollen on a bee.

"I never should have listened to you," I hiss. The darkness is all around us now, so thick and heady I can no longer see the light and the glory of our home. We have been cast out, exiled, separated from the Creator. Now we are falling with the others, spiraling into darkness.

"Chotus, I will take care of this." He brings the tip of his wing around in the clotted darkness and touches the tip to my wound. I feel searing pain as the wound closes. My essence is no longer leaking away. Chamas wraps his arms around my weakened wings and tries to glide. Through a gap in the darkness, we see the tiny green-and-blue dot, the Creator's latest obsession glittering against the blackness of space like a welcome jewel.

"Is that our prison?" I mutter through clenched teeth.

"That is where we are exiled, Chotus. But we will recover from this. We will arise. The Master will make things right."

I pull myself into a ball against the dark frigidity of space and wait for the pain I know will come once we plunge into the substance of this new world. The black matter tears away and we pass through a membrane. It sizzles with energy and flames. Across the horizon, I see millions of my fallen brothers similarly piercing the barrier the Creator made. Once we pass through it, we are bound to this new world and its fate. The pain is electrifying and it courses through every fiber of my being as Chamas and I pass through the barrier.

He falls away and tumbles through the atmosphere. For a fleeting moment, he is a fiery star falling to earth. I stay hunched in a ball and the flames dance around me, searing my wings and burning the wound in my side. I close my eyes and then I am rolling, scraping, floundering through sand across a plane of heat and desolation. I discover a piece of the darkness tucked into my wound. It is small, infinitesimal, and an abomination to this world. It will be a seed of future destruction. I press it deep into my wound, deeper into my substance until I have surrounded the seed of darkness with my very being. There, it slumbers in wait for the day when I need it.

As the fire and heat dissipate, I stumble to my feet and look upon this new world. Something jointed and plated hurries toward me. It is as large as my body, with huge pincers and an arching tail. At the end of the tail, a stinger drips poison. The thing shoots toward me with alarming speed. In the time Before, we moved through the dimensions of space as easily as this thing moves over the sand dunes. I try to pierce the veil of this world's limited space-time dimensions. It is like moving through a tiny crack—then I am in complete darkness. It is not the darkness of the absence of light; this darkness is profound, spiritual, disconnected from reality. And yet, in this lightless dimension, I sense movement and sound and my living-dead fallen companions. Their cries of pain and agony fill my mind. Below me are levels of suffering and torture. Torture! We never knew this in the presence of the Creator. Oh, what we have lost! Oh, what we have thrown away! We are no longer in the presence of the Creator, and our only option is this place? What is this place? I try to move on to other planes of existence but find myself back in the hot, dry desert. The thing that attacked moves about in a clumsy, confused fashion, then it scuttles over the dunes and disappears.

"We can move in and out of only one dimension other than the dimensions of this world," Chamas says as he appears from the interdimensional substance through which we once moved with abandon. His skin is seared from his entry into the atmosphere. "I sensed your presence and followed you here, Chotus."

"That barrier we passed through means we are prisoners here. Or can we move into that dark place? I do not wish to stay there! The master has much to answer for. Chamas, we have given up eternal bliss in exchange for eternal torment."

"Do not despair, Chotus. This is far from over."

"You are lying to yourself, Chamas. The Master has exchanged Truth for a world of lies. And what of the Master? Did he escape God's wrath? I hope not!"

Chamas tries to wipe the black char from his once-luminous skin. "He is here with us, Chotus, and he is gathering the fallen over that dune. He has a plan."

"I hope it's better than the last one."

Back in the present now, I realize with horror that my host is on the verge of consciousness. I am trapped! His awareness is barely a flicker, yet I am paralyzed. I cannot escape while he is still conscious. Someone is coming! I hear the door open.

"You've been busy!" I cannot see the human speaking because of the weakness of my host. "A sacrifice? How precious! How endearing! Wait, that picture—how dare you put that picture on the wall of this place!"

The human is near now, but I cannot see it. There is sudden pain—the human is kicking me! Stop it! If I could just escape from this body, your punishment would be incredible!

"What's this?" I hear the human say. It has found the chest! No! I feel the heat of its body as it leans over me. "I'll just take this for safe keeping." I hear it take the chest from the end of the altar. Gold and jewels flash. It has taken the Knife! In seconds, the human is gone. I didn't even see who it was. How am I going to get the chest back?

Another sound from the door. Is it returning? No, the odor is different. The presence is different. This human is standing at the other end of the altar table, and I sense in it an evil whose long shadow stretches centuries into the past. It is a shadow of powerful substance and it is from a different faction from those I have dealt with before. It does not know I am here on the floor. It followed the other human. What does it want?

I feel my host's body stirring. He is awakening. His eyes are fluttering. I can barely see now. I see the other human's hands. They are hovering over the end of the altar table. What's this? One of the hands is holding a golden object. It is cylindrical and fits into the palm of the human's hand. A foul memory stirs deep within. Where have I seen this thing before?

The demon mind that resides within that human is more powerful than I am at the moment. I have to be quiet. If it hears me stirring, it may kill this host. I must recover my strength and then retrieve the other items. Then I will find the first human, who took the chest.

The second human with the golden object is gone now. I feel the strength returning to this body. Slowly, I get up. I lean against the end of the altar table and breathe in deeply.

"You idiot!" I scream. "You let the human take the chest!" I unleash my anger and fill my host's mind with pain. It grows weak again and I risk killing it. Not yet! I withdraw the pain and manage to stumble to the head of the altar table. The sacrifice's face is bleeding. I pull the black cloth back over its lifeless features.

Outside, the night air is hot and humid. I realize my host needs rest. I will let it rest and then I will return to get the other items. And after that, I will find a new host and finish this business. I will have the chest!

Chapter 7

Josh Knight

I JUST DIDN'T GET it. What was so freakin' awesome about Ms. Pac-Man? I mean, it was an old game from the dark ages of 8-bit—like, ancient! But there it was, blipping away when I woke up in the morning. It was like someone came in the middle of the night and played the game. Could have been Vivian, that freak! She always popped up when you least expected it. My mouth felt like a dead skunk had slept in it and my armpits really reeked of BO. Too bad Vivian wasn't there for me to rub her face in my armpits. That would show her!

I must have fallen asleep on the couch in the games room. I jumped up, cracked my neck, and shoved the Ms. Pac-Man video console away from the wall, which wasn't easy since it was as heavy as Theo. I jerked the plug out to shut the thing up.

The room was suddenly quiet. Too quiet. Over a dozen video consoles stared back at me like they were dead or something. It gave me the willies. Hey, this house gave me the willies!

I first saw this place when I was possessed by the thirteenth demon. I only remembered flashes of it, but I couldn't get rid of the memory of that thing being inside of me. It was like being squeezed way down into a tiny ball and shoved somewhere in the dark where I couldn't breathe. But Jonathan saved me. Man, those weird eyes of his freak me out! He was kind of creepy. Yeah, like Theo and Uncle Cephas aren't?

I went to my new bedroom and made my way through the unpacked boxes to my duffle bag. I really did need to unpack, but doing that would mean putting my house and my past behind me. My house in Dallas had almost burned to the ground, and my lawyer said it would have to be torn down. Except for a few things from my room, most of the stuff from the house was in storage now.

I zipped open the duffle bag and my old monkey, Boobo, peered up at me.

I glanced at the door to make sure Jonathan wasn't there. The dude could show up anywhere, anytime, like a ninja. Boobo had lost one ear and both hands, but he was the first thing I remembered from being a kid. Mom used to act like a monkey and dance with Boobo to make me laugh.

I held Boobo up to my nose and inhaled. For a second, I could smell my house and my mother, and I was sad. She had shoved Ketrick into the furnace to save Emily Parker from being sliced and diced. I ached inside. I missed her. I put Boobo on the bare mattress of my bed. I didn't give a rip if Jonathan saw him!

I pulled on a tank top over my boxers and a new odor filled the air. Bacon? I followed the fragrance down the stairs. My stomach growled. Dude, I was hungry! Uncle Cephas stood over the stove with a spatula in his hand.

Theo hovered beside him. "Your special recipe is very similar to mine, Papaw."

"After you cooked for us last night, it seemed the least I could do to make pancakes, which is the only food I am good at cooking." Uncle Cephas flipped a pancake on the metal griddle.

Theo was wearing a huge, bright-orange football jersey with the Texas Longhorns logo on the back.

"Hook 'em horns?" I said.

Theo tore his gaze away from the pancakes. "That's for you, my man."

"Dude, I prefer the Tigers, but I'll let it slide." I picked up the plastic gallon jug of orange juice from the island and swigged from it.

"LSU? You from Texas, my man. Traitor!" Theo pulled the jug out of my grasp and poured orange juice into an empty glass. "Man, we don't want none of your cooties!"

"Cooties, really?"

"You stink like one. Man don't drink from the jug in my kitchen."

"*Your* kitchen?" Cephas said.

"Papaw, you a parrot or something?" Theo plopped the jug back on the countertop. "I am the chief cook and dishwasher in this house. And don't you forget it."

"I thought you were the treasurer." Cephas plopped four pancakes onto a plate and placed it in front of me. I dug into the pancakes. They were good. In fact, they were freakin' unbelievable! "Hey, Uncle Cephas, these are some awesome pancakes. Where is Jonathan?"

"Running." Cephas smiled and straightened his moustache. "Now, Theo, I hope that Josh's testimonial will convince you to, on occasion, allow me to be a guest in *your* kitchen, which, by the way, is in *my* house!" Cephas poured more batter onto the griddle. "We seem to have a competition brewing."

I cut another bite and shoved it into my mouth. "So, Theo, your recipe is better?"

He crossed his huge arms over his massive chest. "My pancakes will be the best thing you've ever put in your mouth. Papaw here claims his recipe is better than mine. But I have a secret ingredient." He slid a plate of scrambled eggs across the island toward me. "Now, these scrambled eggs are to die for. Try them. *My* recipe!"

I nodded and took a bite of the scrambled eggs. They were good too. Maybe having Theo around wouldn't be such a bad thing.

"You stink."

I turned as Jonathan came in from outside. He had on a long-sleeved athletic shirt and a pair of shorts. He was soaked to the skin with sweat. "Look who's talking?" I said back to him. I mean, for real, the man never cut me any slack! Was I always going to have to put up with his crap from now on? I turned my back on him and felt my face grow warm. "The first time I saw you was right after a run. Bro, you reeked!"

"Sorry." He said. "This is what you smelled like the first time we met. You need some D.O for the B.O."

For a second, there was a ghost of a smile on the man's face. I squinted. "Wait! Dude, did I see a smile? Hey, Theo, did you see the big man smile? What about you, Uncle Cephas?"

Cephas pointed the spatula at Jonathan. "I definitely saw a spasm of the muscles surrounding the mouth. In any other person, I would call it a smile."

"Very funny," Jonathan said. But his face betrayed him. He was actually trying to suppress a smile.

"Once you eat some of my eggs, you'll definitely be smiling." Theo put a plate in front of Jonathan.

"You feeling okay?" He asked Theo.

"My nerves are little rattled, but it'll take more than a Taser to stop Theophilus Nosmo King!" He grinned. "If you recall, I took out an army of vampires with one hand tied behind my back."

Jonathan sat beside me at the island and ate some eggs. Cephas placed a small stack of pancakes onto his plate. Jonathan tried both. "They're good, Theo. Very good. Where did you learn to cook pancakes, Cephas?"

"I learned to cook them for a little girl—" He suddenly fell silent and turned his back on us. I glanced at Jonathan and he shrugged. Theo ignored

41

Cephas's sudden change in demeanor and tapped the plate of eggs. "Even after being tased by a demon lover, I still got the touch. And when you taste *my* pancakes, you'll agree that I am the king of this kitchen!"

A knock on the door interrupted our breakfast. Theo opened the door to reveal a uniformed police officer. He wore mirrored sunglasses and a brown cowboy hat. Yeah, a cowboy hat. On his tan uniform, a patch read, "Caddo Parish Sheriff's Department." Parish? That's right. We were in Louisiana. No counties, just parishes.

"Mr. King?" He said.

"That would be me," Theo answered.

"You called to report an intruder?"

Jonathan stood up. "Come in."

The man hesitated and then stepped over the threshold. "I'm Deputy Sheriff Prescott. Why don't you tell me what happened?"

Theo told his side of the story. Jonathan told his. The deputy sheriff scribbled in a small notebook. He never took his sunglasses off. Theo plopped the Taser down on the island. "This is what she tased me with."

"How did she get in?"

"She had a key," Theo answered.

"Well, it'll be hard to justify breaking and entering if she had a key. Especially since she used to live here. She probably thought you were an intruder."

Theo stiffened. "Listen, man, she kicked me in the chest after she saw who I was. I want to press charges."

The deputy nodded. "Mr. King, I checked you out on the network. You are a wanted man in Dallas."

Jonathan moved between Theo and the deputy. "Judge Bolton released him from his warrant. He is in my custody."

The two of them stood almost nose to nose. They were about the same size and build. The deputy took off his sunglasses. His eyes were as creepily blue as Jonathan's. "And you must be Jonathan Steel."

"Yes, I am. Vivian threatened us with an axe."

"A woman axe-killer? Really? Sounds like a bad cliché." The deputy closed his notebook and tucked it into his pocket. "I think this whole thing was probably a mere misunderstanding. I'll get Mrs. Ketrick's side of the story and let you know." He reached for the Taser but Theo stopped him.

"I'll keep this, if you don't mind."

"It's evidence." The deputy said.

"You just told us there was no crime," Jonathan said, moving closer. The air was full with tension and I was afraid we were in for a Jonathan Steel thunderstorm.

"Hey, dude, forget it. We're cool." I said. Jonathan glanced at me. "Jonathan, man, calm down. We don't want you back in jail. Okay?"

That got to him. He stepped away from the deputy. "Theo is keeping the Taser. Just in case another intruder comes back."

"No problem." The deputy put his sunglasses on and tapped the brim of his hat. "I'll keep you posted."

Theo slammed the door after him. "What was that all about?"

Jonathan eased back onto the stool by the island. "This was Ketrick's territory, Theo. He was rich and powerful. Vivian has his last name. She probably pulled some strings to bury what happened last night. Forget it for now. With Vivian, we are on our own."

"So what was up with Vivian last night?" I asked.

"She said something about a wooden chest left behind by Ketrick," Jonathan said. We were driving in my mother's old, battered truck down Bert Kouns Industrial Drive in Shreveport.

"Uncle Cephas said the basement was empty."

"Cephas thinks there are some hidden compartments in the walls."

"So that's why she had the axe." My mind was whirling. "Wait a minute, dude! Are they going through the walls right now?"

"Yes."

"I want to help! I mean, think of the things that could be hidden in those walls. I'll bet he had zombies in there. Or a mummy or two. Maybe an alien!"

"That is why you are with me."

I sank back into the seat. "You're afraid I'll see something scary?"

"Yes."

"Jonathan, I was possessed by a demon that celebrated a good day by chowing down on human hearts while they were still pumping. And then I spent a week with a clan of vampires and was almost skewered on their spears of destiny. I think I can handle some old skeletons in somebody's closet." We pulled into a car dealer. "What are we doing?"

"We need some new vehicles. We can't drive the RV around town, and this truck is on its last legs." He killed the engine.

"Okay, I want that cool-looking SUV right over there." I pointed.

Jonathan patted the seat. "*This* is your truck, Josh. Do you know how many guys would kill to have a chick magnet like this?"

I looked at him. "Chick magnet? Did you just say 'chick magnet'?"

Jonathan shrugged. "What?"

"Dude, it just doesn't sound cool coming out of your mouth. Just be yourself, okay? And this old truck is far from being a chick magnet."

Jonathan got out of the car. "Fine. But you'll regret it later, and then all you'll do is complain. Maybe I can get us some cheese to go with your whine."

My mouth fell open. I closed it. "Did you just try to make a joke?"

"Did I?"

"Stop! Now. Before you hurt yourself."

There was a ghost of a smile again. I followed him to the showroom floor. "Bro, there are certain constants in the universe. There's the speed of light. There's the fickle nature of girls. And there is Jonathan Steel. Don't try to be something you're not. The universe might implode."

We came home with an SUV after all. It was dark blue and white and could go just about anywhere. For Theo, Jonathan picked out a huge pickup. I hated giving up Mom's old truck as a trade-in, but I had to move on. I drove the SUV and imagined myself cruising the beach in front of Jonathan's beach house. I would stop and the girls would swarm my ride and climb inside and we would—

"Josh? Josh?"

I looked up at Jonathan standing beside the closed window. We were in the driveway of the lake house and I had the air conditioning on super-high. I opened the window. "Sorry, dude. I was, uh, thinking."

Jonathan glared at me with those squirrely turquoise eyes of his. They really grated on my nerves. Like he was from some other planet or something. Sometimes, I could imagine Jonathan from the frosty planet of Uranus. Hey, that was a good one! He pointed at the new truck. "I thought you were right behind me."

I shrugged. "I took a shortcut around the lake. I wanted to see how the new ride handled."

Jonathan glared at me some more. He really needed to perfect a different look of disapproval. But, he was, at times, a one-dimensional dude.

"I need a new iPhone so you can call me," I said. "My old one is in Transylvania."

"Then order one online."

"I will as soon as I set up the wireless network. We've been here less than twenty-four hours, dude. I'm the only tech-savvy guy around."

"Yes, the rest of us are living in the Stone Age." Another joke? The world was tilting. Then I remembered Uncle Cephas and the hidden compartments in the walls of the basement. I hopped out of the car and ran into the house.

Uncle Cephas was waiting at the top of the basement stairs. He looked at me quickly with a sideways glance that spoke volumes. He had found something and he wasn't sure I needed to see it. So I ran around him and hopped down the stairs.

Theo was standing behind that huge desk of Uncle Cephas's, looking down at a piece of leathery fabric.

"What is this? The skin of Bigfoot?"

I heard Uncle Cephas breathing heavily behind me. He leaned over the desk. "We found this on a shelf in the wall."

There was a man-sized opening into the interior of the wall where Vivian had started pounding away with her axe. "I thought she was looking for some kind of chest. Anything else in there?"

"Just this fabric. It is leather. Very old. These lines on it indicate it was wrapped around a rectangular structure."

"Let me guess," Jonathan said. "The box described by Vivian?"

"Yes. The dimensions fit. It was removed and this wrap was left behind."

I peeked in the opening in the wall and looked at the shelves. "Think she came back?"

"No." Theo towered over me. "We had to bust out the rest of the wall. The hole was too small for anyone to get inside, even Vivian."

The inside of the wall smelled of dry rot and mold. Dust covered all of the shelves except for the one on which they had found the leather scrap.

"The wrap was tossed aside as if someone had torn it off the chest. And," Uncle Cephas said, "if you will look down at the floor beneath the shelf, you will see one set of footprints."

A pair of cowboy-boot-shaped footprints was stamped into the dust. But something was weird. There were two sets of prints leading in and then out. "Those are yours and Theo's?" I asked.

"Yes, Josh. What is odd about the single set of prints?"

"There aren't any prints leading to the shelf or away."

"Precisely. Jonathan, I don't believe anyone broke into this wall to retrieve the chest."

Jonathan leaned his head into the enclosure. "So how did this person remove it?"

I shook my head. I couldn't believe what I was about to say. "Beam me up, Scotty?"

Chapter 8

Cephas Lawrence

THERE WAS A time in my life when the idea of working with a colleague was acceptable. But that was before the terrible tragedy that I kept hidden from everyone. I did not dwell on those days anymore. Living in New York City had been my way of isolating myself so I could devote my remaining days to discovering the denizens of evil that plagued my existence. And so it was odd to find myself in a partnership with another individual in my battle against evil. But then, there was no one on the face of the Earth quite like Jonathan Steel. I did not think he realized his own special nature or his nascent abilities. I hoped to live long enough to see him realize his full potential. The results would be breathtaking.

For now, I had to trust that my partnership with the extraordinary man would bring about the revelation of the evil enterprise that dwelled and thrived among us before it was too late. It was true that my plan to move to this southern climate was ill-advised after I had discovered that this house belonged to Robert Ketrick and the thirteenth demon. But I had learned that man's plans were never as clever as God's. For reasons yet to be learned, God had seen to it that we ended up here, in the very edifice where one of those heinous creatures had performed his evil work.

I had sent the others back upstairs. My great-nephew was excited about our new vehicles and went off to take one for a "spin." Theo was "whipping up some supper" in the kitchen. Having spent most of my life on the northeastern coast of the United States, I had never once eaten "supper." Not even during that dreadful time, long ago in Texas.

Theo had helped me to set up some of my equipment on a bench along an inner wall of the basement. I put on a pair of gloves, then picked up the fabric and placed it under a special scanner that used several wavelengths of light to capture images. By fusing the images together using a computer program I had designed, I would be able to bring out any latent images on the leather fabric.

The device gave a mournful *ding* to indicate that the last of the scanning sequences was complete. I sat down at my computer to bring together the multiple sequences. I had placed key reference points on the fabric and used them as points of commonality for each image. After I had finished fusing the images together, I left the program to process the data. It would take a while.

I retrieved the fabric and placed it in another scanner. This one was a modified magnetic resonance imaging device. It had been a prototype of a small "open" MRI for imaging joints. The problem for the clinicians had been the low magnetic field strength and subsequent longer scanning time; patients couldn't sit still for an hour while the instrument took images of ankles, wrists, or elbows. But I had found a way to use the flat surfaces of the open magnet to image ancient manuscripts and artifacts. By using high-energy radio frequencies that would have harmed human tissue, I was able to produce three-dimensional images of most inanimate objects.

The magnet looked like a huge tuning fork with round, flat tines. It was between these tines, on a round Plexiglas sheet, that I placed the fabric. I could only image one quarter of it at a time, but by using the right pulse sequence, I would be able to image each quarter in less than ten minutes.

An hour later, I had finished the MRI scan. I placed the piece of leather on the desk. By now, the fragrance of supper was drifting from the kitchen down the stairs, redolent with Cajun spices. Perhaps jambalaya? Theo had said he cooked excellent Cajun and Tex Mex. I made a mental note to take my antacid medication before we ate. The programs were still running, so I headed upstairs. And yet, something uneasy crawled across my mind. I was halfway up the stairs when the sound came. I felt rather than heard a faint *pop* behind me. I whirled around to look at the desk. The fabric was gone! The air smelled faintly of ozone. I looked around, but the room was devoid of any human presence. Still, the unmistakable presence of evil was overpowering. Someone or something had taken the leather wrap from under my very nose.

Jonathan Steel

"I don't understand."

Cephas slumped into a chair at the table and ran his hands through his hair. "I was working on scanning the fabric. It was firmly attached to a

Plexiglas scanning frame. I placed the frame with the fabric on my desk after completing the scanning. And then—"

"What happened?" Josh leaned forward over the edge of the dining room table.

"I was coming up the stairs and I heard this strange sound. A rustling noise, and then a popping sound. When I turned around, the fabric was gone, but the Plexiglas frame remained." Cephas closed his eyes and leaned back in his chair. "How did they do this to us?"

Theo placed a plate laden with cornbread muffins on the table to accompany the bowls of gumbo already waiting. He sat down. "So, Papaw, you're saying the thing just—what, disappeared?"

"Like I said earlier," Josh said, grabbing a muffin and biting into it, "beam me up, Scotty." His voice was muffled by a mouthful of cornbread. "Man, these are awesome!"

"My grandmama's recipe. Secret ingredient is bacon bits. And something else." Theo scooped gumbo out of a huge bowl on the table and ladled some into his own bowl. "Somebody beamed up the chest and the fabric?"

"When I was looking for Josh in Dallas, Rudolph Wulf transported himself across the room to the stage," I said. In my mind, I was back in the old building in Dallas, dressed up as a vampire to meet Rudolph Wulf at the Bloodfest. I had gone there with Bile, the fangmaster who had designed my fangs. He knew the ins and outs of the local vampire clans and had agreed to accompany me to the vampire gathering.

"Wait, you're saying that Rudolph Wulf just poofed himself across the room?" Josh grabbed another muffin.

"We know that demons and angels have access to other dimensions of space. You learned that with the thirteenth demon."

"Oh, yeah. How could I forget that ride I took on a giant scorpion through space?" Josh said through another mouthful of cornbread. He stopped. "What? You're giving me that look."

"What look?"

"*That* look."

"Don't talk with your mouth full," Theo said. "That's what the look means. You're wasting my good muffins."

Josh gulped his iced tea. "You sound like my ..." His voice trailed off. He placed the half-eaten muffin onto his plate.

Tension filled the air and I glanced at Cephas for help. He sighed. "We're all dancing around the issue here. Josh, I know it hurts to lose someone. I lost someone."

I raised an eyebrow. Really? I didn't know much about the man's past.

"You lost someone. Theo has lost someone," Cephas said.

"You have no idea, Papaw," Theo whispered.

"And Jonathan has lost someone." Cephas reached over and patted Josh's hand. "Let's acknowledge it and move on. We're all in pain, but we have to press on. We have to keep living, Josh."

"I know, Uncle Cephas," Josh whispered. "It's just that I made so many mistakes. It's my fault my mother is dead."

"No, it isn't," I growled. I was growing weary of all of this self-recrimination. "We know who the enemy is. That thing inside of you duped you into inviting it in."

"Bro," he said, turning moist eyes in my direction, "I let it in."

"So you screwed up," I said. "We all screw up. It's not like you knew where it would lead. Live with it. It hurts, but your mother made the choice to die to save us. *She* made the choice, Josh, just like you did. No one forced her. She did it because she loved you." My heart felt like it was filled with molten lead.

I looked at the bowls of steaming shrimp gumbo Theo had placed before each of us. Cephas slurped up a spoonful and blinked. "This is quite good, Theo. However, my taste buds are not accustomed to your heavy Cajun spices." He reached for his glass of water and drank it quickly. His eyes watered and he wiped a tear from his face. "We can wallow in our misery later. I think we can assume that powerful demons can sustain their hosts while they move through other dimensions. That is what happened to you, Josh. You moved through other dimensions, yet you were not physically harmed."

"So someone, or something, teleported itself into the wall and took the chest?" I said.

"Yes."

"That explains the boot prints," Theo said.

"And then, that same someone—" Cephas started.

"Or something," Josh said.

"Or something came back for the fabric."

"Why?" I asked.

Cephas scraped the last of his gumbo from his bowl. "Give me an hour with my scanner data and maybe we will find out."

Chapter 9

Vivian Darbonne Ketrick

THE SUN WAS setting. I should have been amazed by the view from the windows overlooking downtown Shreveport. The Red River cut through the expanse of trees and rolling hills like a bloody serpent. Speaking of serpents, I wished I had a poisonous asp right about now. *That can be arranged*, the leech demon whispered in my mind. I ignored it.

"So we don't have any claim on the house? Is that what you're telling me, you shark?" I said, turning away from the view afforded by my lawyer's penthouse office.

Lynn Alba, a stately, middle-aged woman, sat behind her huge mahogany desk. She was impeccably dressed in a dark-purple three-piece suit and her features were faintly Mediterranean. Her salt-and-pepper hair was brushed away from her face and held back by a golden band. A large jewel hung from a chain around her neck. "I have been called worse, Mrs. Ketrick."

I paced the room. We had wasted an entire day in contract reviews and consultation with the local parish offices of whatever hick government controlled these deeds and successions. I wanted to lash out and kill something! *Let me!* the shark demon screeched in my head. I rolled my eyes and told it to shut up. "Ms. Alba, my Lakeside office told me you could handle anything. My patience is growing thin. I want results!"

"Vivian, my specialty is getting results. Right now, I am personally coordinating the details of the governor's visit this week. He will be speaking at the Chamber of Commerce Convention and the event will culminate with a picnic in the countryside. I can guarantee results, Vivian. However, your needs are small compared to a visit from the governor." Alba got up slowly from her desk. Her every movement seemed perfectly controlled. She moved across the office to a wet bar. "Would you like some sherry?"

I couldn't believe her insufferable patience. "No, I want the artifact! I could care less about the governor of this redneck state."

"That man is rumored to be the next president of the United States. He is a deliberate and patient man. Patience, Vivian." Alba poured herself a small glass of amber liquid, then turned and studied me for a moment. She raised the glass, sipped, and sighed. "Sherry must be savored. Why don't you sit down, calm your nerves, and let me do my work."

I plopped into a huge leather chair. "My administrative assistant, Reggie, said you were good. But what does he know?"

"He is *your* employee." Alba walked across the office, moving precisely as if even her steps were carefully planned and predetermined. "Vivian, you have no idea what I am capable of. My abilities and influence extend far beyond this state. Far beyond this country. I moved from Spain to this small city in order to consolidate our legal holdings here in the United States. Although my first duty is to my oil and gas clients, I will find this artifact for you."

"I just need access to the house, Alba. Get me a court order."

"Of course," she said with her back to me. The phone buzzed and she touched a hand to her earpiece.

"Yes." She turned to study me with dark eyes. "I see. I want you to do whatever it takes to find this artifact for Mrs. Ketrick. Yes, she claims it is located at Robert Ketrick's previous residence. I have, of course, assured Mrs. Ketrick we will do everything in our legal power to gain access to that house. You will? Good." She tapped her earpiece and sipped more sherry. "That was one of my associates. We may have access to the house by tomorrow, Mrs. Ketrick."

That really wasn't good enough, but I could see that badgering this woman wasn't going to do me any good. Maybe I could unleash one of my demons on her. They screeched with joy within me at the thought and Alba suddenly blinked and rubbed at her right eye. She reached into her jacket and removed a small vial. She began to put drops in each eye. "Forgive me, Mrs. Ketrick. I have allergies." She blinked a few times and retrieved a monogrammed handkerchief from her desk to dab her eyes. "We may have a court order by tomorrow."

"Good. Then you will call me in the morning?"

"I will let Reggie know. Until then."

I walked out of the building into stifling heat that had not relented with the sunset. Alba's office was across the street from my hotel. I paused on the street corner and watched the tourists heading for the casinos on the riverfront. They seemed so ordinary, so happy. I could be happy, too, if I wanted. I could take my frustration out on the casinos. With my powers, I could arrange to win everything. But I already controlled two massive international corporations and their funds. Money was no longer attractive to me. Only power. And the power I wanted was on the Council of Darkness. My cell phone rang.

"Hello?"

"Vivian, it's Juan."

I sighed. "I told you I didn't want to hear from you."

"I just wanted you to know I haven't given up looking for your artifact," he said.

"Juan, I am on the right track now so there is nothing you can offer me."

"I disagree, my dear Vivian." His voice suddenly changed. The man was growing confident and I didn't like that one bit.

I glanced around at the crowds moving down the sidewalk and hurried across the street into the cool lobby of my hotel. "Let me set you straight. I used you, Destillo. I wanted access to Ketrick's artifacts and that was it. We had some fun. You're a pretty boy, but it's over. Go back to you young bimbo and don't call back." I ended the call and turned my phone off.

Outside the lobby, a Caddo Parish Sheriff's car pulled up. A tall and wiry deputy sheriff got out of the car. He entered the lobby and passed me on his way to the front desk, where he conversed with the clerk. The clerk pointed in my direction. The deputy glanced at me and pulled off his sunglasses. There was a flicker of interest in his bright-blue eyes as he approached.

"Are you Mrs. Ketrick?" He drawled in a soft Southern accent.

"Who's asking?"

"Deputy Sheriff Prescott." He extended his hand. It was warm and supple. "I have a few questions about something that happened at a house on the lake last night."

His grip lingered and I gently pulled my hand away from his. Let me handle this, Summer whispered in my mind. I relaxed and blinked my eyes. "You must be talking about that man in my old apartment. Oh, it was just horrid!"

I stumbled back toward a chair. He took my arm and gently assisted me into it. "Thank you. It was just so horrible!" I took a handkerchief out of my purse and dabbed at my eyes. "First, my husband dies and I have to handle the transition of his estate and his business." I frowned at him. "Such a complex thing, his business. It was so hard trying to understand all the proceedings and the legal mumbo jumbo. And then I find out he was a murdering fiend! I had no idea! So I come back to town to get some of my things from our house so I can get on with my life, and I find out someone else is living there! Robert sold the house right out from under me!"

I shook my head and wiped a tear from my eye. "I went to my old apartment. I lived there before Robert and I were married, of course. And there was this huge man in my bedroom. My bedroom! I always keep a Taser on me for protection and before I knew it, I had shot him with it!" I started sobbing gently and covered my mouth with the handkerchief. "I'm sorry. It was so horrid!"

The deputy nodded. "Sounds like it, ma'am. I thought this was just one big misunderstanding. Don't you worry your pretty head about it one minute more. I'll close the book on this issue."

I stood up and moved closer to him. His eyes were such a deep blue. *Don't,* I told myself. *You don't need this.* I pushed Summer and her seductive ways back into the corner of my mind, but still, his deep-azure eyes drew me in. My heart skipped a few beats. He had that rugged man-smell of sweat and aftershave.

"Honey, when do you get off duty?" His eyes widened and he blinked. I reached down and took his hand. No ring. "Looks like you're single."

He opened his mouth and then closed it in surprise. I touched his lips with a finger. "Let me buy you a little old drink later this evening. I'm lonely and I could use some company. No harm in that, is there, sugar?"

He smiled slightly and nodded. "Okay, ma'am. But … you just lost your husband."

"Well, I am a practical woman, Deputy. Truth is, Robert Ketrick was a bit of a monster. I'm sure you've heard about the bad things he did. I need to put him behind me and get on with my life. Can you blame me?"

"Well, no, of course not! I'll come back around eight?"

"I'll be waiting."

The deputy nodded and left the lobby. I drew a deep breath and started for the elevator. The clerk was ogling me. He was fat and balding with a scraggly beard that did nothing to hide his double chin.

"What are you looking at?"

"You're good."

"And you're *you!*" I said as I stepped into the elevator. There had been more than just a physical attraction between the deputy and me. I could have him accompany me to serve the court order. That would put Jonathan in his place. Jonathan. The name brought a bitter taste to my mouth. And yet, as I returned to my room to get ready to meet the deputy for a drink and who knew what else, I couldn't clear the image of Jonathan's turquoise eyes from my mind.

Chapter 10

Jonathan Steel

I SAT AT CEPHAS'S desk in the basement while he hunched over his computer. Josh was hovering nearby, his hands twitching in anticipation. He wanted the keyboard. Theo lumbered down the stairs and plopped into a chair on the other side of the desk.

"Anything?"

"I don't know," I said.

Theo nodded and propped his feet up on the desk. "If that freaking Vivian has been popping in and out of here, I want to know. I'll be waiting for her with her own Taser."

"I don't think Vivian has that capability. Wulf could do it, but he'd been working with his demon for years. Vivian's demons are still new at this. I doubt she can transport herself like that."

"She can," Josh said.

"What do you mean?"

He glanced at me and swallowed. "You remember that night on Sandia Peak?"

"When you scattered your mother's ashes?"

"What are you talking about?" Cephas asked.

"Claire's favorite place. Sandia Peak," I said. I recalled the evening I had spent with her on the porch of the missionary house in Lakeside. I saw her face illuminated by the setting sun as she told me the story of her husband's death on Sandia Peak in New Mexico.

Cephas studied Josh for a moment. "That was the last place you saw your father, wasn't it?"

Josh nodded. "Yeah. He went hang gliding and disappeared when I was eleven. Died somewhere out in the desert. Mom still hoped he would show up one day. Every year, on the anniversary of his death, she would go back there.

I thought it would be a good idea to spread her ashes there, Uncle Cephas. Jonathan took me."

"I left you alone for about fifteen minutes," I said quietly. "Tell us what happened."

Josh Knight

I looked across the valley at the city of Albuquerque painted orange and red by the setting sun. The breeze was cool on my head. I had cut away my dyed hair and the piercing in my lower lip was healing up. Jonathan told me I had cleaned up pretty good. I wished my memories of the thirteenth demon would clean up as well as my wounds had. My mind was still raw and wounded from the thing that had lived inside me.

"The last cable car down is leaving in a few minutes. You want me to stay?" Jonathan asked.

"No, I want to be alone."

Jonathan nodded and reached into his backpack. He took out the brass box and studied it for a moment before handing it to me. The box wasn't really heavy, but to me, it felt like it weighed a ton. This was all I had left of my mother. "This was her favorite spot. Thanks for bringing me here."

"I'll wait for you at the cable-car house." Jonathan walked down the stone path and disappeared into the fir trees.

I made my way down the winding path to the edge of the precipice. This was the last place I had seen my Dad. Now it would also be the last place I'd see what was left of Mom. I stood with my toes on the lip of the cliff and felt the wind hurtling up from the darkening valley. I glanced over my shoulder at the spot my Dad had launched himself on his hang glider so many years ago. I followed the path, my eyes drifting out to the clear air hovering over the city below. I was alone now. They were both gone. All I had left was Uncle Cephas. And Jonathan Steel.

"Well, Mom, I'm here to tell you goodbye," I said, my voice cracking. My eyes watered. "I don't know how to say I'm sorry. I guess that's something I'll have to learn to live with."

I opened the top of the box and the ashes were caught by the gusting wind. They swirled up into the air in a whirlwind of gray dust, twisting and drifting out over the valley, following the path of my father's hang glider. Sorrow hit me hard. I groaned in pain. But then, the pain was suddenly replaced by a new feeling, an overpowering sensation of heaviness, oppression, anxiety. Evil! The hair stood on the back of my neck.

"Oh, Josh!" Behind me, darkness had swallowed the mountain path; the setting sun was hidden behind the mountains. From the far side of the small clearing, Vivian Darbonne appeared, dressed in a black jumpsuit. Her white face floated in the still, cold air. "Looky here what the cat dragged in. Did you really think I would just go off and leave you?" She stepped onto the mountain path and smiled.

"Vivian? What are you doing here?"

"I've come to party! And this time, I brought along some friends." Dark, shadowy figures appeared among the fir trees and slipped into the scarce light afforded by the moon. They moved lithely, like cats stalking prey. There were seven of them, clothed in black. They came to stand beside Vivian. One of them, a girl, smiled as she moved to Vivian's right. "Hello, Josh."

My eyes widened in shock. "Ila?"

"It's time to come home and play, boyfriend. I've missed you so much." Ila's lips parted and her tongue ran across fanged teeth. Fangs? "Vivian said you're all empty inside. We're here to fill you up again."

I shook my head in fear and closed my eyes. The wind died down behind me and I stumbled back toward the cliff face. My feet scrambled for purchase on the crumbling edge.

"No! I've changed." I felt myself slipping. Suddenly, a strong wind lifted me and pushed me back onto the ground, away from the cliff edge. A single butterfly flew into view. It glowed pale blue in the moonlight.

Vivian watched the butterfly float through the cool night air until it came to rest on Ila's arm. "A butterfly? Really? That's the best you can do?"

It was the butterfly from my dream. "That is no ordinary butterfly," I said.

Vivian laughed. Suddenly, Ila screamed in pain. She swatted at the butterfly but it evaded her hands with ease. The wind rose up behind me and my shadow stretched dark and long in front of me as something glowing and massive rose up the cliff face. Before I could even turn, a maelstrom of glowing, blue butterflies swirled around me and streamed toward Vivian and her demonic friends. Vivian cringed as the light from the butterflies cocooned her. Ila followed her friends into the forest, still screaming and swatting. Vivian was surrounded by a thousand flapping wings. I could barely make out her dark, glittering eyes through the glowing mass.

"This isn't over, Josh!" Vivian hissed. Then she disappeared in a puff of wind. The butterflies fell away and dissipated into glittering particles. A lone butterfly paused just in front of my face, and then it flew off into the darkness above the valley.

Jonathan Steel

"Now I understand why you felt compelled to help Ila," Cephas said.

"I'm not even sure she was really there, Uncle Cephas. Vivian could have been trying to fool me. But she did teleport right out of existence from the midst of all those butterflies."

"Raphael helped us all out," I said. "And I know why he chose a butterfly."

Raphael was an angel who came to our aid during our final confrontation with the thirteenth demon. On the front porch of the missionary house, Claire had shared her terrible secret with me, and she had compared death to a cocoon, to a caterpillar becoming a butterfly. I cleared my throat and blinked away moisture. "So Vivian managed to teleport herself away from the mountain peak. Then I suppose it's possible she came for the chest."

"Dude, do you think she'll come back for me?" Josh asked.

"If she does, I'll be waiting with the Taser," Theo said.

One of Cephas's machines warbled. He clapped his hands and pointed excitedly to a large printer attached to his computer. "Let's see, Josh."

"Dude, you have a 3D printer?" Josh's eyes widened as he followed Cephas around a crate to stand in front of a huge device the size of a refrigerator.

Cephas lifted a door in the front of the device and reached inside. "I do, Josh." He removed a pale-brown object and handed it to Josh. "If you would be so good as to take this to the desk, I will bring the other half."

Josh looked up at me with admiration in his eyes. "My Uncle Cephas has a 3D printer! Cool!"

"What is a 3D printer?" Theo appeared behind me. Cephas lifted out another object and nodded toward the desk.

"It is a device that uses plastic polymer to create a three-dimensional image of an object. Let me show you how it works." Josh placed his piece on the desk and Cephas slid his piece up against it. The two pieces joined to make one large object. "As you can see, this matches Vivian's description." It was a facsimile of the chest Vivian had described. "The principle of my scanner is that an object will leave a latent image on the surface of anything in contact with it. Oils and salts from human sweat were deposited on the object, which led to the deposition of chemicals over time. By combining methods of scanning, I can put together various versions of these latent images and fuse them into a three-dimensional approximation."

Cephas pointed to the base of the object. The surface looked like the grain of a heavy wood. At each of the four corners was a triangular object. "The bottom of the chest is composed of wood and four brass cornices."

I was dizzy. My head began to hurt. The room grew blurry as an image of the chest rose from the depths of my lost memories. "Cephas, I've seen this chest before." My flashback took me into the past.

Chapter 11

Jonathan Steel

Lakeside, Louisiana

I STOOD AT THE end of the red-clay driveway. The insects in the bushes did not take kindly to my intrusion and fell silent. Above me, the stars shown so brightly, the sky glowed with a luminescent glory that could never be seen from the city. Fireflies flickered in the distance, hovering in the tree line behind the still, dark house. Would its occupant notice the sudden silence? If so, then so much for the stealthy approach. I was bone tired from chasing the ghost of my father and I no longer cared for stealth. Time for a more direct approach.

The silence dissipated and crickets started to sing again. Frogs filled the night with a symphony of croaks. Once, I had appreciated the beauty of the nature that surrounded me. Now I could care less. I drew a deep breath and walked up to Dr. Brown's house. The front porch sagged on crumbling cinderblocks and the old wood creaked as I stood in front of the door and knocked. The sound echoed in the night air. For a moment, the crickets and frogs fell silent again, then they picked up their tempo and slid easily back into the natural rhythm of the night.

From deep within the recesses of the house, I heard muffled swearing and then the sound of footsteps. The door burst open, letting out pale light and a stale odor.

"Who the heck could want to see me this time of night?" A voice rasped from the other side of the screen door.

Dr. Daniel Brown leaned precariously against the inner doorframe. He was dressed in boxer shorts and a faded flannel shirt with only the bottom two buttons fastened. His hair stood on end like a bush and he clearly hadn't shaved in days. He was a squat man with an obvious curvature in his spine. His bulbous eyes were red-rimmed. He was drunk.

"Dr. Brown, we need to talk."

Brown wiped a hand across his mouth. He was buying time while he tried to get his brain cells to work. "Just what on God's green earth do you have to talk about at this hour?" He squinted, and then a curtain seemed to lift. His eyes opened wide. "You!"

He tried to close the door but I jerked the screen open and shoved the door back into his face. Brown's forehead bounced against the door edge. He fell backward. I watched him tumble, seemingly in slow motion, over a couch and into a disaster zone.

In the center of the living room sat a recliner surrounded by crumpled newspapers, discarded food wrappings, and empty whiskey bottles. Magazines and empty boxes of crackers and cookies created a maze over the floor. A television cast flickering shadows on the ghostly piles. The reeking air was stale and greasy with body odor. It sickened me. I lifted Brown off the dirty carpet. Blood trickled from a cut on his forehead.

"Now, Dr. Brown, you're going to get sober and then you're going to answer some questions. My patience is wearing thin. So we're going to take a little shower, understand?"

Brown blinked as he tried to regain composure. His eyes finally focused on my face. "You son of a—"

I cut him off with a stranglehold around his pudgy neck and pulled him across the living room floor. Stacks of magazines and boxes toppled as I dragged his struggling figure. I paused in the hallway behind the living room and glanced into the kitchen. Dishes covered in petrified food remains probably dating from the Bush era filled the sink. Another hallway to the left led into the back of the house and the bathroom. I pulled aside the shower curtain and shoved Brown into the tub. He tried to get up but I pressed him back against the tiles and turned on the cold water with my free hand. He screamed as the water hit him in the face.

I backed off, feeling strangely familiar with the ritual. Every time Brown tried to get out of the tub, I gently pushed him back under the stream of water. Finally, he collapsed in the tub.

"I'm going to make some coffee. That is, if you have anything in this house besides booze. If you try to get out of there before I come back, I'll personally sit on top of you to keep you in the tub. You understand?" I said through clenched teeth. I slammed the bathroom door behind me and flipped on the light in the kitchen.

Several roaches, Brown's only companions, scurried into hiding. I searched through cabinets full of dirty glasses and chipped dishes until I found an unopened can of coffee. It had probably had been a housewarming gift. The coffeepot was hidden in the corner behind a pile of food-encrusted pans. I pulled the pot into the open and paused to listen for the sound of the shower still running. I hoped Brown wasn't drowning. No mouth-to-mouth for him!

After I got the coffee going, I went back to the bathroom. Brown was sitting in the tub covered in the recent contents of his stomach. He was still heaving. I held his head until he stopped, then I pulled his shirt off over his head and tossed it into the trash. Crouched in the tub without his shirt, the man looked even more like a frog than usual.

"What happened to turn you into this?" I turned off the cold water and turned on the hot. "You stink. Clean yourself up."

Brown looked up at me. The fight had gone out of his eyes. He nodded. I opened a nearby cabinet and found him a towel and a musty washrag.

I began my search in the living room and found five unfinished bottles of whiskey and scotch. I took them to the kitchen and emptied them into the sink. I went through the rest of the house and searched all the hiding places for the rest of his stash. I knew exactly where to look. I had done this before.

The bathroom door opened and Brown emerged with the towel around his waist. His hair was plastered to his skull and water dripped from his stubbly chin. He was hunched by the curvature of his spine. "If it's okay with you, I'm going to my bedroom to get a robe."

"When you get back, we'll talk." Brown stumbled into the bedroom and cursed. He re-appeared in the door with a robe pulled around him. "Where's my stuff?"

I pointed to the sink as I poured coffee into two of the cleanest cups I could find. "Down the drain."

Brown's face reddened. "Who gave you the right to come in here and mess up my life?"

I reached into the refrigerator, retrieved two ice cubes, and placed them in the cups of coffee. "Looks like you took care of the messy part. I'm here to help straighten it out. You can go on killing yourself after I'm off the scene. But for now, I need you sober. Sit down and drink this coffee." I pushed the cup toward him. "If you don't, I'll hold you down and pour it down your throat."

Brown stumbled to the kitchen table and collapsed in a chair. He sipped at the coffee and made a face. "It's nasty."

"I put some crushed aspirins in it. Found them in the medicine cabinet. You'll need something for the pain. Now, drink it all, and then you can start on this second cup."

Brown gulped down the lukewarm coffee and set the cup on the table. I placed the second cup in front of him and went to get a third. After the fourth cup, Brown's eyes began to clear. He gagged.

"Keep it down, or I'll make another pot."

"Why don't you just let me die?" Brown whispered.

"I don't know." I had pondered that question too. I had not come here to help this man.

Brown wiped his eyes and looked down at his hands. "My God, what have I done to myself?"

"How long has it been since you were sober?"

Brown sipped at his coffee and grimaced. He rubbed his head. "Weeks, months? I don't know."

"You need help, Dr. Brown."

"Yeah, I've heard that one before. I've been to all the programs. I know the drills. I play out the script and they let me go. Then I come home and pick up where I left off." He studied me with his intense brown eyes. "You can't save me. No one can."

"I didn't come here to save you. I'm here about the Ark."

Brown flinched and his coffee cup clattered onto the tabletop. Hot droplets of coffee showered my hand. He looked away. "I can't tell you anything. I'm sworn to secrecy."

"Of course you are." I took out my wallet and retrieved a card. "Here's my cell phone number. When you get ready to talk, give me a call."

"Yeah, right."

I stood up and glanced around at the man's hellhole. "Enjoy your brief sobriety."

Brown studied the card and I left him alone with his misery. I hopped off the front porch and moved into the trees beside the house. I waited until I saw the window in Brown's bathroom light up. I had opened the curtains slightly so I could see inside. Brown had taken the top off the back of the commode. He had a small candle and was pouring a small pile of white powder from a plastic envelope into a spoon. Heroin.

I eased around to the back of the house. I had unlocked the back door during my inspection tour. Quietly, I entered the house, slipped down the hall, and kicked open the bathroom door. Brown screamed as I slapped the syringe out of his hand and shoved him back into the tub. The shower curtain tore loose and Brown fell over, wrapped in the curtain.

I slammed my bare fist down on the lighted candle and hot wax sprayed across the bathroom counter. I picked the syringe up from the floor and squirted its contents into the commode. Then I broke off the needle against the hard tile of the wall. Brown struggled up out of the tub, swearing and swinging. I dodged his feeble blows and caught him by the neck.

"I could kill you with one squeeze, Brown. I'm a desperate man on a mission and right now, you're in the way. Don't push me any further."

Brown gasped in my stranglehold and his eyes bulged. My vision faded, and then it was my father hanging from my hand. His face was covered with blood and his hair was matted. His breath was rich with alcohol as he managed a swollen smile and mumbled, "Go ahead and kill me, kid. I deserve it."

I gasped and released Brown. He tumbled back into the tub with a thud. My father had been drunk like this. How many times had I sobered him up?

Brown looked up at me and started to sob. The sobs wracked his body and snot streamed from his nose. He sat up and wiped his face. I handed him a wad of toilet paper. "Where's the rest of your stash?"

Brown blew his nose and stared blankly at the wall. "Under the kitchen sink. In the wood box by the fireplace. In the old cigar box by my bed. That's it. I swear."

"Stay in that tub until I get back. Understand?"

Brown nodded blankly while blood trickled from the cut on his forehead, staining his crumpled white robe. I went through the house as meticulously as the junk would allow me to and found three more stashes. While I was going through a roll top desk in the second bedroom, I found an envelope full of newspaper clippings.

The clippings detailed the death of a well-known city councilman two years earlier. It seemed that while performing minor surgery on the councilman, Dr. Daniel Brown had injected a cocaine-like solution directly into the patient's skin. One article explained that this was common practice, but Dr. Brown had made the solution ten times stronger than it should have been. The patient suffered a massive stroke and died twenty-four hours later. Subsequent investigation proved that Dr. Brown had been drinking the morning of the procedure. The articles detailed the ensuing investigation and the lawsuit filed by the patient's family. Brown had gone to jail for a few months and then had been released. His license to practice medicine had been revoked.

I placed the clippings back in the envelope and took it into the den. I tossed the envelope onto the cold ashes in the fireplace, made sure the flue was open, and found a match on the mantle. I lit the envelope and watched Daniel Brown's past go up in smoke.

Back at the desk, I found one last item: a savings account book with figures written in longhand showed two deposits of $10,000 in the last six months. Interesting.

When I opened the bathroom door, Brown was standing in front of the mirror, combing his wet hair away from the bloody cut on his forehead. "I look terrible."

I took him by the arm and led him out to the living room. I kicked magazines and boxes out of the way and brought him over to the couch. He winced as he sat down.

I shoved aside a pile of magazines on a shelf nearby and picked up a book I had spied earlier. I opened it and studied the inside cover.

"It says here you received this Bible on the day you were baptized, twenty-five years ago. Doesn't look like you've opened it in a long time. I'm guessing this was your home as a child and your parents are dead. At least, I hope they're dead. I would hate for them to see their son in your condition, turning their home into a pigsty." I dropped the open book onto Brown's lap. "The book of John. Read it. Out loud."

"What?" Brown said.

I reached into my pocket and pulled out a small envelope of heroin. "Indulge me or I'll have a chat with the sheriff. I don't think you want to go back to jail."

He glanced over at the glowing ashes in the fireplace. "What did you do?"

"Erased your past. Now read."

Brown drew a deep breath and blew it out. The blood from the cut on his head had dried in a long line down his right cheek. He scratched at the clotted blood and squinted as he looked at the page. "In the beginning was the Word." He looked up. "You're not serious, are you?"

"Go on."

For over an hour, Brown droned on as he read the book of John. At first, his words were halting and he stuttered; the alcohol and drugs in his system were still affecting him. In time, reading became easier. He finished and looked up, his eyes drifting off toward the ashes in the fireplace. "It's been a long time since I read the Bible. I should thank you. You have always cared more for me than anyone else. We were friends once, weren't we?"

"Before that," I said, pointing to the smoldering newspaper clippings. "Before you changed. Before the Captain."

"You mean when I was still normal." He looked away and wrung his hands. I held up the packet of heroin.

"Is this how he controls you?"

Brown grimaced. "I can't live without it. The pain is so bad. So bad. I keep seeing that man's face."

"You mean the one you killed?" I said.

Brown's eyes filled with tears. "I can't go back to jail."

"Did the Captain get you out of jail?"

"Yes."

"Why?"

Brown shook his head and held up his hands in a defensive posture. "I can't tell you! He would hear. He knows. He'll come here and kill me."

I picked up the Bible and ran my fingers over the warm, leather cover. "I didn't come here to help you. But let me tell you, you can live without the heroin and the alcohol. You can live with the pain. I should know. You can hide from the Captain."

"No one can hide from him." Brown shook his head and wrung his hands. "No one. Except for one person."

"I don't care about him. Now, where is the Ark?"

Brown froze. He seemed to shrink into the couch. "No! I can't talk about that."

"The Captain wants it. You've been looking for it, haven't you?"

Brown shook his head and glanced at the front door. "I don't know where it is. I swear."

"It's here in Lakeside, isn't it?"

"You need to leave now. If he finds you here, he'll torture you. He'll want his own answers. Forget the Ark. You know who he is looking for. He'll get it out of you. You can't resist him. I know." Brown began to sob and blubber. I stepped toward the couch and he cowered like an animal cornered by a monster. I wasn't the monster.

The front door slammed open. A crimson glow illuminated the face of the Captain. He wore his white Panama hat and was clenching his meerschaum pipe between his teeth. Two men in black sweats stood behind him.

"Hello, son. It's been a while."

"Jonathan! Wake up!"

Cephas was hovering over me. I tried to clear my mind and sat up. I was on the floor of the basement. "What happened, Jonathan?"

"Another flashback, Cephas. It was about Dr. Brown."

"You mean the dude in Lakeside?" Josh asked.

"Yeah. I was in his house—but it was long before you and I met. I was searching for something called the Ark."

"The ark?" Theo tapped the box. "Do you think this thing is the ark? I doubt if floats."

"Not like Noah's ark," Cephas said. "A chest containing something of great value. Dr. Brown had the chest—I mean, the Ark?"

"I was looking for the Ark. For all I know, I was talking about the Ark of the Covenant. That's all I recall." My stomach was queasy and I felt dizzy. "I have to stop thinking about it. You know what happens."

Cephas nodded. "Some kind of suggestive conditioning to keep you from remembering. It is deeply disturbing that your father may have also been looking for this chest, if it is indeed the ark of which you spoke."

I swallowed back the nausea. "Maybe it was a coincidence the Captain showed up then. Maybe he has no connection to this chest." I tapped the box.

"There are no coincidences," Cephas said. "Why don't we move on for now and see what we can discover?" He brushed away plastic dust from the top of the 3D-printed object. "This should be the top of the chest." The surface appeared to be a wooden slab with a circle covering most of the top. Etched into the circle were symbols. I glanced at the secretary, beat Cephas to it, and threw open the doors. The frame was empty. Cephas gasped. "It's gone!"

I slammed the door shut. The wall vibrated with the shock. Cephas stepped back, stumbled, and almost fell. Theo caught him and helped him to a chair.

"What?" Josh said. "What happened?"

"There was a document. Cephas showed it to me last year. It has a symbol for each of the twelve demons. He had it framed in protective glass and placed right there in the secretary." I slammed a fist onto the desktop. "It matched the image on the top of the chest so they took it too!"

Josh stepped back. "Dude, calm down! What's so important about an old piece of paper?"

Cephas took a deep breath and tapped the top of the chest. "I call this image the demon wheel. It is similar to the image on the document." He leaned forward and studied the top of the facsimile. "The Ark, as Jonathan has named it, must have contained something important to the twelve demons."

"Okay, so what is in this Ark that would be related to the demon wheel?" I asked.

"I am afraid, my friend, that I am as confused as you are. I believe we are on the cusp of arcane knowledge that could turn the tide against this cadre of demons."

"The Dark Council, Vivian called them," I said.

Cephas nodded weakly. He seemed suddenly very tired and fragile. I was worried about him. "Cephas, there's nothing else we can do tonight. We can't stop this … entity from teleporting into the basement, so I suggest we let it go for now. You need to rest."

"I suggest you look in that crate, Josh," Cephas said, pointing. "Inside is a set of perimeter motion alarms I used in my old building. Set them up and we will be alerted if this person shows up again."

"And if they show up, what do we do?" Josh asked.

Theo smiled. "We tase them, bro."

My cell phone warbled and I plucked it out of my shirt pocket. "Hello?"

"Looky here, honey." Vivian Darbonne Ketrick's southern drawl oozed from the speaker. "Have you ever heard of Alba, Bartley, and Cummings?"

"Vivian," I growled, "you have the nerve to call here after what you've done?"

"I told you I would get the best lawyers in town. Well, sweetie, these guys are the best in the world. I will be over there tomorrow with a court order and a sheriff to come into *my* house and find *my* chest. Do you understand? And if you try to stop me, Jonathan, I'll have you thrown in jail!" The phone went dead.

"Who was that?" Cephas asked.

"Vivian," I muttered. "She has retained a lawyer. She's coming tomorrow to get the chest."

"What?" Theo thundered. "Let her show her pretty face and I'll tase the smile right off of her."

"No, wait," I said. "She still thinks the chest is here. That means she isn't the one who took it."

"Then who is?" Josh asked.

I looked at the plastic facsimile on the desk and a chill ran down my spine. "Who are we dealing with?"

Chapter 12

Nosmo Theophilus King

I DON'T TAKE TOO well to sleeping on a cot. But considering I had been sleeping on a trash pile in Dallas, I guess it could have been worse. Jonathan thought I was overreacting, but I didn't believe Vivian for one second. I wanted to catch her and give her a dose of her own medicine. I set up the cot in the corner of the basement behind a bunch of crates. Josh and Cephas had set up some kind of alarm system, so if our visitor popped in, it would let me know. I held Vivian's Taser on my chest, fully charged and ready to pop. Ready to give that witch a taste of her own medicine!

Cephas seemed to be worried that she, or whoever it was, would come back for more. More of what, I wasn't sure, though. Some of that scanned-in computer stuff, I guess. Who knew?

I lay back on the cot and heard the wood groan with my weight. Cephas had installed some nightlights from his New York place, so there was this low-level glow that made the ceiling of the basement look really weird. I had to close my eyes because I kept seeing things.

When I had tried crack, I had seen lots of stuff that wasn't there. But the demons I saw in the caverns with Wulf had been worse than any of those nightmares. I hoped I didn't see anything worse tonight!

Josh had set up the alarm signal to trigger my earpiece and send a signal upstairs to Jonathan. We didn't want Vivian to know she had been caught before I could zap her. I put the earpiece in and listened to the low hiss.

Josh seemed pretty smart. I guess that thirteenth demon he talked about hadn't messed with his mind the way things had messed with mine. He had hated me at first. Couldn't say that I blamed him. I had been pretty strung out that night at the mall when I tried to rob them. Jonathan had come after me instead of staying at home with Josh, so Josh had ended up the prisoner of the vamps. But then the kid had decided go after his girlfriend on his own and got all wrapped up in trouble with that vampire clan. That I understood. I had gone after Lydia.

When I closed my eyes, I could still see my church before me. I saw my face up on the big screen. I heard the Amens and the Hallelujahs from my people. After what I had done in Los Angeles, I had felt the calling of God. Probably due to all the guilt. Oh, baby, did I look good in that fancy suit under those bright lights! Bringing the word of God, My Salvation! I had put my sins behind me and Andrea had helped. I met her right after my dismissal and she brought me to her church. Soon after, I heard the call. It took me only two years to become the pastor of my own church. Two years of bliss! And then I had thrown it all away.

I could still see Andrea's face as she sat in the front row. Right behind her was Lydia. Lydia had been my Delilah. She had seen through my mask. She had sensed the sin hiding deep within me, and I had followed her into the abyss. I lost Andrea and the girls. I lost the church. Now it was a strip joint. I ended up with the homeless crackheads in Dallas, Texas, totally alone even though I was with Lydia. I couldn't really blame Lydia; I knew the real reason I had fallen. I hadn't been able to get the sight of those dying eyes out of my head.

The alarm went off! A shadow moved across the ceiling. I sat up and winced as the cot creaked. The shadow halted. I threw caution to the wind, jumped up, and ran around the crate. I held the Taser in front of me and, as I made out the form of a man, I pulled the trigger. The darts buzzed and electricity crackled. The figure jerked and fell forward onto the floor.

I turned him over. He had dark hair, a goatee, and Hispanic features, and he was probably in his mid-thirties. He was dressed in a black jacket and jeans. In his hands was the three-dimensional model of the chest.

"Well, you're not Vivian, but you'll do."

The man's eyes opened. They glowed lime green. Suddenly, he bolted upright to his feet. I felt the air crackle around me and I grabbed the man, wrapping my arms around him.

Something happened.

Some thing happened.

So me th ing hap pen ed.

It was dark and it was light. Colors moved around me and I tasted them. Lights flashed and I heard them. Sounds moved over me and I smelled them. My face was an inch from the man's face. His glowing green eyes bored into mine.

"Righteous pig!" he hissed.

I tasted his words. Around us, the universe unfolded into wave after wave of glowing strings and pulsing beads against a black fabric that moved and surged like dark velvet under water. Heat and blinding darkness shrouded me. From that burning ebony night, the dead eyes of my past reared up over the man's shoulder and glared at me.

"You ain't no different!" Cracked, purulent lips blubbered at me, and then the faces vanished in a puff of purple smoke as a blinding point of light and warmth appeared. A face formed in the pinpoint of light. Grandmama peeked over the man's shoulder.

"Chief, what you doin' here? You gotta stop this thing! He gonna hurt people! Good people!" she said.

I tried to reach for her, but my arms were still around the man.

Something unhappened.

I fell onto a hard concrete floor.

"We'll see how long you last in here," the man said. He opened a heavy metal door, went through it, and slammed it shut behind him. I heard a deadbolt turn. I was in a room with only dim light coming through an old-fashioned grate like at a movie theater. The room was small and the walls were bare.

I slowly sat up and looked around. Grandmama was nowhere to be seen. She shouldn't have been, anyway. She'd been dead for years. The dead men's eyes had disappeared. Nausea hit me suddenly and a pain like none I had ever experienced shot through my head like lightning, and I fell into darkness.

Grimvox Interlude #4

Chaos

I LOCK THE HUGE man in the room. It was the closest place I could go without giving myself away. Maybe he will rot in there. Already, my host's body is growing weaker and weaker. If I pass out here, the others might find the fake chest. I transport myself to an alleyway in a city far away. With one mighty squeeze, I crush the chest to pieces and toss the remains in a dumpster.

Pain! I am feeling incredible pain in my chest. I breath more deeply and the pain lessens. I am sweating and my muscles are aching. But there is one more thing to retrieve. I close my eyes and think of Ketrick's basement, and I am there. Hurry! There is some kind of alarm going off! I move across the room, embrace the last item, and move through dimensions. Something is wrong! The pain is now unbearable.

Back in the alleyway, I dump the other items into a trash bin and clutch my chest. The pain! I wander toward the street. Two people are coming my way. I stumble and fall. They lean over me.

"Mister, what's wrong?"

"My chest," I whisper. "Pain."

The female human uses a cell phone and calls 911. But I am gone.

It is black and I am still trapped.

Flickering lights, exquisite pain. White coats are standing around me. Faces filled with concern. The pain is going now and my host is dying. I reach into the dark corner of the human's mind and pull his soul up from the depths of his imprisonment.

"No! I've changed my mind! I don't want this!" he is pleading.

"Too bad. You made the choice and now your time has run out. It is time to go."

His soul is eclipsed by the dark, hideous form of the shadow of death, and he is dragged away kicking and screaming into the eternal darkness preserved for my kind. I leave the body and find myself in an emergency room. The man's body is limp and pale on the stretcher. The doctors and nurses leave and finally he is totally alone. He is dead and his soul has been harvested. I have nearly completed my plan. Ah, the Plan. Memories return to fill the emptiness and I am back with Chamas at the beginning of the Master's plan.

Primeval Earth

We search for miles and miles across the empty desert. The Master, resplendent in his shimmering robes and still shining as bright as he did before the Fall, floats above the crest of a sand dune. He slowly rotates and turns his gaze upon us. Chamas falls on his face in the sand. But I refuse to bow down. A sea of prostrate Fallen surround me and the Master floats my way.

"Chotus, you refuse to acknowledge your new Master?" His voice is unctuous, flowing, smooth, and seductive.

"I should never have followed Chamas. He told me you would become equal to the Creator. What is this falsehood that has cost us eternity with the Creator?"

The Master smiles. "I am the father of falsehood, it seems. We do not need eternity. This is now our world. We shall have dominion over it. And, Chotus, once we have conquered this world, we will rise up once more against the Creator, and the throne of heaven will be mine."

Heads stay bowed around me. I alone defy the Master. "Have you not learned already of the futility of resisting the Creator?"

The Master's hand locks around my neck. Pain lances down my back and flows into my healing wound. Suddenly we rocket upward into the air and soar over the sea of Fallen. The Master's grip does not relent. He presses his beautiful face close to mine as the world flies beneath us. "I have a plan, Chotus. I will show it to you, and you alone. End this resistance to my reign, join me as my second, and I will make you a master in your own right. Behold!"

We hover in midair and the Master gestures toward the ground. Beneath us is a bright-green jewel spread across the sand dunes. Even from this height, its beauty is breathtaking. Trees sway in gentle breezes. Creatures roam over the gentle rolling hills. A glittering field of energy contains the entire garden. It is a bit of heaven on this harsh world.

"What is it?"

"The Creator has fashioned a new creature called 'man.' He has placed man here in this garden to show it a little of heaven. Man is pure and undefiled."

"As we were before you rebelled?"

His grip tightens and pain shoots through my chest. "Man will become our servant, Chotus. We will be their gods."

"How?"

"I will go into the garden as one of the most beautiful creatures. There is a tree, the fruit of which will give man the same knowledge as the Creator."

"You would lie to them? You would defile them? You would have them fall even as we did?"

"Yes. And once man sees our wisdom, we will have our own creation to reign over." His smile lights up the sky. No wonder we followed him. He is a pale reflection of the Creator.

"The Fallen shall reign over the fallen? I want no part of this, Lucifer." I speak his name with contempt. "We are forever separated from the Creator's glory and it is your fault."

Lucifer's eyes burn with power and he flings me away from him at the far horizon. I hear his voice as the world spins beneath me and I fall once again into darkness. "You made the choice, Chotus. Now live with it. Forever!"

Back in the now, I live with the results of my choice. This man has died because of his choice. He lies before me, cold and motionless, a victim of the Fall. Time to move on.

Chapter 13

Josh Knight

I HAD JUST FINISHED playing BioShimmer IV for the third time when I heard the alarm go off. Jonathan and Uncle Cephas had wanted me to put a receiver for the alarm in the kitchen, but I had made sure it was tied to my laptop. So just when the bad-dude character was telling his tale of betrayal and all that at the end of the game, the little red light popped up on my screen. The teleporter had returned!

I bolted down to the kitchen, where Uncle Cephas and Jonathan were already heading for the stairs down to the basement. Downstairs, Jonathan rushed down and flipped on the light switches. Man, where was his head at? I passed Uncle Cephas hobbling down the stairs and beat Jonathan to the desk. He held out his arm and I ran into it. It was like falling off my skateboard onto a handrail.

"Hey, what'd you do that for?"

Jonathan clamped a hand over my mouth and I jerked away. "Stop it!"

"Would you be quiet?"

"Why?" I whispered. "Dude, you've already turned on all the lights. I think we've lost the element of surprise!"

But Jonathan ignored me. "Where's Theo?"

"Jonathan, we may have a problem." Cephas picked up the Taser gun from the middle of the floor. "Theo shot someone." He glanced at his desk. "And the chest is gone. Someone took it. But not to worry, I have the original information on my computer."

Theo's cot was empty. The computer desk was also empty. "Ah, we have another problem, Uncle Cephas. Your computer is gone."

"My computer too?"

"If Theo shot someone, where are they?"

"Where's Theo?" Jonathan said. His face reddened and the muscles at the corners of his eyes twitched. Not good! Jonathan was not a pretty sight when he was angry, which was more often than not.

But it was Uncle Cephas who shocked me. He tossed the Taser across the room. "Satan, you fiend! Get out of here!"

I put a hand on his shaking shoulders. "Calm down, Uncle Cephas. Dude, you don't want to stroke out."

"I am so tired of this!" He roared. His bushy hair was a mess and I noticed for the first time he was wearing flannel pajamas covered in tiny red robots. I wanted to laugh. I wanted to cry.

"I fight them and I fight them. They hurt us and they kill us. They take away everything we love! I hate them! I hate them!" He collapsed onto the concrete floor. I looked at Jonathan, whose anger quickly faded into concern. I helped Uncle Cephas up from the floor and into the desk chair. Jonathan drew a deep breath and put his hand on Uncle Cephas's shoulder.

"Cephas," Jonathan said, "we all need to calm down. This is exactly what the enemy wants us to do. We can't lose hope."

Uncle Cephas rubbed his face and mumbled something. It sounded like a name. Molly? Who was Molly? He looked up. His eyes were wild.

"Man, don't get wiggy on us," I said.

"Wiggy?"

I wiggled my finger in a spiral motion at my temple. "You know, ditzy, loony, gaga."

"I am not going gaga or ditzy or wiggy. I'm merely frustrated, young man."

Jonathan sighed and leaned on the edge of the desk. "Theo must have zapped the intruder. But then what?"

I snapped my fingers. "Wait! The camera!"

"What camera?" Uncle Cephas asked.

"I hooked up my old webcam to one of your computers to stream video to my laptop. Wait right here." I ran up the stairs and into my room, grabbed my laptop, and ran back down to the basement. I plopped down at the desk and pulled up the video file. "I didn't tell you guys, but I wanted to check out this cool video-monitoring program I downloaded. I wasn't sure if it would work." I tapped the keys and another thought surfaced. This would make Uncle Cephas's day. "Oh, I backed up your data files onto our network hard drive. Go ahead, say it: I'm a genius!"

Wait for it! Wait for it! I glanced up at Jonathan and his face reddened again. Okay, so maybe I shouldn't push him too far.

"You're a genius," he mumbled.

Uncle Cephas's eyes filled with moisture. "My son, I have underestimated you. Again."

For a second my heart skipped. I had never known Uncle Cephas very well. He had always been the strange mad-scientist dude, but my mom and dad had had good things to say about him in spite of his weirdness. Mom and Dad. Sorrow hit me hard for a moment. I wanted to wallow in the feeling of loss and despair. It felt good sometimes. But the video that appeared on my laptop drew my attention back to the present. I examined the time code at the bottom of the screen and moved the scrub bar to about ten minutes before the alarm went off. I could feel Jonathan hovering over me and I smelled Uncle Cephas's Old Spice.

"Nice pajamas," I said.

"We must, sometimes, reconnect with that which reminds us that we are still young at heart. I speak, of course, of those of my generation. I had a pair of pajamas like these as a child." His voice had gotten stronger.

I pressed the play button. "Here we go. Ten minutes ago."

On the screen, there was a tiny flash of light and then a man appeared in the center of the basement. He hurried to the desk and grabbed the chest. Something huge obscured the camera view and when it cleared, Theo was there. He fired his Taser. The flash of electricity lit up the man's face. He fell and Theo rushed across the room. As Theo bent over him, the man suddenly flipped backwards and landed on his feet, still hugging the two halves of the 3D-printed chest against his jacket. Theo grabbed the man in a bear hug. There was another flash of light and they disappeared.

"He took Theo with him," Jonathan said.

Two minutes later, the man reappeared in the video. He walked toward the computer desk. The camera was only about two feet from his side. He grabbed the CPU and there was another flash of light. The camera went to static.

"Lost the signal," I said. I listened to Jonathan's ragged breathing. He looked off into the distance, deep in thought.

"It was so easy. He took Theo. And the computer. We have to protect this house." Jonathan began pacing. I watched the arteries pulsing in the dude's temples. His face grew red.

"Uh oh, here it comes," I mumbled.

Jonathan grabbed an empty wooden crate and hurled it across the room. It struck the back wall of the basement and Styrofoam peanuts filled the air. "I am sick of this! Why can't you give us one break?" He glared up at the ceiling. "Just one freakin' break? But no, you keep letting them come at us, over and over!"

"Hey, Jonathan," I said. My voice was shaky. "Calm down, dude."

Jonathan clenched his fists as he breathed hard and fast. "Don't tell me what to do!" Those turquoise eyes of his were really freaky when he lost it. "I'm tired of being calm. Tired of waiting for help from God! Sick of all of this! You hear me? Sick of it!"

"Stop!" I shouted. "Would you just stop for a second, dude? I mean, come on! Getting all bent out of shape isn't going to do us any good. Or Theo. Before you know it, you'll be smacking me around again like you did in that Dallas courtroom." It was stupid, but I stepped right into his line of vision. "Dude, if it'll make you feel better, then let me have it. The sooner you get this out of your system, the sooner we can find Theo. Or if you want to, you can tell me to find a new mother again!"

Jonathan stiffened and stepped back from me. He raised his clenched fists and looked at them. "What did you tell me once?"

I knew exactly what he was talking about. "For someone who wants to help people, you sure are violent."

He relaxed his fists and reached toward me—but he wasn't going to hit me. He placed both hands on my shoulders. Those weird eyes of his filled with moisture. "Thank you, Josh. You're right. This is exactly what the enemy wants us to do. Lose control. Get angry. Run off in total chaos." His grip was hurting me, but I tried to not to let on. He relaxed and patted me on the chest. "Okay, so we need a plan. We need protection."

He glanced around the room until his eyes came to rest on the desk. I noticed for the first time the picture frame and the box of Uncle Cephas's stuff. "Cephas, how did you protect all the stuff in your building?"

Uncle Cephas looked at me and nodded. I guess I had done well. "I never worried about it. Frankly, I didn't attract that much attention after I moved in."

"Until I came along," Jonathan said. "How can we protect ourselves from these demons? They just pop up at will. Come on, Cephas. You're the expert here."

Uncle Cephas nodded and drew a deep breath. He pointed to one of the glass-fronted bookshelves. "Josh, bring me the notebook labeled 'The Third Dimension.'"

I opened the door to the bookshelf. The smell of paper and glue wafted over me, old and ancient. A black leather-bound notebook with *The Third*

Dimension stamped on the spine sat amid several others. I wanted to look at all of the labels, but Uncle Cephas was waiting. The notebook was heavy, two inches thick, and bound by a leather thong. I placed it on the desk in front of Uncle Cephas. He untied the leather thong and opened the book. The pages were crinkly and covered in precise handwriting. "You've got good penmanship, Uncle Cephas."

He nodded and leafed through the pages. "The best remedy for emotional extremes is to engage the intellectual side of the mind. In the beginning, God and his angels dwelled in the heavenly dimension—the first dimension, if you will. Then, God created our universe. Within this second dimension of man, we have at least four space-time dimensions. God and his angels can move in and out of them. There is also a third dimension."

Cephas paused and retrieved his reading glasses from his pajamas pocket. "This comes from *The Kingdom of the Occult* by Walter Martin. I will read it to you. 'The third dimension is one of spiritual darkness, controlled by Satan and his hosts. The Bible describes it as hell, or the alienation of the spiritual nature of man from fellowship with his Creator. It belongs to the "prince of the power of the air, the spirit who now works in the sons of disobedience" (Ephesians 2:2).' Let's see, my next note from that book reads, 'Perhaps this dimension is best described in terms of the condition of its occupants, who are portrayed as "wandering stars for whom is reserved the blackness of darkness forever" Jude 13 ... Some of the fallen angels were already chained in the darkness of hell, awaiting judgment.' Ah, and here it is: 'It is possible, then, that hell may be one dimension with many levels, some restrictive and some not, since Satan and an unknown number of unknown demons are still free to roam the earth.'"

Jonathan sat down opposite Cephas. "These demons can move through this third dimension and back into our dimensions at will?"

Cephas nodded. "So it would seem. The doorway from that dimension is opened from our side, Jonathan. Humans who dabble in the occult, who have a fascination with evil, are the conduits for demonic power. Anytime humans engage in spiritual activity that is connected to Satan in any way, they open a crack in the inter dimensional barrier. We are the reason that demons are moving so easily through our world. It was the first sin, the first disobedience, the first rejection of God's command that tore a hole in the fabric of our protection from that dimension."

"How did Lucifer get into the Garden of Eden in the first place?" I asked.

"That is the subject of many a theologian's dissertation, but I believe the answer must be that God allowed him in. Without Lucifer in the Garden tempting humanity, we would have been without free will. God wants our love. He does not coerce it. We chose poorly in the Garden, and that choice condemned mankind to always be at the mercy of Satan."

"Does that mean that Theo went through hell?" Jonathan asked.

"He may have touched it briefly. More than likely, he sensed the inter dimensional nature of our universe but only briefly tasted the third dimension."

I reached back in my memory to my trip through those dimensions on the back of a huge scorpion, the thirteenth demon. "When I was in the church at Lakeside and the scorpion took me into the baptistery, I didn't sense this third dimension, Uncle Cephas."

"Ah, but that is because the thirteenth demon took you into the presence of a microscopic black hole and protected you from destruction by the power of the physical universe. You never actually teleported. You squeezed through a very improbable and impossible hole in space as you journeyed from the sanctuary of the church in Lakeside to the basement," Uncle Cephas said.

I drew a deep breath. "I do have a question. If God loves us so much, why does he send us to hell?"

Uncle Cephas took off his glasses and studied me with his tired pale-blue eyes. The wrinkles in his face had deepened and increased over the last few days. "I have the answer right here." He tapped the book and then slid it over to me. "Read the Bible verse at the top of the page."

The faded handwriting was precise and angular. Uncle Cephas must have written it years ago. It read: "God did not spare his angels who sinned, but cast them down to hell and delivered them into chains of darkness, to be reserved for judgment (2 Peter 2:4)."

"Okay, so what does that mean?"

"For whom is hell reserved?"

I read the words again. "The angels who sinned?"

"Precisely. Does that verse say anything about hell being reserved for sinful men?"

"No. But then why do people go to hell?"

"I mentioned three-dimensional realities earlier: heaven, our universe, and hell. Where else is man to go if he rejects God but to the only other dimension that exists besides ours and heaven? Hell is a place where you are literally separated from the presence of God for eternity. It was designed for the original sinners, the angels who rebelled against God. It was never intended for man. But when we rejected God, we were kicked out of the Garden of Eden and denied access to the Tree of Eternal Life; mankind was destined to die. When man dies, his soul must go somewhere. If a man rejects God, why would he want to spend eternity in the presence of God? Unfortunately for us, the only other alternative is hell. It may have been designed as punishment for the fallen angels, but it will also be the final resting place of those of us who totally reject the creator God of the universe."

"I don't like that," I said.

"I don't either. I wish it were different. I wish we could all go to heaven. But you can look at it this way: It would be as much of a punishment to put a person who has rejected God in God's presence for eternity as it would be to send that person to hell. Ultimately, our eternal home is determined by our choice. Love God or reject God. There is no other way." Uncle Cephas shook his head sadly. "No other way."

Jonathan sat forward and rested his hands on the desk. "How does this help us protect ourselves against these demons?"

"It does not. What this information tells us is that we have no protection. We cannot block these demons from accessing our dimensions." Cephas took the notebook from me. "But there is hope to be found in these verses from Ephesians 6:

Finally, my brethren, be strong in the Lord and in the power of His might. Put on the whole armor of God, that you may be able to stand against the wiles of the devil. For we do not wrestle against flesh and blood, but against principalities, against powers, against the rulers of the darkness of this age, against spiritual hosts of wickedness in the heavenly places. Therefore take up the whole armor of God, that you may be able to withstand in the evil day, and having done all, to stand.

Stand therefore, having girded your waist with truth, having put on the breastplate of righteousness, and having shod your feet with the preparation of the gospel of peace; above all, taking the shield of faith with which you will be able to quench all the fiery darts of the wicked one. And take the helmet of salvation, and the sword of the Spirit, which is the word of God; praying always with all prayer and supplication in the Spirit, being watchful to this end with all perseverance and supplication for all the saints.

"I think all we need to do is to go to God. Don't mess with the devil and his demons. God will take care of the devil. We are like a guard who sees the enemy army coming. He could grab his sword and run out and fight the war.

But what he should do is go tell the commander. The commander will be our champion. In the Scriptures, Jesus said all authority was given to him." Uncle Cephas grew quiet and his gaze shifted and grew distant. "I'm sorry for sounding so negative. I've been trying to bind up Satan for decades."

I looked helplessly at Jonathan. "What are you talking about, Uncle Cephas? Bind up Satan? With what? Brimstone tape?"

Cephas stood up shakily and began to pace. He paused before the secretary and touched the wooden door behind which the document had once been. He glanced over at the box on the desk and the facedown picture frame. "Once, I stood in an old abandoned building trying to cast out demons for three hours until I was blue in the face." His voice was quiet, but intense. "None of them went anywhere. And the boy with the demon kept kicking me until my legs were bleeding. I was standing in a pool of my own blood. Throughout that empty building, demon voices were talking and screeching and screaming. I quoted Scripture. I quoted entire sermons I had memorized, some from my favorite preacher, James Stewart. Over and over, I tried to send them to Tartarus, that part of hell where the worst demons are chained. I would have sent them anywhere, you name it!"

I did'nt known Uncle Cephas had once cast out demons. Jonathan had a concerned look on his face. Had he known?

"Well, guess what? They didn't go anywhere. I was trying to do the wrong thing. I realized then that God takes care of those things. I couldn't just walk around the room and chant, 'I bind you up, Satan.' If that were all it took, Satan would not be loose to work his devilry in the world today. We need to protect this place, but we must appeal to God for that. Only God can close up the dimensional cracks through which these demons can travel."

"Okay, so what do we do next?" Jonathan asked.

"We get on our knees and pray," Uncle Cephas whispered. "We pray earnestly that God will send someone to protect us. It may not be Raphael, but whomever He sends will suffice, because He is sufficient to meet our needs."

I looked at Jonathan and felt all strange and wiggly inside. I had never prayed on my knees before. Jonathan's fists relaxed and he let out a long breath. He helped Uncle Cephas to kneel on the floor beside the desk. This old man, my great uncle with the Einstein hairdo and robot pajamas, reached out and took my hand. I knelt beside him. The floor was cold and hard on my bare knees. I should have put something on over my boxers. Cephas reached out with his other hand and motioned to Jonathan. Jonathan knelt beside us, but the look on his face made me realize he was just as uncomfortable with this as I was.

Uncle Cephas bowed his head and started praying. I don't remember much of what he said. I just know that after a while, the cold pain in my knees went away. And ... something happened. I felt the air thicken as if a thunderstorm were coming and lightning were dancing on the ceiling. I felt the hair stand on the back of my neck. And as Cephas's words and pleas with God continued, I saw tears drop to the floor in front of his bowed head. I started shaking. I realized we were in this thing for real. This wasn't a fantasy. It wasn't a video game. I already knew that, but I hadn't really *known* it. A weird thought came over me. I remembered in the Gospels, Jesus had told his disciples dozens of times that He was going to die. Over and over, he told them. And yet, the dudes didn't have a clue. I had never understood why they didn't get it. Now I understood. I had been possessed by the thirteenth demon. I had faced off against the twelfth demon. And yet, until this moment, kneeling in an old man's pool of tears, I hadn't gotten it. This was war. This was not a game. We needed help.

Light seemed to blossom around us. I looked up. Jonathan's head was bowed. Uncle Cephas's eyes were closed. Standing just a few feet away was a figure who smiled at me. It was Raphael. There was another figure beside him who also looked like an angel but was tall and thin and dressed in green surgical scrubs. Raphael clapped the other angel on the shoulder and pointed at us. The other angel smiled, and then they both disappeared. It was then I felt the tears on my own face. For the first time in a long time, I knew we were going to be all right.

Chapter 14

Vivian Darbonne Ketrick

IT WAS SOMETIME after midnight. The handsome deputy sheriff was asleep in my bed. He had been quite attractive in his uniform. I had expected some kind of redneck clumsiness, but that had not been the case. He had been charming and remarkably adept in his dinner conversation. In some strange way, he reminded me of someone.

I slid quietly out from under the covers and walked across the hotel room. The cool air dried the sweat on my skin. I slid into the hotel robe and pulled it tight around my body. For some reason, I had never felt this exposed before. I had initially told myself that I needed the deputy to serve the court order on Jonathan Steel and company, but in reality, I did not wish to use him. I did not wish to dominate him. I only wished for company, something besides the demons that pulsed inside of me. Something human.

I stood at the window overlooking Red River and watched the stars glittering in the cloudless sky. As a child, I had longed to see the stars at night. In the deep countryside where I had grown up, the stars had been like a million flashing jewels on a bed of black velvet. I studied the deputy's slack features and his gentle snoring, and then I remembered something painful and beautiful. He reminded me of my father.

"Hurry, we don't want to miss the meteor shower."

I picked up my yellow Curious George blanket and my Suzie Strawberry flashlight. "I'm coming, Daddy." I couldn't wait to see what Daddy had described as the most wonderful sight in the universe.

I ran down the hall and stopped outside my parents' bedroom. I tiptoed past the closed door. We wouldn't want to wake up Momma. A pain hit me in the gut when I thought about her waking up. I prayed to God she would keep on sleeping. I thought the pills she had taken and the stuff she drank every night would probably do their trick and keep her asleep.

Daddy was waiting by the back door. We both had our coats on. He was tall and handsome with dark hair, bright-blue eyes, and a smile that could melt the North Polar ice cap. He grabbed my hand, pulled me outside, and led me across the yard into the clearing next to the pasture. We used to have lots of cows and horses, but Momma's problem cost us a lot of money, Daddy said, so he had to sell all the horses and cows except for that one mean old horned heifer, Ludie. I hated her! I gave the cows hay in the winter. Ludie would gouge all the other cows out of her way so she could get to the hay first. Nobody wanted to buy Ludie because she was too old and tough. Well, I had known that already!

Once, Momma had brought Ludie an apple. For some reason she liked that old cow. Maybe it was because they had a lot in common. Ludie had rushed so quickly to get that apple that she had almost gotten Momma with her one horn. If Momma hadn't been so relaxed from her medicine and all, Ludie would have hurt her.

Daddy spread an old blanket over the ground. It was cold and the grass was frosted. We settled right by the fence that separated our yard from the pasture. I looked through the barbed wire for Ludie, but the old heifer was nowhere in sight.

"Now that we've put down the blanket," Daddy said, "we lie down, cover up with the other blankets, and wait." Daddy took off his jacket and made a pillow out of it. He patted the spot next to him and I lay down there. I settled into the old blanket. It smelled like fried chicken and butter. The smell made me feel good. It reminded me of sitting in the kitchen while Daddy fried chicken. Momma sometimes ate.

Daddy pulled the blanket up over his chest and pointed at the sky. I had never seen anything so beautiful. I guess at night I had never stopped playing or running and hiding from Momma long enough to look up at the sky. Millions of stars twinkled in the cold, clear air; they were like jewels spilling out of a jeweler's bag onto a sea of black.

"See that cloudy-looking bar across the sky?" Daddy pointed.

"Yeah."

"That's the milky way," he said.

"Can we get milk from it?" I asked in wonder.

"No, honey. That's not real milk. That's the rest of our galaxy, billions of stars."

I smiled and scooted over until I could feel my Daddy all warm next to me. He made me feel safe. He made me feel loved. Momma didn't make me feel that way. She made me feel ugly and stupid and cold and afraid. But tonight was our night, for just my Daddy and me. Suddenly, a white light flashed in the sky and streaked across the heavens, leaving behind a brilliant tail.

"Oh, Daddy, did you see that?"

"That's a shooting star. Make a wish!"

I closed my eyes really tight and wished that Momma would go far, far away and leave me and Daddy alone. I opened my eyes and they were filled with tears. The tears ran down my cheeks and got cold in the night air. More shooting stars filled the sky until there were dozens and dozens filling the night with magic.

"Oh, Daddy, they're so beautiful. Just look!"

"It's called a meteor shower. And every single shooting star is a wish you can make." He patted my hand. It was the most perfect moment in my eight years of my life.

"What you two doing?"

I heard the coarse voice in the darkness and sat up. Momma lumbered toward us with an old flashlight. The light danced like crazy around the bushes. She stumbled into a tree and fell down. I felt Daddy go tense.

When Momma got up, there was blood running down from a cut on her head. She touched the blood and swore out loud. She swore and swore and swore until her face was as white as a sheet and the blood was still running down her cheek.

Daddy got up and brought her over to the blanket. "Sybil, you should have stayed in bed. You're drunk."

"I'm always drunk!" she screamed. The flashlight danced around the sky like a dizzy searchlight. My stomach began to hurt and I wanted to crawl under the blanket or float up among the beautiful stars to get away from her.

Something snorted loud in the darkness. I looked through the barbed wire and Ludie lumbered up. Her huge curled horn glistened with frost and her eyes glowed in the light of the flashlight. She stopped at the fence and eyed Momma. She probably thought Momma had an apple.

"Well, at least the cow is glad to see me!" Momma screeched. "Why are you sneaking off into the night with our girl? You gonna kidnap her and run off like you threatened to last week? Huh? You worthless shell of a man!" Momma said. She jerked out of Daddy's grasp and fell onto her backside on the blanket. She turned her reddened eyes onto me. Behind her, stars fell from the sky.

"What you looking at, pumpkin? Huh? Look hard, cause this is what you'll be some day. You'll marry Prince Charming and then find out life is horrible. That's all you got to look forward to. The only thing happy to see me is a cow! My own daughter and husband don't want to be around me!"

She struggled to her feet and went for the fence. Ludie backed away. I guessed she had realized Momma didn't have an apple. Daddy tried to stop Momma. He grabbed her shoulders but Momma shoved him up against the barbed wire. I saw Daddy grimace in pain. He turned his back to me and I saw blood run down his shirt. He was cut by the barbed wire. I picked up his jacket to hand to him. Momma cussed me and shoved me back down onto the blanket. And that was when heaven fell.

A blinding ball of light came out of nowhere, burning like a flare, etching itself onto my eyeballs as it streaked across the sky toward the pasture. A loud roar followed in its wake. It hit the ground and the explosion rocked the trees and echoed in the distance. Light rushed over us.

Ludie reared up on her back legs and rushed the fence. Her horn exited through Daddy's back. She backed up with Daddy impaled on her horn and ran off into the darkness, trailing barbed wire. Momma stood there with the sickeningly whirling flashlight. I couldn't speak. I couldn't breathe.

She looked down at me. "Now look what you've done."

Something touched my neck. I jerked and whirled away, ready to unleash the power of one of my demons. The deputy was standing there. He raised his hands.

"Sorry, I didn't mean to scare you, baby. Why are you crying?"

His face was all shadows. I could barely make out his intense blue eyes. I touched his bare chest and felt the warmth of his beating heart. "Just a bad dream," I whispered.

He placed his hands on my shoulders and tenderly pulled me into him. No! I did not want this. I did not need this. He gently pressed my face to his chest. I inhaled his scent, heard his heartbeat, felt the warmth of his embrace, and melted into him. I cried. Hot tears poured down my cheeks and onto the deputy's skin. My demons wanted them to be acid. They wanted the tears to eat away at his compassion. They wanted more than anything for me to push him away and hurl him through the window, out of my life! But I didn't. I was getting weak, and it was the fault of one man. He had saved the kid from the thirteenth demon. He had forgiven Raven in the caverns under Romania. He had saved Theophilus King when the man should have gone to prison. He could have sent my demons to Tartarus while he was in my apartment in Dallas. Did he think he could save me too? Even here, in the arms of this deputy, I could think only of one man. In that moment, I hated Jonathan Steel more than I hated his God.

Chapter 15

Jonathan Steel

CEPHAS APPEARED AROUND the corner of the kitchen in his pajamas just as the rising sun peeked through the French doors of the hearth room. He looked at me with bleary, swollen eyes.

"You're drinking coffee."

I looked down at the cup in my hands. I seldom drank coffee. I didn't like it. But after having been up for the remainder of the night trying to figure out what to do about Theo, I needed something to clear my head.

"Yeah, and it's nasty. I think I made it too strong."

Cephas poured him a cup from the pot and sipped it. He grimaced. "Yes, quite strong. If you do not mind, I will make a some coffee that is more digestible." Cephas emptied the pot and refilled it with water. I watched him pour water in the coffee-maker and measure out scoops of coffee. I had used twice as much. No wonder the stuff had been so strong. Cephas turned on the machine.

"Let's go sit outside while this brews."

Cephas led me through the dining room and out onto the patio. The back of the house was still cool. I sat at the patio table and watched the grayness give way to light. Out on the lake, a sailboat was already plying the waters. Its tall white sail was tinted orange by the rising sun. A cool breeze wafted over us. About a hundred yards off shore, a man in a ski boat lowered a pair of binoculars. He started the engine and moved behind the sailboat, out of view. I wanted to be paranoid. I wanted to be concerned. But I was just numb.

Cephas sat down across from me. "What now?"

"I keep seeing the same man in a ski boat looking at us through binoculars."

Cephas chuckled. "More than likely, he is looking at the house next door. I read on the Internet that a famous movie star is staying there while acting in a movie being shot in the area. Perhaps you are being a bit too paranoid.

But after what happened last night, I can't say that I blame you. However, with the prayers, I believe we made some progress. We should be safe now."

"So what happens now? Guardian angels with supernatural swords stand watch around this house?"

Cephas nodded. "Something like that."

"Come on, Cephas. Guardian angels? Really?"

Cephas stood up and went inside. He returned with two cups of coffee. "Have you forgotten the angel who helped us with Wulf in Lakeside? This angel, Raphael, did not come of his own volition. Angels are messengers, Jonathan. They can only protect when given direction by God."

"Josh seems to think he has a guardian angel in this Raphael." I sipped my coffee. It was not as bitter as my pot of coffee. In fact, it tasted pretty good.

"I understand you saw the angel in the cavern with the vampires." Cephas said.

"I did. But the details are fuzzy. I remember what Claire told me when she appeared to me from her 'other dimensions'. She said our minds could not retain what we perceived from the other dimensions. Maybe this is why we have problems clearly remembering the presence of angels or demons."

"And thus, the guardian angel question." Cephas slurped his coffee. "In the twelfth chapter of Acts, Peter is freed from prison by an angel. When he comes to the house of Mary, the servant girl tells the others she was speaking to *his* angel. There is an implicit understanding here that God gives us angels to watch over us. And let us not forget the angel that appeared in the furnace with Shadrach, Meshach, and Abednego. I have to believe that God will send an angel to protect us from the demons."

I studied the man's puffy, swollen face and his wild, bushy hair. "You never told me you'd cast out demons."

He gazed out at the lake. "There are many things I've never told you, Jonathan. A man has a right to his secrets."

"How badly were you hurt?"

He looked down at his leg. "You don't notice my limp, do you?"

"I never have."

"I hide it well," he said.

"When were you going to tell me?"

Cephas rubbed his huge moustache. "I guess now. This limp came many years later. But there is always a first time. You are interested in the box on my desk. It contains trinkets from my first encounter with a demon."

Cephas Lawrence

October, 1963
University of Dallas Library Rare Book Collection

"Boo!"

I jumped and dropped my book about demonology. I whirled around to see Father Caskey's grinning face in the dark shadows in the library basement.

"James, you frightened me to death!" I picked up the book.

"Cephas, my friend, you should know better than to come down into the basement alone," he said with his faint Irish accent. "Strange things be happening here! And reading about demons? I thought you didn't believe in demons. Or angels. Or Satan. Or God."

I closed the book and slid it back into its slot on the shelf behind me. "Just because I don't share your delusions doesn't mean I am not interested, James. I am planning to write my dissertation on the alleged phenomenon of demon possession and to prove there is nothing behind it but psychosomatic disorder."

"So you've come to a Catholic university to prove God doesn't exist and demons are just made up to scare cranky six-year-olds." James' brown hair was ruffled and he wore a brown jacket over his black shirt and white collar. His eyes danced with mischief. "I did scare you though, didn't I? Tell me, laddie, why would you be scared down here in the dark with a book about demons in your hands if you didn't believe just the tiniest bit that there might be some truth to it all?"

"You haven't made me a believer yet, James."

"How did you gain access to the rare book room if you aren't a Catholic?"

"I told the librarian you and I were dorm mates at NYU."

"Well, now, did you tell her how we really became friends? How we bested the brightest chess players at NYU? Of course, you'd have had to reveal who the real master chess player was: yours truly." He poked himself in the chest.

"I remember well our games and all the bets I lost. My poverty is earned. Yours comes from your vows." I pushed past him out into the open aisle between the rows of ancient books. Tables were positioned down the center of the aisle and illuminated by pale-green lamps. There was no one else in sight. The dim, flickering overhead lights hung from bare concrete trusses. It was a dismal and gloomy atmosphere for the university's oldest and possibly most valuable books. I

really had to speak to the head librarian about setting up a proper environmentally sound room for the oldest books. "I never imagined Lover Boy would take the vow of celibacy and become a priest."

"And I never imagined the cold-hearted Cephas Lawrence would go to medical school and become a regular Dr. Kildare." James laughed.

"I'm in graduate school. Anthropology. I am not pursuing medicine. Just a doctorate."

"Well, if you'd answer my letters or return my phone calls, I might know more about what you're doing with your pitiful life."

"Pitiful life?" I paused and glared at him.

"Come now, Cephas me boy. How long has it been? Two years? You come to my town and you don't even bother to give me a call? The least you could do for your old college roommate is to visit a local pub."

"We're in Texas, James. They're called saloons. How did you find out I was here?"

James hopped onto a table and crossed his legs. He was a strikingly handsome man in contrast to my seedy disarray. When we were college room mates, I envied his good looks and his easy manner with others. I was more studious and withdrawn. But our friendship had soured over the years thanks to our differences on the existence of God and the supernatural.

"I have an agreement with Katherine. She calls me whenever anyone asks about books on demons. It's one of my areas of interest, you see. And, when she called and said a Doctor Lawrence had shown up, I couldn't believe me ears. Could it be my old pal, Cephas Lawrence, I asked myself. So, here I am. So, you're not a doctor, yet? Probably for the best. You have a terrible bed side manner."

"What?"

"See what I mean? Still cranky as ever."

I nodded and waved my hands around at the bookshelves. "So, why are you looking for those interested in demons?"

"Someday, Cephas, someone will show up who has found the book."

I rolled my eyes. "The Book of the Vitreomancers? Are you on that again?"

"Don't play games with me. I know you're looking for it too. The Vitreomancers worked magic by harnessing the power of the angels, Cephas. If I could learn how to work hand in hand with an angel … Imagine the things I could do. I could heal. I could see the future. I could raise the dead!" For a moment, his eyes had a strange, deluded look. Then he laughed. "Sorry, laddie. I probably sound a bit insane, don't I?"

"If your angels do exist, James, I doubt very much that their boss would allow them to follow your whims willy-nilly. Others have tried to go where you want to *go. It is a dangerous and slippery slope, and you know it."* I rubbed my moustache and retrieved my satchel.

James hopped down and patted me on the shoulder. "Well, Cephas, enjoy your skepticism. I have an appointment with a congregation member who claims to have seen a demon! If you want to play a wee game of chess, just give me a call. Katherine has my number."

"Katherine? You aren't straying from your vows, are you?" I asked.

James laughed and raised an eyebrow. "Katherine is happily married with three children. Her husband and I play golf. But, I still have the charm, don't I, Cephas laddie? Don't stay down here in the dark too long. You don't have the kind of spiritual protection I do. The demons might get you!" He laughed and hurried off.

What he had said was true. I, too, was interested in the Vitreomancers but I would never let him know. I opened my satchel and removed the book I was returning. It was the only modern reproduction of a tome written in the middle ages. It would be irresponsible to have taken the original autograph. The book had served me well as a source of material for a portion of my thesis. It contained a reference to The Book of the Vitreomancers, the manuscript I was hoping to find. I sat at the table in the meager light and opened the reproduction. I was engrossed in the material when a shadow passed over the table. Expecting James again, I cleared my throat and prepared an appropriate insult. I looked up into the eyes of an angel.

Her dark hair was lustrous and cascaded down her shoulders. She wore a simple red dress with a black belt tied around her narrow waist. Her brown eyes were moist and she clutched a small purse to her chest. "Excuse me, I'm looking for information on demons. The librarian said there were some old books down here and that a Father Caskey could possibly help me."

I stood up slowly and drank in her dark beauty. My heart raced and my mouth was dry. She was mesmerizing. "Father Caskey just left. But I am his old friend, Cephas Lawrence."

A look of pain and worry crossed her face and she slumped into the chair across the table from me. "I was hoping to speak to the Father. I don't even think he'll believe me."

"I'm not a priest, but perhaps I can help?"

She pulled a pale handkerchief from her purse and dabbed at her eyes. "It's my daughter who needs help."

I blinked. A daughter. That would imply a husband. Why was my mind drawn in this direction? "What about your husband?"

"He died in the war. Mary and I are all alone. And now she is ..." The woman *collapsed in sobs. I moved around the edge of the table. I held her shaking shoulders and comforted her.*

"There, there. Try to calm down and then you can tell me everything." I sat in the chair beside her and noted how my arm stayed draped across her shoulders.

The woman regarded me with wet eyes. "My daughter is being visited by two demons. She claims she can see them and that they want to hurt her. I've been to the doctor and he told us it was just nightmares. This is more than bad dreams. Something is going on, Mr. Lawrence. I need help."

I patted her shoulder and placed my hand over hers. "What is your name?"

"Please, call me Molly." It was the most beautiful name in the universe.

Cephas fell silent and stared out over the lake. I tapped his arm and he jerked.

"Is that all you're going to tell me?"

Cephas's eyes were moist with emotion. "That is all I can speak of today. Give me some time."

So the picture on his desk was of this Molly? He had called out for her last night in his confusion—I had heard him. But I could sense from his silence he would say no more today. "I can't blame you for holding back, Cephas. I have the same reaction to memories of my father."

He gazed at me and nodded. "I am sure you will tell me more when you can. And I will return the favor. Now, we must focus on finding the chest and, of course, Theo."

"We find one, we find the other," I said. "If Vivian isn't the one who took the chest, then who are we dealing with?"

Cephas sipped his coffee. "I hate to say this, but perhaps another demon, Jonathan."

The thought had crossed my mind. Josh walked out onto the patio with his laptop cradled in one arm. He was wearing pajama bottoms and a tank top. He looked like he had been up all night.

"Dude, I think I found something."

"Have you even been to bed?"

He glanced at me and then seemed to notice the sky for the first time. "Bro, I guess I didn't. No biggie. I can catch a few once I finish."

He seemed amazingly alert. Ah, the vigor of youth. "So what did you find?"

Josh placed the laptop on the table and brought up some images. "Dude, I pulled some frames from the video. We have a clear image of the teleporter."

He moved his finger over the trackpad and one image filled the screen. "Here is the guy's face."

The man was Hispanic, with a heavy five-o'clock shadow, a wispy moustache, and a goatee. His eyes were dark and his hair was short and curly. "I don't recognize him."

"It's not Vivian, that's for sure," Cephas said.

"So what does this mean?" Josh slid into a chair between us. "Does he work for Vivian? Or is this guy a new player in the game?"

"Vivian still thinks we have the chest." I sighed. "I hope he's not a new player. We've got enough to handle as it is."

"He must be associated with a powerful demon to be able to teleport Theo along with himself," Cephas said.

"I don't know, Bro." Josh tapped his trackpad. "This guy is definitely hurting when he returns. Watch." The man reappeared and doubled over as if catching his breath. Clutching his chest, he hurried across the room to Cephas's computer. He was definitely panting and gasping for air, and his was faced contorted in pain.

"The second trip cost him something," I said.

Cephas leaned back and his finger strayed to his moustache. "Moving through other dimensions is not possible for the human body, much less the human mind. We are incapable of sustained existence outside of our dimensions. I imagine multiple trips would take their toll. How many times did Wulf teleport at the Bloodfest?"

"Once," I said.

"Then it is likely that humans cannot withstand multiple trips in a short period of time. I imagine they would require a recovery time in between."

"But our visitor had no choice," Josh said. "He had to come back and get the computers when he realized the chest was a 3-D printing."

"And he knew that we would have been alerted because Theo had caught him red-handed," I said.

"So where do we start?" Cephas asked. "Check the hospitals for emergency visits?"

"In what city?" I asked. "We have no idea how far this man is able to teleport."

"It can't be that far," Cephas said. "The stress would be too much for the human body."

I studied the video playing on a loop and something caught my eye. "Wait! Josh, what is that written on the man's jacket?"

Josh peered at the screen. "You mean over his breast pocket? I don't know. I think I pulled some frames from this video. Let me check." His hands played over the keyboard and then several frames appeared on the screen. He zoomed in on the front of the man's chest. Some white letters were stitched over the breast pocket of his dark-blue jacket.

"Can you clear that up?" I asked.

"Let me try a couple of filters," Josh said. We watched the image change as Josh played with image filters. Suddenly the three letters became legible. Josh gasped. Cephas sat back in surprise. I stood up and headed into the kitchen to get my cell phone.

"Josh, print me out the best picture you have of that man's face. I'm going to have to call an old friend." I picked up my cell phone.

Cephas was right behind me. "You're calling—"

"Special Agent Franklin Ross," I said. The three letters were *FBI*.

Chapter 16

Theophilus Nosmo King

I SAT UP SLOWLY on the cold concrete floor and found my left wrist. That was a major accomplishment, considering it was somewhere on my arm and I had to struggle to remember where my arm was. I tried to drive the cobwebs out of my mind and then found my watch. Six hours had passed. Nothing else had happened. The teleport guy had left me in the room alone.

The only thing on me still working was my watch. The rest of me hadn't fared so well. Earlier, I woke up and had the dry heaves for over an hour. Then a headache had set in, followed by muscle pains, and I had passed out again. Using smack hadn't hurt this bad!

I stood up and then fell back down. I stood up again. And fell back down. I decided to compromise and crawled over to the wall opposite the door. I managed to sit up against the wall. The room was about ten by twelve with a metal chair in the corner and a folding table pushed against the wall to my right. The metal door had a small window in it that had been painted over with opaque black paint. The walls were cinderblock and the ceiling was concrete. I couldn't see any kind of security camera on the ceiling. The only illumination in the room was the light from the small metal grid next to the door.

I drew a deep breath and gagged at the odor of something nasty. I guess my smell hadn't been working earlier. I wished it was still broken. The room smelled like an old slaughterhouse. I squinted at the table and noticed it was crusted with a dark residue. Blood? God, please let it not be blood!

After an eternity, the pain subsided and I managed to stand up again. This time, I didn't fall down. I stumbled to the table and fell up against it. The table toppled over as I slid down to the floor. I was showered with dry, crispy debris. Something hard hid me in the face and I rolled away from the overturned table. I sat up in a panic and tried to brush the stuff off of me. It

96

smelled like rotten flesh and with a shock I realized it was old, clotted blood. In the dim light, I made out the skull that glared at me from atop a pile of dark bones.

I crawfished away from the horror and ran into the door. In full panic mode, I managed to stand up and jerk on the door handle. It was locked. Big surprise!

I made it across the room to the chair and avoided the dead person on the floor. I was sick again, my head swimming from the odor of decay and old blood. Where was I? What was this place? The man with the teleporting demon must have known where this place was. Which meant, he knew there was a body here. Which meant he had something to do with the dead person who had become a pile of bones. I knew from my police training how long it would take for a body to get like that. Weeks, possibly months. This was not a fresh kill.

The air grew hot and stuffy and sweat poured down my back. I took off the long-sleeved football jersey I was wearing over a tank top and wiped my face. The old blood was mixing with my sweat and now I stunk to high heaven. Okay, Theo, don't panic again. Stay calm. You panic and you'll end up a pile of bones like your friend.

I stood up again and went back to the door and I put my ear against the metal. I could make out a distant throbbing sound and the rush of air moving around the top and bottom edges of the door. That meant that air was moving in; so it had to be moving out. There had to be some kind of return vent in the room.

Footsteps approached. I stepped back from the door. What to do? Play possum. I lay back down on the floor and closed my eyes. Something scraped against the door and it opened. Harsh light filled the room. I resisted the urge to squint.

"I thought I heard something fall down here." The man paused. "Who are you?"

I opened my eyes. The man in the doorway was illuminated from behind, so I couldn't see his face. He was wearing black pants and a dark jacket. His eyes were hidden by sunglasses.

"I'm the man you locked in this room!"

"How did you get here?"

I squinted into the light and tried to make out the man's features. "You've got to be kidding. You can tell Vivian I'm not playing her game. She'd better not go back to Ketrick's house for the chest."

"What game would that be?"

"Man, are you stupid or something? You'd better let me out of here now." I stood up and started toward the door. He pulled a pistol out of his inner coat pocket.

"That's far enough." He motioned to the body. "Well, the previous owner of this establishment left some playthings behind. Did he leave you, too? I don't think so. Even as big as you are, you would be dead by now."

I swallowed. "You gonna tell me what is going on?"

He waved the gun nonchalantly and laughed. "The chest, you say?"

"Yeah, the chest at Ketrick's house. The one Vivian is looking for. Did she take it?"

"Well, I can't answer that, but I will make sure and find the answers. Soon. Time for a visit to Ketrick's other house." The man slid the pistol back into an inner pocket. Then, he reached into his other pocket and pulled out an object. Before I could take another step, I saw the electric blue sparks as he pressed the trigger of a Taser. The needles plunged into my chest. Again. I fell back into the pile of bones as he slammed the door. For the second time in two days, I had been tased.

The room swam in shadows and the light from beneath the door fragmented and moved around the room like the reflections off a disco ball. I was somewhere else.

I stood in front of the man hanging from the meat hook. The plastic ties around his wrists had cut into his flesh and blood trickled down his arms and onto his bare chest. I lifted his chin. His empty eyes were fixed on something in the far distance.

"I asked where to find your partner," I growled.

The man drew a deep breath. He tried to focus his eyes on me. "Who are you?" he said hoarsely.

"I told you who I was. Sad thing, man, is that you don't remember what you did. And that makes me even angrier."

His gaze shifted to my uniform. "I want my lawyer."

I laughed until tears rolled down my face. "Listen here, you dirt clod, don't nobody on my force know you're here but me. I'm gonna see to it that justice is done. Now, I'm going to give you one last chance to tell me where to find your partner before I pull this trigger." I put the barrel of my nine-mil in the center of his forehead. His eyes crossed looking at the gun. Then he closed them.

"I want a lawyer. Now."

"Sorry." I gritted my teeth. "All you're gonna get is a head full of lead." I pulled the trigger.

I was back in the room now as the electric charge stopped, and I felt the old guilt, the old pain eating away at my insides the way they had done for years. I started crying and the skull came into focus through my tears. The dead condemned me! I looked away and up at the dark ceiling. "God, I thought you had forgiven me for that. I thought we were done." I guess not. My sobs filled the empty room.

Jonathan Steel

"Jonathan Steel."

Franklin Ross sat behind a desk in a small office at the regional FBI headquarters in Dallas, Texas. Cephas and I had shared the driving from Shreveport and I had managed to catch some sleep during the three-hour trip. Ross had insisted we talk in person after I said there was an issue with a rogue FBI agent. I think the real reason he had made us drive over was because he knew it would irritate me. We have a history. We had left Josh fast asleep in bed.

Cephas and I sat down across from him. I put the photos down on the desk. "How's Sue?"

He looked at me. Beneath his perfectly combed dark hair, his face was tense. Nothing about him had changed. He still wore his signature red tie and black blazer. "We're not speaking."

"Not surprising," I said. When I had last seen Ross at the hearing for Josh, he had left to have lunch with Lieutenant Sue Kane of the Dallas. She had seemed slightly smitten with the man.

Ross shrugged. "High maintenance."

"And you're not?"

"I *was* talking about me. So what's going on?"

I pointed to the pictures. "This guy stole something from our basement."

"'Our basement'?"

"We moved into, uh, Ketrick's house," I said.

Ross's lips slowly curled into a smile. He looked at Cephas. He looked back at me. "You're kidding me."

"No."

"It was an excellent buy," Cephas said.

Ross laughed out loud and sat back in his chair. "You're living in Ketrick's old house? There is justice in the world after all."

My face grew warm and I tried to suppress my desire to rip the man's throat out. I had broken his nose more than once before. "When you're done laughing, maybe you could answer my question."

Ross stopped laughing and wiped tears from his eyes. "You never asked a question. You just showed me a picture."

I tapped the printout. "This man came into our basement and took something that belonged to Cephas. Then he kidnapped Theo."

"Kidnapped the big guy?"

"Yeah."

"Did he have an elephant gun? Loaded with major tranqs?"

He started laughing again and the fury took me. I leaned over the desk, grabbed his tie, and pulled his face forward until his eyes were level with mine. "That's enough! Theo's in trouble."

He shoved me back and bolted from his chair. His hand went into his jacket and returned with a gun. "Don't give me a reason to pull the trigger."

"Are you going to kill me for rumpling your tie?"

"That's enough!" Cephas said. "We don't have time for this! Theo is in danger."

Ross put the pistol back in his shoulder holster and straightened his tie. "If you want my help, I suggest you back off."

I leaned back and tapped the photo. "One of your agents came into our home, stole an artifact, and kidnapped Theo. This is not my problem, Ross. It's the FBI's."

Ross picked up the photo. "Do you know how many employees the FBI has?"

"No. I only care about one."

Ross sat back down and studied the picture. His face paled. He picked up his phone, dialed a number, and waited. "Regina, get into my office. And bring that folder we were looking at earlier. Yes, that one." Ross looked at me. "Where were you this morning?"

The question took me by surprise. "In the basement of our house in Shreveport. This guy had just left."

"Impossible," Ross said.

The door to his office opened and a woman walked in. She was short with red hair and wore a black pair of pants and a beige blouse. She looked at me and then at Cephas. "Trouble, Ross?"

"This is Special Agent Regina Cornelius. Do you have the file?"

Cornelius cast a wary look in my direction and then handed Ross a file.

He opened it and looked at the contents, then he held up a small photo. "This man look familiar?"

"Yes, that's him."

Ross closed the folder and rubbed his jaw as he looked off into space. Finally Cornelius spoke up.

"Ross, what's going on?"

Ross handed her our printout. "Jonathan Steel here claims he took this photo in the basement of his home in Shreveport this morning. And I'm assuming that is some kind of security camera time stamp?"

"That's around the time we got the alarm that alerted us that someone was in the basement."

"This is impossible," Cornelius said.

"Why?"

Ross handed me the personnel folder. "Look at the top sheet."

It was from a Dallas hospital and it detailed, in very messy handwriting, the admission of one Juan Destillo, special agent to the FBI, into the emergency room at 2:47 a.m. He had had chest pains and died thirty minutes later from a massive cardiac arrest.

"He's dead?"

"Died from a heart attack. At 3:18 a.m. That's less than forty-five minutes from the time you claimed he was in your basement. There is no way he could have gotten from Shreveport to Dallas in forty-five minutes."

I looked at Cephas. "The stress must have been too much."

Cephas nodded. "I agree. That means we have just lost our only lead to Theo's location."

"I'm not worried about his location," I said. "I'm worried about his health. It killed this man. What could it have done to Theo?"

Cornelius pulled the folder down so she could look into my face. "You said 'it' killed a man. What is 'it'?"

I glared at Ross and frowned. He shook his head. "Oh, no. No you don't, Steel!" He stood up. "Do not say it. Do you hear me?"

"Say what?" Cornelius asked.

Cephas placed a hand on her arm. "That your colleague was killed by a demon."

Chapter 17

Josh Knight

I WAS HOT. I mean, I was stinking hot! The sun was directly overhead as I stood at the end of the pier overlooking the lake. I had on my LSU sweatshirt and sweatpants, and they were soaked with sweat. I needed to cool off.

At the end of the pier, something stirred in the water. What the …? I looked down as something pale floated deep in the water. I got down on my knees and leaned over the edge of the pier. What was it? A fish?

The pale thing came closer, nearing the surface. I made out the dark shapes of eyes. It was a face. Someone was under the water. A corpse? Someone had been killed and sunk in the water!

It came closer. Dark hair floated around the face. The eyes suddenly opened clear and sharp. Hands came up out of the water, grabbed me by the shirt, and pulled me in. I held my breath as I tumbled into the water and the hands pulled me down. It was Vivian. She smiled and pulled me deeper. The pressure of the water was killing me. My lungs ached. I tried to get away, but her grasp was too strong. And then I felt something around my ankle. I looked up toward the surface. A hand was holding my ankle. I looked back at Vivian. Her face was twisted in hate and anger. Her grip weakened and I broke loose. The hand pulled me upward, but not quickly enough. Darkness closed in on me. I wanted so badly to breathe in the cold water. With a snap, the hand lifted me up out of the water. I landed on the pier, gasping for air as I rolled over to look at the man who had saved me. He was wearing the same helmet he had been wearing on the last day I had seen him. He pushed his goggles up over his forehead. I recognized those eyes. They had glared at me many times after I had done something wrong.

"Dad?"

"Wake up, Josh. You're dreaming."

I sat bolt upright in bed. The sheets were soaked in sweat and wrapped

around me so tightly I could hardly breathe. The open window had allowed the afternoon sun to shine on me full force. No wonder I had been hot. It had all been a dream. I hadn't dreamed about my Dad for a very long time. My chest hurt, not just from the dream.

I unwrapped myself and went to the bathroom. After a well-needed shower, I stood in front of the misted mirror and looked at myself. I'd cut my hair short after the thing with Wulf, but it was beginning to grow back. The piercing holes in my lip and ear lobes were healing. Again. I had re-punctured them in order to join Armando's vampire clan. But I was done with all that now. Things were different. I was different. I didn't need all that stuff. Ila, my old girlfriend, was at home with her mother, where she belonged. I pulled on shorts and a T-shirt and hurried down the stairs. It was after five. I had slept the whole day.

"Hey, guys, I'm up. What's for dinner?"

I stopped in the empty kitchen and remembered that Theo was gone. Kidnapped. Missing. The memory hit me like a blow to the stomach. The doorbell rang. It took me a minute to figure out which door to answer. It turned out to be the side door off the kitchen, by the driveway. The door had a large window in the top half. Sadie, the real estate lady, was looking in at me.

I opened the door for her. She smiled at me as she came in, her arms full of plastic sacks. "Hello, Josh. How are you?"

"I'm fine," I said as she put the sacks on the island. The odor of barbecue filled the kitchen and my stomach growled. "What's up?"

"Jonathan asked me to check on you. I guess he's not back yet?" She took out Styrofoam containers and placed them on the island.

"Where'd he go?"

"To Dallas with Dr. Lawrence. He said he left you a message on the phone."

Dallas? I hurried over to the telephone and pressed the message button. "Josh, Cephas and I are running an errand to Dallas about the picture. Ross won't help us unless we go over there. You can't go because of Judge Bolton, remember? You need to rest anyway. Sadie is coming by later to check on you. We'll call."

I slammed a fist on the countertop. "That's not fair! They went off to my hometown and didn't even take me."

"Sweetie, from what I understand, you *can't* go back to Dallas. Something about a court order, right?" She opened some of the containers. "I brought by some barbecue from Hickory Stick. Figured you would be hungry. So if you're all right, I'll be going. I have a house showing at 5:30."

I glared at her and nodded. She smiled and hurried out the door. I was mad. I was furious. How dare they go off and not even tell me. I noticed a second message and clicked the play button. While it played, I made a sandwich out of the brisket.

"Josh, we've found something. I can't talk right now but we have to spend the night here. Don't worry. I asked Liz Washington to come and stay with you tonight. Once she gets there, give me a call and I'll explain. Better yet, when we get to the hotel, I'll call you." Jonathan's voice echoed in the kitchen.

In spite of my anger, I was ravenous. I ate three sandwiches. The stuff was good, really good! I even ate the beans, although I knew I would regret it later. The doorbell rang again, and this time I saw, through the window, an elderly woman with chocolate skin and short white hair. It was Liz Washington. I had first met her in Lakeside when she had helped Jonathan with the thirteenth demon. I hadn't been able to fool her much. She was wicked smart. She had stayed on in Lakeside to supervise the archeological dig at the old church site.

I opened the door, and she turned and smiled at me. She stepped into the kitchen and opened her arms. "Come here, son. How are you?"

Something inside me broke. It was like a dam bursting and crumbling. When she took me in her arms, it all came through. Fast and furious, the loss and the sorrow and the pain flooded over me. "Mama Liz," I said. I didn't know why I called her that. I supposed in my fantasies and dreams, Liz had become the grandmother I had never known. I started to cry. I cried. And I cried. Like a baby, I cried. With my nose streaming, I cried. She held me and patted me. In this weird whirlwind of sorrow and loss, I fell and fell and fell and let it all come out. All the anger and fear and worry just poured out of me. I didn't know how long she held onto me. She didn't stop until I opened my tear-filled eyes and looked over her shoulder at the girl standing in the doorway.

She was about my height, with long black hair and dark-brown eyes. She was watching me with wonder. She was beautiful. She was perfect.

I pulled away from Liz and turned away to try to find some tissues. I grabbed a kitchen towel and wiped my face and blew my nose. "So how are you, Mama Liz?" I sounded like I was talking through an elephant's trunk.

"'Mama Liz'?" she said. Her hand rested on my shoulder. "Honey child, I am honored. I'm fine. I guess you're better now?"

I turned back to her and my eyes flicked to the girl. She was looking elsewhere. "Yeah, thanks. Who's with you?" I whispered.

Liz studied me with her warm brown eyes and a smile played on her lips.

"She's too old for you. She's a freshman in college," she whispered back. "Ashley Milford, this is Josh Knight."

Ashley looked at me and I melted. My heart skipped a beat. She was gorgeous. I put out a hand and realized with horror that it was covered with snot. I shoved it behind me. "Nice to meet you." I blew a snot bubble out of my nose. How much worse could this get? "Want some barbecue?"

Ashley looked at the spread. "Hickory Stick? Awesome. I'd love some."

I stepped away to try to compose myself and clean up my face and hands while Liz and Ashley got themselves some food.

"So what's happening?" I asked.

Liz bit into a piece of brisket. "Jonathan asked me to come over and check on you. Ashley is just dropping me off. I'll stay the night until they get back tomorrow. So Ketrick's house? That's poetic justice."

"Yeah, Ketrick's house. Yeah. That's what it is. Yeah." My face reddened. I was a total dweeb.

"Dr. Washington tells me you were possessed by the thirteenth demon," Ashley said. She had barbecue sauce all over her mouth. It was beautiful. "Did you gain any insight into the historical consequences of the demon's influence over ancient culture?"

I opened my mouth and then shut it. She might as well have been speaking Mayan. "I don't remember much," I said, and I frowned. I tried for pity. "It was a very painful time for me."

Ashley looked over at Liz. "Oh, I'm sorry. Here I am talking academics and not appreciating what you went through. Sorry." She wiped the sauce from her face with a napkin. "Well, I really have to be going. Dr. Washington has me on a tight schedule."

"I could tell you more about that demon," I said. Liz smiled at me and put a hand on my arm.

"She really does need to get back." Liz turned to Ashley. "I'll call you in the morning once I hear from Mr. Steel."

Ashley nodded and let herself out. I stepped up to the window in the door and watched her climb into the car and drive off. "I think I'm in love."

Liz laughed. "You're just infatuated, young man. And Ashley has a boyfriend. He's on the offensive line with LSU. Much bigger than you."

I turned and shrugged. "Doesn't hurt to try."

"In this case, it would." Liz smiled at me. "Now, do you feel better?"

I looked away. "Sorry. I don't know what came over me."

"You needed to get rid of all that. Jonathan did the same thing."

"Jonathan? You mean he cried?"

Liz bit into her sandwich and nodded. "Like a baby."

I smiled. I had something on the big man so now was the best time to call him. I ran up the stairs to get my laptop and brought it back down to the kitchen. "I'm gonna Skype him." I turned on the program and waited while it looked for Jonathan. It was almost 6:30 p.m.; they should have made it to the hotel by now. An image popped up and there he was sitting in his hotel room. I could see Cephas laid out on the bed behind him.

"Josh, what's up?"

"Bro, I'm here with Dr. Liz Washington," I said professionally. "I have just completed an exhaustive interview regarding her unique capability to bring out the inner child in all of us."

Jonathan looked as confused as he would have been watching a Japanese anime. He shook his head. "What are you talking about?"

"She said you cried like a baby." I leaned into the picture. "I didn't know you had it in you."

Jonathan's face reddened. "And you didn't cry when we went back to your house in Rockwall?"

A cold chill came over me. Advantage Steel. "I'm just an emotional teenager."

Jonathan frowned. "Is Liz there?"

I turned the laptop so the camera could catch her. "I'm here, Jonathan. Josh called me Mama Liz. I think that should become my official designation. Do you have any objection?"

I felt my skin crawl. I should never have messed with either of them. "No objections, Mama Liz."

In the background, Uncle Cephas sat up and looked at the camera. "Maybe the two of us should get together and work out an agreement about our mutual roles in the boy's life."

Liz laughed. "Nice try, old man. Any news on Theo?"

"Turns out the man who appeared in our basement is dead. He had a heart attack just minutes after leaving the basement with Cephas' computer," Jonathan said. "I don't think Theo will have had the same problem. He only teleported once. This guy did it twice in a matter of minutes, and one of those times was with Theo hanging on for dear life."

"So the dude was an FBI agent?" I asked.

"Yes, and Ross is going to take us over to a storage warehouse where all of Ketrick's stuff is being sorted. That's where this guy was working."

"Do you think Theo is there?"

"I don't know, Josh. Regina worked with the man. She's looking into his address for us."

"Regina?" I asked.

"Special Agent Cornelius," Cephas said from the bed. "Quite attractive."

Jonathan rolled his eyes. "We're meeting her in the morning to check out any places this guy was associated with. I'll call you once we know something. Liz, you don't mind staying the night with Josh?"

"No, honey. I'm going to beat Josh at Ms. Pac-Man."

Chapter 18

Jonathan Steel

REGINA CORNELIUS KNOCKED on our hotel door at eight o'clock that night. She was wearing jeans and an FBI T-shirt. "I'm here to see the video."

I glanced over at Cephas. He was spread out on his bed in an undershirt and rumpled pants. We hadn't known we would be spending the night away from home. Cornelius didn't seem to notice. "I thought we would be going over that in the morning."

Cornelius shook her head. "Nope. I'm heading over to your neck of the woods in the morning to head up the joint security task force for the governor's visit. I'd rather get this over with tonight."

"Ross isn't coming?"

"He has a big meeting tonight about reassignment. I think he's getting brushed off and put into the field somewhere unsavory. Seems his last two cases have cast a shadow on his career. Thanks to you."

Cephas had gotten up from his bed and he was pulling Josh's iPad out of my backpack. "I have the video on an iPad. Josh transferred it."

I hadn't thought much about the video. All I could think about was finding Theo. Regina sat down at the small table in the corner and watched the first video of Destillo appearing in the basement. Cephas paused it to show Cornelius Destillo's face.

"Is that your agent?" He pointed a crooked finger at the screen.

"It looks like him." Cornelius frowned.

Cephas brought up the second video and again paused it on the clearest image of Destillo. There was no doubt. She was silent as, in the video, Destillo disappeared in a flash of light. She sat back and rubbed her eyes.

"Your teenager could have edited it," she said.

"He didn't have time."

Cornelius stood up and paced at the foot of our beds. "Ross told me about you two. Told me about your demons. I don't believe it for a minute."

"But?"

She glared at me. "The video is disturbing. Destillo dies in Dallas and you have a picture of him in your basement thirty minutes before. Something is up. What was that chest he took the first time?"

"A facsimile of an object missing from the basement," Cephas said. "He also took my computer."

"Well, it might be at his house. I'm going over there right now."

"Let's go." I wasn't about to miss the chance to check out Destillo's house. We might find a clue to Theo's whereabouts.

Cornelius put out a restraining hand to me. "I never said you could go."

"Then why are you here?"

"To see the video."

"We could have emailed it to you."

Cornelius frowned. "Fine, Ross insisted I come get you before going over to the house. He wants your opinion of any hocus pocus I might run into."

"Ross is on my side for once? That's a first," I said.

"Don't let it go to your head. We play this by the book. You do exactly as I say."

"You're the boss."

Cephas motioned to the bed. "I'll stay here. I need my beauty sleep." He looked tired and drawn.

Cornelius drove the standard four-door car issued by the FBI. We headed out toward the northern side of Dallas, up past the George H. Bush Parkway. There was heavy construction going on all around us. Dallas was spreading like a cancer, engulfing small communities with unstoppable vigor.

"I don't believe in demons. But Ross said to ask you about them anyway," Cornelius said.

"It's complicated."

"I read your case file."

"Which one?"

"Both of them." Cornelius glanced at me. "So-called number thirteen in Lakeside with Robert Ketrick. Alleged number twelve in Transylvania. You really believe in demons?"

"Yes." I felt my face grow warm with anger. "If you don't believe me, then why search Destillo's house? What does Ross suspect him of?"

"Fair enough." Cornelius nodded. "Destillo had been acting strange. He was responsible for cataloging Ketrick's collection of weapons and torture devices. Some of them are missing. We think he might possibly have been … well, inspired by Ketrick." Cornelius turned the car into an old subdivision with small, low-level houses built in the 1950s ranch style.

"Sort of like he's been in league with demons?"

"I already said I don't believe in demons." She pulled up to a house . The yard was overgrown. Papers littered the driveway. The windows were dark.

"Cornelius, I think Destillo is in league with a demon. Demons have the ability to move in and out of other dimensions. Number twelve, as you call him, was capable of teleportation with Rudolph Wulf."

"You've got to be kidding." Cornelius put the car in park and turned to glare at me.

"You saw the video. You saw Destillo and King disappear."

"Let me get this straight. Destillo teleported into Ketrick's basement and kidnapped King? Why?"

"He wasn't after King." I studied the papers littering the driveway and the weeds choking the yard. "He was after the chest. Doesn't look like he's been too attentive at home. Maybe he has been busy with other things."

"And distracted." Cornelius looked at me. "Ross told me about Lakeside and Rudolph Wulf. He told me things that weren't in the final report. Ross is a hard man. He doesn't buy into religious nonsense, but he said that what happened to you was real."

"That surprises me," I said.

"He also said you'd had your differences in the past."

"Still do."

"You realize I'm finding all of this hard to believe." She rubbed her eyes and yawned.

"Am I boring you?" My face burned. "I can take you to the cavern in Transylvania. I can show you where the assassin Raven died saving Josh Knight. I don't want to believe this stuff either. But I don't have a choice."

"Sorry, I'm far from bored. Just tired. I've been burning the candle at both ends, leading the investigation of Ketrick and now being assigned to the security task force for the governor's visit to Louisiana. I've got a lot on my plate, and now Ross is probably going to be transferred somewhere far away. I'm left holding this bag of, well, your demons. I have a background in forensic science. I can't believe in anything that defies logical explanation. So I'm going to be very skeptical."

"Good," I said. "I wish what happened to me weren't supernatural. It would make life so much simpler."

She climbed out of the car and I followed her to the front door. She pulled keys out of her pocket and unlocked the door. We stepped into the stale interior. The air held a disturbing mustiness and the unmistakable odor of decay. I reached for the light switch but Cornelius stopped my hand. She shook her head and took out a flashlight from her back pocket.

In the meager light of her flashlight, we surveyed the living room. It was a mess. There were TV-dinner trays scattered around the room. The smell of beer and rotting food became stronger as we went into the small kitchen. Flies buzzed over a moldy hunk of luncheon meat on the counter. I reached for the back door and opened it. Cornelius didn't stop me; she wanted fresh air too. With the front door ajar and the back door now open, fresh air poured in from outside and began to wash away the foul odors.

The house had two bedrooms. One was a makeshift storage room full of dirty clothes and stacks of magazines. Most of them were dedicated to pornography. Destillo's bedroom was a mess; sheets lay halfway off the bed and dirty towels were tossed onto the dresser. Cornelius touched the towels. They were dry.

"So just what is this chest that you claim Destillo took from your house?" Her eyes were dark pits in the shadows.

"I don't know. But it was important enough for him to risk his life by moving through other dimensions."

"Other dimension? Okay, just stop! You're giving me a headache. Let's just find the chest. Do you see it anywhere?" Cornelius asked, flashing her light around the room.

"It could be hidden anywhere in this junk." I drew a deep breath. "I'm looking for Theo. I couldn't care less about the chest."

She paused and her flashlight backlit her silhouette. Her red hair gleamed in the halo of light and she turned to face me, her face dark planes of shadow. "What is it with you? You give me the creeps."

"I give you the creeps?"

"Those eyes of yours. What's up with them?"

"They're turquoise. I can't help it."

"For all I know, you might be a serial killer. All this talk of demons. Let's get something straight. I'm here because of your claims of kidnapping and something weird happening to a dead FBI agent. Since this alleged chest is at the center of your claims, finding it might lead us to your friend."

Suddenly, I got that strange, oppressive feeling that I was in the presence of evil. I looked around at the chaos of Destillo's life and motioned to the kitchen. "I need some fresh air."

Cornelius led us back through the kitchen and out to the backyard. A one-car garage sat at the end of the driveway, separate from the house. I took in the hot, humid night air and tried to get the smell of rotting meat out of my lungs. "Cornelius, you said Destillo's personality had changed."

She nodded. "What we just saw in there doesn't fit the personality of a man who was assigned to catalogue Ketrick's things because of his meticulous, compulsive nature. His cataloging became disorganized, even chaotic. Some days, he would show up extremely late. He didn't come in at all yesterday."

Deep in thought, Cornelius studied Destillo's yard. "And then there was that spat he had with his girlfriend. She was trouble, I can tell you. She made fun of my clothes." Cornelius crossed her arms over her chest. "But I refuse to think that it was due to anything, uh, supernatural."

A rusty grill stood at one side of the small patio. The rest of the yard was empty, without even a single tree. The grass had not been cut in weeks. "Something in Destillo's life opened a door to the influence of the, uh, supernatural. Maybe he was fascinated with the occult."

Cornelius shook her head. "I don't buy it. I didn't see pentagrams or black candles in there. I saw a pathetic, lonely man who went off the deep end."

"Maybe," I said. I studied the garage. "What's in there?"

"Let's see." Cornelius led the way. "We found his car at the warehouse, so the garage should be empty."

The sliding door of the small garage was locked, but there was a side door. Cornelius tried to shine her flashlight through the door's small windows but they were painted over with black. A padlock secured the door. She leaned back and kicked the door hard. Wood splintered and the door flew open. The smell of death and decay rolled out of the garage like smoke. I gagged. Cornelius covered her mouth.

"You might want to call in some backup," I said with my hand over my mouth. "I don't think that's roast beef."

Cornelius glared at me and stepped into the garage. In the center of the room, a wooden platform had been constructed out of plywood. It had been painted black, and arcane symbols were scrawled around the bottom. On top of the platform was a body. There was dried, caked blood that had run from the body and over the symbols. Cornelius moved closer and ran her flashlight over it. It was a woman. Her chest and abdomen had been ripped open. Her face was covered with a black cloth.

My heart raced and the hair on my neck stood up. I sensed the unspeakable evil in the room just like what I had sensed in Destillo's house. On each corner of the platform, black candles had melted into puddles of wax. "There are your black candles."

Cornelius pointed the flashlight around the room. "Do you see the chest anywhere?"

I covered my mouth and fought down nausea. "Who cares about the chest?" I stared at the dead woman.

Cornelius glanced over her shoulder at me and her eyes caught the light. For a moment I saw that she was terrified and not hiding it very well. She swallowed several times and moved the flashlight beam up to the ceiling. A red circle had been painted there on the sheetrock. The numbers one through twelve had been written in blood around the circle. At four equidistant points, north, east, south, and west were marked. I gasped and regretted it.

"That was on the chest," I said, pointed at the ceiling. "A circle with numbers. A number for each demon. Cephas calls it the demon wheel."

Cornelius slowly lowered her gaze. "The demon wheel? It looks more like a compass." She played the beam toward the far wall. It was a huge portrait of a woman's face. A second later I realized the portrait was entirely made up of photographs. The same face looked back from each. Blood had been smeared in a circle around the portrait.

"Know her?" Cornelius said.

Bile rose in my throat. "Vivian Ketrick."

"That's the woman who broke up with Destillo a few days ago." Cornelius took out a pen from her pants pocket and used it to lift the black cloth from the dead woman's face. She had black hair and Asian features and her eyes were filmed white. It wasn't Vivian. "I don't get it. Looks like he was obsessed with Vivian Ketrick. But this isn't her body. I'm pretty sure this an intern who worked with Destillo. College student."

I shook my head. "He didn't want to kill Vivian. This is not a murder. It's a sacrifice. It's an act of worship."

Cornelius glanced at me. "Worship?"

I needed to take pictures of the room. Cephas would have to see this. "Destillo worshipped Vivian and her demons."

Chapter 19

Theophilus Nosmo King

I WAS HUNGRY. REAL hungry. I was thirsty. I had enough fat to live off of for a long while. But lack of water would kill me. I stood up again and paced the room avoiding the pile of bones. Nothing had changed. The mysterious man had not reappeared. There had been no offer of room service. I had examined the door and realized that if I could pop off the hinges, I might be able get out. The chair had plastic and metal on it. But the table could be most useful. It would mean touching the coagulated blood.

The door handle rattled, the lock clicked, and the door opened. The man from before stood there, lit from behind. He liked that silhouetting thing. It worked for him. He placed a tray of food on the floor. "Just in case the chest isn't there. If it isn't, we'll be interrogating you tomorrow." Before I could answer, he slammed the door.

I picked up the tray. A peanut butter sandwich and a bag of chips lay on it. The sandwich was prepackaged, probably bought out of a machine. A bottle of water lay on its side. I guess I had gotten used to the smell of the pile of bones. If you're hungry enough you can eat under any circumstance. *What the heck?* I figured. If they had wanted me dead, I'd already be dead. And given my experience with mind-altering drugs, I knew that if they drugged me I would probably just get sleepy. The first rule of captivity was to survive. I wolfed down the sandwich and chips and drained the bottle of water. I waited. Nothing happened.

So this wasn't the guy who had teleported me from the house. And this guy was looking for the chest too. If he was going after it tomorrow, then Jonathan, Cephas, and Josh were in trouble, and I could do nothing but wait. But what if they came back for me in the morning? I had a plan, but I had to be ready. Rested. I said a silent prayer for strength and wisdom, and then I stretched out on the floor in front of the door so that if it opened, it would wake me.

I woke up in the middle of the night, confused and sweating. My head hurt and the room swam around me. I sat up slowly. The meager light from under the door stretched across the room.

"You done a bad thing, King." The bones had come together into a complete skeleton. The blood stained skull wiggled as it laughed at me. The dried blood swirled up off the floor into a cyclone around the bones and filled in the gaps with flesh. Soon, a man was standing there in the room. He was in his underwear and his skin was bruised and covered with cigarette burns. His legs and arms were purple and green from the beatings I had given him. I swallowed, closed my eyes and reopened them. He was still there.

"You can't be real."

"Of course I can. I was real enough when you killed me. I'm just borrowing these bones so I can taunt you. How do you like that word? Taunt!"

"You deserved what you got," I said.

"You were a man of the law. Who made you judge, jury, and executioner?" He walked toward me. Pus ran from his sores and dripped onto the ground. The air was full of the odor of decay. "You thought you could hide from it all by becoming a man of God, didn't you?" His mouth leaked black blood. I backed into a corner and shook my head.

"You're not real. You one of those demons. Get out of here."

"I'm not a real demon, King." He leaned over and a couple of his rotting teeth fell into my lap. "I'm the demon you hide from the world. But you can't hide me from God." He started to laugh. His fetid breath made me gag. I fell into darkness. I woke propped up in the corner. Had it all been a dream? I glanced down at the pile of bones before me. They had moved across the room!

"Good Lord, forgive me!" I sobbed. "Forgive me!"

Vivian Darbonne Ketrick

Alba called me the next morning. There had been a delay and the court order would not be ready until the next day. She said I could come by and get it before lunch tomorrow. Which meant she was too busy getting ready for the governor's visit to take care of my problems.

I called the deputy and told him the news. He volunteered to take me out that night and then make sure I made it safely out to Ketrick's house the next day. I hesitated, but something inside me longed for the feelings he had brought out in me the night before. I told him to pick me up at seven.

He showed up on time in a big pickup truck. He was dressed in jeans, a multicolored western shirt, and a huge cowboy hat. I hadn't been quite prepared for that. I slipped back upstairs and changed into my black jumpsuit. It was as country western as I could manage. He took me to a steakhouse in one of the casinos. I had to admit, it was the best beef I had ever eaten. Then he took me to some country western club where we danced the night away.

Afterward, he walked me to my hotel room. I wanted to ask him inside, but instead, I gently pushed him away and went inside before he could protest. I leaned against the closed door, feeling his presence on the other side. I turned and looked through the peephole. He was standing there with an amazed look on his face. He slapped his hand against his jeans and stalked away.

Later, I woke up and reached for the other side of my bed. There was no one was there. What had I done? I wanted his company. I wanted to feel his warmth against mine. And suddenly, the door hurled open on a hot gust. The deputy stood there, silhouetted against the hallway.

I pulled the sheet around me. "How did you …?"

His head swiveled in my direction and his eyes burned like two fiery coals. I slid away from him and fell off the bed onto the floor. My heart raced and I scurried toward the window. He walked across the bed and hopped down into a crouch before me. He pushed his cowboy hat back off his forehead and frowned.

"Vivian, why didn't you ask me in?" he rasped. Those burning red eyes gleamed with anger.

"Who are you?" I clasped my arms around my bare chest.

"I am your Master, Vivian. I am here to make sure of your loyalty. You're slipping. You're being enticed by the promise of a normal life." He stood up and his body was shrouded in shadow; only his gleaming eyes were visible. "Do I claim your soul now, or will you continue to serve me?"

I felt hot tears stream down my cheeks. "I just want to be—"

"What?" He prodded my bare leg with his boot. "Loved? Vivian, Vivian, Vivian. You should know by now that hate is much more powerful than love. Love is overrated. They all leave you in the end. Don't they, Lucas?"

Lucas emerged from the shadows of the room, his pale chest alive with his many tattoos. He smiled. "So sorry, Vivian. I had to tell the master you were slipping."

"Lucas! Where have you been?" Lucas had been indispensable in defeating the thirteenth demon, but he had been absent during my ordeal with Wulf. "Why didn't you help me with Wulf?"

"You didn't need help then. Now you do. You're weakening, Vivian. You don't see the obvious when it is right in front of you. Find the chest. The Master needs it."

I turned back and the deputy's face was only inches from mine. I could feel the heat from his eyes. "Find the Ark, Vivian. Nothing else matters. Including your loathsome self-pity. And your Jonathan Steel surrogate. Understand? And to make sure you realize this is more than just a dream, I am taking away some of your powers. No more moving through space. Ever." He opened his mouth and a thin, forked tongue appeared. It writhed through the air and caressed my cheek. My demons convulsed inside of me and a cold, freezing pain stabbed through my heart.

I gasped and sat bolt upright in bed. I looked around the room. No Lucas. No deputy. The room was empty and cold. I slid out from under the covers and backed across the room. Had it been a dream? Or had the prince of darkness paid me a visit along with his right-hand man, Lucas? Either way, the message was clear. I pulled on my clothes and stood at the window looking down on the riverfront. My ability to teleport was very limited. My demons were nothing compared to Wulf's. But I could move hundreds of yards through space if I wanted to. I imagined myself standing on the bank of the river and reached for my demons' power—it wasn't there! It had been more than just a dream.

I contemplated finding the deputy and ripping his heart out. But I still needed him and didn't want a mess to clean up. Instead, I went downstairs and walked to the riverfront. The casinos were still hopping, but I wanted to saunter along the riverfront and try to clear my thoughts.

I moved along the glass-and-concrete railing overlooking the river. Below, the waters of the Red River were a murky red illuminated by the lights along the riverfront. I found a bench, sat down, and thought very hard about what had happened in the last twenty-four hours.

The deputy had made me happy. And I had not been happy in a very long time. He offered the promise of things like stability and being ordinary. But Lucas and my Master had just reminded me that I was not destined for those things. My demons squirmed inside of me. They did not like what was happening to me, either. But I did. I kept seeing Jonathan Steel in my mind. His turquoise eyes. His lean face. His—stop! I buried my face in my hands.

I heard them coming before they jumped me. I looked up into the faces of three guys dressed in football jerseys and low-riding jeans with their caps worn sideways. They were a multiracial group. The lead guy held a silver pistol in a loose grip.

"All right, sweet thang, you not gonna scream, or we cap you."

I smiled and laughed in the man's face. "Or you'll cap me? You idiot! You have no idea who I am."

"I don't care if you the first lady. We gonna have some fun. We gonna dance."

So this was what being ordinary would gain me: a cool walk in the evening right into the hands of hoodlums. How trite. How could I have ever wanted this? I shrugged and stood up.

"You want to play with me?"

The lead guy nodded. "You got no idea."

"You want to meet my friends?"

"Bring 'em on."

"Is that an invitation?" I asked. I opened my mouth and let three of the demons out. They boiled out of me and the three guys stepped back as the three demons swirled around their faces in smoky clouds. The lead guy tried to run, but the shark demon got him and flowed inside him. They *had* invited them in. The other two didn't make it three feet.

Then they turned and looked at each other. The lead guy aimed his gun. The second one pulled out a knife and slashed at the third. They fought, screaming at first, until they became a quiet, bloody pile on the ground. My heart pounded with the smell of blood. This was what I was meant for. This was who I was. I stood up and sighed. "So much for affection. Time to get back to business."

The three demons flowed out of their hosts and back into me. I turned to head back to the hotel when I noticed a black SUV parked in the shadows. It had been in a position to see everything that had just happened. I started toward it but the engine suddenly came to life. It pulled away and hurried down the parkway along the river. For a second, I saw the flash of light on mirrored sunglasses. Who would wear sunglasses at night?

Chapter 20

Cephas Lawrence

"I AM NOT AS fragile as you presume, Jonathan." I stood at the door to the garage. Jonathan had returned to the hotel room during the night but had not told me of the grisly findings in the garage until I awoke this morning. He had pictures on his cell phone, but I wanted to see the real thing. He had advised me not to eat breakfast and said that FBI Special Agent Ross wanted me to study the sacrifice.

Jonathan looked tired. It was not quite seven in the morning. I dare say he had not slept more than four hours. "Cephas, you said you were involved in some kind of exorcism in the past. That tells me you've have had experience with rituals gone bad."

I waved my hand at him and sighed. "Jonathan, you have no idea what I have seen. I think I can handle this."

He looked up as the beautiful FBI agent, Cornelius, came around the corner of the house. She did not look as radiant as she had the evening before. Her eyes were rimmed in dark circles. Ross was right behind her, wearing his long black overcoat even in the August heat.

"Dr. Lawrence, I see you made it," Cornelius said.

Ross lit up a cigarette and blew smoke at Jonathan as he leaned against the garage wall. "Sorry to get you involved in this, old man. But Jonathan said you had some knowledge of these kinds of rituals. And I need to wrap this up quickly. I'm up for a transfer."

"I thought you quit smoking," Jonathan said.

Ross sucked on his cigarette. "I thought you quit nagging."

They sounded like two old hags. "I would like to go in alone," I said. "Has the body been removed yet?"

"No." Cornelius glanced at Ross. "I objected, but Agent Ross insisted the room be left untouched until you got here. We haven't even let the crime lab in."

"And that is a shame."

Lieutenant Sue Kane walked down the driveway followed by two uniformed Dallas police officers. She had an acid look on her face. Her short hair swayed in the breeze and she was wearing dark slacks and a dark blouse, but the fire in her eyes lit her face up like a Christmas tree. She went straight for Ross. "So were you going to inform me that a homicide had taken place in my own city?"

Ross blew smoke right into her face. The man had no sense of propriety. "I called your office but no one answered."

"You called at three in the morning," she growled. Kane looked at me and Jonathan. "Don't tell me you two are involved."

Jonathan shrugged. "We didn't ask for this. Theo was kidnapped by Destillo. Agent Cornelius asked me to come with her last night to check out his house. We found that." He pointed toward the closed door to the garage.

Kane squeezed the bridge of her nose and closed her eyes. "I cannot believe this is happening." She removed her fingers and scowled. "You're still here."

I rubbed my hands together. "I assure you, Lieutenant Kane, that we are very real. And as soon as you allow me to view the crime scene, you can get your crime people—"

"*Our* crime lab," Ross said.

"I don't think so!" Kane erupted. "This is city property. You have no jurisdiction."

"Destillo was an FBI agent, Sue." Ross tossed the cigarette butt away. He glanced at us. "Now you know why I started smoking again."

"That had nothing to do with your job, Franklin. It had everything to do with your intimacy issues," Kane said.

Jonathan's face twitched and I saw that ghost of a smile. "Intimacy issues?"

Ross pointed a finger at me. "Get on with it." He pointed the finger at Jonathan. "Back off!" Then, he turned to Kane and grabbed her elbow. "And we need to talk." He led her toward the driveway.

"Agent Cornelius, do you have a flashlight?"

She took one from her belt and handed it to me. I turned it on, took a deep breath, and walked into a nightmare. The odor hit me hard and I was grateful not to have eaten breakfast. I knew the body was in the middle of the room, but I chose to examine it last. I played the flashlight beam across the walls.

Each wall had been painted black and strange symbols had been scrawled in red and white paint on them. At least, I hoped it was red paint. It could have been blood. Ah, there was the demon wheel Jonathan had mentioned. It was disturbingly similar to the document in my secretary, as well as to the image on the chest. The addition of the compass points was a new element.

The back wall was especially interesting. A collage of photos of Vivian covered most of the wall and formed a large image of her face in a photomosaic. Putting such a thing together would have taken a great deal of effort. I leaned closer to the image and pulled out my reading glasses to study the photographs. They were candid pictures of Vivian in various conditions. She had been spied upon. These pictures had been taken without her knowledge.

Around Vivian's face, a red circle had been painted, along with a tiny dot in the center right over her nose. Atop the circle was a smaller circle, and atop that one was a small cross. I recalled this symbol from the Demon Wheel. It was the symbol for chaos.

On a shelf at the base of the picture, black candles had burned all the way down and had puddled around some objects. They were mundane things like a hairbrush, an earring, and a wristwatch. They most likely had belonged to Vivian.

I turned slowly to the altar table in the middle of the room. It had been used for sacrifice, of that, I was certain. The symbols etched around the base of the platform left no doubt. As my eyes came to rest on the eviscerated body I suddenly grew dizzy. Sweat broke out on my forehead and I stumbled. My vision swam. The body changed and became someone else.

"Mary?" I gasped as the old sorrow engulfed me. Her mouth moved. What was she saying?

"Cephas?" a man said. "Cephas, are you all right?"

I shook my head and Jonathan crouched beside me. His hands supported me under my armpits. "What happened?"

"You cried out. I came in and you were about to pass out."

I examined the dead woman's face. She was not Mary. Then I noticed something odd about her eyes. I leaned closer. The eyeballs were shrunken.

"Is Ross still out there?"

Jonathan nodded and stuck his head out the door to call for Ross, who came in after a moment.

"What?"

I pointed at the woman's eyes. "What do you make of this?"

Ross looked at her face. "Make of what?"

"Her eyes. They have lost their fluid." I leaned closer and blinked. "And there, at the corner of each eye—see it? A tiny puncture mark."

Ross leaned over me. Over the stench of death I could smell the cigarettes on his breath. "I think you're right. Are you saying someone extracted the fluid from her eyes?"

Something tickled at the back of my mind. Where had I read of such a thing? "Why would someone do this?"

Jonathan pointed to the door. "Let's think outside."

I followed him outside into fresh air. Ross nodded at the crime lab personnel. "You can take her now."

"You look very pale, Cephas. What happened?" Jonathan asked.

"Bad memories," I said. Visions of Mary pushed the thoughts from my mind. I tried to recall where I had read about fluid being removed from eyeballs.

"Sometimes they take the fluid for tests." Ross exhaled smoke from his newly lit cigarette. "But they do that in the autopsy suite."

"Agent Ross, I think perhaps they should." I looked at Jonathan. "I really need to sit down. Perhaps in the car."

Jonathan took me by the arm and led me down the driveway. Already there were almost a dozen vehicles from the Dallas police force and the FBI parked along the road. I settled into the front seat of our car. Jonathan started the engine and cold air from the vents blew into my face.

"What happened in there, Cephas?" Steel asked.

I blinked and rubbed my moustache. "I was back in the past."

"Are you ready to tell me more?"

I looked into his intense turquoise eyes. "Some of it, yes."

Molly sipped her coffee and studied the cold wind whipping through the trees outside the café. I ate the last bite of my omelet and sopped up the butter with the last bit of my toast.

"You're unusually quiet this morning," I said.

Molly smiled, making my heart skip a beat. "Oh, Cephas, you have been so good to us these past weeks. Mary no longer sees her demons. And ..."

I reached out and took her small hand in mine. She sighed as I lifted it to my lips. "I would do anything for you, Molly. And for Mary. I think the hypnosis has worked well. In time, her demons will completely disappear. I believe she is still working through the loss of her father."

Molly slowly pulled her hand away from mine and rubbed it with her other hand. "As am I."

I winced inwardly. Why had I mentioned her dead husband? Bad form!

"Thanksgiving will be here soon." She peered out the windows and smiled. "The president is coming to town and Mary's class is hoping to sing for him. I just want her to be normal and to have a chance to create wonderful memories. Everything is getting better, Cephas, and I have you to thank for it."

The words poured from my lips before I could stop them. "Molly, I love you."

She blinked and sat up straighter. "Cephas, I'm flattered. But until Mary is stable, I can't allow myself to become emotionally tied to anyone. She needs my undivided attention."

I mentally kicked myself. I tried to remain calm and patted her hand. "I am willing to wait. I can be patient."

The door to the café banged open and Father Caskey swooped in on a gust of cold air. He wore a dark-brown overcoat and his face was pale. His gaze traveled over the room until it came to rest on Molly. He shoved his way through the crowded aisle and stopped in front of the table.

"Molly, I have to talk to you. Now!" He glared at me. "Without this bloody atheist around. It's about Mary."

I stood up, my face growing hot with anger. "James, I have everything under control."

James fixed his wide eyes on me. His breath stank of wine. "You have hypnotized that poor girl into a listless, uncaring state. You have made her a prime target for those demons. They will take control of her and then she will be worse off than before. All so you can make a move on Molly!"

So he had feelings for Molly too. My lips quivered and I poked him in the chest. "I have approached this whole affair with scientific objectivity. There is nothing wrong with Mary that hypnotism and psychotherapy won't cure."

"Stop it! Both of you." Molly slid out of the booth and came between us.

I saw the way she looked at James. My heart sank. "You've been going to see James? Molly, tell me you haven't. He's a priest."

Molly's eyes lingered on James and then she looked at me. "I have been talking to James about Mary. I didn't see any harm in covering all the bases."

James, she had said. Not Father Caskey.

"And I am convinced that soon, very soon, unless I act, the lass will be possessed by demons!" he shouted at me.

I glanced around at the café patrons. They had stopped to stare at us. How many of them believed in God and Jesus and demons? How many of them were scientifically objective, like me? Or were they just frightened of the unknown, desperately seeking the truth of what lay outside the human brain's capacity to understand. I sighed and nodded.

"Very well, Molly. You have chosen. I will not abandon Mary. I will return and continue the hypnotism only if you desire. I will see to it she sings for the president. If you desire. You have my phone number."

It was the hardest thing I had ever done. I glared once more at my old friend and then turned my back on the woman I loved. She would have to choose.

Chapter 21

Jonathan Steel

"VIVIAN AGAIN! EVERYWHERE we turn, it's Vivian. 'Looky what the cat dragged in!' I'll drag her."

"Jonathan! This is a sixty-five-mile zone."

I swerved around another slow driver. "I'm only doing eighty!"

Cephas's hands were braced against the dashboard. "Let's not land you in jail again, shall we? Slow down. Please!"

I let off the accelerator and tried to calm my racing heart. We had left the awful garage in the capable hands of the crime scene investigators. Cephas had fallen silent after his tale of woe. Now we were headed for Vivian's office. "Destillo sacrificed that woman to Vivian. To Vivian!"

"Perhaps she had nothing to do with it."

"She had everything to do with it! Whether or not she told him to do it, she led him along looking for this Ark. She is to blame. And when I get my hands on her—" I slammed on the accelerator again.

Cephas reached over and grabbed my arm. "Jonathan, slow down! Now! Destillo sacrificed that young woman as a tribute to Vivian. I believe he reveres Vivian. But she may not be the one behind his actions. There was a symbol above the picture of Vivian. It was the symbol for chaos. If you recall, that symbol corresponded to a number on the demon wheel."

"What?"

"The eleventh demon. Jonathan, there is more to this than a horrible killing by a deranged man. When the thirteenth demon was defeated, it didn't take long for number twelve to show up to claim number thirteen's territory. Wulf is gone, so it makes sense that number eleven would move into his old territory."

I pulled off the interstate and headed into downtown Dallas. "Are you sure it was the chaos symbol?"

"Yes."

The prospect of the eleventh demon being behind all of this made my mouth go dry. It was happening again.

Ross and Cornelius had preceded us to Ketrick's office building to talk to Vivian. I pulled in behind their car and drew a deep breath. "I'm sorry, Cephas. It's just that Vivian shows up every time evil rears its ugly head. I'm tired of it. She may not be directly responsible for that murder, but she still has something to do with it. And I intend to find out what. She ended up helping the last two demons. That means she is connected with number eleven in some way."

I got out and slammed the door. Ross and Cornelius were waiting on the sidewalk. I ignored them and headed straight into the building. A security guard met us in the lobby. Ross flashed his ID. As we rode the elevator to the penthouse floor, I tried to get my anger under control. When the door opened, the man I saw in reception was the last person on earth I had expected to see. He was arguing with someone else.

"Bile?"

Bile glanced up from his desk. His long, stringy white hair had been trimmed and he wore a three-piece suit. "Mr. Steel?"

"The last time I saw you, a spear was sticking out of your belly."

Bile had been Rudolph Wulf's last convert. "I made a miraculous recovery. And please call me by my proper name, Jerome."

"Well you won't recover from my personnel review if you don't find Mrs. Ketrick for me," the other man said. He was a compact man with thinning black hair and rimless glasses. He was clutching a tablet in his hands, clinging onto it like a drowning man hanging onto a life preserver. "I need to speak with her this instant."

Bile smiled. He still had his fangs. Bile had been a renowned "fangmaster" for vampire clans. He had fashioned me a pair for our infiltration into the Bloodfest in my search for Josh. Wulf had made Bile's fake fangs permanent. "Mark, you can't talk to her right now. What more can I say?"

Mark put a thumb up to his mouth and bit the nail. "If she presses on with this ridiculous legal maneuver, she could open up this corporation to a lawsuit. I don't know why she consulted Alba, Bartley, and Cummings in the first place when she has her own legal department. That house in Shreveport was sold long before she,"—and here he spat the word as if a gnat had flown into his mouth—"*married* Mr. Ketrick."

I interrupted him. "What house in Shreveport?"

Mark glared at me. "And who are you? What business is it of yours?"

"I probably live in that house now."

Mark reddened. "Oh, my! Look, she didn't know that Mister Ketrick had already sold the house. You must understand."

"When did he sell it, then?"

"Six months ago. To,"—he glanced down at his tablet computer—"Sadie Thompson, a local realtor. He leased it from her until he could build his new home on that plot of land along Redcross Bayou."

"So Cephas Lawrence bought the house from Sadie, not from Ketrick?"

"Technically, that is correct. Do you see the problem? Mrs. Ketrick has no claim to any property left in that house. She can't demand to remove anything. When she signed her rental agreement for the garage apartment, she agreed that if she left the property, any remaining items not removed would revert to the owner, once Robert Ketrick, now Ms. Thompson. I tried to tell Vivian's attorney that, but Ms. Alba is very stubborn."

"But didn't she marry Ketrick?"

"So she claims! But the date on the papers is long after the house was sold right out from under her!"

"Mark, you should be careful how you talk about your boss," Bile said.

"Oh, and you would run right in there and tell her, wouldn't you?"

"Could the two of you have this cat fight later?" Ross said, interrupting. "We need to see Vivian now. It may be a matter of life and death."

Mark's mouth opened and closed like a fish out of water's. "I was here first. If she tries to serve these court papers to go into that house and retrieve her property, the owner could sue." His face grew pale and he glared at me. "You wouldn't do that, would you?"

"Not if I can talk to her first."

"Well, all of you can just go have a nice, long breakfast. Mrs. Ketrick isn't in town." Bile said.

"I knew it!" Mark bit his thumb again. "She's in Shreveport, isn't she?"

"She was at Ketrick's house," I said.

Mark's eyes widened. "What?"

"She took an axe to our basement walls."

I thought Mark was going to collapse. "She didn't!"

"She did."

"I have to get to legal. The minute she gets back, I have to see her, Jerome." Mark hurried off and disappeared into the elevator.

"Jerome? I like Bile better. Suits you," I said.

"Wouldn't do for one of the wealthiest and most powerful women in the country to have an executive assistant named Bile. What can I do for you?"

"We're here to see Vivian," Cornelius said. "We have two dead bodies. One of our agents and his intern. We think the agent killed the intern and Vivian Ketrick is a person of interest."

"As I said, she isn't in this morning," Bile said.

"Listen, Bile," I said. He glared at me. "*Jerome*, there was a murder and it involves Vivian. And your little shark-bait of a lawyer probably should have stayed. Mrs. Ketrick may need his services."

Bile sighed and tapped away at the keyboard in front of him. He turned the computer monitor around to face us. "Be my guest. Check out her calendar. Here's her flight itinerary. She flew to Shreveport on Monday in the corporate jet. She's staying at the Remington downtown. She had two meetings Monday afternoon in the Lakeside office. Tuesday, she met with her local attorney, Ms. Lynn Alba. Yesterday, she met again with Ms. Alba and then had a meeting with the real estate agent to close the sale of Ketrick's log cabin on Redcross Bayou. I can get you names and numbers, Agent Ross. As you can see, she hasn't been in town. I hardly think she's had time to drive back to Dallas, commit a murder, and then get back to Shreveport in time for these appointments."

I studied the calendar. "Ketrick had a log cabin?"

Bile glared at me. "I shouldn't tell you, but to assuage your suspicions about the Ketrick house, I will. Robert Ketrick owned a one-hundred-acre strip of land north of Lakeside. It was a hunting lease before he bought it. There's an old log cabin on the property, but most of the land is undeveloped. Mrs. Ketrick sold it to a local state senator. I believe Ms. Alba is arranging the governor's picnic as a guest of the senator on the property."

"That's true," Cornelius said. "I'm driving over tonight to oversee security there."

"Mr. Steel thinks Vivian may have had something to do with the murder of a woman. But according to Cephas, the murder was a ritualistic sacrifice. It is possible her life may be in danger," Ross said.

"Agent Ross," Bile said, showed his fangs as he smiled, "no one practices human sacrifice anymore. I can call and leave a message for her, if you'd like."

"Why can't you get her on the phone for me?" I said.

"She has a spa appointment this morning. It lasts four hours and she cannot be interrupted." The man was lying now.

"What was Mark talking about?" Ross leaned over the desk.

Bile shrugged. "Mrs. Ketrick obtained a court order to let her onto Ketrick's property. She's going out there with a deputy sheriff."

"What? The only person there is Josh."

Bile lifted an eye and laughed. "The kid? Don't worry, Vivian won't hurt him."

"You need to call her now. Tell her not to go to the house. Tell her what Mark said."

Bile patted the desktop. "I'll call and leave a message. Good enough?" He looked at his watch. "In fact, I'll have Mark call her. That should just about seal his fate."

I whirled around and marched toward the elevator. Ross and Cornelius followed. "Where are you going?" Ross said.

The door closed behind us. "Back to Shreveport. I don't trust Bile. And I sure don't trust Vivian."

They followed me out of the building. "Steel, let us handle this," Ross said.

"I will. But, I'm not letting Vivian anywhere near Josh." I slid in behind the steering wheel of my SUV. "Cephas, call Josh. Now."

I slammed the door closed and rolled down the window. "Ross, do what you can to find Theo. I left Josh alone once to go after Theo and I'm not doing it again."

Cephas pressed a button on his phone. "I got the answering machine. I told him to call us on your cell. What is going on, Jonathan?"

I started the car and threw it into gear. "We have to get home. Now. Josh is in danger."

Chapter 22

Josh Knight

"ARE YOU SURE you'll be all right?"

I pushed Mama Liz toward the kitchen door. "I'll be fine. Jonathan and Cephas are coming back this afternoon."

"What are you going to do for the rest of the day?" Liz paused outside the door with her overnight bag in her hand.

"I have lots of video games to play," I said. "Unless you want me to come and help out your assistant. What was her name?"

"Very funny, young man." Liz grinned. "I don't need Ashley distracted this week. We're trying to get an entire crate of artifacts catalogued before the summer is up. And speaking of artifacts, have you seen my lion stick?"

"That's right, you left it with Jonathan when we were in Lakeside. I think it's in the RV."

"I'll come back later to get it." She smiled at me.

"Send Ashley to pick it up." I raised an eyebrow and she laughed as she walked away. Then I realized that Ashley was in the car, of course. I waved at her and walked right into the edge of the door. What a dork! I retreated from their view and waited until the car pulled out of the driveway to let loose with a few choice words. It was still early and I hadn't showered yet. But what was the hurry? I had no place to be and nothing to do but wait. I could at least go get the lion stick for Mama Liz. Yeah, then I could call Ashley and get her to come back and pick it up. We'd surprise Mama Liz. And Ashley could bring her swimsuit and then we could take out the jet skis!

The lion stick was Mama Liz's prized possession, a wooden walking stick with the head of a lion carved at the top. She had gotten it from some African chieftain and she used the thing to prod rocks while looking for snakes. Yeah, she liked snakes! That made her even cooler in my book.

I hurried out to the RV and jerked open the door. The inside was as hot as an oven. Jonathan had turned the RV into a rolling command center,

130

but after the wreck in Lakeside, much of the equipment had been broken. I glanced at the driver's seat. My mother had driven the RV through the wall of the jail to free Jonathan. I reached over, touched the back of the seat, and swiveled it around. She wasn't there. Suddenly, I couldn't breathe.

I bolted out of the RV and slammed the door. What was I doing here? Why wasn't I back in Dallas with my old friends and Ila and my band? I shook my head to chase away the engulfing sorrow. I had a new life. It was strange and weird living with Uncle Cephas, but I had to put the past behind me. I had to find something to divert my attention. Forget Ashley for now. Forget the lion stick. I went to the games room.

I played Centipede.

I played World of Warcraft.

I burned forty-two matches.

I ate some cold pizza from two days ago. I spit out the pizza from two days ago and shoved it down the garbage disposal. I put the forty-two matches down the garbage disposal, too.

Okay, so I was bored. Very bored. Hanging out alone is not what it's cracked up to be. I looked out the windows of the games room. We had a pool! I'd forgotten we had a pool!

I changed into my swimsuit and ran down to the pool, tripping over one of the overturned tables and skidding across the deck. Deck burn! Man, it hurt. It was probably best to clean out the scrapes. Like, with chlorine.

I jumped into the pool. The pool guy must have just checked the chemicals; they were really strong. My scrapes hurt like heck! But I was Josh Knight. I had survived demon possession and an army of vampires! I would not let some road rash stop me. I swam for a while. I did cannonballs. I jumped off the diving board. I dreamed of Ashley floating on an air raft. I floated.

Eventually, I got hungry, so I went inside. I realized I didn't have a beach towel with me. There were some towels upstairs. I ran up and dried off, then I went back to dry off the stairs. I slipped in the water on the kitchen floor and landed on my butt. I think I preferred boredom.

I made a sandwich with the barbecue left from the day before. I waited for Jonathan to call. And waited! I burned forty-three matches, one by one. I logged on to check my Facebook page: messages from familiar faces I had left behind. They stared up at me and I felt nothing for them. No messages from Ila. The judge had forbidden her to contact me, or else she would end up in juvie hall for her involvement with the vampire clan. I closed my MacBook Air and glanced at the clock on the wall.

It was almost three o'clock. My, my, where had the day gone? I stood at the French doors off the hearth room and looked at the boat dock. I could take the boat out for a run. If Ashley were here. Ah, if Ashley were here, I would—

The doorbell rang. Could it be Ashley? I ran to the door and skidded to a halt when I saw Vivian standing outside.

"What do you want?" I opened the door and came out, but I blocked her way so she couldn't go in. "We threw your axe in the lake."

"I have returned with a court order—" And then something really weird happened.

First, there was a policeman with her. I hadn't seen him until he climbed out of his car, which was parked back toward the garage. He was the Caddo Parish sheriff's deputy that had taken Theo's complaint. Jerk!

Second, Vivian backed away from me. She had this look on her face like I had rolled on a dead skunk.

"What is it?"

"What have you done?" she hissed as the deputy came up behind her.

"I haven't showered yet today. But I went swimming. I guess that doesn't count? Sorry for the smell. Let's see. Do I care? No!"

Vivian backed into the deputy and turned to look at him. She was upset. She was confused. She wasn't her usual lovely, demonic self. "I can't go in."

"What should we do?" the deputy asked.

Vivian pushed away from him and backed up some more. "I can't go in! What did you do?"

It hit me. The prayer from the other night and the vision of Raphael and the other angel came to mind. Was it possible? I leaned forward, put my hands in my armpits, and made my arms look like chicken wings. I flapped my arms up and down. "What's wrong, Vivian? Angel got your tongue?"

She hissed at me. You know, like in one of those horror movies when the evil woman opens her mouth and hisses likes she's some kind of creature instead of a real human being. Which is kind of redundant when it comes to Vivian. "I can't go in there."

The deputy frowned. "You ask me to help you, but now all I get is another cold shoulder. Look, I have other business to take care of. Do you want me to wait or not?"

There was an air of tension between them. Vivian shook her head. "No, get away from me. I'm done with you. I'll work this out."

The deputy looked like he was chewing on broken glass. He stormed to his car and drove off down the driveway.

"Have a fight with your boyfriend?"

"You could invite me in."

"What?"

"Come on, Josh. Just ask me to come on in and let me go down to the basement to check out that hidden compartment." She was closer now. She reached out a finger and touched my cheek. What was she doing? Wait! She could only come in if I invited her! Got it!

"Sorry, devil chick." I slapped her hand away. "No way am I inviting you into this house. We are protected. You might recall a flock of butterflies on the mountainside? Remember?"

Vivian paused and hissed again. She backed away and turned her back to me. She seemed to be deep in thought. Then she turned back. "Truce?"

"I'm not the one demanding to come inside."

"Look, Josh, I need that chest."

"Why?"

"I can't tell you. This is my business, not yours."

"Too bad."

She paced and paused with her eyes directed out toward the bayou that ran along the side of the house. "It is the Ark of the Demon Rose, all right? Does that mean anything to you?"

"Rose? Like the flower?"

"Rose as in a compass rose. Rose as in a flower, you idiot!" She frowned. "Why do I even try?"

I was about to say something else when a black SUV pulled around the corner of the driveway and came to a halt between us. I jumped back as the doors opened. Six men in dark suits hopped out. They were regular Men in Black; they wore sunglasses and carried guns. I didn't know what kind of guns they were, but they looked like the Uzis I used in my video games. Three guys on the other side of the SUV grabbed Vivian and pulled her around the car toward me. Two guys on my side had me by the arms before I could run.

"Hey! What's going on?" I shouted.

Vivian cursed and struggled as she was dragged next to me. The three men held her tight. The driver turned to face Vivian. He held up his gun and pushed the barrel against her chest. "Where is it?"

Vivian blinked and looked over at me. For a moment she was confused. She looked back at the man. "Where is what?"

He backhanded her across the face with the end of the gun. Blood splattered from her lips and hit me in the face. "You know what we're looking for. The Ark. Where is it?"

Vivian looked at me again and I saw fear in her eyes. I started shaking. This thing had gone south in a hurry. We were in big trouble. These dudes meant business and they didn't mind slapping Vivian around. What had I fallen into? The main guy pulled off his sunglasses and turned to study me. His eyes were completely white. They were freaky snow-white orbs. "And who are you?"

"Josh Knight," I said.

"What do you know about the Ark?"

I blurted everything out. "She thinks it's in my basement, but it isn't. Someone came and took it, along with the fabric it was wrapped in and the 3-D model Uncle Cephas made. They kidnapped Theo."

Vivian studied me with renewed interest. She kicked White Eyes in the leg. "Hey, the kid is telling the truth."

He hit her again with the gun, then nodded to one of the men holding her and pointed to the house. "Reason, go check out the basement. Take the interdimensional sextant and check it out. If it's here, we'll find it." Had he just called one of them "Reason"?

The man released Vivian and took off his sunglasses. His eyes were normal. "Yes, Mind Gamaliel." "Mind"? "Gamaliel"? Were these guys from Mars? He pulled something out of his pocket. It was golden and looked like an old sextant, only it was engraved with dark symbols and had several jewels worked into the arms.

Gamaliel pointed to the lake. "Let's go find us a boat."

They led us around the corner of the house toward the boat dock. I searched the waters for a boat, any boat that might spot us, but it was the hottest part of the day, so most of the fishing boats were back in the tree line. A momentary flash of light came from the nearby trees. They shoved us along the dock and down into the ski boat. One of the guys hopped in and held the gun on us. Gamaliel pointed to the third man. "Voice, you and Reflection see if you can find some rope and an anchor."

Two of the men disappeared into the storage room. I felt nauseated. I didn't like where this was going. There was only one reason they would want an anchor and some rope. I glanced at Vivian. She was pale. She shook her head slightly. What did that mean? As if I would try something with the guy holding a gun on us!

Voice and Reflection came out of the storage room with a yellow ski rope and a heavy anchor. They stepped into the boat and placed the rope and anchor in the back. Voice aimed his gun at me. Reason, the guy with normal eyes, came back from the house, holding up the sextant. There was some kind of glow coming from the jewels. Gamaliel studied it.

"He's telling the truth. Someone has taken the Ark." He glared at Vivian. "And yet you were looking for it, too? That means you thought it was still here."

She ignored him. Gamaliel jumped into the boat. "Let's go for a ride. There's a quiet alcove back in the tree line where we won't be seen. Name and Voice, secure the woman."

I had left the keys in the ignition from two days ago. Gamaliel took the boat took out of the berth and headed along the southern shore toward the wooded fishing area. I was getting scared now, really scared. These dudes were going to ice us and feed us to the fish. Just like that! My stomach churned and suddenly, I vomited. The vomit hit Voice or Reflection or Name, whoever, in the face. Vivian grabbed his gun and started firing. I fell back as the boat lurched and I landed on the floor. One of the men fell over me. I saw that the back of his head was missing. Brains and blood ran all over me. I shoved him away. Vivian was still firing at the other men. One man caught it in the chest and fell overboard. Another grabbed at his throat as bullets ripped through his neck. He went into the lake, too.

Gamaliel spun the wheel of the boat and we lurched sideways. The other remaining man threw the rope over Vivian and cinched it tight around her, locking her arms at her side. The gun clattered across the back of the boat. I grabbed it, tried to aim, and pulled the trigger. Bullets plowed through the floor of the boat and across the engine block. I heard the gas tank hiss. Flames roared up from the rear of the boat. I guess shooting guns in real life was harder than in video games.

Vivian flipped up into the air and backwards over the man with the rope, coming to rest behind him. She leaned over his shoulder and clamped her teeth down on his throat. There was a spray of blood and the man screamed as she literally ripped out his throat like some kind of shark. He collapsed. Gamaliel raised his gun at us. Vivian kicked it out of his hands. He grabbed her and heaved over the side into the water. The yellow rope and anchor followed them.

I kicked up the seat in front of me, grabbed a life preserver, and jumped over the side after them. They were sinking quickly, so I released the life preserver and dove after them. I don't know why I did it. I didn't care a bit about Vivian.

She could die as far as I was concerned. The thing was, she had saved my life. I saw her latch her teeth onto Gamaliel's face. Blood gushed into the dark-green water. Fish appeared out of nowhere, drawn by the blood. I swam through them.

Vivian and Gamaliel fought and sank as the anchor pulled them downward. More blood came. I didn't know what to do. Vivian was head-down now, with the yellow rope and anchor wrapped around Gamaliel's neck. He was clawing at his bleeding face. The tightening rope around his neck made his white eyes bulge. Vivian struggled for air. I swam down and grabbed Vivian's ankle. I didn't have a knife. I could just let go and then they would both sink to the bottom. But I couldn't do that. I realized I was still holding the gun.

I pressed the end of the barrel against the rope on the side trapping Vivian and pointed it away from her. Would the gun fire underwater? I pulled the trigger and the staccato sound of the bullets echoed. The rope came loose and we floated toward the surface. Gamaliel sunk out of view.

A huge explosion rocked the water as the gas tank on the boat ignited. My ears felt like they had ruptured. I was stunned, unsure what was up or down. The gun slipped from my grasp and I saw the orange glow of fire on the surface. Parts of the boat started to drift down. They were pretty. They were glowing. It was so nice and warm and it was getting dark.

Something tugged me upward. My head broke the surface of the water. The fire was close by but the air tasted sweet. I gasped for breath and looked into the face of Vivian. She pushed the life preserver into my hands. A huge gash on her head leaked blood into the water.

"We're even now," she whispered. Then her eyes rolled back into her head and she sank below the water. I grabbed her by the back of the neck and pulled her back up. She had passed out. I turned her around and put my arms under hers. Using the life preserver as a float, I kicked away from the burning boat. Jonathan was not going to be happy.

A shadow passed over us. Only then did I hear the sound of a boat motor. The front end of a ski boat sliced between us and the fire. I glanced up into the bright sun, barely making out a man with a pair of binoculars hanging from his neck leaning over the side. He snared Vivian with a boat hook, leaned forward to grab her by the collar, and pulled her into the boat. I started sinking again. My arms were weak, my legs were useless, and the life preserver slipped away. I felt the man's hand grip my wrist. He pulled me up out of the water into the boat. I was fading now. The last thing I heard him say was, "I've got you, Josh."

Grimvox Interlude # 5

Chaos

AFTER MY FUTILE search for the chest, I return to the altar room, hoping the unknown human who took the chest from me will return. I suspect the human's identity, but I am not sure, so I have issued it an invitation. The room has been cleaned. All of the pictures are gone and the altar table has been disassembled. All that is left is the odor of decay and blood. Ah, sweet! Now, if only the human would accept my invitation and return. Waiting here in this fetid silence, the memories come again: a similar scene, a similar odor, a similar ending.

1ˢᵗ century
Jerusalem

I leave the crippled man to die in the human refuse along the Jerusalem dirt road. No one notices. No one grieves. No one cares. His soul now belongs to my accursed Master. I have performed my duty and now it is time to move on. Whenever I enter the mind of a human, for a short season, my memories are dampened, my pain is suppressed, the insanity is avoided. But now, the past is once again a burning reality in my mind; it floats free and flowing through the wretched masses around me.

"Chotus, where have you been?"

Chamas appears before me. I have not seen him in centuries. It is hard to believe there was a time we were as one. "I have been about the Master's business, ruining lives and cursing souls to hell. What else is there to do?"

Chamas looks good in his regal robes. His wings are full and powerful. His face is not lined with time. He has been loyal to the Master. "Chotus, I know we have had our differences, but I come to you now with an unprecedented opportunity to regain favor with the Master."

I laugh. "Why would I care about such a thing?"

"Because the Creator is now here among us."

I study his eyes. Are they filled with mirth? Or insanity? "That is not possible."

"If you had been paying attention to the world around you, Chotus, you would have seen this man, the Creator, in the flesh. He commands the Fallen as if we were chattel. In His presence, it is as if we were back in the realm of His glory!"

"Then His thirst for revenge must be great. Is His punishment not already enough that He must come here to confront us?" I walk away and Chamas follows after me.

"That is not his mission. We don't fully understand it, Chotus. But come with me now. The Master is here in Jerusalem. He has gathered his finest Fallen to him. He is offering us a mission of our own. Will you not come and give him one more chance to win your favor?"

I pause and feel Chamas's hand on my shoulder. I have missed that connection with my brother. "Very well. I will go with you."

The sound of the building creaking and expanding under the August sun awakens me from my reverie. Outside, the heat is building as the bright sun beats down on the garage. I relish the warmth and the fragrance of death and decay. I relive the delicious memories of the streets of Jerusalem. Such fun!

The door opens and the human steps in. It is deep in shadows and its face is obscured by darkness. It holds the chest in its arms.

"I got your invitation," it says. "I want to join with you. I want to complete this work."

I materialize in the form of the chimera uncoiling my snake tail. A human head and a goat's head protrude from my back and eagle's wings complete my form. I hear the human gasp in horror. Or is it wonder?

"How marvelous!" it says. "You are truly beautiful!"

I nod and my snake's head bobs along with my human head. I flick my tongue in the human's direction and hiss. "I can make you beautiful, too."

"I've tasted the evil. I want this. I want the power. I want to help you with this work. But there is a problem."

"What is this problem?" I ask through the human mouth.

"The other faction is here. What about them? They will try to stop me."

The other faction? What is it speaking of? Then I recall the hands hovering over the sacrifice's eyes, and I feel an emotion I am most unaccustomed to. He is here! We have not dealt with each other in decades. This means the Council is involved. For an instant, I feel fear. But I cannot let this human see me fearful.

"Whether or not you are associated with this other faction is immaterial," I roar through the lioness's mouth. "We will triumph. Will you let me in?"

It stares at me in wonder and nods. "Yes."

Chapter 23

Theophilus Nosmo King

I WAITED. IF EVERYTHING went as planned, I would soon be out of this room. I heard footsteps coming down the hall and I rolled up against the foot of the door. The lock clicked and the door opened. It bounced against my hips. It bounced several times. I pretended to be asleep.

"What is it, Lydia?" I mumbled.

"Get up, you tub of lard," the man said. "I have some questions for you."

I rolled away and stood up shakily. The man pushed the door open. He was soaking wet. Blood dripped from a burn on his neck. His sunglasses were askew and he was shaking. Blood trickled from teeth marks on his cheek. He had been in some fight, all right!

I swung the leg bone from behind my back and pounded the man across the head. He fell backwards and rolled away from the door. Clearly, the fight had taken the wind out of his sails.

I ran out into the hallway. It was cinderblock, just like the room. I headed to the right and in the direction the man had come from. There was a flight of metal stairs at the end of the hallway and I bolted up them bursting through the door at the top of the stairs and out into blinding sunlight. I was outside some kind of huge log cabin. Woods surrounded the place and a driveway led away from the log cabin through the woods. There was a farm house or something with a barn nearby. A limousine sat in the driveway. There should have been a tractor! A window on my side rolled down. A pistol appeared, held by a gloved hand. Couldn't go that way!

I turned and ran in the opposite direction. The woods behind the barn were thick and the underbrush was full of vines and thorns. I didn't hesitate; I barreled through them anyway. I kept the afternoon sun before me so I could be sure which direction I was heading. Right now, that was away from the cabin.

I heard some shouting and the sound of the man tearing through the woods after me. I hurried on, deeper and deeper into the trees. I heard more shouting and the crack of a gun. A bullet whistled through the brush near me.

I was getting winded and the lack of water and food was getting to me. Soon they would be right on top of me. I came up over a slight rise and halted. Before me, the ground dropped away in a steep incline to red clay along a river. The water boiled with eddies and whirlpools. I had no choice. I slid down the embankment, lost my footing, and rolled into the water. It was shockingly cold, but I didn't mind it. I lifted my head and sucked in air just as the man appeared on the shore above. I dove down into the water and let the current take me.

Bullets whizzed close by. I stroked deeper into the heart of the current, waited until my lungs were about to burst, and then surfaced to grab more air before going back down. More bullets pinged through the water, but the current was fast. It would take me far beyond the distance he could run through the dense underbrush. When I next came up for air, I had turned a bend in the bayou and the man was nowhere in sight. Now I had to stay alive in the water. As I had told Josh, I didn't swim very well.

The current was strong, tumbling me about. I tried to swim toward the shore, but I couldn't get out of the current. I knew that my waning strength would cause me to drown. I closed my eyes and sank into the water. I tried to find peace. I prayed for help and resurfaced. The back of my head hit something. It was an ice chest. I grabbed the handle and pulled it toward me. The thing was empty but the lid was tight, so it was very buoyant. I managed to drape myself over it and let the current take me faster and faster. I looked up at heaven and gave thanks.

Cephas Lawrence

"Jonathan, this is not making a lot of sense," I said.

"Tell me about it. Why have an eight-lane highway around Dallas if it's just going to be a parking lot!" Jonathan swerved around a slow car and leaned on his horn. We were still two and half hours away from Shreveport.

"I'm talking about the murder."

Jonathan glanced at me with those piercing turquoise eyes. "Oh."

"Vivian wants the Ark. Let's just call it that from now on. And then someone teleports in and takes the thing and all evidence of its existence.

And yet Vivian is going back to the house today to get it. It must have some kind of significance. I haven't had the opportunity to discuss it with you yet, but I discovered some significance to that the diagram that may help explain what is happening."

"We have plenty of time!" Jonathan slammed on the breaks and we screeched to a halt in the heavy traffic. "This freeway is nothing more than a parking lot! So tell me."

"It is a kind of compass, if you will. Each point on the circle represents one of the demons of the Council of Darkness. Now, what is significant about the Ark, I do not know. Perhaps it contains items that relate to each of the demons."

"Would these items give someone an advantage over the demons?"

"Yes, that is the question. It is legend that if you know the name of a demon, you can control it. But, that is pure conjecture and not scriptural. However, to know the nature of a demon is to know what it has done in the past. I believe the more powerful demons, such as the ones who would constitute this Council of Darkness, each have a skill or ability they have developed over the millennia. Knowledge of these skills could be useful. The size of the Ark would not allow much, though. The exploits of demons who have been busy with Lucifer's plan for over two thousand years would probably fill a library." We started moving again. "When I studied images of the Ark, Jonathan, I discovered that the plate on the top is a fusion of three different diagrams."

"Okay," Jonathan said.

"There is the circle or compass, similar to the one in my document. Superimposed on that is an inner circle with names. I cannot make them out without a more direct image. And the third diagram is the innermost circle, with what appear to be gems or stones along with names. In the very center of the plate is a rose."

"A rose? You mean, the flower?" Jonathan asked.

"A compass rose. It is a well-known entity found on maps. Anyway, this Ark, I fear, is very important in the struggle against the Council, Jonathan. Whoever ends up with it will have considerable knowledge about the inner workings of these demons."

"And, perhaps, the identities of their hosts?"

"Yes," I said. "Jonathan, it is possible that Vivian is not helping the eleventh demon. She may be competing with it. They may both be looking for the Ark!"

We finally left the traffic congestion behind. We had just passed the Louisiana-Texas line when Jonathan's cell phone rang. The call was from Josh.

"Josh, where have you been?" Jonathan gasped. "What? You're where? We'll be right there."

"What is it?" I asked.

"Josh is at the hospital. Someone tried to kill him."

"Vivian?"

"No, they tried to kill her, too. They're together."

Chapter 24

Jonathan Steel

I ran into the emergency room waiting area and left Cephas to park the car. Josh was slumped over in a chair. He looked up at me and ran across the room. My anger built. I was ready to knock some sense into him. But he grabbed me and held on for dear life, squeezing me in a bear hug. He held on and on. I finally put my arms around him and hugged him while my anger dwindled. For a moment I thought he might be crying, but he drew a deep breath and pushed away from me.

"Dude, they tried to kill us! I tried to stop them and almost shot one of them and then the boat caught on fire and Vivian fell in with the rope and the anchor around her and she was going to drown and I didn't know what to do, I mean, do I save her or just let her sink? But I saved her and then the boat blew up. Then this man pulled up in a boat and saved us." He paused for breath.

"Slow down. Tell me everything."

He sighed and sat back down. He told me everything. My heart sank when he told me about the men in the SUV. And the idea that he had been at the mercy of Vivian during this whole ordeal almost drove me mad.

"Where is the man who saved you?"

"I don't know. I passed out about the time he was pulling me onto the boat, and I woke up in a police car. I guess he called 911."

"I'd like to thank him," I said.

"He was driving a ski boat and he had binoculars, I remember. But, that's all, Jonathan."

Binoculars? Was it the same man I had seen that first day? But what of it? He had saved Josh. That was all that mattered. I glanced back at Josh's bruised face and his soaked clothes.

"Are you hurt?"

"Nothing but a few bruises. They checked me out and told me to wait until you got here." I looked up. Cephas was standing behind me. He had heard the entire story.

"Where is Vivian?"

He pointed to the double doors. "Still inside."

"Stay with Josh, Cephas." I headed for the double doors leading into the emergency room. A nurse came through the doors and I slid inside. I had been in this emergency room before, on the night Claire had died. But right now, my anger kept me from dwelling on the pain of her loss. On a dry-erase board, I read which room Vivian was in. I pushed open the door to the room and ripped the curtain aside.

Vivian Darbonne Ketrick

His name was Weston. I had never even bothered to ask. He was standing by my hospital bed in his spiffy deputy uniform.

"I never should have left you. I'm sorry," he said.

He held his cowboy hat in his hands, working his fingers around the brim. I tried to avoid his bright-blue eyes.

"I told you to get lost," I whispered. It was the best I could do after Gamaliel had choked me.

"I know. Who were those men?"

I shrugged. I had already told the Shreveport Police everything I knew before Weston showed up. He'd heard what happened through the grapevine. "I really have no idea."

"The kid is okay?"

"Yeah."

The door to the room burst open and Jonathan Steel rushed in. He ran into Weston's back and the two of them stumbled toward me. Steel stopped, surprise etched onto his face as he regarded Weston.

"Who …?" He glared at me. "You! I ought to kill you!"

Wrong thing to say. Weston grabbed Steel by the arm and jerked him away from my bed. Steel pulled himself out of Weston's grasp and shoved him back. Weston fell over the rolling stool. He was up in a flash, his hand going to his pistol.

"Hey!" I managed to croak. "Put the horses in the pen, you two!"

Weston stopped and his face grew red with anger. Steel didn't know which threat to go after.

"I'm usually flattered when two men fight over me. But right now, my head is about to explode, so both of you be still and be quiet!"

Steel and Weston eyed each other. Steel finally put up his hands. "Look, I'm sorry. I didn't know you were in here. I want to talk to Vivian."

"Yeah? Right after you kill her?" Weston picked up his hat. "I think you need to leave."

"I *need* to find out what happened to Josh," Steel said.

"The kid? He's fine, I hear."

"Weston." I could just reach his arm. I patted it. "Let me talk to Mr. Steel alone. It'll be fine. We have a history."

Weston tensed at my touch and then glanced at me. Those eyes were filled with true emotion, true caring. I shuddered to think that they had been glowing orbs of fire the night before. He nodded. "I'll be right outside the door. If you need me, you let me know." He bumped against Steel's shoulder as he stepped outside.

"New boyfriend?"

"Yeah."

"What do you need from him? Protection?"

I leaned back into the bed. My neck was sore and my head was throbbing from the sutured cut along the side of my forehead. Once I got my wits about me, I would use the leech demon to heal it before it became an unsightly scar. "He came to Ketrick's house with me to serve a court order."

Steel clenched his fists and paced. "And where was he when these men attacked?"

"I sent him away. We had a falling out."

"What happened out there, Vivian?"

"Someone doesn't want me to have the Ark of the Demon Rose."

"The ark of what?"

"The Demon Rose. It's figurative. Rose as in rose compass. Rose as in the flower of flowers. Rose as in a circle of overlapping petals, interlocking and interwoven. The Master's prized possession. Figure it out. I'm tired." I waved my hand at him.

"You almost got Josh killed," he said.

"I didn't call in those goons, Steel. Besides, I saved his life."

"Where did they come from?"

"Look, I had no idea those men were coming. I still don't know who sent them or even who they are." I sat forward and swung my feet off the bed. The floor was cold on my bare feet. The nurse had placed a folded set of surgical scrubs by the bed.

"It sounds like Josh saved *your* life," Steel said.

"Well, don't punish him for it." I began to slide out of my hospital gown. Steel's eyes bugged out.

"What are you doing?"

"Putting on these scrubs. My jumpsuit is ruined. I'm getting out of here." I dropped the gown on the floor and Steel turned away. "What's the matter, honey? I didn't know you were such a prude."

"Come on, Vivian. Is this how you seduced that deputy?"

I pulled the scrub pants up and cinched them around my waist. Inside, Summer the seductive demon whispered Jonathan's name. I shooed her away and put on the scrub top, groaning at the pain in my muscles. "He came to me, Steel, after you reported my little visit."

He turned around and glared at me with those intense turquoise eyes. "It wasn't a visit, Vivian, it was breaking and entering."

"Not the way Weston saw it." I straightened the scrubs and tossed the hospital gown into the trash and stumbled with brief dizziness. "It really doesn't matter now. Someone has trumped us both."

"Who?"

"I don't know." I blinked in surprise. I had grabbed his arm to stay steady. I released it. He seemed not to have noticed. "Jonathan, it's hard for you to think I could have a normal life, isn't it?"

"You can't have anything normal, Vivian." He glanced at the arm I had touched. "Whatever you touch, you destroy."

The shark demon surged and I lashed out and slapped him hard across the cheek. It felt good. I punched his arm with all of my diminished strength and he winced. "Get out of here! Now!"

Steel rubbed his cheek. "Not until I get some answers."

I massaged my aching head. "Look, these guys showed up to take the Ark. But Josh said it was already gone. That's all I know. Now, you tell me what you know. Who took the Ark? And how?"

"Fair enough." As Steel told me about the teleporter taking the Ark and Theo, I grew cold. Someone else had the Ark. Had they opened it? Would they know how to use it? And unlike little old me, whoever had taken the Ark could teleport. "Teleportation takes a very powerful demon. It must have cost the host plenty."

"It did. He's dead," Steel said.

"How do you know?"

He reached into his jeans pocket and took out a piece of paper. "Know this guy?"

I gasped. "Juan."

"Destillo."

"Yeah. He was one of the FBI agents who came and took Ketrick's things. I went to the FBI warehouse to see if the Ark was there but they wouldn't let me in. It took a while, but I worked my magic on Destillo and got a look at the catalogue of items."

"What kind of magic?"

"You really have to ask?" He actually blushed. I handed him the printout. "The Ark wasn't at the warehouse. That's why I came back to the lake house to find it. What happened to him?"

"He had a heart attack."

"That's what trying to carry Theo around will do for you. His body couldn't take the strain. So Destillo has the Ark?"

"He *had* the Ark. We searched his house. It wasn't there. Just the dead woman."

"Dead woman?"

"He sacrificed a woman, Vivian." He fiddled with his cell phone and shoved it in my face. The image of a gutted woman filled my field of vision. "This is Zoe Reynolds, Destillo's intern. He sacrificed that woman to *you*! He worshipped *you*," he said through clenched teeth. I swallowed. My shark demon writhed in ecstasy at the images. I felt nauseous. She deserved it, Summer said. I looked away and drew a deep breath. "How is this my fault?"

"Did you lead him on? Did you give him the idea of sacrificing your competition on a demon altar?"

I glared at him then poked him in the chest. "Listen, sweetie, we all have the capacity to choose. And no matter how you slice and dice it, the choice is always yours and yours alone. Someone influenced him to prepare a sacrifice, and he made the choice to do it. And that someone was not me!" Who could it be, then? "The only people who know about the Ark are the members of the Council. Maybe one of them convinced Destillo to take a life."

Steel slid the phone into his shirt pocket and backed off. "So why take the Ark? Is someone going to use it as a bargaining chip? Are they trying to push you out of the succession line to the Council?"

"Stay out of this, Steel."

"I'm in until I find Theo."

"I know where Theo is."

"What?"

"You're not telling me everything. Tell me the rest and I'll tell you where to find Theo. What else do you know about Destillo?"

He filled in more details about the house and the garage. He told me about the symbol above my picture in the garage. "Cephas says the symbol is on this Demon Rose of yours. It stands for Chaos. And it also coincides with the number eleven."

A wave of weakness passed over me and I stumbled toward the bed. Steel grabbed me and eased me onto the sheets. Eleven was here? Now? Did he have something to do with the white eyes? I wasn't ready for this. The Master had taken some of my powers. In a flash, I realized how stupid I had been to let myself be distracted by Weston. It had nearly cost me my life. I brushed Steel's hands away.

"Vivian, Zoe was sacrificed to number eleven in honor of you. No matter how you look at this, you are to blame." Steel said.

I couldn't look into his turquoise eyes. "A sacrifice to number eleven? Don't be absurd. That sacrifice stuff is for amateurs. It means nothing to the Master. It's just for show, to make sure the host is willing to do anything for the Master. You know that. So either Destillo hid the Ark or there is someone else involved who took it from him."

"You don't like the fact the eleventh demon may be involved. You didn't see that coming, did you?" Steel almost smiled. "These people who tried to kill you, will they come for Josh again?"

I relaxed back into the bed and fought the headache. I had to get out of here. "They won't come after you. They're only interested in me. I'll handle it from here, Jonathan. Go back to your precious house and your precious God and your sweet, albeit strange, little family."

"Theo?" he asked.

"Oh, he's in the room next door. They brought him in by ambulance. He looked like a beached whale."

Steel glared at me one last time. His eyes glowed with hatred and then anger and, maybe, just maybe, something else. "You aren't growing soft toward me, are you?" I asked.

He blinked and shook his head. "In the caverns under Transylvania, I did something I never thought I could. I forgave Raven." He looked away. "For a moment, I wondered if I could forgive you. I was mistaken." The privacy curtain swirled around as he left.

I cursed and threw the water pitcher at the door. Who did he think he was? Forgive me? What was there to forgive? For a second, the image of my father impaled on Ludie filled my mind, then it disappeared into the darkness of my memories. I wiped away the tear that trickled down my cheek. No time for this. No time!

Chapter 25

Jonathan Steel

IN THE NEXT room, Theo was spread out over the bed, soaking wet and covered in welts and scratches. He opened his eyes and smiled. "Hello, Chief. Heck of a day."

By the time the ER physician had checked him out, Vivian was long gone. I waited until Theo was ready to move. The hospital loaned him a set of XXXL scrubs. I sent Josh and Cephas to bring the SUV around to the entrance and helped Theo into an extra-wide wheelchair. We were waiting just outside the ER door when I noticed a man standing out front, wedged into an inconspicuous corner ten feet away from the smoking area. He wasn't smoking. I could see just one side of his face. He motioned to me with his right hand, then he turned and walked deeper into the shadows of the loading dock.

"I'll be back in a second, Theo." I patted the big man on the back.

Theo squinted at me as I disappeared into the thick cloud of rancid cigarette smoke hanging around the heads of a pack of nurses and technicians who were babbling amongst themselves. Around the corner, the man was standing at the far end of a narrow alley. He glanced at me once and then stepped behind a dumpster overflowing with garbage bags.

Behind the dumpster, a short set of concrete stairs led up to an employee's entrance. The man was sitting on the top step. He wore jeans and a gray T-shirt with a Dallas Cowboys emblem. I went up to join him and as he looked up at me, I noticed his face was slightly deformed, with one eye a bit lower than the other.

"You look good," he said.

"I know you. You're Dr. Daniel Brown."

"Yes." He just stared at me.

My heart raced. I blurted out the first question that came to mind. "Do you know who I am?"

"I know all about you. I've been keeping an eye on you. You're doing good.

Lucky to have survived that thing on the boat two years ago. I tortured you to within an inch of your life."

"You're awfully nonchalant about it!" My face grew warm. "You tortured me!"

Brown cringed at the sound of my voice and held up his hands in a defensive posture. "Wait! Let me explain. Your father made me do it. I couldn't go back to prison, not after the first time."

I tried to find words and shook my head in confusion. "But ... your house ... Emily ... the kidnappers who took you ..."

Brown relaxed and ran his hands through his thin hair. "Emily was a friend. When she and Thomas couldn't have a child, she came to me for help. Of course, Ketrick had set it all up with her." He wiped at his deformed nose. "But I felt sorry for Emily, so I double-crossed Ketrick. The Captain sent me to Lakeside to find the Ark but Ketrick figured it out. He could have killed me, you know. Instead, he made me help with Emily's pregnancy. Implant his embryo. But, she was already pregnant when it was time to do the procedure. I was going to come to the church and rescue the lot of you, but Vivian found out and sent Lucas after me." Brown's haunted gaze fell on me. "You know what Lucas is capable of. I had to run."

"You were the man with the binoculars. In the boat. You saved Josh."

"What? The man in the boat? Not me." Brown wiped his thick lips. "Someone was looking after the boy. But that wasn't me. Just a good Samaritan out for an afternoon of fishing. I have been watching out for *you*." He rubbed his back and leaned against the dirty brick wall. "My back is killing me. I wasn't always like this, Jonathan. Not always. No, I had to get greedy and listen to the Captain."

"I had a flashback, Brown. I remember the night I came to your house. I asked you about the Ark. What do you know about the Ark of the Demon Rose?"

Brown shook his head. "Oh, no you don't! You led the Captain right to me, that night. It had nothing to with the Ark. It had to do with the other." Brown stood up painfully and tried to back away from me. "After the Captain found me, he threatened me. Used me to torture you for information. Listen, just a word of advice: Forget your father. You've got better things to do. God has a different plan in mind than yours. I'd go with His. You've got to help take care of this kid. Now, there was a surprising turn." He glared at me with his uneven eyes. "What would have happened if that man in the boat had not been there? Eh? You have responsibilities now. Think outside of yourself,

Jonathan. You've been given a gift. Your past has been erased. Don't go looking for it. You won't like what you find. I have to go now. They might see me if I talk to you much longer."

"But, I've got questions—"

"No time. They are watching." He studied me for a second and then leaned forward. I pulled back from his sour odor. "I shouldn't do this, but I can help you remember something. When you do, you'll see that you need to trust me. Listen to my advice. I was your friend. I'm not your enemy." He suddenly grabbed my face in an iron grip and shoved his mouth up to my ear. He whispered a phrase and then I was somewhere else.

Two years earlier
Gulf of Mexico

The room pitched violently to one side and the two men holding my arms moved with the floor. I blinked blood out of my eyes and focused on Dr. Brown. "I thought you were my friend."

Brown grabbed at the bulkhead as the ship shifted again. It was one heck of a storm outside. "You, of all people, should know how the Captain works. I had no choice but to go along."

I glanced down at my naked body, the cuts on my stomach, and my broken fingers. "You always have a choice, Toady."

"Don't call me that!" Brown lashed out with his hand. Blood filled my eyes again as my head snapped back from the blow. I spat blood into the air.

"What are you going to tell him? I'm not giving you any more information," I growled.

He rubbed his hand and nodded to the two men holding me. "Drag him up to the bridge. I tried to protect you, Jonathan. I really did. But now it is out of my hands."

They pulled me up the stairs to the bridge. My legs were weak and my arms numb from the beatings and the drugs. It wouldn't have done any good to fight them even if I had been able. Outside the bridge windows, the storm churned in the blackest night I had seen in years. But the inside of the bridge was dry and the air was hazy with pipe smoke. The Captain turned from his instruments. The pitching of the deck seemed not to affect him. His eyes burned ferociously in the shadow of his panama hat. The lower half of his face was illuminated by the glow from his meerschaum pipe.

"Did he break?"

Brown shook his head. "No, sir. He wouldn't say a thing."

The pipe bowl flared with his inhaled breath and lit up the Captain's relentless gaze. "He wouldn't give up the location?"

"No."

I found the energy to speak. "Why don't you look at me? Why don't you look at your own son?"

The Captain slowly turned his gaze on me. "You had your chance and you chose the wrong side. We've been over this before."

"So what are you going to do now that your Toady failed?"

Brown swore and thudded a bulky fist on the bulkhead. "Stop calling me that!"

"He speaks the truth for once." The Captain said. "Need I remind you that if it weren't for me, you would be rotting away in prison? Look at you. You're a pitiful excuse for a doctor."

The Captain motioned to one of the men who had brought me to the bridge. "Take Toady and throw him overboard."

"No!" Brown screamed. "I can't swim!"

"Then shut up or I'll send you back to prison, where I should have left you to rot. If he can't be broken, then I have no choice but to throw him overboard instead of you."

Brown seemed to shrink. He looked at me with shame and remorse. "Please don't. He was my friend. You turned me against him."

The Captain shoved him up against a bulkhead door. "It's your choice. Either you go overboard or he does."

"But he's your son." Brown wiped blood from his deformed lips.

"I know that." The Captain glanced at me and, for a second, concern filled his eyes. Regret, perhaps? Shame? He picked up a backpack from the corner. "Put something that floats in here and tie it on him. It'll keep him from drowning."

Brown picked up two plastic bottles from the corner. "Take him outside."

One of the men holding me popped the handle on the door and the wind slammed it open. Rain and wind whirled around the bridge. The Captain clamped his hat onto his head and tucked his pipe into his pants pocket. The men dragged me through the open door and out into the maelstrom. Brown held the backpack as the two men put my arms through the straps and fastened them across my chest.

"Now, you listen good." Brown leaned in. I could barely hear him above the roaring wind. Thunder crashed on the horizon and his face was lit by a splinter of lightning. He was crying. "I will find you. I will help you, understand? I will make all of this right. But it will take time. I have to fall off the radar so the Captain can't find me."

Suddenly, I felt the iron clasp of a hand that had gripped my arms and shoulders many times in the past. The Captain whirled me around. His intense eyes burned with anger. The wind snatched his hat off of his head. Rain dampened his short, grayish-red hair and ran down his lean features.

"If you cannot tell me what I want to know, then I will have to risk getting rid of all of your knowledge. Do you understand me? You will stop following me. You will stop hunting me. You will remember nothing of this. Nothing. That is the only way I can let you live. Beware the demon of the spiral eye."

Lightning illuminated his wild features and my mind fell, whirling, spinning into oblivion as his grip released and I fell backwards, down, down into the warm, salty water and down, down into an empty mind where dark specters waited to snatch away my memories and bury them in concrete and steel and where the lightning grew green with the pounding waves and I was no more.

"Chief! Chief! You okay?"

I looked up into the eyes of Theophilus King. He pulled me to my feet and I fought dizziness as I searched the alleyway. Brown was gone, and already, the memory that had surfaced was growing hazy. I tried to latch onto it, but the more I did, the worse the dizziness became, until I felt nauseated. This had happened once before. So I pushed the memory away, hoping I could at least recall some vestiges of it. One thing was certain: Dr. Brown, the man known to me as Toady, had tortured me at the command of my father. But he had also promised to help me. Just who was this man?

Chapter 26

Jonathan Steel

I TRIED TO MAKE pancakes the next morning, but I discovered that cooking was not one of my lost skills. Even Josh turned up his nose at them. We ended up making toast and drinking orange juice. Theo emerged from his garage apartment at about ten. He was moving slowly after surviving a swim in Red River. Someone on the Riverwalk in downtown Bossier City had seen him floating by and called the police. Theo cooked himself six of his famous scrambled eggs, half a pound of bacon, and an entire pan of biscuits.

"I haven't eaten in a while, Chief," he mumbled through the biscuits. "Grandmama's recipe."

I glanced at Cephas and Josh. I hated it when Theo called me Chief. "Theo, you don't have to call me Chief. I'm not—"

"Whoa!" Theo pointed a piece of bacon at me. "Don't you be telling me not to give you respect. You deserve it. You saved my life and you gave me a purpose. I'll call you Chief if I want to. Don't like it, too bad."

Josh chuckled. "I guess he told you. So why do you call him Chief?"

Theo finished chewing his bacon and his gaze drifted far away. "I got my reasons."

"What are they?" Josh persisted.

Theo looked at Josh. His eyes held something painful and far away. "You really want to know?"

"Yeah."

"Well, I guess we ain't got secrets between us anymore, so I'll tell you. You see, I didn't stay in school like you have so far. I didn't do too well in school. They wanted me to play linebacker 'cause I was big. But I got hurt. Tore the cartilage in my knee. Then I was out of luck. Didn't have the credits to graduate." He glanced at me. "My brother, Marcus, had started a café with our Grandmama's recipes. He was older and Grandmama got him first, before she got me. You see, my mother didn't do such a good job with us. She was a

155

dopehead. The apple doesn't fall too far from the tree, does it? Later I got my GED, but I never walked across the stage. In the meantime, Marcus gave me a job. He taught me how to be a chef so I could cook in his café. Then, one day, it all came to an end."

Anaheim, California

I brushed the yeast rolls with butter and put them in the warming rack to rise. The smell of yeasty bread, butter, and cinnamon filled the café with mouth-watering fragrances. I glanced through the open window above the service rack at the tables in the small café. The morning crowd was gone. Only a couple of stragglers still hunched over their pastries and coffee.

"They like my cinnamon rolls?"

Grandmama hobbled into the kitchen. She was small and stooped with a thatch of gray hair over her dark features. She wore a blue cotton dress and walked with a cane made from an old tree limb. I smiled and helped her across the spotless floor.

"Yes, ma'am! I sold every single one we made this morning. Nobody makes them rolls like you, Grandmama."

Grandmama smiled and settled into her chair next to the counter. "Where's Marcus?"

"He'll be back in a minute. He ran to the bank." I took another tray of yeast rolls from the counter and brushed them with butter.

Grandmama tapped her walking stick on the floor and squinted at me. I felt her gaze settle on me like a wave of hot water. I was in trouble!

"What did I do now?"

"How come you didn't walk?" Grandmama asked.

"I didn't have a diploma."

"You got your GED, Theophilus Nosmo King. You got a diploma."

"But I should have walked two years ago."

"You embarrassed?"

I brushed the last roll and turned to put the tray in the warming rack. I felt the walking stick jab me in the back. Grandmama had it pointed at me like a rifle. "Listen here, young'un. I raised you after your no-good momma threw you away just like she did Marcus. I raised you to be proud of who you are. I raised you to fear God and to fear no man. You got nothing to be embarrassed about. Nothing!"

I looked down at the floor. "Grandmama, I didn't belong with those folks."

"You mean you didn't want to be seen as a failure, young'un. You ain't no

failure! You are a success! How many young'uns you think don't ever go back to get their diplomas? You should be proud of what you did. You should have walked across that stage with a strut in your step and showed them all that you are the Chief!"

I smiled and looked up at her. "And I do strut, don't I?"

Grandmama smiled back and tapped her stick on the floor. "Better than most, my child."

I hugged her to my chest. "I'm sorry I didn't walk. But since you the one who raised me, I'll strut now."

I pushed away and strutted across the kitchen, swinging my apron back and forth like a robe. "I be struttin'!" I said and Grandmama laughed. I turned and moonwalked back to the bakery rack. "That was for you, Grandmama."

She chuckled and wiped at her eyes. "That's more like it, Chief."

"You never called me that before. You only ever called Marcus that."

"Man can only call someone that if he respects them, young'un. You already had my love. Now you got my respect." She reached up, pulled me down to her level, and planted a kiss on my cheek.

Without warning, the door to the café exploded inward with a roar as Marcus was hurled across the dining room in a cloud of broken glass. Two masked men followed Marcus through the broken outer door. They both carried pistols. The two customers left in the café jumped to their feet. Without hesitation, each of the masked men shot one of the patrons.

I rushed from the kitchen into the dining room and froze with fear, my mind reeling as it tried to grasp what I was seeing. Marcus climbed up from the floor and stared at the two dead customers. "Are you crazy?"

The nearest gunman stepped forward and slammed his pistol across Marcus's face. Marcus fell back across a table and onto the floor. "Shut up and get us the rest of the money."

Marcus blinked as he slowly climbed to his feet. "All the money we had was in that bag."

The other gunman was nervous and twitchy. His masked face swiveled back and forth. "Smells good in here. Smells like money."

I heard the swinging kitchen door open and watched in horror as Grandmama hobbled into the dining room. "Listen here, you two hoodlums. You get on out of here and leave us be. You done killed two people for no good reason, so get on out of here." She raised her walking stick and poked it at the nervous gunman.

Marcus got up off the floor and threw himself in front of her. "Grandmama, get out of here! Get back in the kitchen!"

"I will not let these worthless buzzards do this to us."

The nervous gunman glanced at the first and shrugged. He pointed the pistol at the back of Marcus's head and pulled the trigger. Blood burst from his forehead and splattered over Grandmama's face. He collapsed at her feet. Grandmama wiped the blood from her face and shock came over her features.

"What have you done?" she shrieked. She raised her walking stick and stumbled toward the gunman. He pulled the trigger again and Grandmama lurched with the impact and fell over Marcus.

I stood frozen in horror, unable to speak or move. The first gunman looked at the second. "Well, I guess there wasn't any money after all. Let's get out of here."

They ran through the shattered glass door even as the sounds of sirens filled the air. I felt the world darken, felt my strength leave me. I fell backward through the kitchen door into the warming tray. Buttered yeast rolls rained down on me, engulfing me in their warm redolence even as I settled into bloody darkness.

Jonathan Steel

A tear ran down Theo's cheek and he wiped at it angrily. "I ain't never told anyone that story. But I never trusted anyone like I trust the three of you."

"Did they catch the shooters?" Josh asked.

"I did. Four years later. I was a policeman by then. I went from being a chef to being a cop."

"So you've shot a man?" Josh asked.

"At least two." He whispered.

"I'd be honored for you to call me Chief," I said. "Theo, the man who teleported you is dead. Why did he take you to that house in the woods?"

Theo frowned. "There was a dead body in that room too old for Destillo to have killed. Maybe his demon had used that room before. I have no idea where it was. I was just glad I ran into the water and found that ice chest."

We sat there in silence for a moment. Cephas stared down into his coffee cup. He still looked tired and his eyes were rimmed in dark circles. Josh had a few scratches on his face, but he didn't look much worse for wear. I decided it was time to lay out my plan. "I think we need to go to the beach."

Josh might as well have been hit with a cattle prod. "The beach?"

"Yes. I think we ought to get out of here for a few days. I need to get some stuff from the beach house. You've got how many days until school starts?"

"Less than three weeks. And my birthday is two days before school starts. It would be sweet to spend it on the beach."

Birthday? I hadn't realized Josh's birthday was coming up. I glanced at Cephas, and he nodded. Theo wiped his face with a napkin.

"Now wait a minute, Chief, this Destillo guy took something from us, and now I know where he took me. We find a big farm house by the river and we can get that Ark back."

"Nothing doing, Theo. No, you and Cephas and Josh are going down to Gulf Shores."

"And just what are you doing?" Cephas put his cup down noisily on the table.

"I'm going back to Dallas to meet with Ross and give him all of this information. We'll let them investigate this building Theo was held prisoner in. We'll let them do their job."

"These men are evil, Jonathan. Of that I am sure. I have seen this kind of evil before. You must confront it personally or it will destroy everything it touches." Cephas pointed his crooked finger at me. "You are a part of this now. These fiends will defy the authorities."

"Are you telling me to take matters in my own hands?"

Cephas breathed deeply. "I just know that sometimes the authorities of this world are not enough. I remember—" He looked at Theo. "Like Theo, I trust you enough to share more of my secrets."

Cephas Lawrence

Dallas, Texas

A cold wind ruffled Molly's hair as she paused on the sidewalk in front of her apartment building. "I need to tell you something, Cephas. That is why I asked you to come here."

I swallowed and tried not to be nervous. I had not talked to her since the incident in the café and had been certain any chance I might have had with her was gone. Now I hoped she was giving me a second chance. "I'm listening."

She stared down the sidewalk. "Mary's father is not dead. He is very much alive, and I do not want him to find her. I've been hiding her from him." She gazed at me with tear-filled eyes. "But she found out about him and then she wanted to meet him. I refused. That was when she started acting strangely."

I patted her shoulder. "That would explain a great deal of her problem, Molly. There is no reason to believe in demons. This is all a textbook case of acting out disappointment."

Molly nodded. "I haven't told her about my past. She can't know what I once was." She led me up the steps into her apartment building. "I'm not proud of what I was, Cephas. James, I mean, Father Caskey overlooks my past. That is why I go to him. But you've been so kind that I will give you one more chance with Mary." Molly unlocked the door to her apartment. She paused and blinked at me in the waning light. "Cephas, Mary does not know about my past."

I placed a hand on her cold arm. "I don't care, either, Molly. You did what you had to for Mary."

Molly led me into a small living room. It was spare and impeccably clean. She took off her coat and hung it on the back of a wingback chair. Her pale shoulders glowed in the wan light coming through the shuttered windows. Light reflected off a green jewel dangling from a silver chain around her neck. "Mary is asleep. I'll wake her."

I reached out and touched the jewel. "A gift?"

She nodded. "It's called the Metastone. Watch." She held up the stone to the weak light from the window. At first, it glowed a pale green. She shifted it slightly and the color changed to red. "It's made of alexandrite. It changes color with your perspective. It is supposed to represent internal and external regeneration. You know, renewal."

I sighed. "Come now, Molly. Surely you don't believe in that hocus pocus."

Molly gazed at the jewel as it twirled on its silver chain. She closed her eyes and shook her head. "Of course not. It's just a gift from James. He left it on my doorstep yesterday morning. All wrapped up in a box with a pink bow." The jewel came to rest on her neck and she frowned. "Cephas, Mary's father wants to meet her." She swallowed and moisture filled her eyes.

I gently squeezed her shoulders. "Tell me about him."

Molly averted her gaze. "Sparky runs a night club. I never told him about Mary. But somehow he knows Mary is his daughter. Cephas, I was just sixteen. I needed the money and he offered me a job as a stripper." Molly drew a deep, shuddering breath and slowly settled into the chair. "I lied about my age. One night I had too much to drink. I woke up in Sparky's office. I was so ashamed of what had happened, I ran away."

I touched her chin. "We all make mistakes, Molly. You did what you had to do. I understand."

Her eyes gleamed with tears. "Do you? A sixteen-year-old girl stripping for those hideous monsters and then getting pregnant? I hid it from everyone until Mary was born. I was going to give her up for adoption, but she was so beautiful. She was my child, Cephas." She swallowed. "And then I did something unthinkable. Just a few weeks ago, right after Mary turned ten, I went back to him."

"Why?"

"Times were bad. I heard Sparky had opened the Carousel Club. I knew he would need someone with bookkeeping knowledge. He offered me the job. At first I was glad he didn't even remember me, Cephas. But then, I was angry because he didn't even remember what he did to me." She pressed the back of her hand against her mouth and sobbed. "So, I told him who I was. It was stupid of me. Why did I tell him? Now, he wants to meet Mary—"

"What's wrong, Mommy?"

Mary was standing in the door to the apartment's only bedroom. She was tall for her age. Her dark hair was tied into two long braids and she was wearing blue, one-piece pajamas covered in tiny robots.

"Hi, Mary."

"Uncle Cephas?" She smiled and ran to me. I hugged her. I heard Molly sniffle behind me. "Are you going to make some pancakes? Pancakes would make Mommy happy and she would stop crying. Wouldn't you, Mommy?"

"Your Mommy was just telling me a sad story that made her cry," I whispered into the girl's hair. It smelled of shampoo.

Mary took her mother's hand. "Mommy, don't be sad. I can tell you something happy."

Molly wiped at her eyes and smiled. "What's that, dear?"

"My friend came by my class today and told me I was going to meet an angel. Isn't that wonderful?"

Molly frowned and glanced at me. "Mary, what have I told you about this imaginary friend of yours?"

Mary looked down at her knees. "You think he's not real. But he is. He gave me a prize."

My mouth went dry and my heart raced. "What kind of prize?"

Mary smiled and ran into the tiny adjoining kitchen. She opened the small refrigerator and pulled out a white paper package. She hurried over and handed it to Molly. "He said we could have it for supper, Mommy. He said your friend Sparky was coming for supper. Mommy, who's Mr. Sparky?"

Molly gasped and looked at me. She slowly unwrapped the package. Her face paled and she lurched up from the chair as the package's contents tumbled out.

An eyeball stared back at us, trailing its optic nerve like a severed worm. Mary's screams joined Molly's as the eye rolled off the chair and onto the carpet, coming to rest looking right at me.

Jonathan Steel

"This 'Sparky' was involved with organized crime. In those days, their methods were ruthless. They were sending Molly a warning." Cephas said.

"What kind of warning?" Josh asked.

"Don't involve the cops," Theo growled. "Right, Papaw?"

"Exactly. I represented the organized authority of this world and Father Caskey represented the authority of the spiritual world. It is within this world from which we operate, Jonathan. We did call the police, but there was nothing they could do. Some of them were probably on the payroll of the mob. But organized mobsters do not utilize teleportation."

"Yeah, about that," Theo said. "We need to find that house by the river. Who knows, maybe the owner is Vivian? Have you thought of that?"

I leaned across the table. "Don't go there, Theo. We're done."

"We have verified that Vivian knew nothing about the teleporter, Theo. But there is a possibility," Cephas said, "that the demon using Destillo knew about the room with the body."

"Excuse me, am I invisible?" I blurted out.

Cephas glanced in my direction. "Did the two of you hear something?" He pretended to look right through me. "I could have sworn someone else was talking. Now, back to our theory."

"No, no, no!" I pounded the tabletop. "You're not listening to me."

Theo began to laugh so hard that biscuit crumbs sprayed from his mouth. "He don't like not being listened to."

Josh nodded. "Dude, there are a lot of things he don't like."

Cephas sipped his coffee. "He thinks he's in charge around here."

My face was growing warm with anger. "Wait, just a moment ago I was 'Chief.' If I'm not in charge, then who is?"

Theo finished his biscuit and rubbed his hands to get the crumbs off. "I think it was Josh who defeated—how many was it?"

"I took out four out of six, Bro," Josh said, beaming.

"Four assassins and saved Vivian's life."

"And blew up the ski boat in the process."

"Bro, if I knew how to handle a gun, I wouldn't have shot the boat engine instead of the assassins," Josh said. "Theo could teach me. He was a cop, right?"

I clenched my fists. I wanted to pull my hair out. "When did I lose control?"

"When you said we would go to the beach before we finished this," Theo said. "Chief, we cannot let these evil men get away with taking the Ark."

"And, taking my document," Cephas added.

"And blowing up my ski boat," Josh added. "I want to go to the beach more than anyone, but we have three weeks until school starts. We can take a couple of days to take out the trash."

"Take out the trash?" I said loudly.

"Yeah, you know, clean up the white-eyed goons. They had weird names, too, like Reflection and Voice and Name ..."

"Did you say white eyes?" Cephas became rigid.

"Yeah, the main dude had these really weird white eyes. You know, he had no pupils. The others called him Mind and Gamaliel."

Cephas bolted up from the table as though he'd seen a ghost. He rubbed his moustache. "Oh, please Lord, please make it not so! I have to get downstairs to my books."

I looked up at Theo and Josh and threw my hands up. "Fine. We'll take out the trash. But we'll take it out my way, understand?"

"Was there ever any doubt, Chief?" Theo finished his eggs in one bite.

Josh nodded. "You're the boss. Let's go see what Uncle Cephas is up to."

Chapter 27

Cephas Lawrence

I WAS MORE FRIGHTENED than I had been in years. Josh's mention of the assassins' white eyes had made my blood freeze. I hobbled down the stairs and across the basement to the nearest crate. The movers put my most precious crate of books next to the desk. I fumbled with the wooden lid. A splinter skewered the delicate skin under my fingernail. I swore, something I rarely do. I sucked the blood from my fingertip and the room swam. I slumped into the desk chair and gasped for breath as my heart raced. I tasted coppery blood and I was back in the abandoned asylum. His blood pooled around my feet and fire blistered the aging ceiling where—

"Need some help?" Theo appeared beside me.

I came back to the present. "Theo, I need to get the lid off of this crate."

Theo grabbed a hammer and got the lid off in moments. Dust puffed from the airtight seal as it was broken. Only one of the four humidity-controlled shelves was ready, but the immediacy of this new threat drove all such concern from my mind. "Now I need a dark leather-bound book titled *Testamanet of the Vitreomancers.*"

"Vitreomancer?" Josh approached the crate. "Dude, that would be a cool name for a band. Josh Knight and the Vitreomancers!"

I envied him. He was innocent in so many ways, yet wise in others. But his wisdom arose from the pains and losses he had suffered. For a fleeting second, I saw his mother's eyes in the eager planes of his face. I missed her. Once again, I felt dregs of guilt for bringing her, and thus Josh, into this unholy affair. "You will not want to deal with these Vitreomancers, Josh. Trust me."

Theo leaned over the edge of the crate and Jonathan shone a flashlight inside. Theo handed me book after book, and I handed them to Josh. He placed them in a pile on my desk. I winced at our handling these books without white gloves, but there just wasn't time. Finally, Theo lifted a huge leather-bound book with pewter clasps and hinges. He placed it on the desk with a loud clump. It weighed over thirty pounds and was two feet by two feet in size.

Josh read the title. *"The Testament of the Vitreomancers.* Who are they?"

I regarded this book that had occupied years of my life. For years, I had searched libraries, bookstores, and university storerooms looking for this book, looking for my answers, looking for my Molly.

"I looked for this book for years, but once I found it, I did not open it." My fingers traced over the leather and touched the metal clasps. My mouth was dry. This was the book I had been searching for when I first met Molly. Since the time of that tragedy, I had refused to open it. Now, I had no choice. I fumbled with the latches and opened the yellowed and faded pages. The odor of the paper was dry and crisp and the odor of the lacquered ink was like death , decay, and evil. Arcane drawings of animals and humans in various stages of vivisection covered the pages. I gasped. The feeling of utter evil seemed to emanate from the pages. I glanced at Jonathan. His face was pale.

"Cephas, this book is evil," he said.

"Yes," I whispered.

"This writing is in Latin," Josh said. At times, he was very perceptive. He was far more intelligent than he let on.

"You are correct, Josh. This book is a collection of macabre and evil sects from the early church. Within these pages are records of evil factions of the church that are lost in history. There is one group in particular I am interested in. Around the time of the Reformation, a group of priests separated themselves from the Catholic Church. They thought the threat of the Reformation would sweep Christianity into the ash heap of history. And in their lust for power and control, they embraced Gnosticism."

"What is Gnosticism?" I asked.

"The Gnostics came from a belief system that predated Christianity. It was their contention that there was a supreme God who created several smaller gods."

"Mini-gods?" Josh asked.

"Very clever, Josh. One of these mini-gods was evil. He created the material universe around us. Thus, in the minds of the Gnostics, all material reality is inherently evil. Now, Jesus comes along, professing to be the physical incarnation of the supreme God. Do you see the problem? For them, Jesus was divine. But His material self was inherently evil since He was made of the stuff of this universe. Only His spirit could be good. If you read the Gnostic Gospels closely, you will find that they portray a very spiritual Jesus who is afflicted by His evil flesh. In fact, many new age religions' talk about a 'Christ consciousness' echoing this idea."

"But these Gnostic Gospels were written 150 to 200 years after Jesus, right Papaw?" Theo said.

"Exactly! They were not written by those who actually walked with Christ. They are fiction. You might call them romance novels with a reinterpretation of Christ in the Gnostic tradition," I said.

"According to that Da Vinci book, all kinds of gospels were left out of the Bible." Josh said.

"And you have just bought into a lie, my son. The original canon of the New Testament, as it came to be called, was established long before these Gnostic Gospels. The Muratonian fragment mentions a list of the books of the New Testament before the Gnostic Gospels were written. They were never included in the official canon to begin, so how could they have been edited out?" I picked up an old book from the pile. "This Bible is over one hundred years old, Josh. If you look at the end of the book of Mark in this Bible, you will find an interesting footnote. Go ahead, look it up."

Josh took the volume. I held my breath. The pages were somewhat sturdy, although the edges were brittle. But he gave the book the respect it deserved as he gingerly turned to the New Testament. I watched his lips move as he read the last chapter of Mark.

"It says here that portions of the last chapter of Mark were not in the original manuscripts. I didn't know that."

I tapped the page carefully. "We have over 5000 ancient manuscripts, Josh, with some fragments dating to before 100 A.D., and if you compare all of those manuscripts, you will find a 99.9-percent correlation! Where there are differences, such as the passage you just read about handling snakes and drinking poison, you will see that the Bible accurately identifies such passages as not having been found in the original manuscripts."

I closed the book carefully and ran my hand over the leather cover. "The Bible does not hide its difficulties. It proclaims them. The early church fathers were adamant about including only those books that were written by eyewitnesses and could be corroborated. This is why the Gnostic Gospels were not placed in the Bible. They were not written by eyewitnesses. They did not reflect real events. They did not portray Jesus of Nazareth and his actions as those of a man living in first-century Palestine. Those books were fiction. You see, Josh, when we cannot tolerate the truth, we twist the facts to fit our version of the story. If you are going to use so-called facts to denounce the truth of the Bible, then use all of the facts—both the ones that support your theory and ones that don't."

Jonathan nodded. "So there was never a conspiracy to cover up the true books of the Bible?"

"Early Christians died because they were convinced of the truthfulness of the canon of Scripture. Felicity is one such early Christian woman who was sentenced to be thrown to the lions in the Coliseum. Her father begged her to renounce Christianity. She pointed to a pitcher of water and said that the pitcher could not be called something else. It could not be remade into another object for political reasons. It was what it was. And so it was with her. She was a follower of Christ, and she could not denounce the truth for a lie. She was thrown to the lions and devoured. Her devotion was to Christ. You will not see a follower of the Christ depicted in the Gnostic Gospels willing to die rather than denounce the Messiah who was God in the form of man!

"If this book was false, then why does it still stand the test of time? How can it still be relevant to us today? Why are the teachings of Christ so timely, so universal? Did you know that every religion on the face of this planet holds Jesus in high regard, as if He alone were humanity's closest thing to a universally recognized religious figure? The reason is these religions are looking for truth and Christ is the only manifestation of Truth. In the midst of their attempts to find God, they at least vaguely recognize God's presence in Christ. They are drawn to Truth. Of course, the real Truth is that Christ is the only true manifestation of God. He said it himself. 'I am the way, the truth and the life and no man comes to the Father except through me.' My point is that the truth of Christ being the Son of God is so overwhelming that even religions hostile to Christianity grudgingly admit Christ was more than a mere man. We *know* He was more than a mere man. He was and is God in man form, the incarnation. So, I tell people if these religions at least recognize that Christ is a compelling figure who is higher than any man then why not start with Christ instead of other religions? Why not start here?" I touched the Bible.

I opened the Bible carefully and turned to the book of John. "Look here, at this passage. Jesus has been brought once again before Pilate. Here, a man of reason, a man of education in the Roman tradition, a man of great power and intellect, is confronted by a carpenter who claims to be God. Look at what transpires:

Then Pilate entered into the judgment hall again, and called Jesus, and said unto him, Art thou the King of the Jews?

Jesus answered him, Sayest thou this thing of thyself, or did others tell it thee of me?

Pilate answered, Am I a Jew? Thine own nation and the chief priests have delivered thee unto me: what hast thou done?

Jesus answered, My kingdom is not of this world: if my kingdom were of this world, then would my servants fight, that I should not be delivered to the Jews: but now is my kingdom not from hence.

Pilate therefore said unto him, Art thou a king then?

Jesus answered, Thou sayest that I am a king. To this end was I born, and for this cause came I into the world, that I should bear witness unto the truth. Every one that is of the truth heareth my voice.

Pilate saith unto him, What is truth? And when he had said this, he went out again unto the Jews, and saith unto them, I find in him no fault at all.

I closed the Bible. "Truth incarnate, Truth born as a man, Truth both physical and spiritual—what would thus be a heresy to the Gnostics—stood before Pilate. A King not of this world and yet over this world, Jesus spoke truth. Jesus is Truth. And what was Pilate's reply? 'What is truth?' The question of the ages, gentlemen. What is truth? The truth, according to hard evidence, is a difficult thing to accept. We do not want to admit that we are spiritually bankrupt beings in need of grace and redemption. We want to be our own gods, so we take the harsh truth and wrap it up in conspiracies and secret societies and rewritten fictions in the hopes that if we live with the lie, it will become truth. We create other religions and spiritualties that are pale echoes of the Truth of Christ. But we all know who is the father of lies, don't we? He is the same master whom these Vitreomancers served. The father of chaos is Lucifer. He spins his web of deception through the ages even into today."

Josh leaned over the tome and pointed to the illustration of a tall man swathed in robes. His hair was long and he held a sextant. His eyes were shrouded in shadow. "Hey, one of those white-eyed guys had something like this thing the guy is holding. Gamaliel called it some kind of sextant."

I closed my eyes and said a silent prayer. These developments were not good. "This man is Simon Magus, the founder of a Gnostic sect in the second century known later as Simonians. His teachings were a combination of Hellenism and Hebraism, Greek thought and Jewish thought. He claimed that God was a 'devouring fire,' an intelligent being, but far different from the God of the Bible. He perverted the Hebrew way of thinking by trying to merge it with Greek paganism. The Simonians used magic and incantations and love potions. Magus conceived of six *roots*, or powers: Mind, Voice, Reason, Reflection, Name, and Thought. These all comingled with the seventh and greatest: the Boundless Power."

"Those were the names of the white-eyed dudes with Gamaliel."

"Six men with the six names of the roots of power conceived by Simon Magus ... Hand me my notebook, Theo." I pointed to a leather journal on the desk and Theo passed it to me. I searched through the pages and stopped. "Ah, here it is. Origen, one of the great Christian fathers wrote this: 'Like Simon, Menander—a pupil and, after Simon's death, his most important successor— also proclaimed himself to be one sent of God, the Messias. In the same way he taught creation of the world by angels who were sent by the Ennoia. He asserted that men received immortality and the resurrection by his baptism and practiced magical arts.'"

"Now, this is where it gets interesting. Many thought the Simonians and their successors, the Menandrians, died out. But during the Renaissance, Leonard da Vinci, consummate anatomist that he was, concluded that light passed into the eye and was somehow transmitted to the consciousness. To the mind, if you will. Imagine the remnants of Simonianism discovering that the eye was the window to the soul. Why then, the eye was the key to accessing the six powers of Mind, Voice, Reason, Reflection, Name, and ultimately, Thought!" I paused and searched through more pages in the book. "Ah, here we are."

The drawing on the page showed a dissected body spread out on a table. Standing over the man were four others. One of them was holding a metal trocar. From its end, liquid dripped into the eyes of one of the other men. Blood streamed from the eyes of the corpse. "Back to our division of heretical priests during the Renaissance: These priests believed that the dead had seen Christ in his secret form and that that image was stored in the liquid within the eyes of the recently deceased. So they extracted the liquid, mixed it with special chemicals, and placed it in the eyes of their followers. They knew that such an action would blind them but they believed it would also give them a very special kind of sight, the secret sight of the dead, along with access to the six powers, and ultimately, the Boundless Power. Thus, they called themselves the Vitreomancers, those who used the fluid of the eye, the vitreous humor, to look beyond the veil of death."

"Only crazy people would believe that," Jonathan pointed out.

"You are so correct, Jonathan. And yet, even into the early part of the twentieth century, a belief persisted that the last thing a person saw before death would produce an image on the retina, much like a photograph. Photographers thought that if they took a picture of the dead eyes, they would be able to see the murderer. Such photographs were called optograms. The Vitreomancer attempts a similar maneuver with only the viscous fluid of the deceased's eyes." I retrieved another book from the pile and opened it at random.

"Were the Vitreomancers really blind?" Steel asked.

"With the onset of blindness, a Vitreomancer would indeed acquire new sight. I believe it was supplied by demons. The real power behind this special sight was the supernatural intervention of demonic powers."

"Wait, Uncle Cephas." Josh pointed to his eyes. "How could these dudes keep their existence a secret if they were running around with white eyes?"

I massaged my moustache and nodded. "Now, they probably wear contacts. There could be dozens of these Vitreomancers among us and we would never know. But in ancient times, Josh, clouding of the eyes was a common malady. There were no corneal transplants or cataract surgeons in those times. People were used to seeing individuals with white eyes."

"So the white-eyed dudes who attacked me were these Videomanics? I mean Vitreomancers?" Josh asked.

"Yes, Josh. And if they are here, among us, then we are in dire straits indeed." I closed both books. "Jonathan, I believe they were at the sacrifice in Destillo's garage. Someone extracted the liquid from the dead woman's eyes."

"But why?" Steel asked.

"Wait a minute, Bro." Josh interrupted us. "Someone sucked out a woman's eyeballs?"

"It's a long story," Jonathan said.

I stood up and paced the floor of the basement. "I cannot be sure. It may have been the entire purpose of the sacrifice, Jonathan. To kill this woman and then extract the secret knowledge she supposedly saw at death."

"Or perhaps the Vitreomancers wanted to see what she had seen as she died. They may be looking for the murderer," Jonathan said.

"This is loopy," Theo said. "No one can use eyeball snot to see the past."

"Oh, I agree, my good friend." I looked at Theo. "But this procedure is not about any magic properties of the fluid. Is about the process of extracting it. Doing so demonstrates to Satan that you are willing to do anything in obedience. Like the sacrifice itself, it affords no special powers to the killer, but further damns his soul."

"So what's next?" Josh asked.

I shrugged. "I frankly don't know. This has gotten very complicated."

Jonathan nodded. "It always does. Have you met these Vitreomancers before?"

I sank into chair. "In retrospect, I believe I have." I felt Jonathan's hand on my arm.

"Does this have to do with Molly?"

"Yes."

"Molly is the hottie in your story?" Josh asked.

I reached over and picked up the picture frame. Molly's face smiled back at us, and my heart sank at the sight of her long, dark hair cascading over her shoulders. In the moment the photograph was taken, she had seemed so happy. "Yes, this is Molly. We both met a man with white eyes."

Jonathan knelt beside me. "Maybe it's time you finished telling her story."

I looked at his taut features, his tightly clenched teeth, and suppressed anger at these creatures we were battling. "Yes, son, it is time."

Chapter 28

Cephas Lawrence

Dallas, Texas
November, 1963

OLD WIND MOANED through the dead trees as I stood outside the entrance to the condemned mental hospital on the outskirts of Fort Worth, Texas. The world was coming to an end. I was certain of it. A madman had assassinated the President of the United States. Mary's class never had the chance to sing to him. But, I had to put all of that aside and find Mary.

The dying light of day painted me in orange and reds. In the few remaining glass panels of the asylum's entryway, my reflection was on fire. I stared at the man looking back at me. My hair was beginning to turn gray around the edges. In spite of every effort to keep it under control, it waved around my head, making me look like the offspring of Medusa. My eyes were tired and my face was drawn. I turned up the collar of my long overcoat against a sudden frigid gust.

It had been a long week searching for Mary and Molly after the 'gift' of the severed eyeball. I had finally gone to James's church and begged the secretary for information. She had claimed that James had disappeared, but I knew she was lying to me. I managed to wear her down enough to show me a discarded note she had dug out of his trashcan. It was the address of this abandoned insane asylum. He was going to attempt an exorcism on Mary. The idiot! I had to stop him.

My reflection lengthened and changed into a pale man who emerged from the glass as if he were smoke. He was tall and thin with white skin, a bare scalp, and glistening red eyes. I stumbled at the sight of this strange apparition. "Who are you?"

"Lucas," he whispered. The air was cold and yet the man's chest was bare beneath his black overcoat. I blinked in confusion—his tattoos seemed to be moving! He closed his coat and tapped a long finger against his chin. "I must confess something to you, Dr. Lawrence."

"I am not a doctor," I whispered.

"Not yet." Lucas smiled. His huge white teeth were obscene. "I have grown fond of the girl. I do not wish harm to come to her. And so I give you some advice: When the time comes, place the Metastone around her neck. It will transform her."

"What are you talking about?"

"She will lie in the shadows between life and death. The Metastone will restore her to life. But it will come with a cost." He drew a deep breath and sighed. I realized with shock that his breath did not steam in the cold air. "All such things come with a cost."

Something knocked against the glass door of the asylum. I jerked my gaze away from the strange man. Once again, my reflection stared back at me. The man was gone! From behind my reflection, another image became clear. Molly materialized out of the dark shadows of the hospital entrance, pushing the door open.

"Cephas, I'm sorry. I had to try. I was scared for Mary after ..." She paused and began to cry.

I glanced over my shoulder and the weed choked-yard of the asylum was devoid of life. Where had Lucas gone? Molly pulled her dark woolen coat tightly around her chest. Her long, lustrous hair blew about in the wild wind. I longed to bury my face in those dark tresses. Her cheeks were red from the cold and her dark-brown eyes were moist with tears. I wanted to be angry with her, but instead, I drew a deep breath and fought the desire to sweep her up in my arms. "There was someone here. A man. Did you see him?"

She seemed not to hear. "I went to James—I mean, Father Caskey. I was afraid that what you were doing with Mary was hopeless."

I closed my eyes and shook my head. "I don't believe Mary is possessed. If she is not possessed, an exorcism would be dangerous! She has a mental illness, Molly. She needs a doctor and specialized tests. Please, come with me and I will get Mary the best neurological help money can buy."

Molly looked away from me. The gesture, though small, cut through my heart. "It's too late. James has already started the exorcism. You need to leave. I have to go be with my daughter."

There was no way I was going to leave her and Mary to that charlatan! I followed her receding figure through the hospital entrance. The hallways were dark and dank and the odor of decay and mold and stale urine burned my nostrils as I caught up with her. "Why here, Molly?" I grabbed her shoulder.

She jerked out of my grasp and glared at me. "She keeps having a vision of a ward at this hospital. James said we had to come here, to the source of the visions, to isolate the demons. If she were only hallucinating, how could she see someplace she has never been?"

"Molly." I reached toward her. "Listen to me. Listen to reason. Mary is a special girl. Maybe she is having visions of these demons. Maybe there is a God and He is trying to tell her something. But I fear her visions will drive her to the brink of insanity. I can help her. You must listen to me."

"Cephas, there is more." She drew a deep breath and clutched at her chest. "I was right about her father." The green-red jewel slid into view and for a moment I thought I saw a flicker of red light at the heart of the stone. I swallowed. The Metastone! "Sparky knows where we live. I just want her to be normal and then I will take her away, far away from this madness."

"Let me take her away from this place."

For a second she seemed on the verge of caving in. Then she whirled around and ran down the corridor. I hurried after her, following her into a cavernous ward. The ceiling was bubbling with peeling paint and stained with black blobs that would have driven Rorschach insane. Old beds and IV stands were shoved to the end of the room, where they lay intertwined like the bones of some dead creature. In the center of the room, a girl reclined on an old hospital bed. Glowing candles filled the air with the odor of wax. Huddled over the girl was my friend, Father James Caskey.

Molly ran over to the bed and reached for Mary's hand. James stopped her.

"Don't interfere, Molly. She might hurt you."

James's face was red from the cold. He looked up at me. He had a patch over one eye. "Cephas, why are you here?"

"To save Mary." I moved slowly toward the bed. "What happened to you, James?"

"You shouldn't be here, laddie. The world of science and faith are separated by a huge chasm, you see. Mary needs the world of the spiritual right now, not your cold, sterile science." He had a purple sash draped over his shoulders and his white collar was stained with sweat. He ran a hand through his hair and turned back to Mary.

"I am here because I am concerned for her safety, James." I stepped closer to the bed and gasped in horror at the sight of Mary. Since I had last seen her just one week ago, she had changed. She was gaunt and looked almost weightless on the stained sheets of the hospital bed. She could not have weighed more than a six-year-old, even though she was ten. Her frail limbs protruded through the armholes and from the lower edge of a hospital gown. Bruises covered most of her visible skin. Her cheeks were prominent against her sunken skin, and her eyes were closed. Her hair surrounded her pale face like a dark stain. She was breathing rapidly.

"Mary," I whispered.

"No!" James pushed himself between us. "You will not speak to her. You cannot interfere, Cephas. You have to trust me. I can save her from, well, from evil."

"James, she has severe depression. She is bordering on psychosis. She needs medical attention."

"No, her illness is not of this world, Cephas," he whispered. "I will remove the demon from her." He leaned closer. Blood was cracked around the edge of his eye patch. "They took my eye, Cephas." He whispered. "I let them have it in a bargain to save her life. Do you understand? If you interfere, they will have her! I can make this right."

Mary touched my hand with a cold finger and I turned away from utter confusion at James' words. "Mr. Lawrence, you came. I want you to know that it was your lack of belief that allowed me to take this young girl." Her voice was strong and far too mature for a child's. "She did not believe either, so she invited me in. And now, we are having a grand time together. If only you had believed! You could have saved her. For if you ever were to become a believer, Mr. Lawrence, you would be quite a formidable foe. Now, I have to stop Chimera's plans." She reached up with one bony hand and tugged on the jewel around Molly's neck. "Mother, you must give me the Metastone."

"No!" A voice echoed from across the room. A figure moved out of the shadows and into the candlelight. It was a short man with dark hair. He had a vaguely foreign look and wore a Nehru jacket. His most striking feature was his eyes, which were totally white. "No one can stop my plans, my little girl. Not even with the stone."

I glanced at James. "Who is this?"

But James was entirely focused on the man. "No! Let me have her!" He put himself between the bed and the approaching figure.

"The deed is done, Father Caskey. Our operative has killed the assassin. Our ploy worked. We no longer need the girl."

"Then let me have her. Let me take care of her and her mother. You promised."

"Lucas promised, not me. I don't keep promises, human. You must realize, Father, that we must gather all of the missing pieces of the puzzle and eliminate them."

"What is he talking about?" Molly asked.

The white eyes moved in our direction. "Your good Father here is in love with you. We used that love to get the girl, and to make our operative believe that he had fathered your child. We threatened that if he did not do as we asked, the girl would die. And so Ruby killed Oswald for us."

"Who are you talking about?" I asked.

"All part of our plans, Mr. Lawrence. In time you will understand for these names will go down in infamy. And, just as Ruby and Lee were enemies, the spirit *within the girl is my enemy. We have a hierarchy, Mr. Lawrence. Some of us are powerful and our plans change the orbit of this world. But, some, like the pitiful spirit within this child are but lost and lonely creatures who shiver and shake in fear of such powerful spirits as mine." He paused and studied Mary with his ice cold eyes. "You should never have left your pigs, lowly one. I am Chimera and all fallen beneath me tremble at my name."*

"Give me the Metastone and I will prove you wrong." Mary said in a guttural voice. She smiled insanely and giggled.

"Not even the Metastone will help against one such as I. The good Father gave it to his love to cement her devotion to him so she would bring you here. It will return to its rightful owner."

Mary laughed. Her deep basso echoed through the ward. "The Metastone will be mine, Chimera. It will complete my transformation."

Chimera's white eyes regarded Mary with utter disgust. "I am growing tiresome of you. I guess we shall have to do this the hard way."

Mary was not the one who transformed. Chimera's face began to elongate, pushing outward as if something hideous within was fighting to escape his flesh and bone. He closed his white eyes and hair sprang out of his head. He arched his back and the sound of cracking bone and rending flesh sickened me. I stumbled back as his body flowed disgustingly, as if it were made of clay. His head transformed into that of a lioness and his body elongated into that of a four-legged animal. A snake sprouted from his back and became a hissing tail. The head of a goat and the head of a human grew from his back like an obscene fungus. The lioness's white eyes opened and it roared. Fire billowed from its mouth. Clawed feet tore at the concrete floor. Ancient tiles splintered into the air as the creature bellowed and screeched. The snake tail snapped in my direction and paused just inches from my face. Two faceted eyes glittered white and pearly and a forked purple tongue danced through the air.

Molly grabbed my arm. "Cephas, what is happening?"

"I don't know."

"It's the demon!" James screamed. "It can't have her!" He reached into his pocket and took out a small Bible. He started chanting in Latin. Mary's laughter continued to build in volume and stridor until her bony hand grabbed James's coat and turned him around to face her.

"You are ineffective, Father. For you are empty. You have forsaken your vows. The Creator is not in you—He never was. For your eye offended you and it was plucked out. Do you not see?"

James's face filled with fear. "No, I am a priest—"

"And you gave it all away for the love of the mother." Mary smiled and her features twisted with an insane power.

James leaned over her with the Bible and began to chant once again. I had to get Mary out of here. I tore my arm from Molly's grasp and reached for her daughter. Mary suddenly sat up in the bed and struck me across the chest with a casual swing of her arm. With a power unlike anything I had felt, she threw me across the room. I landed on my back, the breath knocked out of me, and slid across the wet, moldy floor into a pile of equipment. IV stands clattered down on top of me and I gasped for breath. I struggled against the metal bones and managed to get to my feet.

"Cephas!" Molly screamed. She shoved James aside and grabbed the Bible from his hand. "You can renounce him, Mary. Claim the Lord as your protector."

Mary laughed. "I will release the child now that my true enemy has made himself known." She convulsed as if gripped by a mighty force. Something vile and dirty fluttered in the air above her. For a second, I saw a swirl of dark specks floating above the hospital bed.

"What is this?" the chimera's human head bellowed. "An ancient enemy challenges me? Behold the devouring fire of my god!" Behind James, the chimera reared up on its hind legs and the snake head came forward, spewing flames. The flames rushed across the floor to a tangle of old beds and examination tables, which exploded into flames that engulfed the hovering cloud of black specks.

James roared with anger. "I will stop you!"

"You have no power over me! I have taken your eye!" The chimera's snake tail lashed across the roof, spewing flames and crashing into James. He flew past me into the tangle of metal poles. One IV pole caught him in the neck, tearing through his skin as he collapsed. I ran from the flames to kneel beside him.

"Forgive me, Cephas," he said, reaching for me with bloody hands. "They used me to get the girl, but I never joined them. Never. You have to save Molly." Blood gushed across the floor as he gasped for breath. I grabbed a dirty towel from nearby and pressed it against his neck. Tears streamed from his eye.

"Now, do you believe?" he gasped. His one good eye rolled back in his head. Above me, the swirling cloud of particles from Mary coalesced with the flames to form a multijointed shape. It looked like something with a chitinous exterior and glittering scales. The creature charged the chimera. With a clap of thunder, the two demonic beings collided within the glowing cloud of fire.

Molly screamed. Her cry pierced the darkness and echoed off the cold walls. I looked up to see her holding Mary in her arms. The girl looked lifeless.

"Cephas, do something! Save her!" Molly screamed at me.

"I don't know what to do. I—" Smoke filled the air and I began to cough.

Molly's face was streaked with soot and tears. "You said you could save her. You promised!"

The Metastone peeked out from the folds of Molly's coat, dangled over Mary's motionless body. As it spun, it changed from pale green to dirty red. I ran to her and quickly lifted it over her head.

"What are you doing?"

"I don't know for sure. Lucas said to use the Metastone. It can save her." I placed the silver chain around Mary's neck and placed the stone gently over her heart. Nothing happened.

"Are you crazy?" Molly's gaze shifted from the stone to my face. "Who is Lucas?"

"The pale man," I mumbled. "He said it would save her. He told me to try—"

Molly hugged Mary to her. What was I doing? I was buying into this madness, this insanity! Demons and chimeras and magic stones! I grabbed Mary's still body and nodded toward the hallway. "Go find a phone and call for help, Molly. Go! I will do what I can. Go for help, now!"

Molly took one more look at her daughter and ran out of the old, abandoned ward even as blood from James's body puddled around my feet. Why had she died? Then the Metastone began to glow crimson with a slow pulsation. It drew me into its heart, into its substance. There, gathered for this mortal to see, was a shard of the beyond. For a brief moment, I saw all of eternity, from the unmaking of a perfect creation to the coming of the final judge. I saw! I believed—but it was too late for Mary.

Something burned my neck, breaking the stone's spell. I looked up just as the ceiling collapsed. I rolled aside as burning timbers enclosed Mary in a blanket of flame. I tried to get to her, but the ceiling continue to collapse. I ran out of the ward and into the frigid air. Molly was nowhere to be seen.

I looked up at Jonathan. "I had to decide who to help, you understand. This was in the days before cell phones and 911. I went after Molly and called the police when I reached the hospital. But Molly wasn't there. I tried every hospital in the area, but I never found her. The city was still in turmoil from Kennedy's assassination. No one could help me find a missing mother. The police told me the hospital had burned to the ground by the time they got there. They never found any bodies. I never saw Molly again."

I reached out and touched the picture. "I became a Christian shortly after that. I looked for Molly for years. This is how I became what I am. This is why I fight the demons and evil. One day, I will find Molly. One day."

Theo tapped the desktop. "You're telling me this white-eyed demon blackmailed Jack Ruby into killing Lee Harvey Oswald?"

"So they claimed." I shrugged. "These demonic presences have their hands in all of man's affairs, particularly politics. Kennedy's death and the subsequent conspiracy theories about it changed the landscape of Washington forever. We ended up in Vietnam. We were paralyzed by the oil embargo. Nixon resigned in shame. Authority tumbled and fell out of favor. The United States splintered into factions. And, it began with Kennedy. I had hoped that this secret group had vanished over time. But it would seem they are still very active, and now, they are in search of the Ark of the Demon Rose."

With relief I pushed aside the huge book whose evil still emanated from its pages. "Jonathan, we cannot go to the beach. We cannot leave this place for no other reason than our own protection. It would seem that these Vitreomancers are still working behind the scenes to change the world order in much the same way they did in 1963. I have often wondered how one man could assassinate the president as Oswald did. Whether or not they inspired him or indwelt him, the results were the same. They bring chaos and anarchy, and their master is the father of chaos. I can only conclude that if they get their hands on the Ark, it will further their cause. It will become the Ark of Chaos, and they will let no one stand in their way."

"You said the demon was a chimera?" Jonathan asked. "You also said the symbol for chaos was associated with the eleventh demon on the demon wheel. I think that confirms that we are dealing with the eleventh demon. What could be more chaotic than the form of the chimera?"

I gasped. Why hadn't I put those facts together? I had been in denial about Molly. I had allowed my past to cloud the present. "I have suffered from my own form of blindness. I did not want to revisit these memories but it would seem they confirm your conclusion, Jonathan. Chimera was the eleventh demon and he had white eyes. He is the power behind the Vitreomancers."

"Well, I don't know how things could get worse," Theo said.

"Give it time," I said. "Give it time."

"I met Lucas in Lakeside. In the vision given to me about the day I was born, Lucas was with a teenage Ketrick. And, now, you're telling us you met Lucas in 1963?" Jonathan asked.

"So it would seem. I had not revisited that memory, Jonathan. It was far too painful. Who is this creature?"

"Lucas. Vivian. The eleventh demon. Vitreomancers. Sounds like a typical day for Jonathan Steel," Jonathan said.

Chapter 29

Vivian Darbonne Ketrick

CALLED UPON THE power of my leech demon to heal the cut on my head and take care of my sore muscles. I got a call on my cell phone from the deputy. I ignored it. I was done flirting with normalcy. A few moments with Jonathan Steel at my side in the hospital room had proven too uncanny. I couldn't go down that path. My path was in another direction.

After a long, hot soak in the bath, I slept. The next morning, I walked across the street to Alba's office. I ignored the young thing behind the reception desk and marched straight into Alba's office.

She was sitting at the conference table drinking coffee and eating a piece of coffee cake. The cake was perfectly symmetrical. She had cut off small sections and was carefully placing them in her mouth. She glanced up at me, not in the least surprised I was there. She touched her ear. "Excuse me, Governor, I just had a rude interruption. I can assure you that everything will be in order for the fundraiser. Can I assume you will be announcing your candidacy for the nomination at the picnic? Ah, I thought so! I will have my assistants touch base with you again this afternoon." She touched her ear again and nibbled some more cake. "Good morning, Vivian. I wasn't aware we had a meeting."

"What happened yesterday?"

Alba chewed thoughtfully. She sipped some coffee and swallowed. "The market fell. Again. I had three meetings with the executives of three oil and gas companies. And we finalized the seating assignments for the governor's picnic. I am truly sorry you were not invited. That must disappoint you greatly."

"You know that is not what I'm talking about." I jerked a chair away from the table and sat down. "I went to serve my court order to Steel and someone tried to kill me."

"Kill you? Now, Vivian, don't exaggerate. Did the occupants resist the

180

court order? I hope you called the authorities." Alba tucked an errant strand of graying hair behind her ear.

"The authorities were with me. But you knew that. You waited until he left to unleash your attackers."

"My attackers? Vivian, I don't know what you are talking about."

"Six guys in a black SUV. Did your eye allergies clear up? Still having eye problems, just like those goons?"

"Eye problems?"

I leaned over the table. "White eyes. Big guns. Incredible strength. *Supernatural* strength."

Alba's face relaxed and she smiled. "I'm afraid you have me at a disadvantage. If you need security, I can arrange for a bodyguard."

I slapped the table. The woman didn't even flinch! "I don't know what you are, Alba. But know this: I am in line to take a seat on the Council of Darkness. I have worked toward this for years. I have friends and associates who could make your cronies look like Cub Scouts. Don't mess with me."

Alba carefully placed her knife and fork on the table. She sipped her coffee and slowly stood up. She placed her hands behind her back and walked around the table toward the window. The hem of her long beige dress brushed the carpet. "These 'white-eyed goons' you mention. You seem to think they are some kind of supernatural force. That would imply that you have some kind of supernatural connection. Perhaps you should be more specific."

I was breathing hard now. I followed her across the office. "I took out the thirteenth demon. Then I oversaw the downfall of the twelfth demon. Next week, I'm meeting with the Council of Darkness to claim my seat. And when I do, I will make sure you end up sucking on brimstone in Tartarus."

Alba turned. I was stunned to see her eyes were now white. She held out her hand and showed me two colored contact lenses. "My dear Vivian. I know all about your meeting next week. I'll be sitting at that table, and you will not."

"What?"

"I am number eleven. I will see to it that you never sit at the table, even if it means leaving the seat for number twelve vacant." She smiled. "I started my law firm in Europe. I have offices all over the western hemisphere. I was hoping we could work this out amicably. Do you think it was coincidence that I now represent your companies? I will take them from you and leave you rotting in some alley, Vivian. Then I will use your money to fuel the industry behind my influence on world governments."

I backed away from her hideous white eyes as she moved gracefully across the room. "You seem to think you have some kind of power with your bottom-feeding demons, but they are no better than catfish straining at fish dung. Don't presume to match wits with me, Vivian. I have seen things your demons can't even begin to remember. There is something bigger and grander here than your mortal mind could ever imagine." Those white eyes bored into mine. "I could melt you into a pile of goo right now with a mere thought. The reason I didn't come after you myself was because I have to keep my presence a secret. But know this: I will destroy you, and soon. So enjoy the hours you have left."

"But … you don't have the Ark, do you?" I whispered. My heart was racing and my demons were shriveling in fear of this being.

Alba paused and touched a well-manicured finger to her right eye. She wiped away a tear. "How do you know anything of the Ark?"

"Wulf told me to find it. He said it would give him an advantage over the council. Is that why you want it?"

"We thought it had been lost until you started searching through Ketrick's artifacts. I want my talisman back. It's a beautiful golden syringe I used to extract the eye fluid of a martyr."

"Who is 'we'?"

"The Vitreomancers, Vivian. I have overseen their growth over the centuries. We are the alternative to the Council. Competition is good for our kind. You of all people should appreciate that."

Alba pulled at the silver chain around her neck and slid a translucent green jewel from beneath her blouse. It hovered over her heart. She touched it and a wave of black-and-red energy passed over me. Sunlight gushed into my eyes. I turned around and found myself in the middle of a road. Horns blared. I jumped out of the way just as a pickup truck barreled toward me. The truck pulled over. I tried to sort out what had happened.

A man got out of the truck. He wasn't nearly as handsome as the deputy. "You all right, ma'am?"

I shook the confusion from my head. "Where am I?"

"What?"

"Where am I?" I screamed.

"Outside Baton Rouge," he said.

I drew a deep breath and, for the first time in a long time, felt fear. Alba had teleported me to south Louisiana. Maybe I had bitten off more than I could chew.

Chapter 30

Jonathan Steel

I SENT JOSH UPSTAIRS to play video games and asked Theo to keep an eye on him while I talked to Cephas. We sat across from one another at his desk in the basement. "Cephas, how bad is this?"

The old man ran his hands through his hair and frowned. "Jonathan, we thought the thirteenth demon was strong. Then Wulf showed up with an army of demon-possessed vampires. Now, these Vitreomancers have been killing and working their devilry for centuries. I am very afraid, Jonathan. Not just for you, but also for Josh. He has seen six of these Vitreomancers, as he calls them. And he was involved in the death of some of them."

"How would they know that? None of the assassins survived," I said.

Cephas pursed his lips. "Was the black SUV Josh mentioned still in our driveway when we came home from the hospital last night?"

"No." I kicked myself mentally. I had missed that very important detail. Think, Jonathan, think!

"Who do you think took it? Vivian was still in the emergency room when we left. I am certain these fiends clean up after themselves. The authorities will find no bodies in the lake, Jonathan, because the devotion of the Vitreomancers to secrecy is absolute. They will make certain that anyone who has come in contact with them never live to tell about it."

"That includes Vivian."

"Unfortunately for her."

"Josh said that Vivian couldn't come into the house. He said she had to be invited in." I got up and paced. "Does that mean that our prayers were answered? Are we being protected by a guardian angel?"

"That, my friend, is the only good news of today. It would seem God has afforded this house protection. But the Vitreomancers will not just up and disappear."

"What can we do to stop them?"

"Well, we can't run off to the beach."

I froze and the muscles of my right eye twitched. "I was trying to get Josh out of the line of fire, Cephas."

"And leave yourself out in the open as a target. Jonathan, there is a reason the four of us are together. Theo and I are here to help you with these demonic enemies."

"And to protect Josh," I said. "How do we stop the Vitreomancers and the eleventh demon?"

"I think the key to understanding this entire situation lies in these books and in that image we have of the Ark. If we can decipher what the image means, we might learn why the Ark is so important to the Vitreomancers and to Vivian."

"And our mysterious teleporter."

"Our teleporter is dead," Cephas said.

"But a demon teleported Destillo, and that demon has the Ark, Cephas."

"And I am afraid that that demon with the Ark may be number eleven." Cephas stood up and went to his computer table, and picked up his tablet. "As I mentioned earlier, the diagram on the Ark is more complex than the one on the document that was also taken. There was more than one layer on it."

"Josh said that Vivian called it the Ark of the Demon Rose."

"Yes, and she also mentioned that the rose was like a compass rose."

"Fine, so what is a compass rose?"

"It is the physical representation of north, south, east and west on a map. The rose compass establishes the directions on the map to correlate with the real world." Cephas turned the tablet to face me. He brought up the image of a compass rose on the screen. "There are thirty-two different points named on a compass; naming them is called 'boxing the rose.' The name 'rose' comes from the ornate nature of these illustrations on ancient maps. The Romans favored a compass rose with twelve points on it, each point representing thirty degrees. The most ornate were created by the Portuguese in a colorful style known as Manueline."

I looked at the colorful images on the screen. Some were incredibly ornate with overlapping lines and shapes and multiple colors. Some were very simple with triangular arrows for each of the four main directions. "The Romans used a twelve-point compass rose?"

"Later on in the Middle Ages, the compass rose used sixteen points. So if the image we saw on my document is indeed part of this demon rose, then it dates back to Roman times." Cephas turned the laptop back toward himself.

"According to the legend of the thirteenth demon, Satan chose his twelve demons when Christ chose his twelve disciples."

"Which would have been during the time of Judea under Roman rule. Could your framed document date back that far?"

Cephas shook his head. "I had it dated. I believe it is a copy of the original. But that doesn't change the fact that the diagram had twelve points, one for each demon. And, the compass rose has twelve points. Here, beneath the number eleven, is a symbol." He picked up a pen from the desk and scrawled a symbol on a pad. A large circle sat beneath a smaller circle. He placed a dot in the larger circle and then drew a small cross atop the upper circle. "This symbol was also painted over the image of Vivian in Destillo's garage. It is the symbol for chaos. Jonathan, if I am not mistaken, the Ark of the Demon Rose is somehow being sought by the eleventh demon. The chimera is a symbol for chaos also. The eleventh demon is here and somewhere, somehow, involved in all of this. I just don't know how."

I stood up and leaned over the table. "Then I need to let you get to work on these composite images from the Ark, don't I?"

Cephas nodded. "I will do my best to see what other layers were added to the original twelve-pointed diagram. I imagine the metal seal on top of the chest is the final part of the demon rose, as Vivian called it. And if so, it could literally point the way to each member of the Council of Darkness."

"If the eleventh demon is here," I said, pausing at the foot of the stairs, "where do the Vitreomancers fit in?"

Cephas's tired eyes widened and he shook his head. "The thirteenth demon had his Eagle Warriors. The twelfth demon has his army of vampires. It would seem the eleventh demon has the Vitreomancers."

Josh Knight

"Dude, I'm not staying here," I shouted at Jonathan. "I'm going with you and Theo."

"No, you are not going, Josh." Jonathan picked up the keys to the truck. "You're staying here with Cephas while he researches the demon rose."

I slammed my hand on the island. "I am sick and tired of staying behind, Bro."

Jonathan grabbed my arm and pulled me up off of the stool in the kitchen.

185

His face was red and I realized I had pushed him too far. His iron grip hurt like heck. "You are protected while you are inside this house, Josh. These Vitreomancers are dangerous and they will be coming back for you. Understand?"

I jerked my arm out of his grasp. "That hurt!"

"Not as much as the Vitreomancers will hurt you." He looked away and calmed his breathing. "I'm sorry. I can't lose you again, Josh. I can't."

I rubbed my arm and settled back on the stool. "What makes you think meeting with the FBI would be dangerous?"

"Agent Cornelius asked us to meet her at Ketrick's old office. She's here for the governor's security task force at the picnic today. But she said she found something that links Vivian and the Ark. Vivian may be there, and I don't want you around Vivian."

"Afraid I'll save her life again?"

Jonathan leaned into me with those freaking eyes of his. "Afraid you'll get killed this time. The Vitreomancers are out there somewhere, and they don't leave loose ends. You're not leaving the house."

"Can I at least go swimming?"

"I don't know, Josh," Jonathan rasped. He was breathing hard as he paced at the end of the island. "I don't know what to tell you. We have protection while you are *in* this house. Vivian couldn't come in. I don't know if that includes the pool. There isn't an instruction manual for all of this." He frowned. "Why did you save Vivian?"

I wasn't expecting that. I shrugged. "I don't know."

"You couldn't let her die, could you?"

"I could." Theo closed the kitchen door behind him. He was carrying a gym bag. "Let the Vitreomancers have her."

"No one deserves to die, Theo. We all need a second chance," Jonathan said.

"Wait a minute, Chief. I thought we were just meeting Cornelius at Vivian's office to put the FBI on the trail of these Vitreomancers. You saying Vivian is going to be there?"

Jonathan nodded. "Vivian needs to know what she is up against. She needs to know that the eleventh demon is coming after her with his Vitreomancers."

"Why?" Theo asked. "Man, I say let her fry."

Jonathan was very still. "I can't, Theo."

"Dude! Don't tell me you feel sorry for her," I said.

"She helped us and she said she saved your life."

I squirmed on the stool. "Yeah, so?"

"When God tells me to save someone, I have to listen. It's why I came after you when the thirteenth demon took you. It's why I went after Theo."

"Did God tell you to save Vivian? She's the queen of demons, Jonathan!" Theo shouted.

Jonathan picked up the keys and headed toward the door. "He didn't tell me not to."

Chapter 31

Vivian

I WAS SHAKEN. I was scared. I was mad! How dare Alba pull this cheap parlor trick and teleport me to Baton Rouge! I had my private jet pick me up and was back in Shreveport by the afternoon. By two o'clock, I was pulling up to the office in Lakeside in the rental car. I had to figure how to deal with this. Alba was the eleventh demon? And she controlled the white-eyed army that could be turned against the Council? I mentally kicked myself for not having expected it. Of course there were rivals to the Council. Hadn't the thirteenth demon been a loose cannon?

A police car pulled up behind mine and I recognized the man behind the wheel. Weston stepped out in his hat and sunglasses. "Vivian? I've been looking for you. Jerome said you were going to your Lakeside office."

For a moment I was irritated, but then Summer showed up inside my mind and whispered, *You can use him.* Maybe he could help me inside. "Weston, honey child, am I so glad to see you. I have an axe to grind with a certain lawyer who is operating very much outside the law." I leaned up against him and felt the compact heat of his body. "I know we had a little tiff, but I'm willing to let bygones be bygones. Will you help me?"

"Of course, Vivian."

"Then come with me to my office while I set up a meeting with Lynn Alba. Then you and I will go pay her a visit and straighten all of this out."

I marched up the stairs into reception. Reggie was sitting at the desk and talking on the phone. When he saw me, his eyes widened in shock. He slammed the phone down onto the cradle.

"Mrs. Ketrick? I didn't know you were coming in today."

I ignored him and headed for my office. He ran out from behind the desk and intercepted me. "You might not want to go in there."

I glared at him. He was sweating and it was more than just the August heat. "Why?"

"Since Mr. Ketrick died, we decided to redecorate the office for you." he stuttered.

"You're a terrible liar, Reggie."

He glanced over my shoulder at Weston. Suddenly the fear was gone and his countenance changed. He smoothed down his polo shirt and nodded. "Go on in. They know you're coming now." He opened the door for me.

A man sat behind my desk with his back to me. Two men in sunglasses and dark suits stood at either side of the door. The man behind my desk turned. His sunglasses were pushed up into his hair. His white eyes gleamed at me. He pulled at his collar where his neck was covered in rope burns and an ugly red bruise. My teeth marks marred his cheek.

"Vivian," he said.

I turned to run from the room but Weston blocked my way. He pulled off his sunglasses. His eyes were white. "Don't run, Vivian. It is better this way."

"You traitor! Get your hands off me before I unleash my demons." I tried to jerk out of his grasp.

"My demon would eat them alive." His white eyes began to glowed with that crimson hue. "Honey child!"

"You pretended to be the Master?"

Weston nodded. "With his permission, I might add. We had to get you back on track to help us find the Ark."

I pulled away and backed into the room. "Who are you people?"

"We are the Vitreomancers, Vivian," Gamaliel said.

"That means nothing to me."

"Of course it means nothing to you. We came here looking for the Ark, but you don't have it. If you had found the Ark of the Demon Rose and managed to open it, we wouldn't be having this conversation."

"If you are so powerful, what good is the Ark to you?"

The man shrugged. "I'm not the person who wants it."

"Alba." I practically spit the name out. "What does she want with it? What is in the Ark?"

"What do you think is in it?" the man asked.

I could lie or I could tell the truth. I chose a mixture of the two. "Secrets," I whispered. "Names, organizations, power and influence over the Council."

"Not bad." Gamaliel came around the desk. "But your expectations are very, very low, Vivian. He who controls the Ark of the Demon Rose controls all of the master's minions."

So it was true. That was why Wulf had wanted it. A realization dawned on me, and my eyebrows arched. "Twelve disciples, twelve demons. Ark of the Covenant, Ark of the Demon Rose." My skin crawled at the implications.

"You are slow, aren't you?"

Reggie entered and whispered in his ear. Gamaliel nodded and looked at me. "You have visitors, Vivian. But I'm afraid you are going to be indisposed."

He pulled a Taser out of his coat pocket and aimed it at me. I was about to get a dose of my own medicine.

Theophilus Nosmo King

Should I tell Jonathan? I drove the truck toward Lakeside and glanced over my shoulder at my gym bag sitting in the back seat. I had very few items left from my former life. After the crack house had burned down, I had nothing. But I had hidden a small lockbox behind the crack house and retrieved it before we left Dallas for Shreveport. One of the items inside was my collapsible ASP baton from my days with the police. After Vivian had Tased me, I had dug it out of my lockbox. I got the feeling Jonathan didn't like guns. And, it was a much better club than a bloody leg bone!

"Chief, do you own a gun?" I asked.

Jonathan looked at me with those weird eyes of his. "No."

"What are we going to do if these Vitreomancers show up?"

"Fight them."

Jonathan may have saved my life, but he had a lot to learn about the street. "Jonathan, you ever wonder why God sent you to save me?"

"Sometimes."

"Maybe God sent you to save me so I would have your back. Let me ask you another question. Why do you care so much about Vivian?"

Jonathan glanced out the side window. "I don't know. I don't like it, but, I can't give up on her. I almost gave up on Raven, but God told me to give her a second chance. When she turned away from her bad side and embraced God again, it saved all of our lives. I guess everyone deserves a second chance. You of all people should understand that."

"I haven't tried to kill you two times."

"No, you only tried once."

Ouch, that hurt! I swallowed and nodded. "You're right. I was supposed to shoot you that night. But I didn't, Jonathan. The good Lord stopped me."

"When He wants me to stop saving people, He'll stop me, too,," Jonathan said.

We entered downtown Lakeside and Jonathan gestured at the southern-mansion-style office building on the south side of the street. "That's Ketrick's old office. Cornelius is supposed to be there."

I pulled into a parking spot and killed the truck engine. "Chief, do we have a plan?"

Jonathan was silent as the hot August afternoon soaked into the truck. "Just keep that baton of yours ready." He got out while I tried to hide my surprise.

I slid the ASP out of the bag and tucked it into my right sock, then I followed him up the steps into the building. "How did you know?"

"You got my back." He held the door open and we stepped into the cool interior.

"Man, you keep surprising me."

At the reception desk, a young man was talking on the telephone. He finished his call and smiled at us.

"How may I help you?"

"We're here to see FBI Special Agent Ross," Jonathan said. He headed for a hallway to the left. "He's supposed to meet us here along with Agent Cornelius."

"Sir, you can't go in there." The man stood up.

"Then stop me." Jonathan's voice faded. I looked at the guy and shrugged. I followed Jonathan. He pushed open two huge wooden doors and led me into a big office that was empty except for a chrome desk and chair in the middle of the room. The chair swiveled around. The man sitting in the chair had a rope burn around his neck and empty white eyes. Steel was over the desk and onto the man before I could even move. I felt hands grabbing me from behind. I whirled around, pulling out of the grasp of two men in black suits flanking the doors.

"You missed me, didn't you?" I shouted. "Hallelujah, Jesus, I need to kick some demon butt!"

I plowed into one of the men, driving him through the open office doors and out to the foyer. The other man pulled a gun and aimed it at me. I grabbed the receptionist's phone and hurled it across the room at him. The wire tore out of the wall and the phone hit the man dead in the face. As he fell back, the gun fired, but the bullet went through the ceiling. The man I had knocked onto the floor somersaulted back up into the air and landed on top of the reception desk. He kicked out and his foot caught me in the left cheek. Pain exploded through my head, but I had seen it coming enough to roll with the blow. I grabbed the man's foot and pulled him down with me. He fell and landed on the edge of the desk with a thud.

The gunman had recovered from the blow to his face. His sunglasses were shattered and fell away in tinkling glass. I could see his white eyes glaring in my direction. He raised the gun again and I whirled around, swinging the first man by the foot and hurling him into the gunman. They both flew through the doors back into the office. I got up from the floor, my face stinging, and followed them in. Steel and the rope-burn man were grappling on the floor.

Suddenly, I felt cold metal kiss the back of my neck. "If you don't want to see your partner's brains all over the wall, you'll stop now!" I glanced over my shoulder. The receptionist was holding a gun to my neck. "My name's Reggie, by the way."

Jonathan stood up slowly and let the rope-burn man get up off the floor. He straightened his tie and pushed Jonathan toward me.

"I should have killed you at the cabin. Now, the two of you will cooperate, or one of you will die," he said.

I looked at Jonathan. He shook his head slightly. I guess we were playing along. Reggie was holding the gun in my face now. "I ain't never been taken prisoner by a secretary before."

Reggie's face twisted hatefully. "There's a first time for everything." He backhanded me with the gun.

Chapter 32

Cephas Lawrence

HERE WERE THREE levels to the grainy images I had extracted from the fabric that had been wrapped around the chest. I began an exhaustive search on the Internet for similar images. The compass rose from the Roman era was the most prominent feature. The twelve Roman numerals must each correlate to a demon. That made sense. Someone had drawn the original circle diagram during the Roman era, when the original twelve were chosen.

I closed my eyes and tried to imagine the document. I was such a fool for not having made a backup. Think, Cephas! There had been several more images beneath the numerals. Some of the words were in Latin. This made more sense now that I knew the compass rose dated from the Roman era.

I pulled up an image of an overlapping diagram that had been dropped onto the original circle. It was a ring contained six pointed, narrow triangles that radiated from a small circle containing a strange image. It looked like a head surrounded by three legs at an angle with the feet forming a kind of spiral. Surrounding the strange head and legs were the petals of a rose.

Each one of the six triangles pointed out to the periphery of the ring. Surrounding the ring were eight figures. I had studied the rose of the winds, a rose compass with letters that stood for the names of the four winds, Boreas, Burus, Notus, and Zephyrus. At the top of the circle, there should have been a fleur-de-lis, and the East point should have been a Maltese cross representing Jerusalem. But in this diagram, the fleur-de-lis had been replaced by an inverted cross, and instead of a Maltese cross, there was an inverted V. What could this mean?

The letters at the other points of the compass rose were symbols I could not identify. Nestled in the gap between two of the inner circles was a tiny figure that looked like a cross with two small circles at the top. I squinted. A syringe? The inner symbol for number eleven looked like a syringe. In the warehouse with Molly, Chimera had said something about his talisman—his syringe! Was that what was hidden inside the Ark? Could the Ark perhaps contain the talismans belonging to the members of the Council?

Beneath the syringe was a multifaceted stone. In fact, an inner ring matched a stone or gem to each of the numerals and their symbols. I placed several filters on the image and magnified the stone beneath the syringe. Underneath it were four letters in Latin. I mouthed them and my heart almost stopped. "Meta?" I said out loud. "The Metastone!"

I heard the landline ring and heard Josh upstairs answering it. I met him at the top of the stairs. His face was pale and his eyes were wide.

"They said I have to go outside," he whispered.

"What?" I looked at the portable phone in his hand. "Who said to go outside?"

"Gamaliel. He survived the boat explosion. He said if I want to see Jonathan and Theo alive again, I have to go outside."

"Absolutely not!" I took the phone from him. "Josh, we're safe in here."

His face was white as a sheet. "Uncle Cephas, I just remembered that one of the six dudes came inside this house to see if the Ark was here. How did he do that if we're protected?"

"Was he wearing sunglasses?"

Josh's brow furrowed in thought. "No, come to think of it. And his eyes were normal!"

"An apprentice. There is always an apprentice in each sextet. He is not under the control of demonic forces. He can go anywhere."

"Then why haven't they sent an apprentice in here?"

"Because the only apprentice in this area is dead. They probably don't have another one."

Josh started for the door. "I can't let them kill Jonathan, Uncle Cephas. I can't."

Before I could stop him, he opened the kitchen door and stepped outside.

Josh Knight

I've done some pretty stupid things in life. Running out the back door was definitely one of them. But I wanted to keep Uncle Cephas safe. Instead, the old man ran out after me. I turned and shoved him back toward the door.

"Get back inside. Someone has to stay safe, Uncle Cephas. Someone has to get us out of this mess."

Uncle Cephas stumbled back toward the door. Three shadows fell over the ground around me. Three Vitreomancers were standing in the driveway. One of them was a woman with bright-red hair. Her eyes were normal.

"Agent Cornelius?" Uncle Cephas gasped behind me.

Cornelius reached up to her eyes and pulled out a set of contacts. Her eyes were dead white. "Sorry, Dr. Lawrence, but I need your nephew."

Uncle Cephas backed into the kitchen door. "Josh, if you hurry, you can get back inside."

"And they'll kill Jonathan," I said. "Just get inside and send help."

Uncle Cephas looked stricken. One of the Vitreomancers moved toward him. Cephas stepped back inside just as he tossed what looked like a hand grenade at the open door. Uncle Cephas gasped. I lurched in his direction but Cornelius latched onto my arm. The grenade bounced off of thin air, rolled back toward us, and began emitting tear gas.

We all stepped back. Cornelius grabbed my other arm from behind. Her grip was tight. "Too bad you came voluntarily, Josh. You gave up your protection. Let's go."

She led me away from the house. Uncle Cephas disappeared behind the growing cloud of smoke. They shoved me into the back seat of the SUV. Cornelius sat beside me. The other two Vitreomancers were in front.

"No apprentice?" I asked.

Cornelius flinched and turned her dead eyes on me. "Vivian killed him. I had to act fast to replace the other members of the sextet. Reflection, let's go," she said to the driver.

I settled into the back seat and tried to calm my racing heart. It didn't take long to circumvent the lake and arrive in Lakeside. We passed the old church site. I saw a flash of Mama Liz and Ashley, but they were oblivious to the passage of the car. A mile from the old church, the SUV turned onto a long driveway lined by towering oak trees. After a while, the road opened up onto a clearing. A huge log cabin sat in the center and a lawn stretched out in front of it. Tables covered the open area as far as the eye could see. Near the log cabin, a dais had been set up with microphones and a stand. People milled about the lawn, preparing the tables and equipment.

"What is going on?"

"The governor will be announcing his candidacy for the presidency this afternoon." A security agent with an FBI badge motioned us past him. I tried to lower the window, but it was locked. We pulled around behind the cabin and the driver headed into the woods. Tree limbs scratched at the car and it came to a halt on a low rise. I looked out over Redcross Bayou. This must have been where Theo had fallen into the water.

"Why are we here?"

"Because, young man, you are minding the getaway boat. Remember how you and your accomplice, Vivian Ketrick, tested out your getaway on Cross Lake and blew up the ski boat?" Cornelius opened her door. One of the other Vitreomancers opened mine and pulled me out.

"What?"

Cornelius led us over to the edge of the bluff. Twenty feet below us, a bass boat was tied up and bobbing in the current of the bayou. "Unfortunately for you, I will stop your escape. I will be using lethal force, Josh. One has to when the governor has been assassinated."

I stood there open-mouthed as she got back into the SUV, leaving me in the hands of a Vitreomancer.

Chapter 33

Cephas Lawrence

I WAS DISTRAUGHT BEYOND reasoning. What could I do to help Josh? I started for the back door but a shadow passed through the dissipating grenade smoke and coalesced into the face of a young girl. Her hair was long and greasy and her eyes were tiny irises floating in a sea of red. She opened her mouth and cockroaches fell out. It was Mary.

I closed my eyes and backed away from the door. "No, you're dead!"

"Hello, Cephas," her voice grated through the window. "Won't you invite me in to play? I'd like to play with you. You left me to die in that fire. Don't you remember?"

I turned away from her memory and hurried across the room to the stairs leading down to the basement. My heart was pounding and my head was killing me. I reached my desk and sat down, gasping for breath.

"You're only a demon trying to deceive me," I mumbled. "Lord, I need help. Take these apparitions from me."

"Well, it's about time."

I looked up to see a young man sitting across from me. He was thin and probably in his early twenties with short, dark, curly hair, and he wore a set of green surgical scrubs.

"Who are you? If you are a demon, then I cast you out in the name of my Lord and Savior, Jesus Christ!"

"Good. You should have said that earlier. Of course I am not a demon. We serve the same Master, Cephas."

My mouth fell open in shock. "You are an angel?"

"I am a messenger of God sent to this house to afford it protection. Isn't that what you prayed for?"

"Yes, yes, that is what we prayed for. But Josh and Jonathan and Theo are not here."

197

"All will be well, Cephas. Do not let the enemy shake your faith. What you have just seen upstairs cannot exist, can it?"

I stared at the desktop in thought. "No. She died decades ago. It was my fault."

"Humans must live with the consequences of their decisions, Cephas. So must we. Every creature that has ever sprung from the mind of the Creator must make choices. Even our Savior. Pain comes from such choices. But there is also joy. Do not dwell on the pain, Cephas. Now, ask yourself the Question."

I gazed into the eyes of the angel. "What is the Question?"

"What is the lie?"

I thought about his words. *What is the lie?* The demon was lying to me. Deception was the most powerful tool of Satan. He was the father of chaos. Yes, that was the key! "The young woman could not have returned to haunt me."

"You have burdened yourself with the doubt and guilt of a lie, Cephas. Satan is the father of lies. Throw off that guilt. Relieve yourself of that burden. Cast all your cares upon our Master."

I nodded as a flicker of relief blossomed somewhere in my heart. "What must I do?"

"Go help your friends. The enemy is trying to scare you into staying here, in this house. For, Cephas, you are the key to victory over this demon. But, your guilt has given the enemy power over you. Without that chink in your armor, they cannot stop you."

I felt power grow within me. I closed my eyes and reveled in it. It had eluded me for decades. Now my confidence and my assurance deepened. "Thank you, Lord. Will you go with me?" I whispered. But when I opened my eyes, the young man was gone.

I hurried up the stairs to the kitchen door. The thing was still there. I threw open the door and stepped out of the entryway. The girl backed away. Worms were crawling from her open sores. Spiders were scurrying over her torn and rotting dress. Her face was covered in blisters and pus ran down her neck. "Come to me, Cephas," she hissed.

I saw the thing for what it was. This was not the girl who had come to me for help. This was not the girl whose ordeal had hastened me into the fight against the evil of Satan. I smiled. "Sorry, but you must go away, little one. In the name of my Lord and Savior, Jesus Christ, be gone!"

The thing's eyes widened and it started to scream. It was not an ordinary scream. It was not a human scream. It was strident and unearthly and contained the pain of uncountable millennia. Insects exploded away from her body and the tattered dress fell to the ground, empty. The spiders and worms and cockroaches rushed away from me as the demon disappeared. I smiled. "One down, dozens to go."

A small car pulled into the driveway. I backed inside the open doorway, just in case. Bile climbed out of the car. His hair was in disarray and his tie was crooked. His face was sweaty and pale.

"Tell me she is here!"

"Who?"

"Vivian! I drove over from Dallas to help out. The Lakeside office looks like a fight took place. I can't find her anywhere. I thought she might be silly enough to come back here for that thing she's been looking for." He ran his hands through his thin hair.

"Vivian is not here, young man. I do not know where she is. Jonathan and Theo left for her office to meet her and Agent Cornelius. And the Vitreomancers came and took Josh."

"Vitreomancers? Who?"

"It is a long story. If they are not at her office, then where can they be?"

Bile paced back and forth in the penetrating heat of the August afternoon. "She had nothing on her agenda. Two days ago, she met with Ms. Alba to sign over the log cabin, yesterday, she had a massage appointment ..."

"Wait!" I stepped out of the house into the sunlight. "The log cabin! Ketrick's log cabin! That is why Theo found a body in that room in the basement. It was just one of Ketrick's unfortunate victims. Oh my goodness! The governor is having a picnic there today—" The realization hit me like a ton of falling bricks. I stumbled back and grabbed the threshold of the doorway. "The governor! Oh, no, it's happening again! We have to get to that log cabin. Do you know where it is?"

Bile nodded. "I have it on my GPS. I am supposed to deliver some papers there tomorrow."

I hurried into the house. In our hasty move, I had lost my cell phone. Jonathan was the only one with a phone. I picked up the cordless. No phonebook. How could I get ahold of Ross? But if Ross was with Jonathan and Theo, he might be a prisoner now too. I shuffled out to Jerome. "Let's just go. I'm sure there is security at the picnic. We can warn them."

I climbed into the hot interior of his little car. He slid behind the steering wheel.

"Warn them about what?"

"That someone is going to try to assassinate the governor."

Chapter 34

Jonathan Steel

"THIS IS THE same room I was in the other day," Theo mumbled. "They didn't even clean up the bones."

I paced around the room. My head felt like it had been through a wringer. Since we had awoken in the room, nothing had happened. "We're under Ketrick's log cabin! Why didn't I figure that out! Bile mentioned it in Dallas. And, it's right by Redcross Bayou."

"That's the river I fell into, Chief. And it emptied into the Red River. Chief! Remember what's happening here today?"

I paused. My skin crawled. "The picnic. The governor."

I heard them coming down the hallway. Theo backed away as the lock clicked. The door opened and shadows moved in the hallway.

"Back up or you're dead."

I recognized the voice before she stepped into the room. Regina Cornelius's white eyes glowed in the meager light. "Hello, boys."

"You?" I growled. Another Vitreomancer moved in behind her with a pistol in his hand. "What is going on?"

"I'm just protecting our assets. Of course, in a little while, you'll become liabilities, and I'll have to shoot you during your escape attempt."

"Escape?" Theo said.

"Right after the governor dies." She winked one of those chilling white eyes at me and smiled.

Cephas Lawrence

The terrain was very rough. We had pulled Bile's car into the woods after being turned back by security at the end of the driveway. No matter how I tried to convince them of what was going on, they ignored me. Such is the blindness of bureaucracy. It seemed the governor was still giving his speech to the Chamber of Commerce and was delayed. Car after car pulled up to the driveway. A huge limousine took guests down the road while a valet parked the cars down the street in an open field.

In the papers he had to deliver, Bile had a map of the property. We had taken a dirt road that led in from the side and pulled up to a small barn at the rear corner of the property. Why that road had not been secured was beyond me. Now we were standing at the edge of the clearing just a few yards away from the barn. There were no security forces in sight. Why? Someone moved in the open doorway of the barn's upper level. It was one of the Vitreomancers with gleaming sunglasses and a semi-automatic gun.

"She's up there," Jerome said.

"How do you know?" I was gasping for breath in the heat and humidity.

He didn't answer but ran across the open yard toward the barn. I sighed and shuffled after him. I followed Bile into the cool interior. It was a typical barn with open stalls on each side and a floor covered in old hay and manure. A steep set of stairs led up to a loft divided into right-hand and left-hand sections. The Vitreomancer moved across our line of vision and Bile pulled me into a stall.

"She's up there." Bile pointed up at the second level. "You go up the stairs and distract the gunman. I'll come up from behind."

Before I could protest, he shoved me out into the open. I stumbled, stepped into a pile of dried horse manure, and fell back onto my tailbone on a pile of hay. The Vitreomancer peered over the edge of the upper level.

"You! Stay right there," he barked at me.

I slowly stood up as pain lanced down my legs. The Vitreomancer hurried down the stairs and pointed his gun at me. "How did you get here?"

"I wouldn't shoot that if I were you. It would mess up your big plans," I managed to say through clenched teeth. The man opened his mouth to speak and suddenly lurched. The tines of a pitchfork shot through the front of his chest. Blood spurted over the hay. He dropped his gun and fell over.

Bile was standing behind the man. He rubbed his hands together. "He's been forked."

He turned and hurried up the stairs. I followed, casting a forlorn look at the dead Vitreomancer. Upstairs, Vivian was tied to a chair near the front of the barn, beside a closed door facing the lawn. Her mouth was taped shut and next to her was a rifle on a tripod. Her eyes widened at the sight of Bile.

"Miss Vivian!" He tenderly pulled the tape from her mouth. "Are you okay?"

"Yes, you idiot!" she screamed. "Untie me so I can teach that witch a lesson."

"What is going on, Vivian?" I asked.

Bile untied her and she rubbed her hands. "I am to be the assassin, old man! She wants to pin it all on me. Where is she?"

"The witch is right here."

At the stop of the stairs stood the deputy from the hospital next to a Vitreomancer with a rope burn on his neck. Both had white eyes. Below us, a woman in a long beige dress smiled up at us. "Who's your visitor?"

After securing Vivian again, the man with the rope burn, Gamaliel, had brought Bile and me to the cabin, while the deputy had stayed behind with Vivian. Inside the log cabin, Gamaliel left Bile tied up in the back hallway and shoved me through the doors of a huge, rectangular room. It would have been inviting under any other circumstances. Windows on the outer wall looked out over the yard. Soft leather couches and chairs were arranged on a tiled floor that was dotted here and there with rugs in a Southwestern motif. To my left was a huge wooden table surrounded by thick wooden chairs. At the far end of the room was a spacious kitchen with a small fireplace. The ceiling stretched up to the second-floor roof. The room was dominated by the huge stone fireplace to my right. It was large enough to walk into and the mantel was an intricate interwoven pattern of antlers supporting a mahogany shelf above which hung a painting of Robert Ketrick in his Aztec regalia. His hair was long and black and his bare chest glistened with sweat. His noble features were festooned with colorful streaks of paint, and he wore a heavy cloth skirt. His right hand was raised above his head, holding the reproduction hummingbird knife he had used for his aborted sacrifice under the church in Lakeside.

The willowy woman from the barn had been waiting for me here. Her dark hair was peppered with gray, and around her neck was a silver chain that disappeared into her blouse. She fixed me with a gaze not unlike that of a hungry boa constrictor. Her eyes were not white, but they were, no doubt, covered by contacts. She walked slowly over to a window and pulled aside the curtain. Outside, people were gathering for the picnic.

"The governor will be late," I said. "Late for his own assassination."

"Do you know who I am, old man?" She said in carefully measured tones as she let the curtain close.

Gamaliel pushed me down into a chair and I struggled with my memory. Her face was so familiar. "The eleventh demon, I presume. And master of the Vitreomancers. Does the Council know of your divided loyalty?"

She raised an eyebrow and a thin smile creased her lips. "Ms. Alba will do for now. And as to my loyalty, let us just say that the Master tolerates divided loyalty as long as his plans are advanced. The Vitreomancers may, at times, be adverse to the workings of the Council. But our ultimate goal is the same: chaos." She nodded toward Gamaliel. "You may go keep an eye on Vivian's assistant."

Gamaliel tensed at my side. "Madame, you may be in danger."

Ms. Alba chuckled and brushed her hair back. "I am in no danger, Gamaliel. Dr. Lawrence and I are old friends. Now go."

Old friends? Where had we met? Gamaliel sighed and left through the inner doors, pulling them shut and leaving the two of us in the room alone.

"You have me at a disadvantage, Ms. Alba. Which one of you have I met? The demon or the host?"

Ms. Alba studied me for a moment, choosing her words carefully. She slid a finger beneath the silver chain and pulled. A shining, pale-green jewel came into view, dangling over her chest. "Both, it would seem, Dr. Lawrence."

I slowly stood up. My mouth grew dry and my blood ran cold. "Where did you get that?"

"You placed it around my neck when I was but a child."

"Mary?"

"My full name is Marilyn. I am known professionally as Lynn Alba, but you knew me as Mary. I was but a child when you let me die, Dr. Lawrence. But, as you can see, I'm all grown up now."

"But you were dead. I saw you die. I saw James pierced by the IV pole. Both of you were dead!" I was weak and nauseous.

Alba slowly advanced on me, her dark eyes glittering with malice. "You and my mother left me for dead! The demon came to me and resuscitated me with the Metastone." She touched the jewel. "It takes life and it gives life, Uncle Cephas. But in giving life, it demands complete loyalty. In time I became his host. That was the price for my life. Now, where is my mother?"

"I have no idea," I whispered. My mind was racing as it tried to assimilate this information. "She left to get help. That was the last time I ever saw her."

I felt her cold hand on my chin. "I know you have put every effort into finding her. I knew about the penthouse loft in New York City where you collected arcane artifacts over the years, not to combat evil, but in hopes of finding her. Who do you think urged the city to buy your building? I did, old man. I knew if I took away your last refuge, you would break."

I jerked my chin out of her grasp. "But that did not happen, did it? I am stronger now. I am with Jonathan Steel and together, we will bring your organization to its knees!"

Mary laughed and tossed her hair as she turned and went to the fireplace. "You have no idea who or what you are dealing with, old man. I and the eleventh demon have been working together to infiltrate every country. We have removed leaders who stood in our way. That was my function in the dealings in Dallas: to make Jack Ruby think I was his illegitimate child and to coerce him to do what he did."

"To cover up your meddling?"

"To place the blame where it truly belonged. 1963 is when it all began." She smiled and rubbed the Metastone. "When the Supreme Court outlawed prayer in school, millions of innocent voices crying out to your God were silenced in one glittering moment. It didn't take long until America was mired in Vietnam. Authorities tumbled. Chaos ruled! We broke the world, Cephas! We broke it."

"You're boasting, Mary," I said. "God is still in control."

Mary laughed. "But man still has free will. Every man makes a choice, Dr. Lawrence. No one is ever made to do anything. All I do is facilitate the decision process in our favor. We will establish a legal presence in every government legislature, in every government's executive branch. The Vitreomancers have worked behind the scenes and now our worldwide network is far more extensive than anything conceived of by the Council of Darkness." She paused and glared at me. With one quick motion, she plucked the contacts from her eyes. Her lifeless white orbs glistened, cold and harsh. "I may be blind, but I see far more than any mere human ever could, Dr. Lawrence. I know who will win this confrontation. I know who will one day control this world. It will be my Vitreomancers, and I will be the empress over all of humanity."

"At what price? Your soul? What happens when your master is done with you? What are a few decades of fame and glory compared to an eternity of darkness? This life you live is only due to the power of your Metastone and ultimately, your demon. When he is done with you, you will die. Will your white-eyed minions care when your body lies rotting in its grave?" I shuffled toward her, pointing my crooked finger at her haughty eyes. "You cannot even find your own mother! You had to work behind the scenes to oust an old man from his building to try to find her! Your power is a mirage. You will fail. For

I see far better than you will ever see. I see this world with the reflected light of the Savior. In this world, there is darkness. But He is the light of the world, and one day, every knee shall bow to Him. Not to you!"

"That is a fine speech, Cephas old chap."

We both turned. Father James Caskey stood just inside the doors. His blonde hair was combed just as it had been on the last night I had seen him. His features were youthful and untouched by time. His pale-blue eyes glimmered with mischief. *Both* eyes were blue.

Chapter 35

Vivian Darbonne Ketrick

ESTON TOOK OFF his hat and squatted beside my chair. His ghostly white eyes were inches from mine.

"Did you miss me, baby?" He leaned forward to kiss me. I tried to unleash my demons but the things wallowed in fear of his demon. I bit Weston's lip and he pulled away. I spat his own blood into his face. He smiled.

"I guess we're breaking up?"

I struggled against the duct tape holding my arms behind the chair. "What happens after you shoot the governor?"

He wiped the blood from his face and removed his shirt leaving him in a white tee shirt. "I will tell the FBI that you invited me up to the barn for a little moment of romance. When I saw the rifle, I realized what your plan was, so I overpowered you and tied you to the chair. But while I went off to call for help, you managed to get free and shoot the governor," he said, nodding to the rifle set up by the window. He sauntered over to the door, unhooked the chain, and pushed both doors open. Bright sunshine and fresh air streamed in. Already, patriotic music was playing. The dais was clearly visible from the loft. No one would be able to hear me, even if I screamed. If only I could teleport! But the Master had taken my power and—wait!

"When your eyes were red, were you not the Master?"

Weston shrugged. "It was all a ruse."

I frowned and looked away. I had not been able to teleport right after the incident. Or had I just bought into the lie? After all, meeting the Master face to face was enough to fool anyone. I poked the bat demon out of his corner. He was shaking inside me with fear. Teleport me just one foot to the side, I thought. The demon cowered in fear and I grew angry. Now!

Weston knelt beside me again and put a hand on my cheek. "What's wrong, honey? Cat got your tongue?"

I phased six inches to the side. It was ugly and it was dirty but I did it. I disappeared from Weston's touch and appeared just behind the chair. The duct tape fell to the floor empty and limp.

Weston backed away from my sudden disappearance, bounced into the loft rail, and fell over the edge. I fumbled with the rifle. If I could only get it off of the tripod! The rifle broke loose, tumbled over the edge of the hayloft, and fell into the pile of hay below.

"That was not smart."

I looked up. Weston was back at the top of the stairs. His short, dark hair was full of hay and his T-shirt was dirty. He was holding the bloody pitchfork his partner had been killed with. "You could have shot me."

"I can still handle you."

He lunged at me with the pitchfork and I allowed the shark demon to take over my reflexes. I stepped aside, but he moved just as quickly with as much supernatural speed. I danced aside again and grabbed the tripod, whirling it around to catch him on the side of the head. He stumbled and I jumped across the empty space to the other side of the barn loft. Before I could turn around, he jumped back from the other side and landed beside me, shoving the pitchfork at my face. I ducked, swung my right leg, pivoted, and knocked his legs out from under him. He bounced deftly, rolled, and was back up before I could catch my breath. He ran at me with the pitchfork. I flipped over him and across to the other loft landing on the tripod still in my grasp. The blow knocked my breath away. Weston launched himself across the barn again. I rolled, bringing up the tripod to knock aside the pitchfork. The three legs caught him in the throat, chest, and the stomach. He grunted once as his own weight drove the tripod's legs through his body. He came to rest with his white eyes level with mine, then he grabbed my shoulders and pulled himself further onto the tripod. Blood spurted from his wounds onto my chest as he pressed himself against me. The white orbs were so close now. Slowly, the color of his irises returned. "Vivian? Help me!"

For a second I felt pity as I looked upon the fate that also awaited me. He opened his mouth to plead for more help, but the smoky pixilation of his demon appeared and his breath gushed out of him. I inhaled, snaring his demon even as it tried to escape.

"Sorry. You're beyond my help, honey child. But now your demon belongs to me." And with that demon came every memory, every bit of knowledge that Weston had. Now, to get out of here! I would deal with Alba another day.

Josh Knight

"Dude, you're hurting me." I tried to jerk away from the Vitreomancer's grasp.

"I'm not a dude," he said quietly.

"What are you waiting for?" I asked.

"The signal."

"The signal for what?" I glanced around, trying to find a way to escape from him.

"The shot. When I hear it, you get to hear another one. It will be the last thing you hear." He smiled and pulled off his sunglasses. I stared into his white eyes.

"Not if he has anything to say about it." I nodded toward his back.

"Oh, no. That won't work on me."

"I'm serious. You see, I have this guardian angel. He was protecting our house, but my guess is Dr. Cephas Lawrence sent him to find me. And now, he's going to kick your demonic butt and take names." I smiled. "Dude!"

He frowned and turned around. The angel in the green scrubs was standing right behind him. The Vitreomancer released his grip on me and shuffled backward. He tripped on the edge of the bluff and tumbled out of sight. I ran to the edge and looked down. He was lying in the bass boat, his neck at an ugly angle. I turned back to the angel.

"Got a name?"

"You can call me Dude." He smiled and disappeared. I drew a deep breath and began the long run back to the log cabin.

Chapter 36

Cephas Lawrence

ALBA PUSHED ME roughly aside and stepped toward Father James Caskey. "You!"

"I've come to set things right, lass. It's time to restore the balance." He rubbed his hands together and touched the collar at his neck. He tugged it off and tossed it aside, loosening his shirt. "That's a bit better."

"How?" I asked.

"Well, Cephas my laddie, it is all a bit of skullduggery, unfortunately. You thought I was dead along with the fair Mary in that room. But it wasn't the eleventh demon who was inside of her head at the time. It was my friend here." He pointed to his own head and laughed.

"Now I understand. My Vitreomancers reported to me that the chimera showed up. The chimera is *my* form, not yours!" Alba said.

"Oh, and weren't we a pair, dearie? So many years traveling together." He shrugged and grinned at me. "We were a dynamic duo, don't you know. Why, we could practically read each other's thoughts. When one started a thought, the other finished it." Suddenly, his face twisted with hatred. "That is, until I made the bloody mistake of following my friend on a foolish mission to end all foolish missions."

Alba stumbled into a couch and stopped abruptly. "What have you done with my sight?"

James clapped his hands together and moved to the center of the room. "Well, I am not without me own abilities, now. How else am I going to get you to come out of that weakened, wretched body?"

"What is going on, James?" I asked.

"James? Why, you're awfully familiar now aren't you, Cephas? I'm not your colleague. I just have the memory of him. Thus my little charade. Where the good father is, even I do not know." He winked at me and smiled. "You know, I never had the chance to formally meet you. Your little entourage took care of me. Or so they thought." He grinned madly. "Now, Ms. Alba, is it? Why don't you come on out from your hiding place and let's have at it? In fact, why don't you show me what the chimera really looks like? It's been so long since the last time you took that form. Hasn't it?"

Alba stiffened and dark liquid smoke streamed out of her mouth and nostrils. The oily, inky substance settled on the floor beside her and enlarged into an amorphous blob. As the last of the substance left her, she collapsed like a marionette whose strings had been severed. I caught her before her head struck the floor and together we tumbled onto the couch.

The inky cloud before me bubbled and hissed. Spurs of flame erupted from blisters of black goo. A deformed eye appeared and spun toward me. It was joined by another. The head of a lioness arose from the black substance. The body emerged covered with silvery-black scales and assumed the shape of a lion. Its feet jerked and spasmed into the shape of an eagle's claws. From the thing's back emerged the head of a goat with long ebony horns. A tail covered in green scales sprouted and swung through the air. A huge snake's head formed at the end of the tail and bobbed in my direction. The black skin morphed into patches of fur, short feathers, and reptilian scales. A human head emerged obscenely between the other two heads. Long, silky black hair surrounded a milky face. I gasped. It was the face of Molly!

"Oh, Cephas, darling. How I've missed you!"

"No! Don't defile her memory! You are not Molly!" I screamed.

"But Mary wants her mommy. Don't you, Mary?"

Alba stirred in my arms and opened her eyes. They were normal. She grabbed my shoulders. "I heard her, Cephas. Is my mother here?"

"Yes, dear. Come to Mommy," Chimera said.

Alba sat up on the couch beside me and put a hand to her mouth when she saw the chimera. "No, you are not my mother. You are an abomination. Go away!"

"You can't send me away, dear. You are empty. You are powerless. But once I take care of my old friend here, I'll be back."

Alba grabbed me tighter and blinked her normal eyes at me. "I made a mistake. You have to stop her, Cephas. Stop her!"

"I will," I growled. I tried to stand up but I felt a hand on my shoulder.

"No need there, laddie. I've got this one," James said.

"You have nothing, Chotus. You were defeated by a handful of worthless humans. You are no match for the eleventh demon," Molly's head said. The snake's head shot in our direction and exhaled fire. James flipped the couch away from the chimera and rolled us onto the floor behind its meager protection. Fire gushed over our heads and hit the wall behind me. The logs that made up the wall blistered and bubbled and suddenly burst into flame. James hunched down beside me.

"I don't give a sheep's wool about your life, Dr. Lawrence. But I'll not let this thing win over me. You'd best be getting out of the way." He reached into his pocket and took out a tiny black marble. "Recognize this?"

"No."

"It was in the baptistery of the church in Lakeside. It's me secret weapon. I picked it up during my passage through the dark matter." He wiggled his eyebrows and tossed the marble up into the fire above us. With a powerful whooshing sound, the fire spiraled up into the center of the room. A whirlpool of fire began to spin above us, sucked into a tiny pinpoint of space. I felt it tug on my skin.

"A microscopic black hole? Are you insane?" I screamed. The air in the room began to spin and whirl around us as it was pulled toward the center of the vortex. Papers, plants, and lamps began to tumble along the floor toward the nidus of the black hole. Behind us, wind whipped the burning logs into a frenzy, spreading the inferno along the walls. I pulled Alba away from the couch toward the fireplace.

Chimera dug into the floor with its feet and the snake closed its maw, shutting off the spout of flame. "Do you think this will stop me, Chotus? We fell through the blackness of space! We soared along shafts of dark matter. We burned through the atmosphere of this world. All you will do is destroy the very world you wish to claim." It sank its eagle claws into the floor, tearing through tile into the concrete beneath as it resisted the pull of the black hole. The antler mantle tore loose from the burning wall above us and shattered into a thousand bony missiles. Chimera's lioness head was torn by the hurtling bone fragments. Chimera unfurled its wings and beat against the force threatening to engulf it.

"Having a bit of trouble, Chamas? Why not just slip the surly bonds of earth and give way to the other dimensions?" James laughed and bent over me. "If he does release his physical shape, laddie, he'll be pulled into the other dimensions. It would take him a while to get back here, and I would win. He's not going to let that happen." He pulled us into the fireplace. "Now, I'm not the least bit sentimental, Cephas me boy, but I want you to get a message to your new partner. You tell him that I'm back!

"Now, I'm going to touch you lightly on the forehead and give you a wee bit of memory so that you will understand what Chamas the chimera and I have a beef about. Then you can start worrying, because once I have the Ark and am done with the Council, Jonathan Steel will have to deal with me again."

Grimvox Interlude #6

Chaos

Gehenna, outskirts of Jerusalem

THIS PLACE IS *called Gehenna. I remember it well. The faces of the sacrificed children are burned in my memory, and their desperate cries of pain and anguish as they were hurled into the fire of Baal echo in my mind. Now a great trash heap smolders and burns here. Unquenchable fires glow with unearthly light and send up wisps of stinking vapor. Lucifer hovers above this place. Beneath him, bent low with their faces pressed to the earth, are eleven Fallen. Chamas lands in the remaining empty spot in the ring of Fallen and bows before the Master, completing the twelve.*

Lucifer stares at me as I approach. "Why have you brought this infidel before me, Chamas? That was not my command."

"Chamas tells me you have a new plan to deal with this Creator Son who walks our world," I say boldly.

Lucifer is suddenly before me. His skin looks coarser than I remember. His eyes are darker than I recall and have a deep flame in them. Still he exudes power and charisma. "The Son will soon die, Chotus. I have seen to that. If the Creator is foolish enough to become one of his own creations, then he can die like one of them. And with his death, I will ascend to the throne of the heavenly realms. But to achieve this end, his twelve followers must be diverted. That is why there are twelve here behind me, twelve of my most trusted and powerful Fallen to offset each of the Son's twelve."

"Is this all you can find among the billions of us trapped on this miserable world?" I spit into the fires of Gehenna and they sizzle with my ire. "We are spread across the vast seas of humanity, gibbering and quivering in eternal insanity, at your bequest, wreaking chaos and destruction on these pitiful creatures. Your reign is abysmal, Lucifer."

"And Chotus the great and magnificent knows better than I?" Lucifer says.

213

He grabs my throat in his powerful grip. "You will bow down to me, Chotus. You will serve me."

"Never," I growl. "Put me on this Council of Darkness and I will show you the way to deal with the Creator and his minions. Do you dare?"

"I once offered to make you my second, but you laughed at me." Lucifer tightens his grip and laughs. "Who is laughing now, Chotus?"

I unleash my power then. I have built it over centuries, carefully stoked it and stored in secret, bought it for the price of a million humans bled and sacrificed to Baal and his ilk. I have fashioned it from the bit of star stuff I grabbed during my fall to earth. And now my talisman will be my release. I pull the tiny stone from beneath my wings and hurl it into the air. Instantly, the fire and smoke leap up. Fueled by the growing wind being sucked into the black hole, the fire explodes, engulfing the valley in which we stand, searing the garbage, the discarded, rotting bodies, and the human refuse into a pyre of unquenchable flame. The twelve Fallen are caught unawares and pulled into the fiery tornado. Smoke towers above us. Fire roars around us. For a second, I see the shock in Lucifer's eyes. I snap my finger and the stone returns to my grasp. I smile at Lucifer.

"I'm laughing now!"

And then he moves us both through the darkness and we are somewhere else. His grip tightens. He closes off the flow of energy to my mind. Darkness is coming fast. I knew my prize would have no effect on him, but I did almost defeat him. I almost bested the Master of the Fallen. We fall across the horizon of this world, tumbling through cold air and mist until we land in a vast, barren land. Lucifer releases me and I fall backward into driftwood and bushes.

"You will defy me no longer, Chotus. You could have been one of the twelve." He towers over my weakened body. The unleashing of my power has left me listless.

"I am more powerful than any of the twelve," I hiss.

Lucifer gestures around us. "This is a land untouched by news of the Creator Son. I do not care for it. My business is in Jerusalem. Once I have defeated the Son, I will be the new Creator, and you will have no choice but to bow before me. So for now, this godforsaken land is yours. Rule over it with your pitiful powers and your insane memories. Be the thirteenth demon, but trouble me no more."

And with that, Lucifer vanishes into the frigid morning air of this desert. I sit up. Between my feet, the same creature I first witnessed upon my arrival in this world crawls toward me. It is only a few inches long, but it is menacing, deadly. It is alone, a creature of the desert, doomed to fight against those much larger than itself. It will become my avatar, my image. I will become the scorpion. I am the thirteenth demon!

Chapter 37

Jonathan Steel

ORNELIUS LEANED AGAINST the wall with her gun casually pointed in our direction. The other Vitreomancer had been called up the stairs.

"How does this work?" I asked.

"Vivian kills the governor. You guys are shot trying to escape. The kid is waiting for you at Redcross Bayou with a boat, but he's taken out by my other partner. The FBI are heroes and you, the big man here, Vivian, and the kid are implicated as part of the conspiracy. The old man goes last. He's holed up in the house, where we find all kinds of incriminating evidence in the basement."

I felt my face grow hot with anger. "If you touch Josh, I will—"

"You'll what, Steel?" Cornelius raised her gun and stepped toward me. "You do have the most haunting eyes. Like flecks of turquoise." She glared at me with her empty orbs. She reached into her jacket and pulled out something that glittered gold. "It's not the real talisman, but it is our instrument, Steel." She waved a golden syringe before my eyes. "In the garage, I used it on the girl's eyes to capture her secret knowledge."

"But that didn't help you, did it?" I said. "You still didn't find out anything about the whereabouts of the Ark, did you?"

Cornelius grimaced. "I was growing to like you, Steel. That is why, before I blow your brains out, I'm going to claim both of your eyes as my prize." She leaned into me and I smelled her sour breath. She brought the needle of the golden syringe close to my eye. "I'll have them suspended in Lucite so I can see them every day."

Without warning, Theo shoved her aside. He had the telescoping baton in his hand and he used it to whack the syringe out of Cornelius's grasp. He moved with a degree of deftness that defied his bulk and nailed her in the temple with the baton.

Cornelius spun away with supernatural speed, came up behind Theo, and brought the gun up to his head. "Now, we end this."

But before she could pull the trigger, the room began to shake. The concrete ceiling crumbled and then tore apart. Theo grabbed me by the arm and wrapped his other one around the doorframe. "Hang on, Chief! I don't know what's happening."

The crumbling ceiling was sucked upward and away from us, pulled by some unfathomable force. Wind whirled around us carrying the bloody bones of Ketrick's forgotten victim. The bones pummeled Cornelius and she tried to dodge them as she shot up into the open space above. A whirlwind of fire and crumbled stone and splintered wood hung against the pale-blue sky. Cornelius screamed as she flew into the vortex and disappeared.

Cephas Lawrence

I gasped as the memory, already fading, left me. I tried my best to remember as much as I could, but James just smiled at me. A spiral appeared around his right eye and he laughed maniacally. "Now, when the time comes, you need to work your spiritual magic, old man." He reached into his pocket and pulled out an object made of gold. It was shaped like a hypodermic syringe with a long, thin golden needle. "I have Chamas' talisman. That will give you control over him, but only for a minute, so don't be trying to send us both to Tartarus, old man. Don't be greedy." He pressed the cold metal object into my palm. "Oh, how I hated pretending to be Chimera. I have been waiting for this moment for days. Now I can be my true self, laddie. I'll be seeing you. Count on it!"

He straightened up and his face began to change. His arms elongated and his fingers fused into two huge pincers. His legs curled away from him and in seconds, the huge scorpion Jonathan had faced in the basement of the church in Lakeside stood there, untouched by the flames around him. He skittered away and charged the chimera.

They met in midair and the collision shook the very foundations of the log cabin. The chimera wound its snake head around the scorpion's right pincer, holding it closed, and locked its lioness jaws on the scorpion's head. The scorpion's tail slashed down toward the chimera's human head. The chimera dodged the stinger. The ceiling collapsed upward; huge wooden beams were torn by the gravitational forces. The walls began to splinter. Flaming logs spun across the air. Outside, people were running from the burning log cabin as tables, chairs, and the dais itself tumbled through the air and into the vortex. Debris thudded into the two beasts in the air. The painting of Robert Ketrick flew up into the black hole. The chimney began to disintegrate around us. I knew there was little time left. I held up the talisman and opened my mouth to speak, but my tongue was silent, stuck to the roof of my mouth. My brain was frozen in fear and despair. I had tried so many times to send a demon off to the waiting chains in eternal darkness, but I had always failed.

I felt Alba's hair brushing my cheek. She touched my face with her hands. "Cephas, you must be strong. You did not let me down in the hospital. I let you down."

"You were a child, Mary," I shouted against the whirlwind.

She brought her face close to mine. Her normal eyes were filled with tears. "And you were but a child in the Lord. You must speak the words of power, Cephas, the words you could not speak then." She touched the talisman. "The talisman gives some control over the demon. This much I have learned. I was wrong to accept the demon's invitation to preserve my life in exchange for being used. I have a second chance, Cephas. Most in my circumstances do not get one. I am no longer empty. I was blind, but now I see!"

"Mary, how?"

"I have served Lucifer for too long. Thanks to you, I now know my Redeemer. It is my God and Savior. He holds my heart now. So let me make this right." She jerked the talisman from my hand and shoved the Metastone into my fist.

"Take it. I have been looking for the golem. Find the golem, Cephas, and you will be its master with the Metastone. He will lead you to mother."

She stepped out of the fireplace before I could stop her. The whirlwind caught her and spun her through the air. Her outstretched hand caught the chimera's snake tail; she used it to pull herself to its body. I felt the jewel grow warm in my hand as I screamed. "Stop, Mary!"

"The words, Cephas!" she shouted. "Speak the words of power!"

Words? What words? I was a failure. I had told Jonathan and Josh my story. It was nothing but a litany of defeat in spite of the Scriptures and sermons I had memorized. Suddenly, it hit me: the sermons! My favorite preacher was James Stewart, a man from Scotland who had put to paper some of the most powerful reflections on the meaning of Christ's sacrifice. As I remembered the words of my favorite sermon, I smiled. I stood up painfully against the raging wind and the roaring fire.

"I may have failed in the past, but I know one thing," I shouted to the demons above me. "You think you have succeeded in defeating my God, but you haven't." Then I shouted out the words of the sermon.

"'I find it to be a glorious phrase that He led captivity captive. It means the very triumphs of His foes He used for their defeat. He compared their dark achievements to subserve His ends, not theirs. They nailed him to a tree, not knowing that by their very act they were bringing the world to His feet. They gave Him a cross, not guessing that He would make it a throne. They flung Him outside the gates to die, not knowing that very moment they were lifting up all the gates of the universe to let the King of Glory come in. They thought to root out His doctrines, not understanding that they were implanting imperishably in the hearts of men the very name they intended to destroy. They thought they had God with His back to the wall. Pinned in, helpless and defeated, they did not know it was God Himself who had tracked them down. He did not conquer in spite of the darkness of their evil. He conquered through it.'

"Those were the words of James Stewart. You may have thought you had won here today, but you have not. For Mary is once again whole and beyond your influence. You will fail, foul beasts of hell!"

"It's true!" Alba screamed. "I have chosen to serve another! You have lied to me for the last time!" She plunged the golden needle into the eye of the pseudo-Molly. The chimera shifted and bucked under the sudden pain and released the huge scorpion. Alba clung to the chimera and plunged the needle into the eyes of the human head, over and over. "Now, Chimera, with the power of the name of Jesus Christ, I commend you to Tartarus, where you will begin your eternal punishment!"

I stepped forward, keeping a firm grip on the edge of the disintegrating fireplace. "Mary, turn loose!" I screamed. She cast a look at me and for a second, her eyes were those of the small girl I had once held in my arms. Then she smiled and released her hold. She tumbled into the vortex and disappeared.

The chimera was shrinking now under the influence of the vortex. With a pained, scornful screech, it disappeared from view. But it was not taken into the vortex. Rather, from a point of light, a black filament appeared and wound its way around the chimera's wings. The filament contracted and tightened until it had spun around and entrapped the creature. Then the point of light opened onto utter blackness from which the screeching and wailing of the chained Fallen overcame the sound of the wind. The chimera shrank as it was pulled through the hole. Finally, the dark tear in reality sealed up with a flash of light.

Another figure tumbled through the air. From the basement, Agent Cornelius spun upward into the abyss of the black hole. The scorpion scuttled over to me and began to shrink back into the form of the false Father Caskey. He grinned and snapped his fingers. The vortex shuddered, then disappeared as the tiny marble soared through the air and fell into his hand. He tossed it up in the air and allowed it to fall into the pocket of his jacket. Then he saluted with two fingers and winked at me. "I'll be seeing you around, laddie." He disappeared into thin air.

Debris and dust settled as the whirlwind dissipated. The back wall and the double doors leading to the living room were the only things left standing. The doors opened and Vivian Darbonne Ketrick walked through. She was covered in blood and hay. She glared at me and looked around at the chaos. "Where is that worthless Bile? I need a ride back to the office."

Chapter 38

Jonathan Steel

IN A DRAMATIC turn of events today, the governor's picnic almost became a disaster," the news reporter said. I watched his eager face on the television in Vivian's office. "But local businesswoman and entrepreneur, Vivian Darbonne Ketrick, thwarted the plot of a rogue deputy sheriff to assassinate the governor. Mrs. Ketrick has been invited to a state dinner in Baton Rouge in gratitude for her efforts."

The television went black. Ross tossed the remote control onto the desk in front of him. I think he was angrier about Cornelius's betrayal than about the fact that Vivian claimed to have aborted an assassination attempt on the Governor.

"I don't like this, Steel." He glared at me. "Vivian gets away. Again. And where is Cornelius?"

"Sucked into a black hole with Lynn Alba," Cephas said quietly.

"A black hole?" Ross massaged his temples. "I wish I could join them. This will be a mess to clean up. Regina was in on the whole thing?"

"Cornelius was bad, Ross. She was evil," I said.

He held up a hand and closed his eyes in pain. "Don't even say the word."

"Demon?" Josh asked.

Ross glared at him and then at Theo sitting in another chair. "Are you going to say it too?"

Theo shrugged. "Don't have to. You know it."

Ross glanced at me. "Do you realize what this has cost me?"

"Define 'this.'"

"Cornelius's hidden agenda. One of my subordinates was in on the attempted assassination of the governor. And to make matters worse, the one person credited with thwarting that attempt is listed as a person of interest in those sacrificial murders. My superiors are questioning not only my judgment, but my leadership. So they are sending me to join some surveillance team

220

watching a church of UFO worshippers suspected of bilking the IRS." Ross's face was red. "While they sort it out, they said."

"Ross, you know there was more to this than just Cornelius."

"Yeah, this secret cult you told me about. These Vitreomaniacs. Sounds like a bad Saturday morning cartoon!"

"Vitreomancers, dude." Josh said. "What about the dude that fell off the bluff and broke his neck?"

Ross rubbed his temples. "There were no bodies. No boat for escape. These white-eyed killers are nowhere to be found. Probably picked up by the black helicopters piloted by the men in black."

"And the deputy sheriff?" Cephas asked.

"Oh yeah, the guy Vivian killed with the rifle tripod. We're officially listing Cornelius as his accomplice."

"I wonder what happened to Gamaliel?" Theo said.

"He and the Vitreomancers live to fight another day," Cephas said. "I fear we may face them again."

"Not where I'm going, I hope. I might even try to give up smoking again." Ross stood up. "Since I've got your statements, you can all go. Please. Far away. Don't call me. I'll call you." He walked out of the room and paused to cast one last glance at Vivian, who had just appeared in the doorway of her office. "You can have your office back. I'm out of here."

Vivian had changed into a tight, red-leather jumpsuit and had managed to comb the hay out of her hair. She smiled and patted Ross's cheek. "Oh, honey, it's always nice doing business with the law."

"You came out of this smelling like a rose," I said.

"Yeah, like a demon rose," Josh said.

Vivian shrugged and sauntered into the room. "It's not every day I get to save the life of a governor. I'm a local hero. My desk, please?"

Cephas moved out of her way. "By all means."

Vivian eased into her chair and winked at me. "That must really chap you, Jonathan."

"All I care is that Josh, Cephas, and Theo are unharmed."

"Well, they weren't the only ones you were worried about. I hear tell you came out to my office because you were worried about me. Is that true?"

I glared at her. "I thought you might need saving. I still think that."

Vivian straightened and her eye twitched. "Well, honey child, I don't need you to look after me! Understand?"

The outer door opened again and Bile came in tugging a rolling, black-canvas shopping bag behind him. "Miss Vivian, may I come in?"

"Where have you been? I have been looking for you, Bile."

Bile closed his eyes slowly and fought for control. "Jerome, Miss Vivian. Please call me Jerome."

"I'll call you anything I please. What do you have there?"

Bile pulled the telescoping handles of the shopping bag behind him as he entered the office. He stopped before Vivian's desk, reached into the bag, and pulled out the Ark of the Demon Rose.

He placed the wooden chest on the desk before Vivian. It was beautiful. The ancient wood had been worn down to a dull shine, and the bronze cornice pieces were intricately carved. A circle of shiny bronze sat on the top. It was the Demon Rose, in all of its glory.

"You had the Ark? All this time, you had the Ark?" Vivian flew out of the chair and around the desk.

"It's for you, Miss Vivian." Bile smiled. She glared at him and slapped him hard across the face. Bile's eyes widened in shock.

"Miss Vivian, what was that for?"

"You fool! You idiot! Do you realize what you have done?"

"I did it because I love you, Miss Vivian." He looked down at the floor.

"You love me? I don't want your love, Bile." She slapped him again. "I don't need your love. Or his," she said, pointing at me. "Or God's! Do you realize what a hornet's nest you stirred up, Bile?"

"My name is Jerome," he whispered.

"No, it isn't!" Vivian slapped him once more. His wispy, unruly hair floated around his head, full of static electricity. "You're Bile, Bile, Bile! The eleventh demon and her Vitreomancers—do you realize how dangerous they are?"

"I didn't know they were involved, Miss Vivian. When I found out that Agent Cornelius was up to no good, I got Destillo to teleport and bring the ark to me for safekeeping."

"Cornelius? You knew she was a Vitreomancer? Why didn't you say something?"

"I wasn't sure. I just overheard her talking about going to the garage and taking stuff out of that poor woman's eyes. I didn't know what that meant at the time. So I followed Destillo to the garage. He passed out, and there was the Ark. I knew it was important and that little fool didn't deserve you." Spit ran from the corner of his mouth. "He had your pictures on the wall. *Your* pictures! He didn't deserve to worship you! So I took the Ark. I was going to tell you, but I couldn't get ahold of you. So I hid it for safekeeping until I could talk to you. Please believe me!"

"You're a stupid, helpless shell of a man, Bile." Vivian shoved him and he stumbled and fell. He reached for her feet. She placed her foot on his forehead and pushed him away. "Get away from me!"

Bile glanced at me, his face smeared with tears. I almost felt sorry for him. Almost. He crawled away into a corner and continued to sob. Vivian turned her back on the poor man and leaned over the Ark of the Demon Rose. Her eyes widened as she examined it.

"Innocent people have died for this, Vivian," I said. "Destillo, Zoe Reynolds, and Lynn Alba."

"I would hardly call Lynn innocent!" She glanced once at me and then at Cephas. "I don't know where your little document is, old man. But it would seem that we both want to stop these Vitreomancers and the Council. So I'm going to give you a little help."

Vivian placed her hands on the Demon Rose and twisted. With a click, it released from the lid of the Ark. She held it up and it gleamed in the light of the office. It looked almost three-dimensional, deeper than a simple flat circle. She handed it to Cephas. "We're even, Steel. What is inside is more important than the Demon Rose."

She slid the Ark back into the canvas bag. "Now, it's just the Ark of Chaos. Let's go, Bile. I have a plane to catch." Vivian stormed out of the room dragging the Ark of Chaos behind her. Bile picked himself up from the corner and followed her out, sniffing and panting.

I stood there with my mouth open in amazement. Cephas stood there with the demon rose in his hands. Josh and Theo just shook their heads. It was going to be an interesting summer.

Chapter 39

Vivian Darbonne Ketrick

HAD I EVER been glad to get a shower and a change of clothes! I'd be picking hay out of my hair for days. I recalled the look in Weston's eyes as he had died. He was in hell now, along with the eleventh demon. For a moment, I felt sorry for him. I contemplated my own destiny. My six demons writhed within me. Weston's demon was accommodating to his new friends, and they made sure he remained under control. We lurched again as my jet tossed and turned in the thunderstorms over the Florida Panhandle .

"Why can't the pilot keep this thing steady?" I asked Bile. He was strapped into the only other chair in our small cabin. He had hardly said a word since we left my hotel and boarded the jet. He would get over it in time. His cheeks were still red from my slaps. Served the idiot right!

Bile shrugged. "There's a hurricane moving across Florida. It came up the Gulf Coast and is moving across the Panhandle toward Central Florida. I'm afraid we'll be flying right over it."

I swore and stabbed at the intercom button on the wall. "Hey, this is Mrs. Ketrick. Can you guys fly around this storm?"

The pilot's voice came over the intercom. "It will add a couple of hours to the flight, but yes, ma'am, we can."

"Then do it."

It took about twenty minutes, but the flight finally smoothed out. I fought down nausea and dizziness and pulled the canvas shopping bag to me. I had been waiting for this for so long. I had been planning to wait until we landed, but my patience was growing thin. "Bile, get one of those attachable tables." I pointed toward the front of the cabin.

Bile unlatched his seat belt and retrieved a tabletop from the wall of the cabin. He centered its post in the floor and bolted it down. I pulled the Ark of the Demon Rose from the bag and placed it carefully on the table. It was beautiful!

"Why did you give the compass rose to Steel?" Bile asked.

I studied his limpid eyes as he hunched over the Ark. "Because we don't need that part of the Ark, Bile. It's just there for decoration."

"You're trying to help him, aren't you?" Bile said.

I felt a flash of anger and slapped him hard across the face for the fourth time that day. His cheek was bright red. He looked away from me. "Don't you ever question my orders, Bile. You pledged your allegiance to me so you will do as I say without question. Is that clear? I am in charge!"

For a second I thought he was going to reply, then he looked down at the floor. I drew a deep breath and fumbled with the clasps on the front of the ark. They unsnapped. I could feel my heart racing. I slowly lifted the lid of the huge box and peered inside. A yawning blackness stretched away beyond the natural confines of the box. "It's bigger on the inside?"

I reached into the darkness and felt something cold and metal. I pulled out a long golden knife whose handle was inlaid with jewels. I had seen it before in Ketrick's office. It was the knife Ketrick had used for his sacrifices. I looked down into the emptiness of the box. "Bile, it's empty except for this!" I slammed the lid shut and glared at Bile. "Where are the talismans?"

Bile slowly raised his head and smiled. He reached out and slapped me hard across the face. I strained against my seat belt and I felt Bile's hand as he fumbled for the buckle. It snapped open and in my dizziness, I slid out of the chair and fell across the floor. My vision swam and I tasted blood. The knife fell off the table and came to rest just inches from my nose. Bile knelt beside me and bit his thumb. He picked up the knife and stood up. I was still reeling from the blow. I could only watch as he placed the toe of his right foot against my forehead. He shoved me backwards and my head bounced against the bulkhead. He squatted before me and pressed the cold tip of the knife against my cheek. His normally limpid eyes were full of new power. A dark spiral formed around his right eye. "After I finished Destillo, I found another host. So look who's in charge now, honey child!"

Jonathan Steel

"We'll take both vehicles," I said as Josh put his bag in the back of the cruiser.

"Cool! I can take the SUV down the beach and cruise. After all, it is a chick magnet!" Josh said.

"Actually, I was talking about the new truck and the RV. We've got some things to bring back."

I watched Josh's face fall as he turned away. Maybe I was being too hard on the kid. "Hey," I said. Josh turned back to me.

"We'll leave the truck and you can take the SUV down the beach, okay?"

Josh's face came alive with his huge smile. "Dude, the girls will be falling all over themselves."

Cephas appeared behind him. "Especially when they see how you drive."

"Funny, Uncle Cephas. I don't see any girls following you around."

Cephas raised an eyebrow. "My young man, you would be surprised at the appeal an older man like me has for a woman, especially when I'm in my robot pajamas."

Theo lugged a huge ice chest into the back of the SUV. "Chief, that neighbor of yours from Gulf Shores just called. Said he closed the hurricane shutters on the beach house."

I nodded. A hurricane was moving through the Panhandle of Florida along Alabama's Gulf Coast. It was supposed to be gone by the time we got there. "Good! I don't think it will hit Gulf Shores that hard. So are we ready?"

Josh glanced at me. "Who am I riding with?"

I pointed to the SUV. "Ride? You're driving. It's eight hours. Let's go!"

Cephas held up the portable phone from inside the house. "I have the phone in my pocket! I'll put it up and lock the house. I'll just be a moment."

Cephas Lawrence

I hated to deceive the man I trusted most in the world. I was calling Ross as I stepped into the kitchen and hurried down the steps into the basement.

"Ah, Agent Ross. I'm glad I caught you before you tied up your loose ends. I have finished examining the walls of the basement. I know that you had planned on sending another crew to examine the contents of the walls in Ketrick's basement. There is no need to send a new crew. They are empty."

"That's fine. I want to put all of this behind me," Ross said. "I'm leaving Dallas tomorrow. A new agent will contact you when the cataloguing is finished. As we agreed, you can have Ketrick's artifacts for your, uh, collection once we're done."

"Very good, Agent Ross. Good day." I stood there as the phone died in my hand and faced the partition beside the secretary. I studied the wall in front of me, then I pulled the Metastone out of my pocket and let it dangle from the broken chain. I had not told Jonathan Steel about the reappearance of the thirteenth demon, or about the events in the cabin. He did not know that there had been two demons involved with the Ark of the Demon Rose, nor had I told him that Lynn Alba was Mary. To reveal that would be to reveal even more of my past than I already had. No, I would deal with thirteen myself.

In spite of what I told Ross, I had found something in the wall. I could not allow Ross's agents to remove this object. I was going to need it. Here, beneath the plaster and paint, was the key to finding Molly. If my ancient texts were accurate, then I had found the very thing Mary had been seeking. It was far more powerful than the Vitreomancers. I held the jewel up to the wall and it began to pulsate with a deep-crimson light. I placed my hand on the wall. I could feel the evil within. It was hidden, frozen, trapped, and waiting to be unleashed—waiting to be reborn. And it would have a new master. Mary had been correct. I had no doubt that once I returned from our trip to Florida, with the help of the Metastone and the thing hidden in the wall, I would be able to find Molly at last.

Epilogue

I WATCHED THE VEHICLES pull out of the driveway and let the binoculars sag around my neck. The ski boat tossed in the waves. A storm was coming and the waters were going to get rough. Where were they going? I would have to follow them, of course. I had not been able to keep an eye on Josh while the others had been in Dallas. Business in California had kept me occupied.

But now, the children were safely hidden away from those who sought them. I had time to catch up with Jonathan Steel and his new responsibility. It was a good thing I had seen them in the boat that day; otherwise, Josh and Vivian would have died. Jonathan was slipping! I couldn't count on him anymore.

My cell phone warbled and I glanced down at the text message. "Neph33 and rest of children now missing after hurricane damaged safe house. Need your help pronto," it read. I blinked and shook my head. As always, there was a new crisis brewing just around the corner. I would have to catch up with Steel and company later.

"Don't worry, Josh. I'll still be there for you, son." I started up the ski boat and headed for shore.

Afterword

And, now, I would like to share with my readers the first chapter of the next book in the Chronicles of Jonathan Steel: *The 10th Demon: Children of the Bloodstone.*

***

Chapter 1: Vega Is Taken

```
30.681768,-86.949234
2:46 a.m. CDT
Quantum flux surveillance
Grimvox Raptor Neural Interface
Subspecies "Water Moccasin"
```

THE MAN ADJUSTED his night-vision goggles and prodded a water moccasin away from the stump on which he squatted. The snake fell back into the receding water and slithered off into the night. The man pushed his long hair back under the strap of the night-vision goggles and raked sweat out of his beard. The August night was sweltering and his dark shirt and sweatpants were soaked.

The alien landscape was bathed in pale-green light beneath a darkening sky. Broken trees thrust their bare trunks upward like the splintered remains of a dragon's teeth. Around the bases of the naked trunks swirled water filled with writhing serpents. The air was still and dank with the odor of decay. Just twelve hours before, the wind had been a howling beast breaking the backs of the tall, mighty pines of this Florida Panhandle forest. But now, the hurricane had moved on, leaving vast destruction in its wake. The night was deathly quiet. There were no frog songs or chirping insects in the utter stillness.

If his quarry still lived, she would come down this trail, away from her prison. A covey of doves burst out of their hiding place, the fluttering of their wings interrupting the silence. She was coming!

The girl appeared in the distance as she hopped over a fallen pine tree. She was almost a foot taller than the man. She was wearing a dark, one-piece jumpsuit and her hair was pulled back in a ponytail. In spite of her size, her features were like those of an eight-year-old girl. But this girl was almost seven feet in height. She paused in the center of the trail and turned her eyes in his direction. Through his night-vision goggles, her eyes appeared alien. She was looking right at him. She had night-vision superior to that of ordinary humans.

"Who is there?" the girl whispered.

"A friend," he said back to her.

A snake hung down from a nearby broken branch and came dangerously close to the girl's face. The girl's hand moved incredibly quickly and grabbed the snake by the tail. With one quick snap, she snapped the snake against the tree trunk like a whip and then tossed it into the darkness.

"Are you alone?" he asked.

The girl hurried across the distance between them and looked up at the man on the stump. "I don't know where the others went. Are you with the Major?"

"I'm not with the Major," The man whispered. Then he heard the music. It came down the trail, ghostly and light, floating on the still air like a dank perfume. It pulsed as it grew louder. He felt his head swim. He squinted into the night air. Against the stars, a dark and hideous *something* moved low on the horizon.

The girl turned. Her body grew rigid. "It's them," she whispered.

The music was growing stronger and the man's mind was becoming cloudy. A pale-lavender light exploded toward the ground, blinding him. He jerked his goggles off as the cone of light swiveled back and forth. An alligator scurried into the underbrush. The hovering thing was coming closer and the music was slowly paralyzing them both. The man fumbled in the messenger bag hanging from his shoulder and pulled out a pistol. He squinted into the bright light and sighted along the gun. He pulled the trigger and the explosion ripped through the night, chasing away the music. The light went out in a flash of sparks.

The girl relaxed and the man pulled his night-vision goggles back on. "We have to get out of here, now!" He grabbed her huge hand and tugged her down the trail. They stumbled and tripped over fallen trees and broken branches. Behind them, the thing came closer. The music had been replaced by a discordant hum that traveled along his spine and into his head. He fell forward and his goggles tumbled off into the mud.

"I lost my goggles!" he hissed. Suddenly, he was lifted bodily into the air and tossed over the girl's shoulder. He looked down at the ground as she sped off into the forest. She ran faster than humanly possible along the trail, hurdling fallen trees like they were so much kindling. He bounced and jerked and fought for breath.

They came to a halt, and the girl put him down. They were standing on a high bluff. He pulled a small flashlight out of his bag and risked taking a look. The tiny beam was lost in the mist rising from the Blackwater River below them. The water level was very high, and the brown current churned against the bluff. Logs and limbs bounced in and out of the turbulent waters.

"We're in the wrong spot! My motorcycle is north of here."

Then the thing was there behind them, dark and ominous against the sky. The humming turned to music once again. The man clamped his hands over his ears, but it was no use. The music was hypnotic and paralyzing. The girl, entranced, looked up at the thing above them. The light came on again, this time from the other side of the shadow. It spotlighted the girl. On the underside of the thing, an iris opened to emit yellowish-green light. A spindly figure appeared at the edge of the hole. Its huge lidless eyes fixed on them both. The man wanted to scream. Terror filled his mind—naked, raw, unreasonable fear.

The girl stepped toward the craft. Her feet left the ground. She was being taken up into the underside of the thing! The man knew he had to act quickly. If he stayed, he, too, would be taken prisoner. But if he escaped, he could track them down and retrieve the girl.

"I'll come back for you!" he shouted as he turned and dove off the bluff. He fell twenty feet and hit the water hard. The blow knocked most of the air out of his lungs, and he sank deep into the cold, turbulent current. Something brushed against him. He snared a tree trunk and used it to pull himself to the surface. He gasped for air and looked back toward the bluff. The girl was disappearing through the iris. The underside of the craft glowed a ghostly, pale green and tilted to the side. He could make out a dome on top of the saucer-shaped craft. In a streak of green-and-lavender light, it disappeared into the stars above. A powerful sonic boom echoed down the river. He hung on for dear life.

Resources

Martin, Walter, *Kingdom of the Occult* (Nashville, Tennesee: Thomas Nelson, 2008).

Stewart, James, *Sermons Principally Designed to Strengthen the Faith and Increase the Devotedness of Christians in the Present ... Era* (Charleston, South Carolina: Nabu Press, 2012).

About the Author

Bruce Hennigan grew up in the deep pine forests of northwest Louisiana. There wasn't much for a young boy to do in the country, unless an active imagination and acres of pastures and woods opened the door to another reality. Bruce spent his childhood chasing dinosaurs, giant robots, aliens from Alpha Centauri, and the occasional cow through this vast land of imagination.

In the eighth grade, he saved up his meager allowance to buy a teal-blue portable typewriter and began to write his own stories. He was doomed, captured, enslaved by story! Bruce wanted to write for the rest of his life.

But God intervened. He called Bruce to a profession in the medical field to become the very last thing in the world he wanted to be, a doctor. Bruce continued to write through college and medical school and found success in, of all places, the theater. For fifteen years, Bruce was the drama director at a local church and wrote over 150 plays. Challenged by the questions of his fellow scientists regarding his faith, Bruce explored the field of Christian apologetics, the defense of the truthfulness of the Christian faith.

After suffering through a severe depression, Bruce co-authored *Conquering Depression: A Thirty Day Plan to Finding Happiness* with Mark Sutton (Broadman & Holman, 2001). After the success of that book, he fulfilled his lifelong dream of publishing fiction with the release of two supernatural thrillers, *The 13th Demon: Altar of the Spiral Eye*, and *The 12th Demon: Mark of the Wolf Dragon* (Realms Books).

Bruce has two grown children and lives in Shreveport with his wife, Sherry. He continues to speak on the topics of apologetics, creative writing, and drama. For more information, check out his website at brucehennigan.com.